Flying to Tombstone

a novel

by
Gordon McBride

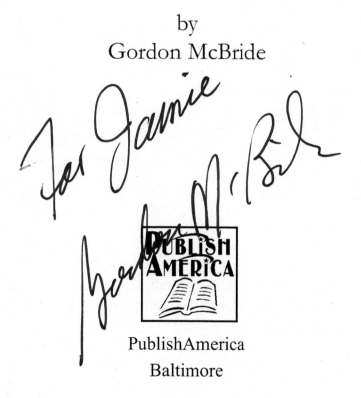

PublishAmerica
Baltimore

First printing

ISBN: 1-59129-743-5
PUBLISHED BY PUBLISHAMERICA BOOK PUBLISHERS
www.publishamerica.com
Baltimore

Printed in the United States of America

As I watched silently, Bob recited his checklist as if it were a litany, fingering switches like beads on a rosary and muttering incantations– "Breakers in!" "Carb Heat off!" "Mixture rich!"–like a vicar at matins, his radio headset and mike the alb and stole of his calling. Briefly he peered in all directions, then opened his side window, shouted "Clear!" in a loud benediction, and turned the key. Almost instantly the 150-horsepower engine two feet in front of our knees coughed alive, shaking awake the Skyhawk. As the slip-stream from the propeller stroked the plane's tail surfaces, the aircraft rose on its landing gear like a churchyard cat stretching from sleep.

–Henry Kisor, *Flight of the Gin Fizz*

For Fred and Hazel

None of the characters or situations depicted in this novel represent real people or actual events. St. Peter's Episcopal Church is a type and not an actual church, and both Bisbee and Tombstone have their own Episcopal Churches. The setting and the issues are genuine as are many of the border incidents that are described.

Many thanks to my wife, Kari, whose encouragement and patient reading and editing have been invaluable.

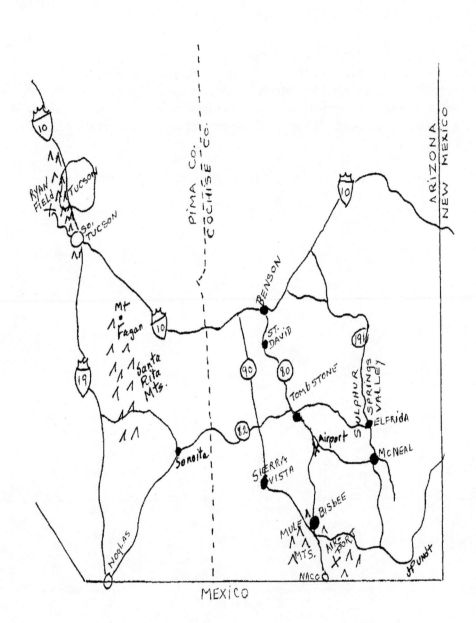

PROLOGUE

The Arizona Border With Mexico

Bernardo Murillo is smart. He knows the score. Using a coyote to get from Mexico all the way to Phoenix costs a lot of money, but it's worth it. Coyotes know where to cross the border—and when.

But even at twenty, Bernardo knows that you can never trust a coyote. They are cowards, and they are mean. After they take all your money, something may scare them, and they run away leaving you in the desert. Maybe with a group of people, maybe alone. And everybody knows what happens next. The police might arrest you and throw you into jail. Sometimes when people go with coyotes, they are never heard from again.

Others tell wonderful stories. They make it all the way to good jobs and to self-respect. And they send money to their families, lots of money. Bernardo wants to be one of those people. Every year except this year they come home at Christmas and at other festival times. Now it has gotten too hard to cross the border; there are too many guards; now you have to pay a coyote each time.

So Bernardo pays the coyote, at least to get across the border. Then he will dump him and make his own way to Phoenix. He is young and strong. He knows he can make it. Not even the desert will stop him.

Everyone says that the most dangerous time is the first hours after you cross the border. Guards patrol the highways. Roadblocks make the best roads impossible to use. On side roads vigilante ranchers wait for you, always alert for the coyotes and their cargo. But Bernardo Murillo has a plan. First he has to get across the border. Then he will strike out on his own. He knows that this is not one of those times when safety comes in numbers.

They cross the border together on foot an hour before dawn. Bernardo counts eighteen of them. They walk about two miles in fear and elation, the coyote prodding everyone to move quickly and to be quiet. Well before they come into the lighted area of the old copper mining town of Bisbee, the

9

coyote walks up to the back doors of a battered white van sitting in front of a dark building. He opens the van's rear doors and tells everyone to get in. "*Pronto!*" The space is so small. Bernardo wonders how they will all fit. The driver's seat is closed off from the rear section where the passengers crowd in. The roof is too low for any but the shortest of them to stand up straight.

Bernardo decides that the time has come for him to go his own way. He holds back, waiting with apparent politeness for the others to get in first, looking for his chance to walk away. When finally everyone else is in, he shrugs his shoulders, as if to say, "No more room," and scuffing one foot on the ground, starts to walk away. But the coyote will have none if it.

"In the van, man," he says.

Nobody knows the coyote's name. The contact who set it up runs a small restaurant in Agua Prieta. He just calls him "the coyote." Like his namesake, the coyote is small, wiry and tough.

Bernardo feels something hard against his ribs, prodding, pushing him toward the still-open door. It's a small handgun.

"*Sí, sí,*" he says. Another chance will come soon enough, he thinks. Surely the coyote doesn't mean to have all of them in this cramped space for very long.

Inside, the van is already thick with the stink of sweat and fear. Someone must have pissed their pants. First one then the other of the van's doors slam shut. The packed humanity inside is as silent as the desert on a winter night. Bernardo hears the sound of the van's engine turning over. There is a jerk as it goes into gear, a slight spinning of the rear wheels on the gravel drive, and then the van lurches onto the paved road, forcing everyone back against Bernardo and pressing him against the doors. Cool morning air begins to pour into the van from an opening above their heads. Maybe this is not going to be so bad after all. Bernardo begins to relax. There's no sitting down in that packed van, but somehow that's okay. It all leads to the goal, to the new life.

They ride this way for perhaps half an hour, then with a violent bump and a swerve that leaves the van's passengers crushing into each other again, the smooth ride of the hard-surfaced road gives way to a bumpy, dusty gravel surface. Still the van speeds ahead. Bernardo feels the tension rise around him. Then, after what seems like a long time, a separate roaring sound, one that grows louder and louder, rises above the rattle and bang of the van and the sound of gravel thrown up onto its undercarriage. It becomes clearer and clearer, louder and louder, the shattering sound of a powerful engine. The sound becomes frighteningly loud, and then, suddenly, it recedes. It comes a second time and then a third. They are being buzzed by an airplane. Terror replaces discomfort. Sobs and muffled shouts fill the van.

Suddenly the van swerves and stops. A cloud of dust settles on it and its human cargo. Coughing now replaces the sobs of fear. Then it's very quiet. A little light is showing in around the solid doors as the new sun of morning begins to rise. Bernardo hears the coyote's door slam shut and the crunching sound of feet on gravel. Suddenly the coyote bangs on the side of the van.

"Be very quiet if you value your lives," he says.

The sound of the airplane comes again, distant at first, and then, as if the pilot has once again located the van, the roar and whine of the plane's engine shatters the air. Bernardo isn't sure, but he thinks he hears the sound of footsteps running away from the van. Then it's quiet.

To hell with the coyote, Bernardo thinks as he reaches for the inside handle on the van door. There is no handle. He tries his weight against the door. It's solid. Sheets of iron, securely bolted into place, cover and darken the rear windows. Bernardo can feel the sweat begin to pour down his face as the temperature rises in the van in the early morning sun. Two other men join Bernardo as they put their shoulders to the door. Still nothing happens. It's impossible to get any leverage in the crowded space.

Somewhere in the van a woman begins to cry, a plaintive, pitiful sound. There are other sobs and moans. Breathing gets harder and harder in the stinking, dusty air of the packed van.

Then the strangest thing of all happens. It sounds a little like the buzz of a gigantic bee, but only for a moment, and a tiny hole of light appears on both sides of the van, mercifully just above their heads. Then there is another.

"They are shooting at us," Bernardo hears someone say. "Everybody down."

Everyone scrambles to get out of the way of the bullets as a second, then a third—a steady stream of them—tears into and out of the van.

Then as suddenly as it began, the shooting stops. Many small holes high up on both sides of the van now emit streams of light that catch the dust particles and give them an unreal, dancing quality in the steaming air. Bernardo hears the crunch of tires on the gravel road. They stop. And then comes the strangest part of this entire bizarre morning. It is the sound of two men laughing and talking among themselves. Then one of them shouts, "I hope you like the air holes, assholes." There is a kind of cackling laughter. "That's rich, air holes—assholes."

The sound of tires on the gravel road begins again. Silence returns. Only the whimpering, sobbing sounds inside the van remain.

Not even someone smart like Bernardo Murillo can do anything about this. He begins to wonder, will I die here today? Bernardo feels a sob escape from his mouth.

CHAPTER ONE

The Last Sunday After Epiphany

*Life begins in Eden, in the presence of God, but something has happened
so that we are no longer aware of that.*
—Marcus Borg

Jerry Hanning took one last look around the horizon before climbing into the left seat of his Cessna Skyhawk. Hank and Teresa's wedding day was going to be an Arizona picture postcard: clear, crisp February air, cloudless cobalt sky and corn-gold sun. Mother Nature would scarcely have dared offer less on that day; Hank Tucker would never have stood for it.

Hank was a prominent rancher in the Sulphur Springs Valley northeast of Bisbee and a member of the local vigilantes. He was also Father Jerry's senior warden at St. Peter's Episcopal Church.

Jerry Hanning had much in common with Hank Tucker. They shared a joint responsibility for St. Peter's Church: vicar and warden. They both had suffered the death of a spouse: Hank had been widowed for sixteen years (followed by a short second marriage ended by divorce), and his two sons both practiced law in Tucson; the death of Jerry's wife two years earlier had left *him* a single parent of nine-year-old Sadie. And both men loved to fly airplanes: Jerry piloted his thirty-year-old Cessna from his home in Tucson to Bisbee on weekends to minister to his new flock; Hank proudly used his airplane, a recently acquired and rebuilt red and white V-tailed Beech Bonanza, mostly to go into Tucson and Phoenix on business and to patrol his thousands of acres of ranch land. Hank's Bonanza brought envy to the heart of every aviation enthusiast in Southern Arizona, including Jerry Hanning's.

Jerry Hanning shared many things with Hank Tucker, but not the older man's determination to defend the land he had lived on for sixty-three years against illegal immigrants from Mexico, laborers mostly, who crossed his place on their way north. Jerry did not in fact know where he stood on that highly conflicted local issue, but he knew he would have to figure it out.

Forty-two-year-old Jerry Hanning's mixed callings as priest and pilot mirrored his complexity as a human being. Unruly brown hair and blue eyes, a rugged exterior and a gentle nature, the single father of a pre-adolescent daughter and a man deeply hurt by the sudden death of his young wife, a nearly rootless vagabond for two years and a believer in the settled lifestyle of the parish priest—Jerry was not someone who could easily be turned into a simple stereotype, any kind of stereotype. At this moment in his life, Jerry felt unsure of himself and uncertain about a faith that had taken him to seminary and which had led him to live the life of a parish priest. He no longer knew who God was or if there even was a God; more importantly, Jerry did not seem to know himself any more—who he was or why he had ever decided to be a priest. Indeed, the two uncertainties were inextricably interwoven.

Hank Tucker—a tall man, slightly stooped in the way tall and active men sometimes are in the upper end of middle age, a full head of white hair creased from hat-wearing, and penetrating dark brown eyes—was one of the most respected men in Cochise County. With his powerful charisma and natural leadership, Hank could have had a political career or just about anything else he wanted. Conservative in an old-fashioned way, he believed in the basic values of hard work, decency and honoring his word. You always knew where he stood and what he wanted. And just now he wanted to marry Teresa Bustamante, a long-time widow and the proprietor of a successful Bisbee hardware store. She was also the mother of five adult children and grandmother of enough grandchildren to field two soccer teams. And there was no doubt who would serve as referee in that or any other kind of family contest. With rich brown skin, gleaming black hair and surprising blue eyes, Teresa was a striking woman with a rich border heritage, a sparkling volatile good nature and an intellect to match. Hank had made the catch of the year in Bisbee, and nearly everybody agreed that it was so.

"Ryan tower, this is Cessna Five-Eight Bravo, holding short at Three-Three," Jerry Hanning had radioed early that afternoon, the day of the Tucker-Bustamante wedding. He moved the small microphone as close to his lips as possible and flashed a grin at daughter Sadie beside him.

"Cleared for runway Six-Right, Five-Eight-Bravo. Squawk zero-three-one-zero, and contact Tucson approach at one-one-eight-point-five," responded the air traffic controller at Tucson's Ryan Field, a general aviation airport fifteen miles west of Tucson International.

"Five-Eight Bravo," Jerry answered, confirming that he had heard the instruction. He began his takeoff run.

The open desert dotted by scattered homes, mostly double-wide mobiles, began to flatten out beneath Jerry and Sadie as the Cessna climbed higher, and the ribbon of the Central Arizona Project canal below became narrower and thinner. They flew directly toward the jagged, low peaks of the Tucson Mountains. The sprawl of modern Tucson spread and boiled like spilled soda on the other side.

When he was not actually doing weddings for St. Peter's senior warden, Jerry gave flying instruction during the week and on weekends led the recently merged Episcopal congregation formed of St. Peter's Church in Bisbee and the former St. Paul's in the neighboring town of Tombstone, which the bishop had closed a few months before Jerry assumed pastoral oversight. Both towns had their origin in mining and their current life in regional business and tourism. Not the least of the bishop's promises at the time of the closure of the Tombstone church was that if the fifteen people of St. Paul's joined the other Episcopalians in Bisbee, an easy twenty minute drive away, there would be a community large enough to have its own part-time vicar instead of whatever "supply" priest happened to be available and willing on a given Sunday. In fact, for at least half of the Sundays of the year, there was no priest available at all. But not even Jerry's smiling face had thus far been enough instantly to reconcile the Tombstonians to their membership in St. Peter's Church, Bisbee—or to satisfy the fears of the St. Peter's congregation about their new fellow parishioners. Still, this small congregation had some real strengths, especially its surprisingly diverse population drawn from the whole of Cochise County. Getting the two major groups of parishioners, especially those from the infamous former gun-slinging town, to accept and bond with each other was probably Jerry's greatest challenge, especially since so much of his energy these days went to dealing with his own ghosts and religious uncertainty.

"Ryan tower, Cessna Five-Eight-Bravo, permission to change frequency?" Jerry called as he approached pattern altitude on a straight ahead departure.

"Permission granted, Five-Eight-Bravo, have a good day, Father."

"Thanks, Mike. Have a great day yourself. Five-Eight-Bravo." Jerry changed the radio frequency and announced himself to Tucson approach control.

Sarah Rebecca Hanning sitting at Jerry's side was the light that brightened his life. She had her father's wide blue eyes, but entirely her own freckles across an up-turned nose and high cheek bones. Her straight blonde hair promised to turn a lustrous reddish-brown in a few years when she spent less time in the sun. With permanent teeth still a little too large for her face and an irrepressible sparkle, Sadie was a great kid. Seldom angry or irritable, she was also good company. Father and daughter, already close, had bonded even more deeply when both had had to adjust to the death of Marjory Little— his wife and her mother.

On that horrible day, Jerry had been attending to his usual parish work, committee meetings, liturgy planning, and visiting sick parishioners in his Western Hills suburban Cincinnati parish. The call from Good Samaritan Hospital shocked him out of his day—and his life as he knew it.

"Is this Jerry Hanning, the spouse of Ms. Marjory Little?" the voice had asked.

"Yes, it is. Is something wrong?" Jerry had felt a terrible dread in the pit of his stomach.

"Ms. Little was brought to the emergency room and rushed directly into surgery. It's a ruptured aortal aneurism. They're doing everything they can."

"Everything they can? What does that mean?"

"It means the doctors are doing anything anybody could do. I think you should get over here as quickly as you can, sir."

And Jerry had gone, breathing formal prayers and fighting a rising fear as he negotiated the twisting streets into the Clifton neighborhood and Good Sam Hospital. But he had been too late. Marjory had died before he got there. Just like that. No warning. No ceremony. No last rites. Nothing. Gone. That was two years and most of the width of the continent ago.

"Daddy," Sadie said into her microphone, "do you think it will be okay for me to read Harry Potter in the church today?"

"Why wouldn't it be?"

"You know, some people don't think magic is okay in church." She laughed easily and openly.

"I know. Too bad for them," he said. "Besides, what better place is there for magic?" he laughed.

"You know what I mean, Daddy," she returned quickly.

"Just don't you worry about it, Sadie. I doubt anyone will say anything. Besides, there's enough going on today to keep everybody plenty busy." Today the people of St. Peter's would be so excited and preoccupied with the wedding of Hank Tucker and Teresa Bustamante that they would have trouble noticing if Harry Potter himself were to turn up.

Jerry leveled off the Cessna at 7,500 feet and adjusted the course to one-hundred-seven degrees. Reaching Bisbee Municipal Airport required either climbing ultimately to over nine thousand feet and going over Mule Mountains, in which old Bisbee is nestled, or flying around the small range to the airport south of town. Much of the way to Bisbee, the route followed the winding green valley of the San Pedro River to the little Mormon community of St. David, where, curiously, a Roman Catholic Benedictine monastery sits among green fields and tiny lakes and ponds. The next major landmark was Tombstone, in the hills twenty miles east of the combined Sierra Vista/Libby Air Force Base/Fort Huachuka valley community, where civilians and army and Air Force installations coexist with the Mexican border. The small well-maintained Bisbee airport is even closer yet to the border. A loud shout from the south end of the runway would be heard in Mexico.

Jerry had gone through all of the necessary motions at the time of Marjory Little's death: funeral, sympathy from parishioners at St. Mary Magdalen, where he had been rector for six years, and from family and friends. But he had kept his grief private, much of it even hidden from himself, and tried to go on with his life as if nothing had happened, rising to the occasion as a professional, he had told himself.

But ultimately, Marjory's death, for which Jerry was ill prepared both emotionally and spiritually, had made it impossible for him to do his parish work. A grief-laden depression drove him into isolation, and he had been unable to muster the spiritual energy to go on with religious rituals like anointing the sick and dying—just as if he still thought his ministrations would actually make a difference to them. His sense of loss and abandonment by God had become so acute that none of the comfortable old rituals or even the sacraments seemed to carry much meaning for him anymore. Instead, he clung to Sadie and she to him so tightly that they could see little more than each other. Not even his parents could penetrate that fog of sorrow. He was only now, two years later, just barely beginning to experience life again, with his belief system still fragile and his sense of himself as a priest deeply shaken. Sadie had seemed stronger and better able to cope than he had been. Many times it was she who offered her father gentle words and reassuring pats.

Jerry had sold the house in Cincinnati along with most of the furniture, and the two of them had migrated west in the Cessna, stopping in Wichita for a few months and in Denver for a little longer, finally settling in Tucson eight months before Hank and Teresa's wedding day. In Tucson they both felt that they had found a new home. There was something about the desert that nurtured Jerry Hanning. Gradually he took on a healthy looking tan and leaned down his six-foot frame to a not-quite trim, but healthy-looking, one-hundred eighty pounds. His recovery had begun.

The taxi to tie-down that day at Bisbee Municipal Airport and the securing of the Cessna took no time at all. Sadie, an old hand at caring for the airplane, scurried around locking doors and climbing up on the struts to stretch canvas on its windows. Jerry pulled out the two collapsible bicycles, which usually rode as mute passengers in the rear seat and luggage area of the Skyhawk, snapped them together and attached the front tires. They hopped on the bicycles and set out on the hilly twenty-minute ride toward the church, wide grins on both of their faces. Regardless of his shaky confidence as a priest, Jerry was content to be doing something that he really loved—facilitating important personal events in the lives of people he liked. Sadie just liked being with her father.

"You're really excited about being an acolyte for the wedding, aren't you, Sweetheart?" he asked.

She grinned shyly. "Aw, Daddy," was all she said.

This afternoon's wedding promised to bring out most of Bisbee's old guard, ranching families from around the area, business owners, teachers and administrators at Cochise Community College twenty miles to the east, the upper echelon of the local government and the Border Patrol, the latter mostly from neighboring Douglas, and even some of the Bisbee artist community. This was the social event of the decade for the small congregation.

St. Peter's was a bustle of activity when Sadie and Jerry Hanning coasted their bikes to a stop beside one of the rear doors into the church and chained them together to the wrought iron fence that marked the boundary of the church's property.

Inside, the chancel of the red-brick church looked like a disorganized flower shop. Altar Guild members hurried back and forth on purposeful missions inside the ninety-three-year-old building. Boxes, lately the containers of flowers, lay across the tops of the front two pews. The altar rail was a draper's cutting room of silk bows and streamers, lace and fluff. Candle stands leaned precariously against the sides of pews and Gothic arches with fresh white candles all fixed with pink bows. Mrs. Elspeth Findlay, the tiny and wiry altar guild head, held court with gesture and nod. With Mrs. Findlay in charge, Jerry could relax in the confidence that order would soon descend on the chaos.

"Hi, Father Jerry. Good flight down?" It was Kate Becker, or Saint Kate as Jerry often jokingly called her for the combination of calm wisdom, good nature and willingness to help out that were her hallmarks. Kate always seemed to be on hand when she was needed.

"Fine, Kate. Looks like everything is underway here." He waved a hand at the disarray.

"Not to worry. We'll be done in a flash," said Mrs. Findlay giving him her impatient smile. Nobody ever called her anything but Mrs. Findlay. Nobody would dare.

"Seen anything of the bride and groom?" Jerry asked, looking around vaguely.

Mrs. Findlay snorted. "Teresa was by earlier, but we haven't seen anything yet of Hank. He's probably off catching Illegals or playing in his fancy new airplane."

Saint Kate flashed Jerry one of her brilliant, knowing smiles as Mrs. Findlay continued.

"Sometimes I think that man is more childish than any of my students ever were." Mrs. Findlay had retired years ago as an English teacher at Bisbee High, but middle-aged men still scuffed their feet in her presence and looked as if at any moment they might say, "Aw shucks."

Kate Becker, a bit of a mystery to the people at St. Peter's, was a pretty forty-something woman who had come to Bisbee from the Midwest a couple of years before to teach business and economics at Cochise Community College. As rumor had it, she had fled a disastrous romance (perhaps even a marriage, some said) and started a new life in this distant corner of Arizona. Jerry found her kind and thoughtful and forthright in the way she dealt with other people. One Sunday he overheard her countering some objections to books that he was using in his up-coming Lenten programs. The complainer, a back-pew-dwelling old dinosaur, had been muttering about how liberal the writers of the books were and how the church was going to hell in a handbasket because of such writings. Kate gave him a little smile and a softly spoken, "Then I guess you won't be coming to the book group, will you." "Damn right I won't," he had answered. She just reached out and planted a tiny kiss on his wrinkled old cheek. Silas Ruhl was so nonplused that all he did was mumble while fighting off a grin of flattered pleasure.

Kate's shoulder length blond hair framed magnetic pale hazel eyes that

Jerry Hanning found mysterious and inviting. Her slim, feminine body perfectly filled out her wardrobe's mainstays, white pants and tailored blouses. Jerry tried, but not very hard, to keep Kate's looks from distracting him. But even as he chided himself for lusting after a parishioner, on the whole he recognized his interest in her was probably a good sign that his grief had begun to pass. He liked it that he found women attractive again.

It had been many years since Jerry had thought of himself as an "eligible man," and the thought of dating gave him the willies. But the sexual and emotional vacuum of the two years of grieving had to end sometime if he were ever to get his life back into balance. Some thought it dangerous or inappropriate for priests to date their parishioners, but he could see no real reason why two single people who seemed to be attracted to each other should not explore that attraction. By the time adults reached their forties it was tough enough to meet compatible and available people without totally excluding the work place.

Jerry had followed the rules in his last relationship. That had been in the second year of his curacy as a priest in Miami, Ohio. He met a woman attorney while giving testimony in a minor civil lawsuit. Marjory Little, ironically very tall, had a combination of beauty, dignity and brains that left Jerry feeling weak and silly in her presence. Their dating had quickly progressed from casual to serious, and Jerry soon concluded that she was the woman with whom he would share the rest of his life. The only serious obstacle they faced while dating was that Marjory had no religious affiliation of any kind. She was unsure that religion had any redeeming social value at all. In the end, she conceded the point to him and agreed that they might have a parish wedding, but the religious issue never entirely went away. Even though Marjory did go to church from time to time, Jerry had to admit that their very different values about religion had always gotten in the way of their relationship, especially considering the kind of work he had chosen.

Jerry's marriage to Marjory lasted just eight years and five months, and Sadie had just passed her seventh birthday when Marjory's death so suddenly ended that chapter of his life and initiated the odyssey that brought Jerry and Sadie to Tucson and then to Bisbee. The irony of Jerry's and Sadie's sad migration was that it carried with it for Jerry a religious skepticism not unlike Marjory's own when she was alive.

So they skipped and hopped across the country in Jerry's Skyhawk, finally stopping in Tucson. "I'll never forget the day we arrived," Jerry had shared in his initial visit with the bishop in Phoenix. "It was early June, and the heat in the desert was so intense when we got out of the Cessna at Ryan Field, that I was momentarily worried about the plane melting as it sat there baking in the sun. I wondered how anything could survive in that heat. We hitched a ride into town with another pilot and rented a car. I found a cheap motel where we both jumped directly into the pool. The rest of the day, we lounged in and out of the sun, doing what I could only describe as bake, and the pain and shared loneliness of the last months were drawn out of us by a kind of spiritual poultice. I don't remember us actually talking about the decision to stay in Tucson, but without ever actually saying it to each other, we both agreed that we felt at home there."

The bishop had just nodded understandingly. He was a good listener.

Jerry and Sadie had spent a week looking around and finding a place to live in Tucson, which proved to be easy at that time of the year when many people had fled the intense heat. They settled easily into a flat-roofed, two-bedroom stucco house with rough-plastered walls and wood floors not far from the university and the downtown area.

In Tucson, Jerry's spiritual and emotional healing began in earnest. He felt blessed by some extraordinary neighbors who helped a lot. Margaret Lopez and her pediatrician husband, Charles, were raising two granddaughters who bracketed Sadie's age by a year on each side. All of the Lopezes offered their unqualified welcome to the Hannings, and the six of them soon became good friends. The three girls seemed joined at the waist almost from the beginning, often spending nights back and forth at each other's houses.

Jerry soon located a spiritual guide in Fr. Benedict at Holy Trinity Monastery in St. David, south and east of Tucson about sixty miles as the Cessna flies. The community at Holy Trinity even put up a windsock for Jerry so he could land his plane on one of their dirt roads. It was companionable being at the monastery where, with Fr. Benedict, Jerry could be fully honest about his feelings of anger and despair—and what he thought of as his loss of faith. At first he made weekly visits there, sometimes spending the night while Sadie stayed at the Lopezes'. Fr. Benedict led Jerry to face his grief and loss honestly, and he encouraged him to get back to work as a priest and into relationships with other people who were dealing with pain in their lives. Jerry resisted at first, but in the end, he looked around and did some fill-ins for vacationing clergy. There were times when he felt dishonest, even fraudulent, with his uncertainties. But it felt good to be active again and to exercise his vocation, despite his doubts about God and about many of the spiritual claims of priesthood. Was there anyone out there listening to the prayers he offered? Why should *he* have any particular access to whatever God there may be? Still, the human contact was good for him, and he felt welcomed and kindly received by the people he saw. In a way he had never been conscious of before, the ministering flowed in both directions, both from and to the priest.

In his initial visit with the bishop, Jerry had confessed his unreadiness for a regular call to parish ministry, but agreed that he was otherwise willing to help out where needed. The conversation must have stuck in the bishop's mind, particularly the part about Jerry flying his own airplane. After a few months Jerry was invited to become part-time vicar in Bisbee, serving there on weekends and still able to live in Tucson during the rest of the week. It seemed like the perfect compromise. He could work with the people of Tombstone as they adjusted to losing their town's church, form solid relationships with the people in Bisbee and Tombstone and combine his love of flying with his religious vocation.

A packed St. Peter's Church greeted Hank Tucker and Teresa Bustamante for their wedding.

"Dearly beloved," Father Jerry began the service in the familiar opening words of the marriage rite. Hank grinned, and Teresa, eyes shining, maintained a dignified solemnity. "We are gathered here to join together this man and this woman in Holy Matrimony." Later in the ritual Jerry asked, "Teresa, will you have this man to be your husband?" She glanced momentarily at Hank and then back at the priest, who continued, "to live together in the covenant of marriage? Will you love him, comfort him, honor and keep him, in sickness and in health; and, forsaking all others, be faithful to him as long as you both shall live?"

"I will," she answered with a smile.

"Henry, will you have this woman...." He repeated the formula. Hank stood there, slightly awkward in his beautifully tailored new suit, string tie, and cowboy boots shined to a gleaming lustre.

"You bet I will," he answered loudly. A chuckle passed through the congregation, and Jerry smiled.

"Will all of you witnessing these promises do all in your power to uphold these two persons in their marriage?" Jerry asked.

Their loud and enthusiastic "We will" gave the priest another reason to smile.

After the wedding service, the party moved in a wave of laughing celebrants toward the Copper Queen Hotel for the reception. Kate Becker and Jerry Hanning walked together. Sadie skipped ahead with another girl her age. The bright and crisp night air was lighted by the brilliance of an almost-full moon. Kate reached out and took Jerry's arm as they walked, a simple, ordinary gesture, one that instantly gave him pleasure—and then self-conscious alarm. His heart raced. Jerry's vulnerable emotions screamed out, forcing him to pull carefully away to shake the hand of one of the guests who spoke to him.

"Father Jerry," Teresa Bustamante Tucker said later at the reception. "I want you to meet our favorite painter. Harold, this is Father Jerry Hanning. Harold is the artist who painted our wedding portrait." She gestured at the handsome oil painting that had been unveiled right before dinner when everyone had reached the lobby of the Copper Queen Hotel. "I can't tell you how much I had to argue to convince him to come tonight."

Jerry nodded to the large man. "I love the picture," he said, shaking the artist's hand and letting his eyes pass to the stunning Latina who stood at his side. Jerry guessed she was about thirty or a little more, dark-complected and dark-eyed. She moved her body with sensual yet understated elegance and seemed to sparkle in conversation, carrying herself with a kind of loftiness that made her different, set apart from the rest of common humanity. Harold Jenkins clearly adored her. It was easy to see why.

"Teresa exaggerates," the big man responded, wiping a hand self-consciously across his shaven head. "I'm a bit shy of big parties. Actually, Teresa is persuasive enough to talk paint off canvas." He paused and smiled. "Let me introduce my friend, Virginia Vega. Virginia is also an artist here in Bisbee."

She smiled at Hank and Teresa, then turned her flashing dark eyes toward Jerry, making him feel very uncomfortable. There was no invitation in those eyes or on the perfectly-formed face that showcased them. Instead, he felt something more like challenge coming from her.

"Virginia," he said and reached out his hand. She took it briefly, and with what felt to Jerry like reluctance.

She turned to Teresa. "What a beautiful wedding. It's an honor to be among your guests." Her voice was cultured, intelligent and as smooth as newly waxed wood.

Jerry stood there, entranced but ignored, feeling as awkward and self-conscious as he had in the ninth grade around his female classmates. It had been a long time since the ninth grade. He did not like feeling that way then, and he did not like it any better now. It must be an aversion to the clergy, he thought, something he sometimes ran into when wearing a clerical collar. He tried to let it pass.

Hank turned to Harold and picked up a conversation that they had been having. "Hear about the van load of Illegals they picked up over by Bisbee today?"

"Yeah, the one shot full of holes?" Harold responded.

"That part's too bad," Hank responded thoughtfully. "But at least the Border Patrol was on the alert. Sent 'em back, I guess."

"Or to prison, more likely," Harold observed gently. "Great lot of help that is."

"At least it keeps them from leaving my gates open and the water running," Hank was quick to reply.

One of Hank's neighbors, Charlie Snow, broke into the conversation with the slurred voice of someone who had been drinking, "Yeah, I think all those wet backs should be sent back where they came from. A bunch 'a stinkin' peons…all the Mexes are!"

"I beg your pardon, Charlie, what did you say?" Hank snarled quietly at the shorter, but powerfully built younger man. "Button your lip or go home." Anyone who looked carefully at Hank Tucker could see that he was very angry, but he managed to keep calm, reaching over and pulling his wife to his side.

Teresa effectively cut off the conversation. "Ms. Vega, what kind of work do you do?" she asked.

"Pencil. Some oils," she said. Like Teresa she ignored Charlie Snow's outburst. "I'm really just getting back to work after a long time away from it." A confused expression of pain and uncertainty showed on her lovely face.

There was something about Virginia Vega that looked familiar to Jerry. When Sadie asked him later if he thought she looked like one of their neighbor girls, Carmen, he thought at first that maybe Sadie was right. Then he wondered if his finding something familiar in Virginia Vega might not be similar to Charlie Snow's open racism, just less violent and nasty, but racist all the same—about all Mexicans looking alike.

Jerry danced that evening for the first time in years, including, amidst much laughter, with Mrs. Findlay as a partner. He had fun. At one point he found himself pressed close to Kate Becker on the dance floor, and she smiled with a gentle, knowing warmth that both moved and stirred him.

When the party ended and he tumbled into bed, Jerry felt exhausted but exhilarated as he called goodnight to Sadie, who had spent the evening running and playing with the other children.

"Have a good time tonight, Sweetheart?"

"Sure, Daddy. It was lots of fun. And *you* danced."

"That okay?"

"Sure. It was cool. How come you didn't dance with me?"

"I'm so sorry. It never occurred to me that you might want to."

"Well, I really don't know how, I guess."

"We'll have to do something about that."

"You promise?"

"Sure." Jerry turned out the light.

"Hmm. That's cool. Night, Daddy."

"Good night, Sweetheart."

Jerry's sleep had Kate Becker's image moving through it that night, and he no longer thought of her in saintly terms. Rather, he remembered about how she looked, and smelled, and felt, and the way she had smiled at him…and taken his arm as they walked. It felt to Jerry a lot like starting to fall in love.

St. Peter's echoed in near emptiness the next morning. Of the forty or fifty people who might be in church on a regular Sunday morning, many probably still nursed hangovers from the night before, but others likely had the conviction that they had already been to church that weekend. And even if the numbers had been more like normal, it would still have been a let-down after the wedding excitement. Months, maybe years, would pass before anyone would see that church filled with so many enthusiastic people and such genuine celebration. For once, the ten people who drove over from Tombstone that morning almost equaled in number the Bisbeeites in the sparse congregation.

After the service, Sadie and Jerry made their way to the airport and began the flight back to Tucson. It was perfect flying weather for a small, private craft piloted by a weekender with a nine-year-old passenger. They tightly circled around Mule Mountains to indulge their ground-watching hobby, looking in the surprisingly rich vegetation for large animals—perhaps deer or a herd of javelina. Flying at barely a thousand feet above the ground— often less—they could see many details. As they approached Tombstone's 4700 foot high abandoned but useable landing strip, Jerry decided to take a careful look at its deteriorating surface for his landing there the next week. Flying this low they would also pass close above Tombstone: the OK Corral, Allen Street, and the Old County Courthouse.

"Daddy, look out," Sadie suddenly shouted into the microphone of her headset, pointing across toward the left front quarter of the Skyhawk. Jerry saw immediately what had startled her. No more than a mile away and at almost the same low altitude, perhaps even fifty feet lower, a shiny red and white aircraft hurtled toward them from around a small hill.

"My God, what is this idiot doing?" Jerry breathed out and pulled back on the wheel, quickly gaining another hundred feet and at the same time banking sharply to the right. The pilot of the other craft must have seen the Cessna at the same time and made an instant maneuver, only diving instead of climbing. When they passed each other, Jerry and Sadie could feel the buffeting caused by the comparatively close call. The one thing that Jerry saw clearly was the unmistakable V-shape of a Bonanza's tail. What on earth, he wondered, was Hank Tucker doing out flying his plane on the day after his wedding? If only he had been able to see the registration number, then he could have been sure it was Hank's plane. But he could not imagine that there would be another craft just like that one in this part of the state. He certainly hadn't seen or heard of one. And what was it doing flying so low? Maybe just looking around the way they were? These were puzzles he could not resolve just then.

"You okay, Sadie?" he asked as the Skyhawk passed over the abandoned Tombstone airport, feeling a bit shaken himself by the near miss.

"Sure, Daddy," she answered.

Once the adrenalin rush had passed, the close call left Jerry with a very unsettled, hollow feeling in the pit of his stomach.

CHAPTER TWO

Last Summer and After

[O]ur concept of God Matters. It can make God seem credible or incredible, plausible or highly improbable. It can also make God seem distant or near, absent or present.
—Marcus Borg

Jerry Hanning had first met Art Gronek and his second wife, Maddie (short for Madeline), at the Cancer Center of the University Medical Center in Tucson. That was just a few weeks after Jerry and Sadie arrived in Tucson, and it was one of Jerry's first forays back into pastoral work. He had been at the hospital making some calls as a fill-in for vacationing priests and stopped by Art's room at the request of Bisbee's soon-to-retire part-time vicar. Art, with the eye and demeanor of a wounded bird of prey, and Maddie, pretty, soft-looking and gently quiet, were a striking couple. Art was ten years older than his wife, but he looked even older. Maddie could be described as petite, but the last thing she seemed was "small." Art stood five-ten and once had been powerfully built. Both had dark hair and eyes, and they looked as much like brother and sister as they did like husband and wife. Even with his widely metastasized cancer, Art had a barely diminished presence and a magnetic personality. For her part, Maddie was one of those women who managed always to look put together no matter what kind of clothes she wore or where she wore them. She was equally at home in loose, long, brightly colored skirts in town, formal clothing for evening, business attire during the week and ranch-life blue jeans at the Twisted K Ranch where they lived. Beneath her loose-fitting clothing or carefully tailored look was a healthy, generously proportioned and athletic body.

Arthur Gronek had bought his Twisted K Ranch outside Bisbee to be a hobby and a getaway. At least that was how he intended it in the mid-nineties right after his Silicon Valley computer business went public. He loved the rugged, isolated country and the varied culture there beside the Mexican border. An industrial engineer by training and a successful entrepreneur by force of personality and intellect, Art had lived most of the year in California where he could be near his business and the three children of his first marriage. Mostly, the ranch near Bisbee was meant to be a vacation spot and an escape from his busy life. Instead it became the place where Art Gronek came to die of cancer at the age of forty-eight.

Jerry stepped into Art's hospital room the day they met and greeted the Groneks casually with, "Hi, I'm Jerry Hanning." He noticed ruefully as both pairs of eyes shifted almost imperceptibly to his clerical collar before returning to his face. "Father Colshaw in Bisbee called and asked me to look in on you."

"Come in, Father," Art responded with a grin. "The clergy are always welcome here."

"Hello," Maddie said softly, the slightest hint of a smile on her face. "Here, sit down." She moved over to a straight-backed chair, leaving the green, plastic-covered lounger beside the bed for Jerry. The chair was warm from her body heat, and it felt to Jerry like an awkward intimacy for him to sit where her warmth remained. But, then, nearly every intimacy felt awkward to him these days.

"I'm a pretty conventional church goer," Art confessed as they talked. "I don't manage to get there every Sunday," he laughed, "but I always make a pledge, and I can be counted on for other gifts when something comes up."

Jerry smiled. "I'll bet you have even been on vestries, committees—the like."

"Oh, yeah. I try to do my part. And I like the liturgy—especially the old service. There's something about the poetry of that language that really gets to me. "

Jerry soon figured out that Art's life had been little affected by the theology or spirituality of the church. But he liked clergy and was comfortable with them, was not intimidated by them. And right from the first Jerry liked Art very much.

"I go to church with Art sometimes," Maddie said. "But I'm not an Episcopalian—not much of anything, really. My mother's Jewish but doesn't practice, and my father's some sort of Christian, I guess. I've never known him to go to church." From her expressions and body language, Jerry guessed that church and religion in general amused her. "I guess my emotional connection to Israel makes me more or less Jewish," she said, "but that seems…ah…political, or cultural, I guess, not really religious."

Jerry shifted in his chair and then asked about the elephant in the room. "Your cancer is pretty bad?"

"Yeah, it's damned bad. They tell me that I have less than a year."

"That's crummy." Jerry pushed a pitcher of ice water and an institutional size box of Kleenex out of the way and put his prayer book, stole and pix filled with consecrated communion wafers onto the wheeled hospital table. He looked over at Maddie, and their eyes met. Her pain and his grief acted in that moment to create an instant bond between them. Jerry and Art also hit it off. They simply understood each other.

Jerry visited Art several times during the weeks of his in-patient chemotherapy treatments. They played some one-sided chess—Jerry not really being a match for Art—and some more competitive gin rummy. Art usually won at that, too, but it didn't matter. About a week after Art left the hospital to go back to the Twisted K to wait for the results of the chemo and radiation, Jerry got a surprise call one morning.

"Jerry, this is Art Gronek," the disembodied voice said. Art seemed strangely diminished without the force of his presence.

"Hi, Art," Jerry answered. "How've you been?"

"Not great, but at least I'm finished with the chemo and it's pretty much out of my system. That's the last of that stuff I intend to suffer."

"Funny thing about poison. It makes you sick."

"That's a damned odd pastoral attitude." Art gave a belly laugh. "Anyhow, the reason I called is to see if you have a couple of days free, say Thursday and Friday next week. Maddie and I would love to have you visit. Just say the word and I'll have my ranch manager, Refugio, scrape the weeds and litter off the old runway for you."

"Is it okay to bring Sadie?" It was early August and she still had a couple of weeks to go before school started. Like most kids her age, she would get a real kick out of seeing a genuine working Arizona cattle ranch.

"Sure. We'll put her to work. Ha!" he exclaimed, promising again a newly scraped landing strip and a bright, fresh wind sock in a clearly marked circle beside it.

The month of August is the heart of Southern Arizona's monsoon, a seasonal flow of warm, moist air from the Gulf of Mexico bringing surprisingly high humidity to the desert and the wildest thunderstorms anywhere. Brilliant skies, ominous clouds, colorful sunsets and flash floods with enormous quantities of water vie with each other to offer the best performance in the seasonal drama. The Santa Cruz, the Rillito and other rivers and washes in Tucson and the surrounding area, dry for most of the year, can overflow their banks during the monsoon. Most of the time, these dry stream beds serve as avenues for dirt bikes and four-wheeling or horses and riders. Sometimes, especially in the southern part of the state, they become paths for migrants, the Tohono O'odam historically, and illegal immigrants today. During the monsoon with its ever-present danger of flooding, dawdling in those normally dry beds can be very dangerous. It is also the most treacherous time of the year for small private aircraft. Flying anytime after mid-day can be chancy at best, dangerous or fatal at worst.

The monsoon was in full rumble on Thursday right after lunch when Jerry and Sadie set out from Ryan Field for the Twisted K ranch. Storm clouds, gray-to-black and threatening, had already built-up by ten o'clock around the mountains that ring Tucson, promising a violent afternoon, perhaps a repeat of the day before when high winds and a torrential downpour had broken tree limbs and flooded Tucson streets. Jerry was prepared to divert to Bisbee or Sierra Vista if the weather took a turn for the worse. Just locating the Twisted K was going to be tricky. They had to spot a particular peak on the west side of Mule Mountains just east of the San Pedro Riparian Conservation Area. From there Art's instructions were to look for a bright red windmill.

They flew down the San Pedro valley, already a familiar spot for Jerry Hanning because of his visits to the monastery in St. David, and over legendary Tombstone, which Jerry pointed out to Sadie. They then headed due south, the search for landmarks now beginning in earnest.

Ore-rich Mule Mountains is a compact collection of low peaks, the eastern edge of a discontinuous east-west string of mountains stretching ultimately south into Mexico. Another section of this range, the Huachucas, was the home of warlike Apaches over a century before. The western foothills of Mule Mountains decline gradually into the vegetation of the San Pedro river basin. From this green band, in some places more than a mile wide, the land becomes gradually drier and is covered with occasional mesquite, ironwood and Joshua trees and creosote bushes. The Twisted K ranch house is cuddled in the low hills at the mouth of a small canyon in this area between the river and the mountains.

Jerry was the first one to notice an ominous build up of thunder heads along Mule Mountains to the east and south of the area where they were searching. But Sadie soon saw them too.

"Daddy?" she asked into her microphone.

"Yes, Sweetheart."

"Those clouds are pretty scary, aren't they?"

"Well, just a bit," he confessed. And at that moment the wind blasted the Skyhawk with a sudden micro-burst that drove the plane down almost 500 feet, precariously close to the jagged, rough terrain below. Jerry pulled back on the yoke and fought against the power of the wind. And then the intense burst and downdraft stopped and, at full power, he dragged the Cessna back up to the thousand feet he sought to hold above ground level, only to have the wind hit again, this time from about 100 degrees across their left wing. It felt for a moment as if the vulnerable craft would be rolled all the way over. That was not a maneuver that the Cessna was built to withstand.

"I'm scared, Daddy," Sadie said in a very small voice as he fought with the wheel and rudder pedals against the primal force tearing at them. They pitched up and down, left and right, dropping a hundred feet in one "bump," then were thrown back up again nearly as much.

And then as one they saw the red windmill and, not far from there, what was certainly the Twisted K ranch house and outbuildings. Just beyond the house was an enormous windsock, its shuddering stiffness pointing the direction and intensity of the wind on the ground. A second later the landing strip itself seemed to break loose from the surrounding vegetation to become clearly visible.

The increased buffeting by the wind, which seemed to be coming from all directions at once, would make for a difficult landing. Paying no attention whatever to the niceties of landing patterns, but adjusting the attitude of the Skyhawk and bringing down the airspeed, Jerry prepared to put it on the ground as quickly as possible. The direction of the stiff wind was steady on the ground, but unfortunately was coming thirty degrees off the right wing. Jerry lined the plane up on the runway, crabbed as best he could and dipped the windward wing to stabilize the approach. A cross-wind landing on a dirt strip of dubious smoothness with a thunderstorm rapidly bearing down was not Jerry's idea of a good time, especially with his nine-year-old daughter sitting beside him. Fifteen knots of cross wind would have been easily manageable. This one was running more like thirty and gusting much more. God alone knew what it would be like in another fifteen minutes.

As Jerry struggled with the wind and with the controls, first raising one wing, then the other, Sadie began to cry and said again, "Daddy, I'm scared."

"It's going to be okay," he replied, but felt less confident than he tried to sound. He fought the storm with both hands and both feet, sometimes having a sickening feeling as the plane dropped like a rock and then shot back up again like a piece of balsa wood tossed on a rough sea.

And then suddenly they were down, helped by a momentary lull in the wind's force. Jerry held the plane on its two main wheels with backward pressure on the yoke and continued power to the propeller, keeping the vulnerable nose wheel from the stress of the uneven field. Sadie grabbed his arm and pressed her cheek against it, little quivers of terror, relief and joy passing between them. As soon as he could, he spun the plane around and headed back toward the ranch house, a sprawling, low-roofed stucco building of varying roof lines and heights set in a bare desert patch—and surrounded at that moment by a pandemonium of blowing dust and dry vegetation. Catapulting tumbleweeds lashed the Skyhawk from behind as it raced toward a lone figure waving them toward a solitary tie-down.

"We made it, Sadie. You okay?"

"Sure, Daddy. I really wasn't…too scared."

"What a girl. What a copilot."

The lone helper on the ground was Maddie Gronek, who expertly guided Jerry as he maneuvered the plane onto the center of the triangle of rusty tie-down chains, one for each wing strut and one for the tail. He cut the power and completed the shut-down procedures, dropping his headset unceremoniously on top of the control panel, and jumped out to secure the plane against the buffeting of the increasingly severe wind. Maddie worked on the right wing, while Jerry put out the chocks and secured the left and then the tail. Sadie worked at the side widow covers as usual. Bits of sand tore at their clothing, furiously flapping pant legs, and stinging bare skin wherever it was exposed: legs, arms and face.

"Where did you learn to tie down an airplane?" Jerry shouted to Maddie in some small astonishment.

"Oh, I used to fly, back before I met Art. Some things stay with you, I guess. And this must be Sadie,"she said. "Can I help you?" she shouted above the roar of the wind.

"Please," Sadie responded, also in a shout. "That was pretty scary." She threw her arms around the waist of the unknown adult and held on, partly against the force of the wind and partly in response to what she had just been through.

"I bet it was," Maddie responded with real concern for Jerry's precious passenger. She bent down to look directly into Sadie's eyes. "Let's go in…out of this wind," she said, taking Sadie's hand in hers. They trotted away toward the house.

"I'll be right with you," Jerry called to their backs. "Couple a things to do first." He finished securing the plane on the inside and snapped a piece of fitted canvas over the front and rear windows. "My poor paint job," Jerry muttered to himself. But then he sighed a quick thanksgiving that they were on the ground and in one piece, resolving to get an earlier morning start during the monsoon season. He grabbed the luggage off the ground and ran for the house just as the rain began, at first a few drops and then a deluge. He made it to cover just as the full fury of the desert thunderstorm hit, flooding the hot, dry soil with barrels of shockingly icy water.

Inside, the Twisted K ranch house was a surprise after the drab exterior. The entrance of the house opened onto a four-sided cloister with rounded arches on all four sides opening onto covered walkways. Earth tones of reddish brown and tan and gleaming Mexican ceramic tile in purples, pinks and oranges were the colors of an Arizona sunset and the land it spilled over. In the middle of the cloister sat a lush grassy area with brightly-colored zinnias, verbena and lantana arranged around a tall, bubbling and splashing fountain. Clustered arrangements of wrought iron furniture suggested an invitation to linger—though not in the present downpour. From the cloister, at least a dozen doors opened into rooms of one kind or another. Double doors of dark-stained heavy mesquite carved with farm animals and laboring human figures opened into the broad living room.

The room inside was even more stunning than the cloister and the doors had been. Geometrically patterned rugs softened the red Mexican tile floor, and the wide rustic room was furnished with dark, well-polished old furniture. Against one wall, an enormous fireplace stood ringed by comfortable, slightly worn over-stuffed chairs and a sofa. The high ceiling, perhaps sixteen feet in this room, was made of huge round pine beams supporting stained and polished wood. On the sofa lay Arthur Gronek in the warm light of a circle of softly burning lamps.

Art looked terrible. Not even the rich surroundings masked the pallor of his skin, his sunken eyes and shrunken size.

"How are you, Art?" Jerry asked him, packing many questions into the conventional greeting: Are you in pain? Are you hanging on to your life? Are you depressed? Do you want to just shout—Shit! Shit! Shit!

"Not too bad," Art responded with a wistful look, an obvious and conventional falsehood. Jerry glanced at Maddie. With an expressionless glance she communicated the truth—and Art's lie. Jerry had seen a lot of cancer patients in his work as a priest, and he could not help but wonder about the accuracy of the year the doctors had given him. He felt very sad to think that. "I hear you had a bit of excitement landing," Art said.

"You could say so. But my co-pilot pulled me through." Jerry gave Sadie a little grin.

Despite the pall that hung over the Twisted K because of Art's illness, Jerry and Sadie's first visit to the ranch was filled with many adventures and lots of fun. That afternoon, the thunderstorm having gone as suddenly as it came, they looked over the ranch buildings and became acquainted with some of the ranch animals.

There was a variety of dogs, some with probable wolf ancestors, and the few cats wily or lucky enough to stay clear of the coyotes—who found them a good choice for a quick meal—were wild and unapproachable. But for simple fun Sadie's favorites were the goats—particularly the lively young kids. Jerry and Sadie also rode a couple of gentle old saddle horses. Sadie soon identified a mare as her particular mount.

"See, she likes me," Sadie declared. The mare nuzzled her ears, to Sadie's giggling pleasure.

They learned about the operation of a working cattle ranch from Refugio Mendez, the crusty manager and foreman who ran the ranch: about modern cattle identification using microchip technology instead of branding, about roundups, even about cattle inoculations and medicine. Neither Maddie nor Art claimed any knowledge about ranching. But it was easy to see why they liked living there. The spectacular mornings and the fresh, clean air were reason enough. Watching the thunderstorms roll in across Mule Mountains and from behind a stand of tall cottonwood trees was awesome...and much better observed from the land than from the air.

Both nights of that first visit Art and Jerry stayed up late playing cards and talking. Maddie was in and out of the room as she served Jerry and herself some fine, old single malt whiskey, while Art merely cast regretful glances at Jerry's tumbler and nursed a glass of mineral water. Art talked about the pending sale of his business, and he had strong feelings of loss about that. They talked politics some, mostly the usual dismay over the current world situation. Maddie wrung her hands over the growing intensity and violence between the Israelis and the Palestinians.

Art and Jerry got around to some serious personal conversation late on the second night.

"I really don't want to die," Art said suddenly.

Jerry looked at him, a bit surprised, waiting to see what he would say next. Art had never before brought up his health and what the future promised—or withheld—because of it. In the hospital as Art completed the chemo treatments, Jerry had tried to be the good pastor and offer him openings, but Art had always ducked them. Then as their friendship grew, Jerry stopped pushing and just enjoyed Art's company.

"It really sucks," Art continued after a moment. "Here I am with a great life, a smart, beautiful wife whom I love, lots of money, the promise of new things ahead, good friends…and a body that has given up on everything." He paused as if to get his breath. "There's so much I want to do." He poured some more Scotch into Jerry's glass and pushed the ice bucket in his direction. Dutifully, Jerry pinched a few cubes with the tongs and dropped them into his glass. The air conditioning hummed quietly, making both of them newly aware of it in a silence that had suddenly become oppressive. Candles flickered in the moving air.

"Yeah, it sucks all right," Jerry responded quietly. The silence resumed as the two men looked unblinkingly into each other's eyes. It was a wordless moment that screamed a rage over the helplessness of terminal illness, the finality of death, the emptiness of leaving life and love and challenge. More communication pulsed through that quiet than there had been over the hours they had played cards and chattered away. Finally, Jerry broke the silence that had gradually slipped from intensity into awkwardness. "Have you made all of your plans?"

"Most of 'em, I guess. The business stuff concludes next week when the sale becomes final. My kids get more money than they'll ever need." Art's three children, twin girls aged fourteen and a ten-year-old boy, were seldom around—their mother's choice, not Art's—and Jerry had not yet met them. "Maddie keeps this ranch and enough money that she won't have to worry. Charitable donations and bills and all of that are paid." He paused for a moment. "I guess I've done all the right stuff. But it still makes me mad as hell." Jerry cleared his throat, as if to speak. Art just held up his hand. "No. I'm not running through the stages of dying. I've done all that crap. I just don't want to leave my life."

Jerry leaned back in his chair and asked the question that his pastoral training and experience demanded, "And where are you with God?"

"We haven't been talking much lately." Art smiled mirthlessly.

"Have you tried to open the conversation?"

"I wouldn't know what to say. 'Why me?' Or maybe 'Let this burden pass from me.' But that must be blasphemous. Wouldn't want to be *that*," he snarled cynically. He paused. "I guess I'm not sure God cares."

"Who *is* God for you?" Jerry asked quietly.

"What do you mean by 'who'? 'Lord, God Almighty, creator of heaven and earth,' of course. 'All that is, seen and unseen.' You know—all that power and might stuff."

"Is that a helpful way to think about God right now?"

"Not particularly. In fact it pisses me off to think that God could fix me...and doesn't."

"What *would* help? What do you want from God...here and now?"

"Nothing!" He paused. "No, that's not true. I want the cancer cured. Or...at least some answers. What kind of a God causes things like this?"

"You think God made you have cancer," Jerry said simply.

Maddie just shook her head and wandered out of the livingroom. The thing she did not understand about either Jerry or Art was how people as smart as each of them was could still hold to those old theological notions about God—all of that very dated religious stuff. But then, she never did understand religious feelings at all.

"Not exactly," Art continued. "But he tolerates it. I can't imagine a God who permits such ugly, horrible stuff...like what's happening to me."

"Mind if I preach for awhile?" Jerry seemed more confident than he felt. Inside, he was a confused jumble of feelings arising from his original sense of call, his training and experience, his own doubts, his lack of clarity about God—if there is a God—and his still-smoldering anger about Marjory's death. It had only recently occurred to him that it all did boil down to the "person" of God—just who God is, or who God is understood to be.

"Preach away. It's probably about time."

"Well, then," Jerry began rehearsing some of his own internal conversation, "what if God is not a benevolent father who is 'out there' somewhere and who runs everything, who is the prime mover in everything?"

"You mean that instead of being Daddy, God has gone away somewhere— like the Deist god who is unconcerned, unconnected?"

"No, that's the worst of the anthropomorphic gods. I mean like the 'ground of being' god, or the 'stream of spirit' god, or 'the one in whom we live and move and have our being' god. You know, the kind of god who is radically here, now, all around us, in us, animating us and everything else—giving life, and giving it 'abundantly.' You recognize these words, ones just as Biblical and just as liturgical as old YAHWEH the warrior king?"

"Right," he responded without committing himself.

"You don't have to have the 'big guy in the sky,' you know. In fact, for me, that way of understanding the holy gets in the way." He decided to share his own struggle with his dying friend. "I have just been through a serious crisis in my own faith—probably am still in it. And the bottom line for me has been this: I cannot dismiss the sacred dimension of life; I have experienced it too clearly and too poignantly for that. But I have not entirely been able to reconcile that knowledge with the horror of living and dying as I have recently experienced it. Know what I mean?"

Art nodded.

"Anyhow, I just can't reconcile my experience of the sacred with what happened to my wife and with that distant God...up there, or out there, or...oh, I don't know. The old all-knowing, all-powerful first mover! A big part of my search is to find other ways to think about God—not ones that invalidate the old ideas, you understand—just ones that are more helpful to me."

"I don't know. That seems pretty abstract, maybe too impersonal, at least for me." Art's reply to Jerry's ideas was thoughtful, but unconvinced. "The warrior God of ancient Israel is flawed; I can see that. But still..." He let this thought trail off, reflectively. They were silent for a moment. Then he visibly changed directions, sitting up and looking at Jerry with a fresh intensity. "What difference does it make to my cancer how I think about him—or 'it'? I still have cancer, and it's not going away. I know that. I'm not 'in denial' about that. I just don't understand why."

"You mean what have you done for God to punish you in this way?"

"Exactly."

"Let me ask you a question," Jerry continued. "What are the things you liked best about being in business?" Art's face took on an annoyed expression. "This is relevant," Jerry continued. "What have you liked best?"

Art thought for a moment. "Let me see," he responded. "I always like the 'job-well-done' stuff, of course."

"Right."

"And I like making the money, a measure of worth, though I must admit that that has lost much of its punch. Course there's the challenge in it," he continued. "The excitement. Making something work, out-guessing the competition."

"The thrill of the hunt?" Jerry asked.

"Sure. That, of course."

"And where would that kind of competition be without the possibility of losing? If you always knew you'd win, and if there were no risks if you lost, how interesting would the struggle be? Could there even be such a thing as challenge? Put another way, what thrill is there in sky diving, mountain climbing, fast driving, business—anything that's risky—unless you run the danger of failure, injury and even death. Or what about sports? If both teams will win, and know they will win, what's the point in playing? Sportsmanship? Love of the exercise? Not very likely. Without the threat of loss and failure, along with the possibility of gain and success, there is no real competition.

"*Life* would hold no zest, no thrill, no challenge…if death were not always there, always lurking just around the next corner. Danger. Death. This is the ultimate risk in all competition. Death is, therefore, the father and mother of joy, of exuberance, of *joie de vivre*. Can you imagine life without death? Perpetual life? Just like now, except no end? It wouldn't be life at all. No death, no life."

"Never thought of it that way," Art replied. "Life and death. Flip sides of the same coin." He was quiet for a moment. "And…I suppose that means that death can't only be for the old, but must come at any time and for any reason? Hmm. I'm going to have to think about that." He smiled and asked a pointed question, "Is that why you fly your toy airplane—the risk of death?"

Jerry laughed. "I suppose that's some of it. I used to joke, back in the days when I really worked, that flying was good for relaxation and a quick get-away from parish worries, chronically red budget balances and the like, that in an airplane, without total concentration, you die. Not entirely true, but true enough to leave behind distractions." They laughed together.

"But then there's something else," Art said, turning serious again. "What about heaven? All I've ever thought about it is that it's 'life everlasting.' With your perspective that doesn't become much of an encouragement or hope, particularly for someone like me who is on the fast-track there…or somewhere else even less attractive." He laughed.

"Maybe that's why the Bible, Jesus, St. Paul and the mainstream of the Christian faith really have very little to say about what…specifically…happens after death. The tradition isn't even clear about *when* it happens—immediately after death or at the Resurrection on the 'last day.' For me—and I'm not speaking for the Church, for theologians or for anybody else—for me, it's essential that we not have a clear road map and city plan for paradise—and for the same reason that death's important to really having life. Human beings—no, I need to speak only for myself again—*I* need to have doubts, unanswered questions, ambiguity. Creativity and hope are not, for me, products of certainty, but of possibility. Know what I mean?"

"Yeah, I think I do." He shook his head—almost like a wet dog shaking itself, and moved on. "This is good therapy for me, speculating about God. At least I'm not feeling so sorry for myself. But enough! Deal the cards," he demanded. "Time for me to show you the power of losing."

Maddie and Jerry found some time to begin to get to know each other that weekend, and they found that they had a lot in common, like early rising. Both of them had awakened that Saturday morning before anyone else in the house. They had coffee together in the kitchen, then she invited him to take a walk around the ranch buildings, corrals and pens. They wandered together beyond the little goat pen where the kids leapt and cavorted with each other in the shade of the cottonwood trees. They followed a path in the wash that wound through a stand of black oaks and then up a small canyon. The usually-dry stream bed provided smooth, water-swept, sandy ground under their feet. Art's illness, small talk about ranch life, Sadie's pleasure in being there and general enthusiasm about life, and the goats and their antics occupied them for a time. After a while, Maddie, sitting on an exposed rock, began to talk about herself, something she very badly needed to do.

"It's lonely out here, but I love it. I grew up in Arizona, you know. Tucson, actually. Went to Rincon High and the UA. Then I went to grad school at UC Berkeley."

"I didn't know that. That's where I went to seminary. When were you at Berkeley?" Jerry found another rock to sit on.

"Eighty-nine to ninety-three," she answered. "But I only finished my dissertation a couple of years ago."

"Ph.D.? I had no idea. We overlapped a year at Berkeley. What in, the degree?"

"Medieval French history, actually." She grinned a self-conscious little smile.

"My God. Depths upon depths. You're pretty quiet about it."

"I guess I'm a little embarrassed. All that education and what do I do? Become a ranch wife."

"I may not have thought of you as having a medieval history Ph.D., but I certainly never would have described you as a ranch wife."

"Just how *do* you think of me?" she asked, amazed to find that he had thought about her at all. Art had so monopolized Jerry's time, that Maddie had felt largely invisible. This was normal. Art was such a strong personality, his conversation so magnetic, that he always dominated any conversation. His illness diminished his presence somewhat, but by no means did it eclipse it. Around Art, Maddie always felt that she got a little lost.

"How would I describe you?" Jerry began in response to her mildly flirting question. "Attractive certainly." Jerry seemed to her to be a little embarrassed. "And smart."

Maddie felt the blood rise to her cheeks. "I really wasn't fishing for compliments."

"Well, I'm afraid you'll have to put up with some. You're great with Art, you know." Jerry realized that there was something about Maddie, perhaps her impending widowhood, but he found that she touched him very deeply, and he liked her company better every time they were together.

Maddie just smiled with pleasure, the delight at simply being noticed by another human making a sudden and enormous difference to her. They resumed their walk.

This conversation set the tone for future ones between Jerry and Maddie. There was always a little harmless flirting, regardless of the seriousness of the conversation. She appreciated that in Jerry. It made her feel more whole, like more than a woman who was taking care of a dying husband, a soon-to-be widow. For Jerry, it was an awkward awareness of a sexual tension he felt in her presence right from that first time they met in the hospital in Tucson.

That August visit to the Twisted K was the first of several, and it set the pattern for the ones to follow. Every couple of weeks or so Jerry and Sadie stayed at the ranch and, after a while, they came to feel like family. Art and Jerry talked more about theology and about Art's death. Maddie and Jerry talked about her life before, during and, with gradually diminishing pain, after Art. Jerry shared his story and what life had been for Sadie and him the last couple of years. Sadie played with the goats and became quite good at riding the old mare. She and Maddie spent a lot of time together. In theory the visits focused on the Hannings being there for the Groneks, but Art and Maddie had become central to Jerry and Sadie's sense of place and their feeling that they belonged in Southern Arizona. Once, when Art had to see his oncologist in Tucson, he and Maddie had dinner at the Hannings' little house. All felt blessed in their relationship.

The last of the visits for Jerry and Sadie to the Twisted K came on Thanksgiving weekend. They got to Ryan Field mid-afternoon the day before, already carrying a new excitement for the holidays this year. Halloween had been lots of fun with Sadie trick-or-treating as Harry Potter's sidekick, Hermione Granger, and Jerry living out one of his political biases by frightening children with a grotesque Richard Nixon rubber mask that he had been carrying around for twenty years. They wandered through their neighborhood filling up Sadie's candy bag. Her two neighbor friends, Carmen and Elizabeth (dressed as rock stars) came along, as did the girls' grandmother, Margaret. They had a terrific, uncomplicated time and then went back to the Lopez house for hot chocolate and pumpkin *empanadas*. Later they all visited the neighborhood Episcopal Church and went through a haunted house designed and constructed by its parishioners. Ghoulish actors, all church members, provided frights for the under twelve gang and many laughs for the older patrons.

Little by little Jerry and Sadie had come to feel more whole as a family of two, as if they had always been that number and had never been three. Though Marjory was never far from either Jerry's or Sadie's consciousness, at least life had become less painful. The width and frequency of Sadie's smiles said much about how she felt. The pain of their loss was no longer the dominant theme of their lives.

And now they would celebrate Thanksgiving with their new family. Art Gronek's clearly deteriorating health was ominous, but it failed to dampen their anticipation. They settled into the Skyhawk that autumn afternoon, a bag of fresh vegetables on the back seat beside backpacks and a bundle of books they were taking for the quiet hours.

They had been cleared for take-off and were moving off across Tucson when Sadie asked, "Daddy, do you think we'll have turkey, or do they have some other kind of meat for Thanksgiving on a cattle ranch?"

"Oh." Jerry smiled playfully. "I'm sure they'll have turkey. Or maybe goat," he taunted.

"You think…? Daddy! You're teasing me—aren't you?

He smiled. "Of course I am."

"What's going to happen to Art, Daddy?" she asked suddenly. Jerry had avoided talking too specifically about Art's health with her, not wanting to risk bringing up their own painful memories when everything seemed, and indeed was, so much better for them.

"I think you know, Sadie."

"He's going to die, isn't he?"

"Yes, he is."

"And pretty soon, too?" Her small voice was very quiet and serious.

"Yes, I'm afraid so. Does that make you sad?" The Tucson air traffic controller broke into their silence by advising of a Piper Cherokee that was in their general area. Jerry looked out to try to spot it.

"There it is, Daddy," Sadie said suddenly.

"That's my eagle eye," he said to her and pushed the send button. "Tucson Tower, this is Cessna Five-Eight-Bravo, I have the traffic in sight. Thank you, sir."

"Roger, Five-Eight-Bravo."

Jerry returned his attention to Sadie. "Does Art being sick remind you of what happened to Mommy?"

"Not really. She didn't have cancer."

"No, she didn't."

"I think what she had was much better than cancer. She didn't know she was dying, and she didn't know she would be leaving us. It hurts a lot watching Art get sicker and sicker. I don't like to think that he won't be here any more. What will happen to Maddie?"

Much was going on inside her little head. Not even Jerry had guessed just how much. And now she was asking the very questions Jerry had been avoiding.

"I don't know. She hasn't made any plans yet that I know of. I think she wants to get through each day as it happens." Jerry paused for a moment, realizing that in his tension he had been holding the Skyhawk level by arm strength alone rather than by adjusting the attitude with the trim tab. He made the adjustment, easing the pressure on the yoke. "And I don't like watching him be so sick either," he continued into his headset. "Art has become a very good friend of mine. I guess the best friend I have, besides you." He reached over and lightly touched his daughter's arm.

Sadie grinned back at him.

The sun was just beginning to peek over Mule Mountains, lightening the broad valley west of the Twisted K Ranch when a panicky Sean Groneck, Art's ten-year-old son, beat on Maddie's bedroom door.

Throughout the day before—Thanksgiving Day—Art Gronek had been charming, but subdued, spending the entire time in his wheelchair when he wasn't actually in bed. He was much worse, perhaps even in a lot of pain, though he did not complain, and he was groggy from being heavily medicated. There was little more to him by then than skin and bones.

Deborah Barr Stringfellow, Maddie's mother, came out from Tucson and took over much of the cooking responsibility for the Thanksgiving dinner. All three of Art's children had come for the weekend, ten-year-old Sean and the fourteen-year-old twins, Jamie and Jodi, in full eye-rolling adolescence, addressing the whole world with disdain. Even the self-focused, snotty twins knew that something serious was up with their father and treated him with a kind of consideration that helped soften the outrageous side of their personalities and behavior. Sean was a delight for Maddie to have around, and, in his quiet and thoughtful way, was adored by all. Sean and Sadie hit it off immediately. The two children had long talks as they explored the ranch's delights together.

Deborah, Maddie's mother, had been the life of the party. Five feet of energy and opinions, she had every hair in place and her clothing perfectly arranged, and she gave all assembled the forthright gift of her wisdom. Everyone saw the sparks that flew between mother and daughter. Maddie, for her part, worked hard trying to be the good hostess—laughing, talking, ignoring her mother, sometimes pointedly, and generally looking, she secretly hoped, as if she had not a single problem in the world. But her actions lied. Perhaps it was partly premonition or maybe because she was worried about having let Art's nurse have the day off to be with her family, but whatever the cause, she was profoundly worried about Art throughout the day. He seemed so much worse.

After dinner was over and they had all settled into the living room with brandies and coffee, Art asked to be taken to his bed, saying he felt just too tired to stay up any longer. This time, Sean came along with Maddie and helped get him into bed.

"Just help adjust his feet," she said. "You okay, Art?"

"Sure," he said.

"Is there anything else I can do? Like, you know, to make you comfortable and all," Sean asked his father.

Everyone went to bed early. Jerry Hanning and Maddie took turns during the night sitting with Art. Sean insisted upon doing his part and sat with his father during the final hours before morning. It was during Sean's watch just at dawn that the ten-year-old found that Art could not be wakened for his medication. Sean tried repeatedly to wake him, but with a mounting sense of desperation, speaking in his ear and gently shaking his arm, but nothing helped. Finally, he ran to waken Maddie.

"Yes," she called.

"I'm sorry to wake you," he called back through the door, "but something's wrong with my dad. He won't wake up. It's time for his medicine, and…. Like, can you come?"

"Of course. Just a sec." Sean stood in the chill of the cloister while Maddie put on her robe and slippers before joining him. They ran together to Art's room.

Maddie could see immediately that Art was either very sound asleep or he had slipped into a coma.

"Art," Maddie called. She shook him lightly.

"I already tried that," Sean said.

"Art, it's Maddie. Can you wake up?" No movement. No indication at all that he had heard her. She shook him again, then turned to Sean and said, "How long has he been this way?"

"When I tried to wake him for his medicine…well you see…"

Maddie half walked, half ran down the cloister to Jerry's room and knocked on his door. He answered it immediately. She told him about Art.

"I think we had better get him to Tucson…to the hospital there," he said. "I can have him at UMC in the plane by the time we could drive him to Sierra Vista—let alone wait for an ambulance to come."

"You're right," she said. It would actually take as long or longer to get to the best regional hospital in Sierra Vista as to fly into Tucson. The care he would get there far surpassed anything in this part of the state, and, besides, he had been a regular patient there. They had all his records, and he could be seen by his own doctors.

"I'll get the plane ready," Jerry continued. "Get Refugio and blankets and pillows for him to lie on. Are you up for a ride to Tucson to keep an eye on him while I fly the plane? Is Sadie okay here 'til I get back?"

"Of course," she said. "I'll wake my mother to be with the kids and to alert the hospital."

Jerry quickly ran to his room, glancing at the lightening sky, and reemerged a moment later in jeans, tennis shoes, a sweatshirt and a wind breaker. By the time Maddie had alerted Refugio and rounded up blankets and pillows, Jerry had untied the struts and tail and had the engine idling to warm up. He got out of the plane and removed the right front seat, forming a make-shift bed with pillows and blankets. Maddie sat behind Jerry and beside Art's head which they lay gently on the cushion bottom of the back seat. Jerry, and Refugio and his helper managed that task as if they were lifting a tall rag doll, so terribly thin and wasted had Art's body become.

"You fly carefully now," Refugio said with a typically serious but worried look on his face.

Jerry just nodded.

"God go with you, Father Jerry. Mrs. Gronek," the other man, Francesco, wished them as he stepped back.

They were in the air within minutes. Maddie sat in the rear seat of the plane without a head set and feeling as alone as she had ever felt in her life. She overheard snatches of Jerry's side of a conversation with Tucson Approach Control telling them of the emergency and asking that an ambulance be waiting at the executive terminal. The short flight seemed to her to take forever as she sat there holding Art's head against her thigh, smoothing his hair with her hand and checking periodically to make sure he was still breathing. She could hear the engine, the rush of air outside the plane, and occasionally Jerry's voice when he spoke to the tower.

It had been strange for Maddie to adjust to Art as a helpless, dying man; he had always seemed so dominant to her, so self-absorbed, eclipsing her into his personality. But nobody else saw it that way, certainly not Art. When she complained to him that she seemed not even to exist when he was around, he would deny it and insist that they had a partnership. And he meant it. From Art's point of view Maddie always gave back as good as she got. He never knew where that nimble mind was going next. He worshiped her.

Still, after they met, Maddie quickly put her Ph.D. program on hold. At the end of the term she moved in with Art in his rambling, ultra-modern home in Silicon Valley. A year later they married in a quiet religious ceremony at his Episcopal Church in the Valley. Her mother, Deborah, snorted about the religious part of the ceremony, but came and did her best to control the details. How like her, Maddie had complained. But Deborah and Art hit it off from the beginning. The newlyweds settled down to a life in which Art made money and Maddie took care of him and tried to meet his needs, or at least that was what she had told herself she was doing.

In one area the Groneks failed miserably. No matter what they did, and they certainly gave it their best, children simply would not come for them. They both tested fine, but she never did get pregnant, a source of real loss for both of them. Now it broke her heart. Call it maternal instinct, baby hunger or just her biological clock ticking, Maddie very much wanted a child, Art's child, to love.

Throughout her life, Maddie had struggled with identity issues, torn between the dual heritage she had had with one Christian and one Jewish parent—and all that implied for extended family relationships. Cousins, uncles and aunts—even grandparents—never felt really like family to her—on either side. Then there was the problem of her absent father. His disappearance from the home before she reached puberty was the kind of loss that she had never yet gotten past. It had left her with vague feelings of insecurity that led her to look after her own needs. Her controlling mother made her sense of inadequacy even greater, so that despite her very great ability and strength, she never felt quite equal, quite adequate, quite okay. And so with Art, she felt eclipsed by his brilliance while reflecting that dazzling light in her own glow.

The ambulance was waiting beside the Tucson International Executive Terminal with its lights flashing. The paramedics ran out to meet the Cessna as Jerry shut off the engine. From inside the plane, Jerry and Maddie helped them get Art out and on to a stretcher. He had not stirred throughout the flight, and he did not move during the transfer.

Maddie went with the paramedics in the ambulance, turning just before she got in and said, "Thanks, Jerry." And then, "I'm scared. You're coming to the hospital aren't you?"

"Sure. I'll fly to Ryan and get my car, and I'll be with you real soon."

As the ambulance pulled away, Maddie felt another wave of aloneness. "Please God, if you are there, help Jerry to hurry," she muttered under her breath. Deep inside she knew what was coming and that she would very much need a friend beside her.

Maddie rode in silence and then trailed along behind the paramedics through the trauma center's busy chaos. Doctors, technicians, interns, nurses were busy checking charts, ordering tests, helping patients. The waiting room outside was filled with bloody noses, crying babies, and restless, sneezing, impatient people. The room at the end of the hall where they took Art was sterile, stark and white, brightly lit by flourescent bulbs. They easily shifted him to the hospital bed in the room, and the paramedics left, kindly wishing Maddie the best of luck, but sharing knowing glances with each other. Art was quickly connected to an IV saline drip and a heart monitor, which showed an irregular beat. One of his eyes, glassy and sightless, was slightly open. Maddie was sitting with her chin in her hands at the side of the bed when

Jerry walked through the door. Nothing had happened or changed since she and Art arrived.

"Jerry. I'm glad you got here so fast." She stood up and went to him. He put his arms around her as sobs wracked her body.

"What have they told you?" he asked finally.

"Nothing much. They've just been trying to figure out what has happened. I think they suspect some kind of internal hemorrhage. But I don't know." They sat down. Jerry leaned against the wall and put one foot on the side rung of Maddie's chair.

A nurse came and went, each time checking the IV and the monitor. Once a middle-aged physician came in, lifted Art's closed eyelid and then briefly watched the monitor.

After she had gone, Jerry asked, "Are you ready for the worst?"

They sat looking at each other. Maddie looked down at her hands and again at Art. She just nodded. "Artie," she said slowly, reluctantly, "it's okay. You don't have to struggle any more. You can let go. I'll understand." Again the room was quiet. The yellow line in the green screen of the heart monitor continued in its progress, left to right. The clock on the wall ticked mechanically as the second hand marked abruptly its revolutions. Distant hallway noises filtered into the antiseptic starkness of the room.

And then Art's heart monitor started a furious ringing.

"Oh my God," Maddie said.

His heart had stopped.

Two emergency doctors and a nurse rushed into the room. Jerry pulled Maddie back away from the bed.

"Is there a DNR order on him?" the doctor asked of the nurse. Clearly, she was the one in charge. The nurse checked the chart.

"There's nothing in here yet," the nurse responded. All three looked at Maddie, questioning looks on their faces. Maddie turned to Jerry for help. He just shook his head in the negative. Art had been very clear with both of them that he wanted no efforts made to keep him on artificial life support, nor to resuscitate him. Jerry just looked on, an expression of concern on his face. Maddie echoed his gesture and shook her head. The emergency nurse and doctors understood and stepped back from the bed.

"You're sure?" one of the doctors asked.

"I'm sure," Maddie replied.

The furious activity of a moment ago stopped only to be replaced by a calm as heavy as death itself.

"Shall I anoint him, Maddie?" Jerry asked. "We've talked about that." Maddie nodded in the affirmative, and he pulled out a little purple and white stole and put it around his neck. Then with one hand on Art's head and his Prayer Book in the other, he began to say prayers for the time of death. It was the words, "Depart, oh Christian soul, from this world," that reenforced the finality of the moment. At the end Jerry anointed Art's body, making the sign of the cross with his thumb on his forehead. Maddie just sat quietly sobbing beside the bed.

"Goodbye Art," Jerry muttered under his breath.

The doctors stood silently at the side as the nurse disconnected electrodes and IV from Art's body and turned off the monitor. When she had finished, they left Maddie and Jerry alone with what had been Art Gronek. He looked no different that he had ten minutes before, only now both of his eyelids were slightly open. Nothing had seemed to change. But everything had changed. Maddie remembered thinking later that nobody had pulled a sheet over Art or anything else. Even in that sterile setting, there was something very normal about the way Art's life had ended. No death agonies. No struggle. And yet, at the same time, there was something radically wrong that it should have ended at all.

They sat there for a long time before finally Maddie had enough presence of mind to ask, "What do I do now, Jerry?" When he hesitated she continued, "I mean about the details, not the whole rest of my life."

"I can help you with that," he responded with a small smile. "There will be papers for you to sign at the nurse's station. Are you ready to go?"

"I guess so," she said and reached out and touched the side of Art's face one last time. Deep inside, she could not believe it *was* the last time. Tears filled her eyes and flooded down her face. Jerry, too, felt moisture on his cheeks. This was it, then. Art was gone. They turned away and walked out the door, both of them looking back one last time. Jerry put his arm lightly around Maddie's shoulders and gave her a little squeeze then steered her by an elbow to the busy nurse's station.

Art Gronek's funeral was in St. Peter's Episcopal Church in Bisbee the next Wednesday, an appropriately overcast gray day, gloomy and cold. Sadie and Jerry Hanning sat with Maddie and her family. Art's twin daughters were pale and red-eyed and, to Maddie's surprise, even a little clingy. His son Sean supported her with very great kindness. A handful of parishioners thinly represented the local community as the church filled to overflowing with high rolling friends and business associates of Art's and some of Maddie's old friends from Tucson. All that remained of Art filled a small box covered by a white brocade cloth. But Maddie could not help feeling that there was a kind of consciousness there that day that carried the essence of Art and his life. Jerry Hanning interred the ashes in a small grove back at the ranch following a short ritual and tribute to his friend. Maddie knew she would never forget any part of the moment when Jerry opened the cardboard box, unfastened the plastic bag inside and then quietly scattered the gray ashes all through the small stand of black oaks, intoning the words, "Ashes to ashes and dust to dust." It felt much the same as when her grandmother's coffin had been lowered into the ground after her funeral. It was so hopelessly and miserably final.

Maddie spent the rest of the day feeling as if she were an observer outside of the event, watching, making mental notes, but being largely untouched by it. Even the lively reminiscences of Art and his life did little to break through her shell. It even seemed odd to her that they laughed, sometimes almost hysterically, at one memory or another or at some rather modest joke. There was something harshly unreal about it.

Everyone's lives would go on. Even Maddie's.

The four months following Art's death were filled with the most complex mixture of feelings Maddie had ever experienced.

"I loved Art," she wrote in a letter from Paris to her mother, "and I still can't believe that he's gone from my life, from the world for that matter. I still think of things I want to tell him, and I look forward to his laughter. It feels as if a piece of myself has been ripped out and died with him." And yet, she felt at the same time and in a way that she could not quite admit, as if she had been freshly born, as if she had become a new person—or, more accurately, that she had regained her old person from the reduced self that she had felt herself to be with Art. His illness and then his death had left her no alternative but to rediscover herself as a person and to come to a new self-reliance that she had felt was nearly lost. She had coped with the early stages of his sickness and the inevitability of the diagnosis by completing her dissertation, in effect both denying his approaching death and simultaneously taking care of herself. Then after his death, the months she spent in Paris were about her psychic rebuilding—walking graceful streets, spending hours roaming the galleries and museums, sipping espresso coffee, and even returning to some research. Gradually her sadness dissolved and she began to rebuild her confidence.

"But Paris is lonely," she continued in her letter to Deborah. "Few of the people I knew around the university are here anymore, and I have no interest whatever in meeting new people. I don't want to shock you," she wrote, "but I even sat in Notre Dame and in some other churches—even *Chivetei Israel,* a synagogue—hoping, I guess, that I might find something of solace or at least understanding. But I haven't found anything."

Maddie thought a lot about Jerry's and Art's long religious discussions. They seemed to be searchers after something that was not lost. After all, a thing has to exist in order for you to lose it, and she was not at all sure that God did exist. She loved the great, old French churches as always, but the gnawing emptiness left by Art's death remained largely unaffected by her being in them.

So she returned home to Arizona, at first staying with her mother in Tucson, and then with great difficulty and reluctance going back to the Twisted K Ranch. And to her surprise, it felt like going home...her home. Still, the loneliness remained, and she thought of Jerry and Sadie Hanning

"Hey, Jerry," she said into the telephone receiver. "Remember me?"

"Maddie. How are you? It's so good to hear your voice. Are you in Arizona?"

"Back at the ranch as usual. You and Sadie free for a visit? Kind of like old times." A short wave of sadness passed over her.

"Absolutely. And I have some news." Jerry told her about his by then three-month-old job as vicar of St. Peter's. "You remember. Where we had Art's service."

"Of course I remember. And now you're the vicar? What happened to the other guy?"

"Retired. Anyhow, how about next Wednesday night. That's Ash Wednesday, and Sadie and I will already be in Bisbee. We'll just make the little hop over to the Twisted K."

"I can't wait."

"Me too."

CHAPTER THREE

Ash Wednesday

I invite you, therefore, in the name of the Church, to the observance of a holy Lent, by self-examination and repentance; by prayer, fasting, and self-denial; and by reading and meditating on God's holy Word.
—Book of Common Prayer

The two middle-aged men, Charlie Snow—not drunk and insulting the way he had been at the Tuckers' wedding the weekend before—and Colin Hines, had been arguing all evening. The occasion of their most recent disagreement—Charlie Snow always seemed to be disagreeing with someone about something—was the St. Peter's Shrove Tuesday supper. Lent began the next day on Ash Wednesday, but in the meantime, it was Mardi Gras, as good an excuse for a party as anyone could find. This year's supper as always at St. Peter's featured spicy Mexican food and live Mariachi music. The subject of Charlie's and Colin's argument, illegal immigration from Mexico, was a recurring one between them.

Rancher Charlie Snow, short and stocky with watery grey eyes and receding brown hair, made people uncomfortable with his strong language and opinionated views. He did not even look like an Arizona rancher, never wearing the usual boots and western hat typical of the southwest. Mostly he wore collarless shirts, jeans, white socks, tennis shoes and a baseball cap. Charlie had a thick neck, muscular arms, broad shoulders and a powerful torso—and a very physical way of solving problems. Charlie's issue at the moment—or, more accurately, his obsession—was that he despised the undocumented aliens who flooded into the United States from Mexico through Cochise County. Indeed, his dislike went even to resident Mexican-Americans whose families had been in the country for generations, and hence his outrageous, drunken verbal assault that had even included Teresa Bustamante Tucker, Hank Tucker's new wife, at their wedding reception. Charlie was an unrepentant racist.

INS officer Colin Hines differed from his neighbor, Charlie Snow, in just about everything. Tall, taciturn and shyly introverted, Colin was as careful about his opinions as Charlie was free with his. Yet there was no question about where Colin stood on the issue of illegal immigrants. He was a staunch enforcer of the law, even had a sense of its majesty. Colin had entered the INS immediately out of law school because he felt that the INS offered excellent opportunities for advancement in government service. While Southern Arizona might not seem like an attractive post for most ambitious career bureaucrats, the INS had a high profile there as concern over illegal immigration had grown in the country in the years just before and especially after the terrorist attacks on the World Trade Center and the Pentagon. Now in his early forties, Colin was about ready for a move that would carry him up the career ladder.

Charlie Snow and Colin Hines continued their Shrove Tuesday table bussing duties until the last plate had been picked up and the final glass stowed in the dishwasher tray. Then they sat down beside the serving window between the parish hall and the church kitchen, still deep in conversation as they had been throughout the evening.

Colin smiled a greeting and Charlie nodded when Jerry Hanning sat down with them at their table. "What have you two been debating all evening?" Jerry asked

"The damned Illegals. No offense, Father," Charlie replied.

Jerry dismissed the rancher's apology with a wave of his hand.

"I'm finding more and more trash on my land, gates left open for cattle to wander and other signs that there's a kind of army of them out there," Charlie continued. Both Jerry and Charlie looked at Colin. The INS officer said nothing. "It's not Colin's fault," Charlie said. "There's just too much territory to cover and not enough manpower to go around."

"I guess I'm kind of slow," Jerry responded. "But why's this so serious? So troubling to you in particular?" Jerry found Charlie Snow hard to like.

Charlie responded immediately, "Because they have no right to be here, and they've got no respect for private property. You just wouldn't believe all the junk they leave behind. Besides, they take jobs from local workers. Something's got to be done."

"Just report your sightings to our office and to the Border Patrol," Colin replied.

Jerry knew that Charlie had been one of the ranchers, along with the newly-wed Hank Tucker, who had been rounding up Mexican nationals on their property and turning them over to the Border Patrol, sometimes holding them at gunpoint. Some ranchers shot at the entrants, perhaps even killing and burying them in the desert, or so rumor had it. Government officials could not tolerate any of this.

"I'm every bit as concerned as you are about the law being enforced, Charlie," Colin said, "but I don't think that's any reason to leave those poor people in the desert to die the way the coyotes do."

"Yeah, but we don't have to rescue them, do we?" Charlie looked immovable.

"I definitely support letting the Tucson people put up water stations in the desert. I'm sorry pressure from Washington has made us stop it—at least officially." Colin smiled with a hint of conspiracy on his face. At least the Border Patrol is still able to send out humanitarian patrols to look for people in trouble—like the ones they found in the van near Bisbee last week. We don't, after all, have to be brutes to uphold the law."

"Do you think they'll find out who shot holes in that van full of people?" Jerry asked.

"I doubt it," said Colin. Charlie just grinned—stupidly, Jerry thought.

The priest's perspective differed from both Charlie and Colin. He had grown up in a working class family in the Western Hills of Cincinnati. His father, Howie (for Howard), a labor union member, even served as secretary of his local. Howie was all working man, feisty in his advocacy of labor causes, intolerant and bigoted. His Democratic politics lionized big-labor. Maybe the superficial similarities between Charlie Snow and Jerry's father explained why Charlie could push his buttons so easily. Jerry's mother, Sherrie, taught high school special education, helping the learning disabled fit into a work routine and contribute to their own support. She was yet another kind of Democrat, the "bleeding-heart" variety. Between them Jerry received a political education that made him mindful both of issues of concern to the labor movement—labor/management struggles for power and the inequality of the distribution of wealth—and also of the liberal concern for people who suffered stereotyping in the workplace or anywhere else in the public arena as a result of the accident of birth. Sherry's quiet feminism, advocating women's issues along with opposition to racism and other forms of discrimination, probably drove her husband crazy, just as his Archie Bunker mentality sometimes exasperated her. Jerry suspected that his father would agree with Charlie and Colin and would find the Mexican immigrants a threat to American labor. This would be the real issue for him. Sherry would certainly take the other position and see the resistance to Mexican workers as racist. Jerry could well imagine his mother taking water jugs out into the desert in defiance of men like Charlie—and, frankly, her husband. Perhaps she would even violate the law to do it.

Jerry Hanning was unsure where he stood on illegal immigration, though his usual inclination was to see things as his mother did. But he felt no burning passion for either side. He tried to tell himself that having no strong convictions on this subject was a pastoral strength. That way he could serve parishioners who stood on both sides of the border dilemma. But it did not feel like a strength to him. It felt as if he rather sadly lacked conviction about a terribly important local issue. Pastoral neutrality just didn't wash. But neutral, or something very like neutral, was where he stood.

Jerry knew that the complex immigration problem had to be raised in any congregation that served the border area, and that theological reflection might show just how uncertain the ethical ground could be. They had to confront the hard questions: What certainties can people hold onto in the midst of a world filled with change and violence? How does the Christian faith inform something as complex as the border turmoil confronted by Colin Hines, Charlie Snow and Hank Tucker? How does a person decide between conflicting goods? In the past—before Marjory's death—Jerry had not been troubled in his leadership by ambivalence. Perhaps the political issues he faced in those days were neither so complex nor so new to him as this one was. Now he was so torn between so many conflicting ideas and values that he barely could lead at all. Perhaps it was just a matter of confidence. Perhaps he would never get it back. Perhaps. Perhaps.

The politically charged atmosphere at the table dissolved as Kate Becker pulled off her apron, dropped it unceremoniously in front of her and sat down with the three men. In a single motion she untied the ribbon that held her blonde hair captive behind her head and shook it loose in soft piles onto her shoulders. Jerry noticed that Kate had a faint and freshly sweet scent lingering about her.

"Mrs. Findlay says we served one hundred and eighty-three people. Isn't that great?" she asked.

"Incredible," Jerry responded, impressed.

"I think that's even more than last year," Charlie offered.

Kate sighed.

"That's a lot of people," Jerry said. "A lot of work."

Kate just smiled. Margaret Snow and Sharon Hines came out of the kitchen and stood beside the table, each with a hand on a hip in that impatient posture that says, "enough already," obviously waiting for their husbands, who, standing, took the hint to go home.

"You two have argued enough for one evening," Sharon Hines spoke in mock seriousness to the two neighbors.

Kate Becker and Jerry Hanning were left alone at the table. "Want to go get a cup of coffee?" he asked, his heart pounding with uncertainty and a fear of rejection rumbling in the pit of his stomach...reminiscent of adolescent dating anxiety. It was his first foray in ten years into something that approximated dating.

"Sure," she answered. "Let me get my coat."

"Are you ready, Sadie?" Jerry called to the weary-looking nine-year-old who had worked hard in the kitchen all evening. She nodded and joined them standing beside the table. "You're a great worker. I'm very proud of you," he said as he gave his little girl a hug.

"It was fun," Sadie said.

Jerry finished turning off the lights and locking the doors, and the three of them walked down the street toward the Simmons House, one of the few places where coffee would be available at this hour.

"It was such a relief to be here this evening and away from the college, both students and colleagues," Kate said.

"Is your work tough right now?" Jerry asked.

"About the same as always this time of the year. I'm tired of the students and the classes—and they're sick of me."

"I doubt that," he responded, with a hint of obligatory gallantry.

"Oh, we get along okay, I guess. But by this point in the semester everyone feels the pressure to complete projects. And," she looked over at him and smiled, "we have all figured out that the great resolutions we had about performance, no procrastination and that kind of stuff, have gone the same way they do every other term. It makes us all grumpy. Same old, same old. We're the same people we've always been." She laughed lightly and took Sadie's hand to cross the street. "The bright, new opportunity has become the same tired old habits."

"That doesn't sound like the saint Kate I know: optimistic, positive, up-beat."

"Right!"

They stepped into the Simmons House. Jerry got the key to their room from the desk clerk, saying to Kate, "Be back in a minute."

"Aw, Daddy, you don't have to take me to the room."

"Aw, but I want to," he echoed her as they walked to the room. He opened the door and saw her safely inside. "I'll be back soon, Sweetheart. You get into bed. Okay? Then you can read a little Harry Potter."

Kate had picked out a booth in the coffee shop off the lobby. He sat down opposite.

"So how's the saint of St. Peter's tonight? Tired from all the kitchen work?"

"A little," she admitted. Kate suddenly gazed intently at him, her eyes moving quickly back and forth as she looked at first one and the other of his eyes with an intensity that he had not experienced from her before. "Some saint! I guess you've only seen a part of me. The Sunday part."

Jerry stirred cream and sugar into his coffee, realizing the truth in what she said. He had fallen into the clergy trap of seeing parishioners in their sanitized versions of themselves, lacking complexity, even humanity. "Guilty. And what about those other, less churchy parts? Sounds intriguing to me," he laughed awkwardly.

"The only way to find that out is to 'peel the onion.' You might discover some things there that make your eyes water." Their flirting was cautious but real, and her smile told him it was okay.

Acting bolder than he felt, Jerry reached over and laid his hand on hers, squeezing slightly as he felt a charge of emotional energy shoot up his arm. Was this going too far? But he could not see any harm in it. Two single people. Why shouldn't they develop an interest in each other? He knew he would have to call the bishop before it went too far, but they were nowhere near there, might never be. He said, somewhat emptily, "It's good to be here with you."

"Yes," she answered, simply.

"So, who are you, Kate Becker?" he asked in a voice more pastoral than personal, realizing that not even his rationalizations carried him over a need for caution. "How does a nice girl like you find yourself in a place like this?" He smiled at the cliche.

"Oh, the usual. A job. And a man," she replied, mocking his bromide with one of her own. Still, he felt his insides go a bit cold with anxiety. "Running to the one and fleeing the other." She smiled a little sadly. "I saw the job advertized in the Chronnie, *The Chronicle of Higher Education*, sort of by accident. Ironically on my friend's coffee table—the man part of the story. He was my boss...and married. Like me. Actually the *Chronicle* was probably hers, his wife's. He had been a teacher, but left that to make the big bucks at Canning and Smith, the Chicago investment firm where I was working, fresh MBA in hand and dollar signs in my eyes. Right in the Loop. Instead, I had an affair with my boss, saw my marriage crumble—that's another story—lost nearly all of my self-esteem, and fled back to the safety of the blackboard and the blue book. Not a pretty picture for a 'saint.'"

"But why Bisbee? Surely there were other jobs closer to Chicago than here?" Jerry tried not to seem shocked or surprised by her revelations.

"It was an adventure. That's all. And, you know, I've loved it here—the town itself and the country, the openness and even the barren parts. There is something…something wild and…primitive, that's it, primitive, about it. The rawness, rather than repelling me, draws me in. Gives me a sense of being where everything is painfully real. Know what I mean?" Her intensity framed the question.

"Yes. I think I do. Maybe that's why this is a place where I found I could heal…from the death of my wife."

"I know. That must have been terrible for you—and for little Sadie."

"It was. We…no, I…have been aimless and without purpose for over two years now. I'm just beginning to claw my way back into usefulness." Kate's honesty had served as an invitation for Jerry to share his own life with her.

They sat quietly for a moment. Then she asked, "So, Jerry Hanning, what are *you* up to here—and in Tucson? Your life's desire?" She laughed in her contagious way.

"Oh, I really don't know. One day at a time, as they say."

"Forget 'them.' What do *you* say?"

He found that he did not resent her probing, and that surprised him. "I…I want to return to a normal life. Normal relationships. No more ghosts. And," he thought for a moment, "and I'm willing to follow my nose."

They looked at each other with unspoken questions rising between them: "Can I trust you?" "Are you someone who will hurt me?" "Where *do* we go from here?" "Am I ready for what is happening here?"

Kate broke the silence, seemingly alarmed by what was passing between them. "It's late. I really have to go." The tension was broken, at least for the moment. Jerry nursed his mingled relief and disappointment.

"Can I walk you to your car?"

"Please. No woman in her right mind is ever alone in Bisbee at night. This is a scary place!"

"Not the ghosts of old Bisbee?"

"Hardly. I'm more concerned about the contemporary ghouls."

They stepped out into the night, silhouettes of clapboard building front outlined against the night sky. The short embrace at her car felt to both of them like more than the usual pastoral hug. They both knew that something could happen between them.

The week following Art Gronek's funeral back in November, Jerry Hanning had flown to St. David to spend some time with his spiritual director, Fr. Benedict. Jerry knew that it was not uncommon for people who suffer the death of a close friend or family member to have a crisis of faith; regular church-goers often can't face being in church—sometimes for years. In Jerry's case, knowing about the effects of grief had not been the same thing as dealing with them; he had already learned from Marjory's death that he was no different than anyone else. Then Art died and reopened many of Jerry's healing sores. Fr. Benedict—all two hundred fifty pounds of him, piercing blue eyes, shaved head and grey beard—had provided Jerry's ticket into some new spiritual space. The monk's age (something over eighty), wisdom and the experience of a lifetime helped Jerry resolve his spiritual crisis. It's a truism of pastoral work that you have to move through your own spiritual death and resurrection before you can genuinely help others with their pain. Marjory's death certainly qualified as Jerry's spiritual death, and Fr. Benedict's work marked the beginning of his resurrection. Now Art Gronek's death served both to challenge and to confirm the shaky new ground on which he stood.

So, leaving Sadie in the care of their neighbor, Margaret Lopez, Jerry had flown to Holy Trinity Monastery, easily located from the air outside the town of St. David by its icon and emblem, a fifty-foot-high Celtic cross. He landed just in time for the morning liturgy on that late November day, and, as he tied down the plane to some trees and put the chocks in place, he heard the chapel bell announcing the Morning Office. The chapel commands the entrance like an immobile sentry, presiding over the monastery's buildings and fields like a trooper in front of Buckingham Palace. Its rough-hewn mesquite beams on top of rounded arches of tan stucco hold up a massive ceiling of saguaro ribs and cover a worship space both rustic and dramatic. Inside, there is an altar built out of the stump of an enormous mesquite tree, polished to a high, dark lustre. Jerry had been such a regular guest at the monastery, that he even had his own place to sit in quire. Mass followed the Morning Office immediately.

Fr. Benedict was the celebrant that morning, and Jerry found himself mesmerized by the monk's deep, melodious voice as he read the Eucharistic texts. As always, Jerry found himself drawn deeply into the mass's mystery. He knew of no other place where the liturgy had such simple power, where he could set aside his doubts for a moment and just be.

After the community liturgy, Jerry met Fr. Benedict in the private meditation garden, which combines roses, cultivated everywhere on the monastic grounds, and a small pond with running water and lily pads. If the chapel is very Arizona, the meditation garden is more like England.

Jerry's first visit tó the monastery nine months before, an eight-day retreat only a month after he arrived in Arizona, had been a time of great intensity that came to a stunningly dramatic climax on a windy late July night. Dark monsoon clouds rushed across a brilliantly star-dazzled summer sky as Jerry huddled into himself for a walk in the wind and felt drawn into a quiet corner of the monastic property beside a duck pond and beneath a sheltering willow tree. Its hanging branches made a kind of a tent as the wind's fury raged around him. He huddled there for what proved to be hours, though it seemed like only minutes. Despite the wind howling and whining around his ears— perhaps because of it—he felt a loving presence shielding and protecting him like a soft blanket, not unlike the way the friendly willow tree guarded him that night from the violence of the natural forces. In that protected environment—both physical and spiritual—he had become acutely aware of his own life, both his failings and his successes. Memories flooded back. He remembered relationships that had soared and then soured and both the joy and pain that that had brought him and other people. Especially he recalled his years married to Marjory with astonishing clarity, seemingly every argument and every ecstacy they had ever shared: times he felt he had treated her badly or had blamed her unfairly for his own moods, and the ways he had neglected her for his work; times they had laughed and known the simple pleasure of each other's company. Somehow he was in full possession of the memories, but generally relieved of their burden. It had been an extraordinary night, one that kept him out in that wind-swept river bottom land moving from one sheltering tree or bush to another, until the earliest signs of morning light began to appear in the east.

That night had even carried an intensely erotic dimension, as Jerry relived the shared sexuality of his years with Marjory and other moments with women he had known before her, intertwining the experience of the sacred and the sexual in his consciousness as it already existed in his unconscious. Out of his empty longing, Jerry remembered every detail of Marjory's long-limbed body, the smoothness of her skin, the rise of her buttocks, the shape of her breasts, the hardening of her nipples under his caress—every part of her. He had crystal clear memories of the months when she was pregnant with Sadie, their increasing care in making love as her body swelled, and the little bumps and bulges as the not-quite-yet Sadie moved and pushed in her growing urgency to be born.

Jerry had cried that July night, tears washing his memories and his loss. Nothing would ever again be the same for him. And yet, he knew that night as he had never known before that he could and would go on, that he and Sadie could and would continue to be a family and that their mutual love and commitment could and would grow into an even stronger bond. Marjory would be proud of their child as he too was proud of Sadie. That intense night left Jerry feeling more rested than he had felt in months.

Then, that week after Art Gronek's November death, Fr. Benedict, shuffling along and more than usually showing his age, joined Jerry after the Mass he had just celebrated and sat with him on a bench beside the bubbling little stream where running water entered the garden pond. They chatted amiably for a time, then Father Benedict got down to business.

"Your friend, Art, must have died," he initiated with the kind of startling insight that often made Jerry feel that the monk was clairvoyant.

"Yes," he answered. "It happened the day after Thanksgiving." They sat staring into the pond for a moment. One of the huge goldfish rose lazily in the morning sun.

"Where was God for you in that dying?" Father Benedict asked finally.

"It was a release for Art. He was so tired…and in pain…and just not able to go on any longer."

"And God seems mercy-full with Art?" he asked.

"Yes, I think so."

"But that was not what I asked you, was it?" He shifted his bulk on the bench and crossed his legs under his broad off-white monastic habit. "Where was God in this dying…for you?"

"I…I'm not sure. In some way, I seem better able to cope—certainly better than after Marjory's death. Oh, I'm grieving Art, but in some curious way the old issues have not come up. Sometimes I think I've become callous, but then a wave of sadness will sweep over me, and I know that's not it. Somehow…in a small way at least, I'm okay with his death. I don't feel angry about it, just sad."

"Aha! Then that is where God is for you in it?"

"Yes, I guess so," Jerry answered, though he had not thought about it that way. "Art's cancer and death, though it wasn't *about* me, is *available* to me for my own healing."

Fr. Benedict nodded vigorously as if this perspective was as new to him as it was at that moment to Jerry. But this small insight brought back for Jerry some of their earlier conversations about Marjory's death, especially the understanding that her death had been about *her*, not about Jerry, or even about Sadie.

They talked for a long time that morning. Finally, Father Benedict said, "Why don't you wander around the grounds and then join us for lunch?" Jerry nodded, as Father Benedict made the sign of the cross over his head in offering of his blessing.

That morning, the monastic grounds were the perfect place for Jerry to be alone and to think. Extensively wooded with native vegetation, watered by a series of ponds and ultimately by the San Pedro River, it had a natural beauty that brought a surprise on every trail and around each bend. Jerry wandered beyond the chapel, past the rocky community graveyard fenced off by spiny ocotillo branches and onto a twisting path that had been hewn out of dense mesquites. It was a quiet and protected trail marked by small monuments to people who had been important to the monastery's life. Jerry was walking along deep in thought and nearly collided with a tall young man whom he knew by sight only. The soft-eyed, beardless man with close-cropped hair had changed out of his monastic habit into blue jeans and a checked work shirt, and he carried four one-gallon plastic milk bottles, two in each of his big hands. They were filled with what Jerry correctly guessed was water. A backpack was stuffed with smaller angular packages. He avoided making direct eye contact as he looked alternately at the trees and the ground.

"Oh, I didn't know there was anyone around," he said.

"Sorry." Jerry looked hard at the monk's burdens.

"Just my care gifts...for the Illegals—the immigrants," he said a little defensively. "To keep them from dying."

Jerry knew there were people who did what they could in this way for the undocumented workers who came across the border from Mexico by the tens of thousands each year. He also knew that it was technically illegal to do so.

The young brother put down two of the water jugs and extended his right hand. "Joey, Joey Warnock," he said. His hand—rough, strong and hard—was also gentle. He picked up the water bottles to continue along the path to the west.

"That's great—that you help those people," Jerry said to him. "Anything I can do?"

"No, thanks. This is all I'm doing for now." He walked away and quickly disappeared into the creosote brush.

The stark, plain liturgy of Ash Wednesday and the smudged cross of ashes on the foreheads of each worshiper, reminded Jerry at the beginning of his first Lent at St. Peter's, if he needed a reminder, of how fragile and insecure life can be. It recalled how close living really is to the stuff and the chaos of creation: "Remember that you are dust and to dust you shall return." The Ash Wednesday ashes, customarily burned from left-over palm branches blessed the year before on Palm Sunday, this year combined for Jerry his personal themes of human impermanence and sacred promise.

Jerry had much to think about that Ash Wednesday. Just where *was* his life headed? What *did* he want? Where did Kate Becker fit into that picture? The tiny thrill he experienced when he imposed ashes on her forehead in the service had nothing whatever to do with the theological principles of that solemn day. He *was* confused. But he was not unhappy about the confusion. In fact, it felt good to have something complex in his life that looked to the future and not exclusively to the past. He also had his usual strange sensation imposing ashes on Sadie's forehead. He knew better than to take this metaphor too literally, but when it came to confronting mortality and his little girl in the same moment, he did not like it one bit. Jerry had every reason to know just how wicked and unpredictable death could be. He doubted he could stand the loss of Sadie to that same evil force. He also thought about Maddie Gronek. He wondered what she would be like when he saw her later in the day. Would she be paralyzed by pain and loss? That was not how she sounded on the phone. What would he feel for her? Pity? Sorrow for the loss they shared? Yes, there was much to think about. Whatever her present state of mind might be, he thought that they both would know more about living and dying than they had the last time they saw each other. And life, he remembered, was both messy and risky.

Despite its being an obvious and slightly tacky tourist attraction, Jerry and Sadie always liked being in Tombstone, the odd little town with the big reputation. That Ash Wednesday afternoon they landed at the abandoned airport and rode their bikes into town to visit some of their new friends there and to make a round of visits to some of St. Peter's parishioners. This was partly to fulfill Jerry's promise to the bishop when he agreed to go to Bisbee—that he would look out especially for the tiny group of Episcopalians in Tombstone, to help them get over the recent closure of their church and hopefully bond with the congregation at St. Peter's in Bisbee. But so far they seemed mostly angry about it.

Shuffling down the boardwalk along historic Allen Street was never dull. You never knew when a saloon floozie or a gun slinger would pop out of one of the shops or there would be a shoot-out between desperadoes and lawmen in the middle of the street, victims dragged off in the general direction of Boot Hill. An antique stage coach might come and go, driven by some rough-looking citizen in duster and ten-gallon hat. All the while tourists milled in and out of the OK Corral and along the boardwalk.

Two small businesses had already become regular haunts of the Hannings: Nellie Cashman's Café, where the food is good and the coffee is fresh, and Ike Clanton's Bead and Craft Shop, operated by Ike "Clanton" McWarder and his side-kick, Doc (Holiday), a sleek Black Lab. Ike was no church-goer, but Jerry had met him at Nellie Cashman's Café, a restaurant owned by two of St. Peter's new Tombstone parishioners, and they had struck up an immediate friendship.

"Afternoon, Ike. Hi, Doc," Jerry called as he opened the shop door.

"Hi, yerseff," Ike said back. Doc wagged his tail furiously. Sadie sat down by Doc and began scratching his ears.

"Get to church today, did you, Ike?"

"'Fraid not."

"How about you, Doc? Did you get your ashes today?" Sadie asked.

Ike smiled at her fondly. Jerry wondered, and not for the first time, if the shop owner had a special liking for Sadie or if he just loved children.

"But I'll be joinin' yer next Sunday afternoon for the God-book class," Ike continued, referring to the Lenten group Jerry would be starting at Nellie Cashman's Café on Sunday. Jerry looked at him as if he were an apparition of the original Ike Clanton up from Boot Hill; Ike had been absolutely frank about his disdain for the church and everything about it. Ike laughed. "Gotcha," he said. "But I'll be there anyhow."

Ike put down some beads he had been stringing, reached over and gave Sadie a little pat on the head and got up. "Wanta' cuppa?" he asked.

"Sure," Jerry answered.

"How about me? Can I have a latte?" Sadie asked.

"Sure, so long as it's really chocolate," Jerry answered.

Sadie just grinned. "Poor Doc has to stay here," she said.

"That's okay. He's due for his tenth nap of the day. Let's go," Ike answered.

Nellie Cashman's Café was a peculiar, even unique, combination of small-town café and big-city espresso bar, with dining tables, overstuffed chairs and a couple of low coffee tables around an ancient wood-burning fireplace. Usually a person could even find a slightly aged copy of the *New York Times* scattered about on the tables. Nellie Cashman's would be perfect for one of Jerry's two Lenten book groups.

There is no current "Nellie Cashman" as such. The original Nellie, known as "The Angel of the Mining Camps," lived in Tombstone during the town's first decades and founded the restaurant, now over a century old, that still bears her name. She amassed a modest fortune in the food, boarding house and saloon business. Being a woman "of virtue," she is reputed never to have actually set foot into the saloon, or so the legend goes. Except for the café, the rambling building has been alienated to other uses, some as humble as storage. The current owners changed the word "restaurant" to "café," as being more in keeping with their vision of the business. These St. Peter's parishioners were recent newcomers to Tombstone, Brenda Litz and Hannah Silver, both of whom jokingly were called "Nellie" by regulars and visitors alike. They publicly and loudly called each other by that name, to the enduring and mirthful confusion of tourists. The Nellies are a couple, have been for over a quarter of a century, and everyone knows it. And they are happy for everyone to know it. There is even some reason to suppose that the "angel," Nellie Cashman, who never married and who had a female companion for many years, may have been of the same sexual persuasion as today's Nellies.

Brenda-Nellie, in her mid-fifties, was a seemingly disorganized, rather large woman, big boned and heavy, a tireless source of energy and good will and, with penetrating blue eyes and henna hair, a real sparkplug. Hannah-Nellie was tall, boney and gray haired, a few years older than Brenda-Nellie, with soft brown eyes and a gentle smile. In another age Hannah would have been described as schoolmarm-ish. While they shared café duties, Brenda tended to be the front room partner, dealing with coffee, customers and staff. Hannah was the primary cook. She was the one who baked pies to die for, though, if you were to ask, either of them would tell you that Nellie baked the pies, just as, if you want a latte you need to "talk to Nellie."

"So Ike," Jerry asked, "what makes you decide to come to the book group? You were serious, I take it?"

"Sure," he responded. "Long as it's not in the church." Ike's receding gray-brown hair and watery blue eyes gave him a friendly, cherubic look.

"What's your problem with the church?"

"I swore thirty-five years ago that I'd never again step foot in one. Places of judgment and smug self-congratulation. A bunch o'empty ceremonies that make the people feel good so they can go out and do whatever they want afterwards." Ike's gentle face suddenly had a kind of fierceness that Jerry had never seen there before.

"And it's okay to come here, have coffee and talk about God?"

"I'm not irreligious. I just don't want that other stuff."

"Fair enough," Jerry answered.

Before leaving Tombstone, Jerry and Sadie stopped by at City Hall, a one-room store front, and said hello to the mayor, Jack Jackson, and dropped in on Jim and Lisa Brown, three solid and willing anchors of the St. Peter's still-reluctant Tombstone contingent. Finally, they paused on their bicycles to take on a little ice cream at Sue-Sue Hawkins's confectionary, another parishioner, to fortify themselves for the three-mile, mid-afternoon bicycle ride back to the Tombstone airport and for the short flight to Maddie Gronek's ranch.

"There it is—the red windmill. And it's turning." Sadie pointed ahead and to the left of the Skyhawk.

Jerry made a long, gradual descent toward the Twisted K ranch buildings and eased Five-Eight Bravo down on the still smooth-graded, but undulating landing strip, the steady breeze comfortably lined up exactly on the runway.

Maddie stood beside the front door of the ranch house waving as Jerry leaned the gas-flow until the engine sputtered and then stopped turning over. Everything at the Twisted K looked just the same, and it felt, to Jerry at least, like he was coming home. Maddie gave each of them a warm hug. Jerry took a long, inquiring look at her. She looked terrific, color good, dark eyes bright and shining in the cool air, and her nearly black hair, a little longer than it had been last November, but still on the short side, ruffled in the breeze.

"It's so good to see you, Jerry," Maddie said.

"You, too."

They walked, the three of them together arm in arm with Sadie in the middle. Maddie genuinely seemed to be in very good spirits.

The living room was much the same. A fire welcomed them in from the chill February air. The coffee table in front of the fire held a gleaming silver tray with six crystal glasses and a half-filled decanter, an ice bucket and an old-fashioned matching soda syphon. All that was missing was Art. A wave of sadness passed over Jerry. Maddie looked up, and her eyes concurred. Sadie shared their feelings. The three of them clung to each other, standing there beside where Art had so often lain. One of the ranch dogs, a cross between a German shepherd and at least one something else, stretched and yawned, tail swinging back and forth, and rubbed up against Jerry's leg in greeting.

"And who are you?" he asked the dog, leaning over to pet him. "I don't remember you."

"I do, Daddy. This is old Charlie," Sadie said.

"He's a fixture around the place, and he's my buddy," Maddie added. "Ever since I got back, he has been at my side, sort of adopted me."

Sitting in front of the fire and looking at Maddie in the gradually lengthening silence, Jerry felt many things for her. Compassion for her loss, a shared emptiness, an existing bond of intimacy, formed around many visits and their joint presence at Art's death bed. Also there was no denying their mutual attraction.

Over supper in the ranch kitchen, Maddie talked about her solitary Hanukkah and Christmas in Paris. "I was so lonely, wandering from church to synagogue, looking for...something. I hardly knew what."

Jerry and Sadie listened, partly empathetically and partly from personal memory, about that emotionally charged time and her loneliness. They had known a similarly empty time, but they had had each other. Maddie cried lightly and quietly as she talked. Both Hannings got up from the kitchen table and touched her lovingly for what felt like a long time. Jerry would always remember watching Sadie's little hand patting Maddie on the back, over and over and over. His pain for Maddie came like the sharp stab of a knife in his chest, and his love for Sadie like a healing compress. His eyes, too, filled with tears.

"I just don't understand how there can be a God when something like...like Art's illness...and death can happen," Maddie said after Sadie had gone to bed and she and Jerry were sitting in front of the fire. "His kids, left without their father, and me...alone and empty. I just don't get it. It all seems so random, so meaningless, so *heartless*! Without God the world is absolutely empty and lonely, I know, but I can't find any kind of god in what has happened in my life or in the lives of my family—like all those Jews who were slaughtered in Europe before I was born. Or all those people at the World

Trade Center." She drew imaginary circles on the coffee table in front of her for a moment and then looked at Jerry intently. "When I say this I feel guilty…that I have denied some essential part of myself as I deny God. It feels crappy." Her tiny, pointed features wore a profoundly serious expression, one of outrage and frustration.

Jerry sat quietly for a moment, letting her distress settle in the room and on him. "That really is the question, isn't it?" he asked rhetorically. "It's like I said to Art, if you can't find God in the life you're living, then maybe you need to change your life. Or change gods."

"Change gods? What a bizarre thing for *you* to say. I certainly can't do anything to change the part of my life that has Art dying. But change gods?" She laughed, but with a hard edge to it. "Give me a break."

"All I mean is that maybe your sense of the sacred doesn't describe reality for you."

"I think you're full of it. Come on, Jerry, don't play with me."

"I'm not playing." He thought for a moment. "You know, this is what the study group in Tombstone is going to be doing. Trying to discard some worn-out gods and move on to something that works better for them. For us. Do you want a copy of the 'God book,' as the locals have been calling it? I have a spare in the plane."

"Sure," she answered, but without enthusiasm, as if to say, *and I'm going to find God in some sort of book?* He had his doubts that she would read it, but he would leave it anyway.

The conversation drifted off in other directions, generally into the future, especially her uncertainty about what came next: A career? Managing the Twisted K? What? It was cozy and comfortable in front of the fire. A big brandy probably helped bring on a glowing sense of well-being. Finally, they parted in the cloister with a warm embrace, the darkness deeper than usual with the new moon only two days passed. He got into bed with a novel, and, after about half an hour, turned off the light and drifted off to sleep.

Jerry had been lightly asleep for maybe fifteen minutes when there was a soft knock at the door, and Maddie stepped into the room.

"Are you awake?" she called.

"Yes," he answered, instantly alert. Was something the matter?

"I'm so lonely," she said as she closed the door and came over to the side of the bed. Without thinking about it, Jerry pulled back the covers and Maddie kicked off her slippers and got in, lying facing toward him. He pulled the covers over her.

It had been a long time since either one of them had shared a bed with another person.

"Is that better?" he asked.

"Oh, yes." She shuddered slightly as he took her into his arms.

They lay that way for what seemed like a long time, looking at each other in the dark, but unable to see more than shadowed outlines. He could feel her hair on his face. She could feel his breath on her cheek. Then as one person they shifted, their mouths meeting, at first gently, but accelerating into urgency, hunger, two people struggling with many needs. Longing and desire overcame both of them. Jerry ran one hand down her back and pulled her against him, her light cotton nightgown leaving little to the imagination. She felt the pressure of his rising hardness against her stomach. As he caressed her back, rear and thighs, she pushed against him. His erection became almost painfully hard, and he felt nearly frantic to relieve his pounding sexual urgency. They were both so hungry for each other—or, as Jerry thought later, were so lonely and needy. It seemed that all of their pain and longing would be expended with each other.

And then Maddie began to cry. At first he just felt the tears on his face, then came the sobs, gentle, but increasingly shaking her entire body. Where he had felt supple flesh beneath his hands now felt unresponsive, remote. He stopped touching her and waited.

"You don't have to stop, Jerry, really you don't," she said between sobs. "I really do care about you, you know. Our attraction has been real, very real, for a long time."

"I know," he answered. "But I…we…do have to stop, at least for now. I know that." He was reluctant to admit that truth, but it was the truth. His body screamed to push forward. But he knew, as she also felt, that this was not the time for them. If it was meant to be, then it would happen. But not just then.

Jerry gently smoothed her hair. She put a hand on his cheek and gave him a light kiss. "Yes, you're right," she said. "I know you're right. I want you very much, but for some reason I just can't stop myself from crying. It hurts so much."

"I know," he answered. And he did. Gently, he helped her turn over on her side, facing away from him and carefully stretched his arm around her waist. They lay that way for a long time. Jerry felt an acute sense of loss in their interrupted love-making, but he tried, not entirely successfully, to assure himself that this was for the best. Maddie was relieved at the turn this encounter had taken. Despite her desire, there was something wrong with right now and right here. Sexual frustration mingled with loneliness and very deep feelings for both of them, feelings that Jerry decided were more brotherly than anything else—it all left him at first wakeful and, finally, they gradually drifted to sleep.

Jerry awoke as the sun was beginning to lighten the room. The first thing he became aware of was that Maddie was still there beside him. Sometime during the night they had shifted and she now lay with both of his arms around her. In fact, he needed to move to get the circulation going again in his left arm. The second thing that occurred to him was that his right hand was cupping one of her full breasts, and he felt himself begin to get aroused again. The third thing he realized was that Maddie, judging from her irregular breathing, was awake. She also noticed that he had wakened and raised a hand to hold what he was thinking of as his rather bold one. After lying a long moment that way, she squeezed his hand, pulled away and got up.

"Good morning," she said, her expression mixing confusion, embarrassment and a kind of playfulness.

"Hi," he returned.

"That was a very nice night. Thanks, Jerry." She bent over and lightly kissed him on the lips. "Thanks for everything." He had nothing to say in response, or at least nothing that seemed to fit the moment, but inside he was a hurricane of emotion—desire, sadness, and a remarkable warmth. "We'll have to do that again sometime," she said as she went out the door, smiling impishly.

CHAPTER FOUR

The Week after Ash Wednesday

All of us deal with the Powers That Be. They staff our hospitals, run City Hall, sit around tables in corporate boardrooms, collect our taxes, and head our families. But the Powers That Be are more than just the people who run things. They are the systems themselves, the institutions and structures that weave society into an intricate fabric of power and relationships. These Powers surround us on every side. They are necessary. They are useful. We could do nothing without them. Who wants to do without timely mail delivery or well-maintained roads? But the Powers are also the source of unmitigated evils.
—Walter Wink

When Sadie Hanning stormed into the house from school a little after three o'clock on the Thursday after Ash Wednesday, she burst into the Hannings' two-bedroom stucco, slammed the door and announced, with a determined stamp of her right foot, "I *hate* Carmen." In a moment Sadie had become a pre-adolescent.

The older of the Lopez grandchildren, Carmen, was several months Sadie's senior and had already turned ten. As nearly as Jerry could tell, she was a great kid. With her long limbs and athletic gracefulness, Carmen Vega promised to become a tall woman, probably even elegant. Her dark eyes missed nothing, and her eldest child's seriousness usually led her into action and problem-solving. Carmen's responsibilities, most particularly for her younger sister, were more complex than for most eldest children because of the death of their father and the absence of their mother. The Lopezes had not seen their daughter, the girls' mother, in over a year. With the exception of occasional phone calls from her, she might as well have been dead, too, for all the participation she shared in her daughters' lives. It was hard for Jerry not to be judgmental about such a parent.

"What's the matter? I thought Carmen was your special friend," he asked his daughter.

This is when the demon of pre-adolescence genuinely made its ugly appearance. Sadie curled her lip, rolled her eyes and said, "Really! Not even!" Five seconds later he heard her bedroom door slam.

From that moment, life in the Hanning home made a not-so-subtle shift. Sadie became alternately the easy child Jerry had always known and the snotty, rude little monster he had glimpsed. Whatever flipped that personality switch inside her, it had no warning light. One morning she would be up, cheerfully getting ready for school, and the next she would whine and cry about what she had to wear, demanding to stay home. She also had begun to complain about tagging along with Jerry to Bisbee every weekend. All the assurances in the world—and he received lots of them from knowledgeable and seasoned parents: "most natural thing in the world;" "don't worry, she'll outgrow it;" "wait until she's fifteen, if you think this is bad!"—none of it eased dealing with this change. Like earthquakes, pre-adolescent personality changes and moodiness may be natural, but you don't have to like them.

Sadie soon got over her momentary break with Carmen, and they were the closest of friends again, making a threesome that included Carmen's younger sister, Elizabeth, an impish kid with a passion for being herself. This playful child took a delight in everything: playing make-believe, posing for photos, playing dress-up. Coloring and drawing were her special passions. The three girls pulled together as closely as ever; they were an inseparable trio. The Lopez grandmother, Margaret, commented when Jerry asked if she had noticed any change in Sadie that she seemed to be a normal, healthy little girl, and even praised him for the "great job" he was doing in raising her by himself.

"You're the heroic one. What would I do without you?" he answered—which was more than flattery, and they both knew it. Still, she smiled with pleasure at the compliment.

Sadie's teacher had nothing new to say about her performance. As a pupil, she was cooperative, good-natured and popular with the other children—all the things Jerry had always heard about her. But at home she continued to behave like a different person, actually like two little girls: Sadie and her evil twin. Jerry was alternately relieved and puzzled as he weathered the change back and forth in dazzling unpredictability.

All that week they argued about Sadie going south to Bisbee with Jerry that weekend. She knew that it was the beginning of the Lenten program, and she didn't want to have to hang around while Jerry conducted his two separate discussion groups: one in Bisbee and one in Tombstone. And he did not blame her. But he was unwilling to leave her every weekend with the Lopezes, despite their assurances that it was fine if he did. Finally, Jerry settled on a novel solution.

"Do you think Carmen would like to come along with us to Bisbee this weekend?" he asked. "Or maybe Elizabeth?"

She thought for a minute. "Can they both come?" she asked suddenly, brightening. "They can teach me some more Spanish." The two Lopez girls had begun teaching Sadie some rudimentary Spanish, not so much the kinds of things one might find in a text book or a travel guide, but words and phrases of interest to nine- and ten-year-old girls.

"Sure," he answered, glad to hit upon something that would move them past the impasse, but he began immediately to regret the gesture. "If it's okay with their grandmother," he said a little less confidently.

"Cool." Sadie began to dance with excitement before his eyes. "I'll go see," she continued and ran out the door. Jerry got right on the phone with Margaret Lopez, who agreed, but inquired about his sanity.

"I'm serious. It'll be great," he answered her, hoping he was right.

His next call was to Bobby Hurschberger, his in-a-pinch driver to and from the Bisbee airport. There would be no room for bicycles in the Cessna that day. Bobby, a seventy-plus-year-old jack of all trades, was always available and willing to do whatever needed to be done, including play piano for the hymns on Sunday morning in the same piano bar style he had used for years.

"Of course, I'll pick you up. Three little girls, huh? It'll be good to have more kids around the church."

Finally Jerry called the Simmons House Hotel to arrange for two adjoining rooms.

When Saturday afternoon came, it was blustery with a high ceiling of scattered clouds at ten-thousand feet. The weather bureau reported a storm on its way from the northwest, perhaps bringing some badly-needed rain to Tucson and Southern Arizona. For the moment there was no real problem for flying, and the storm was expected to pass during the night. Jerry fixed his headset and rubbed a hand over the rough stubble on his chin. One of his Lenten resolves was that he would not put a blade to his face until Easter: shades of ancient Biblical Nazarites like Sampson. He smiled at the happy, excited girls.

The Lopez grandchildren had never before flown in a small plane, and they wiggled with excitement. The constant chatter of "Ohs" and "Ahs" and "look-at-thats" and "can we see our houses?" announced their excitement.

Apart from the novice flying aces and their excitement, the flight was uneventful. Jerry spent that hour stewing over parish worries. The immigrant problem and his stance toward it loomed largest for Jerry. He badly needed to understand the issues better and to develop a responsible stand on it. He also anticipated that there would be some sparks flying between Hank Tucker and Charlie Snow; he had already seen some of that—only hints really, he suspected—at the Tuckers' wedding reception the week before. Then there was the challenge of incorporating little by little the Tombstone parishioners into the St. Peter's congregation; he hoped that the book group at Nellie Cashman's Café would help build some trust between him and them so he could better facilitate their comfort at St. Peter's. And of course, there was his personal life to think about. Sadie's sudden change topped the list. But a close second found Kate Becker and himself definitely on the way to developing a relationship of some kind. And then there was Maddie Gronek. Jerry acknowledged his feelings for her, too. He just did not know what those feelings were. With Kate it was much clearer. They were available, and they liked each other.

"Father, are you *sure* you want to use the ceramic vessels for communion instead of the silver?" Mrs. Elspeth Findlay asked, leaving little doubt where she stood on this small controversy.

"I know you prefer the silver, Mrs. Findlay. So do I, for that matter. But that's part of the point, isn't it? We're modeling lenten simplicity that way. We'll go back to silver at Easter."

"Of course it's up to you, Father..." she grumbled, and stalked away. "Oh, and by the way you seem to have forgotten to shave."

Mrs. Findlay was followed into the office by Silas Ruhl, an elderly and, in Jerry's experience, grumpy widower whose life and hopes remained something of a mystery to him. Silas sat down in the visitor's chair in a way that could only be described as "emphatically." It looked to Jerry as if he were about to be subjected to some kind of pronouncement.

"Father!" he began.

"Yes, Mr. Ruhl."

"I felt I had to talk with you about this book—both of them!" He said the word "book"as if it were something nasty in his mouth, a bitter pill that had he not been so polite, he would have spat out. "I think it—both of them, really—are entirely unsatisfactory."

"What books are those?" Jerry asked, knowing full well that Silas Ruhl meant the ones that the parish would be using in its two Lenten programs, one there at St. Peter's and the other one in Tombstone.

"The one about the Powers, of course—and the other one by that *Borg* person." Silas made a sound very like a snort. "I've been reading it—the *Powers That Be* book…and it criticizes everything we hold dear—even the church. Why don't we just read something about Jesus? A biography or something? Or maybe about the saints? I think that would be more…suitable than this…this…book. It's just going to upset everybody. It's so…so, uh, political. That's what it is—it's political! And the one in Tombstone is just as bad. It criticizes God. That's blasphemy."

"I'm sorry you find the books so upsetting," Jerry responded, trying to avoid being defensive. "Perhaps this isn't the group activity for you right now, and the Tombstone folks picked their book for themselves. Frankly, I have not yet read it carefully myself."

"Well *they* can do whatever *they* want in Tombstone. But I was so looking forward to this study. It's something we've not done for years here in Bisbee. That's why this book is such a disappointment to me. We need something that will reenforce our values, not call them into question."

"It's a pretty feeble set of values that can't withstand some serious examination," Jerry volleyed, but knew inside that what Silas said was true enough, or at least it seemed to be for him. All of Jerry's old religious values were a shambles. But he continued to believe, to hope really, that the road to mature and stable faith could pass through the country of doubt. Jerry prayed that this would prove to be true in his own case. One thing was for certain— no faith he had ever heard of suffered from examination. And that was what he was hoping for both of his book groups this Lent—serious examinations of their faith.

Silas Ruhl even made the classic threat, "I just may have to transfer to the Presbyterian church. And what a shame! I've been an Episcopalian for fifty years!" Silas, a former businessman from Phoenix, had retired to Bisbee; he made one of the largest pledges in the congregation. Jerry reflected ruefully about what the parish treasurer would think about this conversation. But it never helps to let someone hold the congregation—or its priest—for ransom.

"Well, I hope you don't, but if that's your decision, I wish you the best," Jerry said.

St. Peter's Saturday evening Lenten group began with a potluck supper at the church. The little group that assembled, all of whom apparently expected to be there for the book discussion, shared the dishes each had brought— mostly salads and casseroles. Even the newlyweds, Hank and Teresa Tucker, had returned with smiles all around; they also brought a marvelous plate of cold salmon and new potatoes. There was a vague sense of uneasiness in the room. Perhaps they were feeling edgy with the book and the whole idea of "the Powers." Or maybe they shared Silas Ruhl's sense that it would prove to be too divisive and political.

"Isn't a week a pretty short honeymoon, even at your age?" Mrs. Findlay asked in her blunt way.

"My dear," Hank responded, ever the charmer, "we've already been deprived of your company over the Shrove Tuesday supper. We wouldn't want to miss another one." He was repaid for his gallantry by one of Mrs. Findlay's rare smiles.

"Actually," Teresa said in an aside to Jerry, "I couldn't be gone from my store any longer. I had to be there today. But Hank *has* been looking forward to tonight, something about this new kind of demon that you promised him. Sometimes I have trouble following that man!" She swept an unruly lock of hair around behind her head and twisted and tucked it, along with its companions, into a bun at the back of her head. Her bright blue eyes sparkled. A week of marriage had certainly done nothing to diminish her good spirits.

Kate Becker, looking professional and tailored and maybe a bit pensive, her light hazel eyes catching the glow of the single table candle, sat with Jerry and the three girls for dinner. He was pricked by a small jab of jealousy when she focused her attentions mostly on them.

"So, where are you staying tonight?" Kate asked.

Sadie answered, "We're all going to stay in adjoining rooms at the Simmons House."

"It's a *hotel*," Elizabeth chimed in a little breathlessly.

"Of course it is," Carmen said sharply to her sister, as if to say, you stupid little twit, anyone would think that you don't always stay in hotels—which she didn't, of course.

"Isn't that going to be a bit crowded?" Kate asked.

"We have a queen-sized bed. That's enough for us. We do it all the time," Sadie responded. Actually Sadie had two twin beds in her room, and the three of them found various ways of sleeping when they stayed together. At the Lopezes' they usually all slept on the floor, pretending they were camping in the White Mountains—not that any of them had ever been to the White Mountains, but their friends talked about going there and sleeping on the ground.

Jerry changed the subject. "So girls, have you decided which movie to watch tonight?" It was time to get them settled into the former nursery, a left-over from the days when there were lots of families with small children in the congregation. They giggled among themselves for a moment, heads together, and, finally, they nodded in unison.

"*My Best Friend's Wedding*," Sadie responded with a triumphant grin that made it clear that she had gotten her way.

When Jerry returned to the parish hall from seeing the girls settled, the tables had been re-set into a square with chairs lined up around all four sides. Everyone moved to take seats when they saw him, talking a little nervously as they readied themselves to start something new. He counted noses. Someone was missing. Allowing for the three girls, there was still one person short, one less than the even dozen adults who had been there for the potluck supper.

Mrs. Findlay was there, gray and stern, perhaps a bit testier looking than usual, and probably in agreement with Silas Ruhl, who, to Jerry's surprise, had turned up for the supper after all. But now he was nowhere in sight— obviously the one who was missing, Jerry realized with a sense of irony. Kate Becker was very quiet. Bobbie Hurschberger was there as were Charlie and Margaret Snow. Jerry was relieved to see that Charlie was reasonably well behaved this evening. Colin Hines, the border official, and his elementary school teacher wife, Sharon, were there as was Johnny Jewett, the gentle but slow man about the same age as Hank Tucker, his mostly bald head making him seem a bit like a kewpie doll with a face smooth with innocence. Everyone seemed ready to get the group started. In a kind of purposeful stalking movement, the final figure stomped out of the kitchen where he had apparently been taking out the garbage. Silas Ruhl's frosty gray hair and eyes suited well his obviously stormy mood. He was, Jerry knew even before this afternoon's conversation, a generally angry person, unlike Mrs. Findlay, who was stern more by conviction than disposition. Jerry suspected that nothing very pleasant would come from Silas Ruhl's mouth as the weeks of Lent passed—if he stuck it out.

Jerry stood up and pulled a newsprint flip chart from against the wall and stood it by the tables in the middle of the parish hall. On it he wrote, "The Angel of this parish is: _____ " and the phrase, "the Myth of Redemptive

Violence."

"What do you mean by the 'angel' of the parish? I don't get how that term applies to us," said Sharon Hines.

"That's easy," said Bobbie Hurschberger. "It's the original vision that was there at its creation—as in every other organization or business—the telephone company, or Microsoft, or General Motors. This church. The angel is the heart of gold that gets covered up by lots of dirty stuff along the way."

"Then what is the 'Angel' of St. Peter's?" Teresa Tucker asked.

Jerry smiled at the way the discussion was beginning. Everyone seemed to speak at once.

"That's tough. How *do* you get back to any original vision?"

"I think the church's about spirituality. Or at least it ought to be!"

"If the church doesn't do outreach to the poor, then what's it worth?"

"Does that include the immigrants?"

"Absolutely not! We have to take care of our own first. 'Charity begins at home.'"

"Of course it includes them," Colin Hines, the INS official, added softly.

"The church conducts worship services, and its people are the ministers who do the work in the world."

"Promoting learning has to be one of the main values. Like Sunday School...and this class. Thanks Father Jerry," said Bobby Hurschberger.

"No, Bobby, for me this class is more about creating community than it is about education. And we really need to build our community."

"Spoken like the senior warden, Hank," Mrs. Findlay quipped and everyone laughed.

"But what about the other phrase?" asked Silas Ruhl unsmilingly. "The 'myth of redemptive violence.'"

"Yes, what about that?"

Jerry knew this was the moment that might make or break the whole discussion group. "A central claim of Walter Wink's book," he began, "is that human society's long history is a sequence of violent acts based upon the belief that the only solution to evil is to kill or destroy the people who commit evil, and he goes on to say that society believes that is a good thing. As a parallel, the domination of one group of people over others, mostly in class and/or racial terms, represents the mainstream of the history of 'civilized society.' At its core lies the belief that the salvation of human society only comes from violence—imposing virtue through the use of force, the waging of war, or the hero fighting against the villain and killing him."

Wink's strongly worded critique, summarized by Jerry, was exactly what had Silas Ruhl in a lather and which clearly made others in the group uncomfortable, if not with the ideas themselves, then with worry over what the reactions of those around the circle might be.

Charlie Snow became visibly angry. "If some people didn't exercise power and keep the rabble in line, we would live in chaos. And how can the author criticize people for standing up for their rights and their property?" He glared around the table. "Like here on the border. If we weren't willing to use force and guns we would be overrun by the Illegals."

And there it was, the very subject that Jerry both feared and, at the same time, to which he found himself magnetically drawn.

"I get your point, Charlie," Hank Tucker said, carefully keeping his impatience with Charlie out of his voice. "But let's give the book a chance. I for one don't get what he's driving at with this, at least not yet." Hank's expression reflected a studied caution.

Charlie just grumbled. But it was clear by the expression on his face that they would hear more from Charlie Snow.

Finally, Jerry ended the group's first evening together by lighting a single candle as a focus, turning the lights down low and sitting quietly for a few minutes.

When Jerry went to get the three girls, they were asleep on the floor. Their movie was still running, but they lay there in a blanket-covered heap. As he began to wake them, Kate came in to check out his progress. "Do you need a hand?" she asked.

"I'd say I'm desperate for one."

"Let's take them to the Simmons House in my car. That short walk might prove very long tonight," she said.

"Agreed."

As Kate brought her car around to the door of the parish hall, Jerry watched the group members leave. It would be too much to say that they looked stunned exactly. But there was no doubt that the evening's conversation had intrigued and challenged them. He expected that they would all be back next week—maybe even Silas Ruhl. It was a good start. For Jerry, the theological purpose of Lent lay in creating a foundation for the new life that comes at Easter. He felt that on this first Saturday in Lent his personal transformation had taken a step forward—both as a result of Walter Wink's ideas and because of his newly forming relationships, especially the one with Kate Becker.

Kate helped Jerry settle the now fully awake girls into their hotel room. A connecting door to his own and their high spirits seemed to auger ominously for his prospects for a quiet night. Jerry and Kate went to the coffee shop to wind down from the evening.

"They're great kids," she began. "Isn't it wonderful the way they think and act alike? It's almost as if the stages they go through—that we all go through—have more importance than their individual identities, which, paradoxically, each of them is just discovering is *the* most important thing in the world."

"I hadn't thought of it that way, but you're right," Jerry answered with a chuckle of agreement.

"Incidentally, would you let the girls stay with me at my place the next time they come? I've got lots of room, really! I have a hunch they may complicate your life tomorrow morning as you try to get to church and do the service. I would love having them, any combination of them."

"Are you sure about that?" he asked, slightly incredulous. She nodded smilingly. "Let's see how tonight goes," he continued, "and what they would like to do. But thanks for the offer."

"I think it would be fun," she added.

Jerry paid the check and they walked out to her car, which this time was right outside the Simmons's side door on a dark, quiet street. They looked intently at each other for a long moment, then shared a quick embrace. She kissed him on his stubbled cheek.

"Good night," she said.

They looked lingeringly at each other again. Then, feeling very public and very vulnerable, Jerry kissed her lightly on the lips.

"Sleep well," he said.

She gave his arm a little affirming squeeze.

Kate's instincts about the three girls were good ones. When Jerry got back to the hotel rooms, they were wide awake and had no apparent intention whatever of going to sleep. Instead, they sat in three corners of the bed in their room playing some kind of game that at irregular intervals elicited squeals and shouts. With a bit more quiet, he thought, pulling out his old laptop and putting it on the desk in his room, he could probably finish work on his sermon. Inter-generational negotiations brought repeated agreements, which every few minutes fell to ruin amidst more giggles and exclamations as the girls, first Elizabeth followed by Sadie and Carmen, drifted off to sleep.

For the second time in a week, Jerry spent a night in Bisbee with Kate Becker foremost in his thoughts.

CHAPTER FIVE

The First Sunday in Lent

What I come to know in my own experience can be trusted to be true in a way that what we learned secondhand from tradition cannot be trusted.
—Marcus Borg

After church that first Sunday in Lent, Kate Becker caught Jerry as he and the three girls were leaving St. Peter's for Tombstone. "Now don't forget my invitation," she said. "I'm serious about it. I truly would love to have Sadie and her friends overnight. Kind of like a slumber party." She laughed and then once again gave Jerry one of her intent looks. There was something about her intensity that both disturbed and drew him.

"They were pretty good last night," Jerry said. "But I'll bet they'd rather stay at your place than be shushed by me about five hundred times. Let me double-check with them to be sure, but I think you can count on it."

Bobby Hurschberger drove Jerry, Sadie and her two friends, smashed into his old Chevy pickup, to the Bisbee airport. The weather had not changed, but remained what Jerry judged to be just marginally acceptable for flying.

Jerry tried to ignore his feelings about the meager attendance in church that morning, but without success. He had hoped that on the first Sunday in Lent, often a good attendance day in Episcopal churches, more of St. Peter's widely scattered congregation would have found its way to church. Instead, barely forty turned up. And even more disappointing was the slim showing of only four of the Tombstone contingent. He knew all along that his greatest challenge at St. Peter's lay in merging the former Tombstone parishioners successfully into the Bisbee congregation. After three months he had made little progress.

Jerry gave the Skyhawk a quick pre-flight check and started up the engine; they were soon airborne. This time Carmen sat in the right front seat, while Sadie was in the back with Elizabeth. Jerry was charmed by Carmen's obvious fascination with the mystery of the cockpit instruments and with the dual controls of the airplane. The wind had begun to pick up some with a headwind coming at them at three-zero-zero degrees. It would take a few more minutes than usual to get to Tombstone from Bisbee. But for the inexperienced young passengers, the ground speed mattered less than their rough, bumpy ride through the air. From Carmen's and Elizabeth's perspectives it must have been twenty minutes of the roughest carnival ride they had ever had. The main weather system that had just crossed the Huachuca range to the west was coming closer by the minute, and the winds and atmospheric changes were mercilessly throwing the little ping pong ball-Skyhawk back and forth and up and down. Water-laden clouds ranging from light gray to black skittered across the sky much as cars on the Bisbee-Tombstone road below seemed to flee in either direction from the ominous, towering cloud formations. No giggles of delight accompanied this short flight, as the two neighbor girls clung tenaciously to their seats and tried not to look frightened and sick, which they were.

"How're you doing, girls?" Jerry asked, turning half way around so he could look at Sadie and Elizabeth as well as at Carmen beside him. He could see the fear and rising nausea in their faces—all but Sadie's, that is, who was too much of an old hand at flying to have a violent reaction.

"Okay, I guess," Carmen answered. Elizabeth just nodded. No matter what Carmen said, anyone could see that they were *not* okay. Sadie massaged their tender senses with encouraging words.

They finally landed at the vacant Tombstone airport and taxied to the lone tie-down spot Jerry had rescued from the underbrush on an open area at the west end. The propeller had barely stopped turning when all three girls were out of the plane and standing thankfully on the ground beside it. Jerry quickly secured Five-Eight Bravo as the first drops of rain began to fall. Tombstone parishioner Jim Brown waited patiently in his Buick to drive them to his home for lunch before they all went to Nellie Cashman's for the Tombstone book group.

Just before Sadie got into the back seat of the Buick, she pointed to the south. Jerry peered into the growing gloom of the storm, trying to see what interested her. For the second Sunday in a row, his sharp-eyed Sadie had spotted another low-flying aircraft in this same unlikely area as the week before, and, though it was a bit far away to be sure, Jerry sensed that it was the same one as last Sunday. It was too far away to see the flash of red and white, but he imagined he could see the colors as well as a distinctive "V" tail.

The Browns' home was a weathered clapboard that in Tombstone's rough past had served as a boarding house; it sat just three blocks from the town center on a purposely unpaved street that kept the central area looking as people imagined it to have looked in its heyday. Jim and Lisa Brown, now in their early seventies, had come in their fifty years of marriage to seem like parts of the same person. Not that they looked just alike. Jim was tall and slim where Lisa was short and definitely on the plump side—but it was hard to imagine the one without the other. They just fit together. Cheerful, smiling and laughing easily, Jim and Lisa were widely liked and respected. They had been in church that morning, just like every other Sunday since Jerry had been at St. Peter's—and, he suspected, like every other Sunday for many years.

While the exterior of their house fit into the battered old-west look of Tombstone, the inside was a different story. It had thick oriental rugs over highly polished hardwood floors, comfortable, heavy furniture in the living room and crystal chandeliers both in the entrance hall, from which rose a formal staircase to the floor above, and the dining room, where an enormous oak pedestal table was set with gleaming silver and crystal awaiting the arrival of the hungry aviators. A sideboard was already overloaded with steaming dishes when they walked through the door.

Jim Brown, a retired attorney (or, to hear him tell it, country lawyer), was a devoted, if somewhat reluctant, hobbyist. Retirement did not agree with him. After dinner he took Jerry outside to what looked like a ramshackle outbuilding, which inside proved to be a well-designed and fully equipped woodworking shop. Power lathe, table saw, compound miter saw—and an array of other tools whose names Jerry did not even know—were carefully arranged. On the wall hung a baffling array of hand tools and cans and bottles filled with screws, nails, bolts, washers and nuts. The floor was an interconnected series of trails between small mounds of sawdust; the air carried the sweet aroma of newly-cut wood. In one corner stood an as-yet-unfinished rocking chair with sandpaper resting lightly on the seat.

"Wow," Jerry responded, both to the layout and to the chair. He ran his hand over its smoothly sanded top, feeling the power and life of the wood on the tips of his fingers.

"You like my chair?" Jim asked.

"How could I *not* like it?" Jerry answered with a question. "What a beautiful piece of work."

"Then it's yours when I'm finished," he concluded, grinning widely.

"Are you serious?" Jerry asked.

"If you want it," Jim responded.

"If I want it? You've got to be kidding!"

They laughed together. It was easy to be comfortable and relaxed with Jim Brown.

"It'll be finished in a couple of weeks, but I don't know how you'll get it home in your little airplane. I guess I can drop it off for you in Tucson. We get up there to see the grandkids every month or so, you know. It's something to do. Frankly, I find retirement pretty dull."

They scurried together back into the house in the increasing rain. Jerry gathered the girls to leave. They had been helping Lisa Brown put things away and clean up, Jerry's offer to wash dishes having been contemptuously rejected by all four of them. The rain was falling so hard by then that Jim packed them all back into the Buick and drove them the half-dozen blocks to Nellie Cashman's Café, a cozy, warm haven from the rain and blustery wind that sent shivering wet gusts down the necks of unwary pedestrians. Few tourists walked Tombstone's board sidewalks this Sunday afternoon, and most of the shops were closed up tight. Three customers, a couple sitting at a front-corner table by the window and a lone man. They were welcomed to participate—or not—as they wished.

Jerry was worried about the weather. A call to the Weather Service in Tucson from the Browns had confirmed that the storm system was general throughout all of Southern Arizona. It looked to Jerry as if they would have to take the Browns up on their offer to put them up for the night. They were trapped with neither public transportation out of Tombstone nor a rental car agency in the tiny mining-cum-tourist community.

"I hate to see the girls miss school tomorrow," he said to Lisa Brown. "But I can't see what else there is for it. Just one of the hazards of flying." He wondered just how long they would be stranded. Perhaps Margaret Lopez could come down for them in the morning if the weather was still bad, Jerry mused.

At Nellie Cashman's, Brenda-Nellie, her henna hair more in disarray than usual, called to her partner in the kitchen, "Hey, Nellie. Don't you think it's time we closed down and got this show on the road?"

"Right, Nellie," she answered in her precise way, taking off her apron as she came through the kitchen door and setting it down on the café's counter.

"No more espressos folks, but," Brenda gestured to two full pots of coffee on the corner of the serving shelf and in full reach of customers, one regular and one decaf, "there's enough here to keep us alive in the meantime. Just be our guest."

Jerry helped the two Nellies rearrange the chairs and tables into a wide circle and found a place for himself at one of the tables. The three girls and the two Curtain boys, Justin and Joel—the only two children Jerry knew who were at least nominally part of St. Peter's who lived in Tombstone— gathered at one table as far away from the circle of adults as they could get.

"Here's Monopoly," said Hanna-Nellie, and handed the long, thin box to Sadie. The five children went to work setting up for their game.

The senior Curtains, Jillian and Curtis, had already taken a place in the circle of tables. They were much harder for Jerry to like than the Browns— or others of the Tombstone crowd, for that matter. There was a kind of rigidity to them that he and other parishioners found unnerving and uncomfortable. Sadie once said to Jerry in her penetratingly insightful way, "Daddy, I try but I just can't like Justin and Joel. They don't know how to have fun." Jerry could not remember ever seeing any of the Curtains laugh, except in a kind of hollow, mirthless way. It was as if all four of them had been told that they needed to laugh more, so they laughed, even though they hadn't a clue what it was for.

"I'm glad," Jillian said, "that we finally have something here in Tombstone again—even if it's only a book group—and a very poor choice of books, at that," she concluded with a verbal slap at the other members of the group who had outvoted her in making the selection.

Jerry ignored her jibe. It was hard for him to get past her intolerant personality to the much gentler appearance that oddly seemed to hide behind her brittle persona. Her husband, Curtis, was even more humorless than Jillian, if that was possible. At about forty, he was perhaps five years older than his wife. Yes, life was serious business for the senior Curtains, both of whom were bureaucrats for Cochise Country. Their seeming rigidity and their theological fundamentalism would make them uncomfortable with some of the ideas they would encounter in *The God We Never Knew*. Their participation threatened to make the experience uncomfortable for all of the remainder of the group.

With the Curtains sat Sue-Sue Hawkins, the grande dame of Tombstone Episcopalians, still decked out in her Sunday best, in her perpetual look of unregulated enthusiasm, and curls of gray hair piled high on her head. Even in her mid-eighties, she still ran a confectionary store on Allen Street in a converted former saloon. She often drove herself over to Bisbee for church as she had done this morning.

Next to the Curtains and Sue-Sue sat Tombstone mayor, Jack Jackson, and his wife, Linda. Jack was heavy with a round tummy and multiple chins. He was doing his best to provide leadership and to encourage his constituents to make the shift to attending church in Bisbee. Linda Jackson was an athletic woman, strong and a little butch. Her carefully arranged straw-blonde hair was pulled back in a pony tail, and her tanned face was no stranger to the Arizona sun. She looked like the devoted horsewoman Jerry knew she was. It surprised him to find her there at all, since there had been no mention that she would be part of the group. He had not even expected Jack, though the mayor was the church-goer in the family.

Their lunch hosts, Jim and Lisa Brown, were next. They were two of Jerry's favorite people, easy-going, devoted and the kind of straight shooters who would always let you know where you stood with them, but in a way that never left you feeling inadequate or beholden to them. Ike McWarder sat with the Browns, Doc at his feet—a special concession to the not-open-for-business session. Behind their table was a lone customer, someone Jerry did not know, a man in his late twenties or early thirties, with multiple earrings and neglected-looking stringy brown hair. He was reading the *Sunday Times*. Jerry expected him to flee when the discussion began, as the couple who had been sitting by the front window had already done rather pointedly.

The two proprietors of Nellie Cashman's Café finally stopping their hovering and sat down at the last table, beside the one where Jerry, himself, sat alone. Counting the young man—if he chose to stay—there was a total of eleven, including Jerry—one or two, depending on the young man, short of the group size in Bisbee. Most of the Tombstone Episcopalians had shown up.

Jerry decided to seek the fortification of caffeine before getting the group underway, and he turned and walked to the coffee pot, hearing as he went the front door open and close, accompanied by a blast of cold, damp air. The unknown young man had gone out, Jerry thought to himself, and now numbers were down to ten. But Jerry was wrong. Instead, the group's count had swollen to an even twelve, the same number as the group in Bisbee—equivalent to the mythic Tribes of Israel and the named apostles of Jesus and the guests at the Last Supper. Jerry heard Sadie let out a little squeal of pleasure, and when he turned around he saw Maddie Gronek standing in the room with one small, blonde girl hurtling towards her. She and Sadie hugged enthusiastically, while over Sadie's head Maddie gave Jerry one of her enigmatic nodding smiles. He warmed with pleasure at seeing her, then felt a little nervous as vivid memories of their most recent time together flooded over him and made him feel strangely awkward. This was Maddie, he reminded himself, trying to refocus on the task at hand. She took a seat beside the Jacksons, and Jerry launched the group.

"Who is God for you?" he asked, expecting a long, awkward silence.

"Well, not th' nasty ol' tyrant in th' sky," Ike McWarder responded immediately and emphatically.

"Whoa," answered Brenda Jackson just as quickly. "Isn't that a bit harsh?" She stretched her lanky frame, then straightened up in her chair as if she were about to come out of it to glower at Ike.

It was the two non-church-goers who spoke first, though others soon chimed in, beginning with Jillian Curtain. "God is my Heavenly Father," she said. Sue-Sue Hawkins nodded vigorously. "That's what Jesus called Him, and that's good enough for me." Jillian's curly reddish-brown hair jiggled as she shook her head.

"And what does the word 'father' mean for you?" Jerry asked.

"Being protected and cared for," Jillian responded without hesitation. "I remember when my dad would come home from work, he would read to us. Other times he took us places with him. That's how I think about God, too, always there, always ready to listen and nurture—and going places with us. Lots of places." Jillian smiled broadly and a bit smugly. "And definitely not like that bishop who closed our church!"

"Yeah, well I had a very different experience than you did," Brenda-Nellie breathed through her teeth, "though I share your anger over what's happened to our dear little church. Father, humph! Damn, but it's no secret, my old man started sneaking into my bedroom in the middle of the night right after I turned twelve. The word "father" conjures up some very different ghosts for me, and I don't mean Holy ones. If I have to call God 'father,' then I'll have to go without."

The high discomfort level in the room showed in fidgeting and nervous shifting around at the tables.

The long moment of silence was finally punctured when Ike McWarder asked, "Who d'ya think God is, then? That famous tyrant of th' Old Testament, slaughterin' the enemies of th' Chosen People, demandin' blood sacrifices?" He snorted contemptuously.

"No, not that." Brenda-Nellie's come-back was instant. "If I thought that the only way to think about God was either as the Warrior or as the Father, you certainly would never find *me* in church."

"Me neither." Lisa Brown stepped gently into the fray. "That's why I wanted to have our book group be on this subject. I just don't know what to think about God. None of the old ways seem to work anymore, at least not for me, they don't."

"I think it's all a bunch of crap." It was the new young man. "How can there be a god when the world's so fucked up?"

"I'm sorry, but I don't know you," Jerry said, trying hard not to seem judgmental or resentful at his comment...or his language. The Curtains seemed a bit shocked, and Jerry noticed that everyone looked at them co-dependently to see what their responses would be, but otherwise the newcomer's comments seemed to elicit interest not resistance. "Tell us what you mean," he said.

"I'm Cord. None of you know me. I'm from Bisbee, but I heard about this discussion and wanted to see what it would be about." Cord had an undeniably magnetic intensity about him.

"Are you a member of the church there?" Sue-Sue Hawkins asked innocently.

"Naw," he answered simply and dismissively. "But I grew up Episcopalian...even went to Groton School."

"Thanks for coming, Cord," Jerry said. "Flesh out your point a bit for us."

"I'm thinking especially about all the racism, sexism, homophobia, greed...all *that* crap. Everything's about getting advantage—about taking control, about grasping power and hoarding money. I can't believe in a God whose primary business it is to sit back and pass judgment, but who lets all that shit come down in the meantime. If there's a God like that...then...then I just don't *want* to know him." Cord stopped to take a breath. "How could there be a God who sits back and watches people die from sickness and accidents...children...even old people. I just think it's preposterous." Cord's resonant, articulate voice was in sharp contrast to his scruffy appearance, but his strong jaw, clear blue eyes and confident bearing seemed consistent with the sound rather than the mask created by clothes and jewelry. From the faces in the room, Jerry concluded that the others found Cord as intriguing as he did himself.

And so did the five children in the far corner. They watched silently through Cord's intense expression of his opinions, ears practically twitching as they soaked up every word. They loved it.

The conversation mauled all of the adults' old ideas about God, and it carried a strong sub-text of outrage at the bishop's closing of the Tombstone church—the very conversation these people needed to be having among themselves, Jerry thought, pleased by the openness. Jim Brown never said a word, and neither did Hanna-Nellie. Maddie remained largely silent, except at the end to introduce herself, making up for what Jerry castigated himself as his neglect.

"I'm sorry, but I guess you folks don't know me. I'm Maddie Gronek, and I live on a ranch west of Bisbee." She smiled openly and, Jerry thought, winningly. Then she said something that pleased him very much. "I'm a friend of Jerry's."

"Guessed that from Sadie's greeting." Jack Jackson smiled back at her. Suddenly he was the politician, making a newcomer feel at home and being the town host.

"He's the mayor," Hanna-Nellie said in her soft voice.

Maddie nodded. "Nice to meet you, Mr. Mayor. Hope it's okay if outsiders are part of your group."

Jerry took the cue from Maddie's change of subject to bring the conversation to a close. "If you still need a copy of the book, one of the Nellies," he smiled, "will be glad to help you. Blessings." He stepped over to Maddie's table through the general din of conversation and clutter of tables and chairs. She stood and gave him a warm embrace.

"Surprise," she said. "Bet you never expected to have a Jewish girl in your group."

"I like Jewish girls, especially this one," he added. "Just a minute, I want to speak with Cord." Jerry gestured toward the young man who had just picked up a copy of the thin volume from the counter and was looking at it. Sadie and the other girls quickly gathered around Maddie.

"Excuse me, Cord," Jerry interrupted him. "It was good to have you here. Will you be back?"

Cord shrugged. Then after an awkward pause, said, "Sure, why not?" He put down the price of the book and walked out the front door without another word. Soon everyone heard the sound of a motorcycle starting up. It would be a cold, wet ride back to Bisbee on a motorcycle, Jerry thought.

The espresso maker began to rumble and hiss as the good smells of Nellie Cashman's Café began to fill the air again.

Jerry had found himself acutely aware of Maddie's presence, the way she tilted her head as she concentrated, furrowed her brow with a little frown, or smiled when someone said something amusing. He liked having her there, and turned back to her as the group was breaking up and she was talking to the three girls. Sadie had apparently introduced them.

"So how are you planning to get these girls home?" she asked. "Don't they have school tomorrow? This is certainly not flying weather, especially not for these girls," Maddie ended emphatically.

Jerry glanced out the front window. Maddie was right. At that moment sheets of rainwater were pouring down the old-fashioned wood frame windows of Nellie Cashman's Café, and he could see the effects of a nasty, gusting wind, as a hanging wooden sign on the corner of Allen Street shuddered and swung back and forth in the wind. They were going absolutely nowhere in the Cessna today.

"It looks like we'll have to stay," Jerry answered somewhat morosely.

"Or let me drive you back to Tucson," she offered immediately. "I had a hunch you would be stranded. I called my mother, and she's expecting me to spend the night at her place."

"You don't mind?" Jerry asked. She shook her head. "That's terrific," he said. Their intense eye contact carried many unanswered questions—about the night they had spent together, the future of their friendship, and how they felt about each other.

Though Jerry hated to leave his airplane in Tombstone, he accepted the gift with relief. "Thanks, Maddie. Give me a few minutes to make some arrangements? Okay?"

He called the local Arizona State Police office on his cell phone, actually Trooper Joe Hardy, who lived in Tombstone, and asked that he keep an eye on the solitary plane at the otherwise vacant Tombstone airport. Jerry also checked in again with Margaret Lopez to give her an update on their plans.

Within minutes they had all been bundled into Maddie's Audi sedan and were on their way to the airport, the opposite direction of their destination. Jerry checked out the plane and secured it as best he could; their luggage was soon out of the Skyhawk and into the back of the Audi, and they were back on the highway. It would take about ninety minutes, perhaps a bit more, to make the drive to Tucson. In the back seat, the three girls chattered away. Every now and then the adults in the front seat could hear a giggled "*Un elefante se balanceaba*," as Sadie's lessons resumed. "*Dos elefante?*"

They had driven a few miles when Jerry, to his surprise, spotted through the still-intense rainfall a stack-up of waiting cars on the road. "I wonder what that's about?" he asked.

"Roadblock. Checking for illegal immigrants," Maddie answered. Unlike Jerry, she drove these roads regularly.

It took no time at all for Jerry to discover how terribly unfriendly armed and uniformed guards could look and feel. It reminded him of the time he had traveled in Eastern Europe before the fall of the Soviet Union where men in uniform and carrying weapons examined each car as it came through the barrier before passing them through. Jerry found this experience unnerving right from the outset, even before it became more serious. There was a helplessness in their passive role that gave Jerry just the merest hint of what an illegal immigrant must feel. And yet, the immigrant would be without Jerry's stable lifestyle, modest position in the community, ID and cash in his pocket.

When their turn came to pass through the barrier, the experience quickly changed from annoying to frightening. Instead of waving them on, the guard— a big dark-complected man with black hair and a carefully trimmed small mustache along his upper lip—looked both Maddie and Jerry carefully in the face. His dark eyes paused briefly at Jerry's clerical collar, something that often happened to him, but not usually with suspicion and mistrust as was the case at that moment. Then the guard's attention passed to the back seat. One of the girls said, "*Federales*," and then realized that the guard was staring at her and became silent.

"Ma'am, will you please pull the car over to the side?" He stepped back, and Maddie complied. "Father, please get out of the car. You young ladies, too. Everyone come inside. The guard gestured toward the mobile office beside the road.

"What's this about?" Jerry asked, afraid that he already knew.

"I'm going to need to see some ID, especially for those two young ladies." He nodded toward Carmen and Elizabeth.

The mobile office was exactly what someone might have pictured: blonde plastic "wood" paneling, and a counter separating the part of the room that housed three desks from the entrance area. Along the wall of the entrance section were padded, straight-backed, gray-painted institutional metal chairs. Beyond the desks was a door leading presumably to an inner office.

The guard spoke quietly to Carmen in Spanish and she answered him, also in Spanish.

"Father, Ma'am." He gestured toward Maddie. "May I see your IDs?"

"Of course," Maddie answered, smiling confidently. "We have nothing to hide." They all stood nervously in the entrance area.

"We'll see," he responded, looking at Jerry's driver's license and at Maddie's. He also glanced at her auto registration, which she had brought from the Audi. "And now, what about the girls?" With this question he focused clearly in on what most interested him. He pointedly did not offer to give back their documents.

"It never occurred to me that they needed them," Jerry said. He began to feel really tense. "This is my daughter, Sadie." He pulled her to his side, knowing that he had no identification of any kind for any of the girls, Sadie included. Nine- and ten-year-old children had no need for ID in this country, or so he had thought.

"And what about the other two girls?" the guard asked.

"They're our next door neighbors…in Tucson. Sisters. Carmen and Elizabeth Lopez," Jerry said.

"Is that right?" he directed his question toward Elizabeth in Spanish.

"Not really," she answered in English. "Actually our name is Vega."

"What's that?" he asked, looking up at Jerry.

"I'm sorry. I'd forgotten," he said. "The two girls live with their grandparents, the Lopezes, and I had just thought of that as their name. Actually, I knew better. It is Vega."

"I think I need to talk with each of the girls…in private. Please sit down." The guard looked Elizabeth in the eye and smiled, kindly. "Can we start with you, miss? What's your name?"

"Elizabeth," she answered in a small, fearless voice.

"I'm Edward," he said to her. "Let's go back here and chat for a minute."

They were gone for less than five minutes, but it seemed like hours to Jerry and Maddie and the remaining two girls. None of them said anything to lift the cloud of mingled fear and outrage that hung over them. Maddie—as could be seen by her body language and general stiffening of muscles, at least to anyone who knew her well—in her quiet way, had become genuinely angry. When Elizabeth returned with Edward the guard, she was smiling broadly. That was comforting.

"And now, Carmen is it? Can I speak with you for a moment?" he asked again.

Carmen got up and, passing her younger sister on the way, went around the counter and into the private office with the guard. She looked very brave and dignified. They were back in short order. While she was not smiling the way Elizabeth had been, Carmen seemed content enough with her conversation with Edward.

"And now, the third young lady, please," the guard said.

"Now, wait a minute," Jerry began, about to object to his daughter being interrogated, however gently the guard seemed to be doing it. But then Jerry realized the implication of his objection. If the guard had *not* spoken to her and if *he* objected specially in her case, the racist implications of this whole nightmare would have been even worse—for him as well as for the guard and the entire Border Patrol and Federal Government establishment. Ideally and fairly, Elizabeth and Carmen should no more have been questioned than Sadie.

"Relax, Father. There's nothing to be concerned about," Edward, the guard, reassured Jerry.

Sadie gave her father a very adult glance, as if to say, *I can take care of myself*, as she got up and went with the guard. Feelings of pride and fear battled within Jerry.

This time they were gone for no more than a minute. When Sadie and the guard returned he said, "Well, everything seems to be okay. Just as a precaution, let me copy your IDs." He turned toward the small copier, placed the driver's licenses on it and pressed the button. The machine whirred and a piece of paper came out the end. He picked it up and, satisfied, placed it on one of the desks. Then he handed back their licenses. "You can go now. I'm sorry, but we have no choice but to check out anyone who might be entering the country illegally. And, I'm sorry to have to say it, Father, but it's often churches that help them to do it, especially the children, and the extra pressure on the border has created lots of attempted crossings by children to join their parents in the states." He paused for a moment. "Someone in Tucson may want to check up on the Vega girls," he gestured to a form he had filled out, "but I doubt it. Sorry to have troubled you folks. Have a safe ride into Tucson."

They all filed out of the office and resumed their places in the Audi. Maddie's ominous quiet finally exploded, and under her breath she said to Jerry, "That was the most blatantly racist thing I've ever seen in my life. It was about who those girls looked like they might be, not about who they are. This *is* racial profiling—of the ugliest kind. Two little girls! Give me a break!"

"It's okay," Carmen injected from the back seat, showing that they were listening to the conversation, probably picking up every nuance. "He wanted to make sure that we weren't from Mexico, but really lived in Tucson. He was actually very nice."

"I liked him," Sadie added. "I don't think he likes his job very much. He seemed embarrassed."

Jerry remained quiet…and thoughtful. Maddie was right, he thought. Rage, fear and righteous indignation battled for the upper hand in his gut. He thought about rancher Charlie Snow and his anger, about INS official Colin Hines and Hank Tucker, the public spirited vigilante. Clearly, there was more emotion wrapped up in the border situation than he had imagined or understood.

CHAPTER SIX

The First Week in Lent, I

The heart is
The thousand-stringed instrument

Our sadness and fear come from being
Out of tune with love.
—Hafiz

Maddie was in a dark mood as she drove away from the INS roadblock that stormy Sunday afternoon. Singling out those two little girls the way the guard had done appalled and enraged her. And finding religious people— Jerry!—particularly suspect seemed like yet a second level of profiling. In her present frame of mind, she felt that if church people were suspect by a system as blatantly racist as the Border Patrol appeared to be, then she would become one of them. She resolved right then and there, perhaps only out of spite, to continue with Jerry's group in Tombstone. What the hell, she thought as she drove down the road toward Tucson, she might as well be a part of something, at least a peripheral one, just for now.

Maddie had wondered how it would be when she saw Jerry again, and she had been a jumble of feelings that Sunday afternoon at Nellie Cashman's Café. Just screwing up the courage to go into Nellie Cashman's took every ounce of energy she had. But Sadie's demonstrative and uncomplicated joy at Maddie's arrival restored her. Jerry appeared to carry some of his earlier embarrassment, but he soon got over it, and before long it felt almost as if nothing had happened. Almost, but not quite. Maddie was glad that they had not crossed the big line; but it was clear that they had crossed another line— a lesser one, perhaps, but an important one, still. Maddie would never again be able to see Jerry simply as her priest friend, and he wouldn't be able to relegate her to being "Art's widow." Their friendship had endured, transformed certainly, but it had weathered the night together in bed and all of the frustrated passion and longing they both had felt. And it was important to her that their friendship was unbroken; it mattered a great deal.

After they had driven quietly for a few minutes Maddie's anger had begun to abate. At last she said, "I have a favor to ask of you, Jerry. In fact, I must admit that that was the main reason I came to Nellie Cashman's today, not really the search for a new god, as you put it. The weather became just a happy coincidence for me to have this time to talk to you."

"Sure. What can I do? Anything for my devious friend," he responded flashing her a big grin.

The warmth in his voice felt good to her. "I've decided that I want to take up flying again."

"Good for you." He paused for a moment, then asked, "When did you make this decision?"

"I guess I've had it in mind for a while now. I thought about it a lot in Paris. I meant to bring it up the other night, but one thing and the other"— she could not help grinning, stupidly she thought, at the memory—"I just never got around to it."

Jerry smiled back at her, but she could tell that his embarrassment had returned.

"There's more," she continued. "I've learned—just yesterday, actually— about a Cessna 172 for sale at the Marana airport. What are the chances of your driving up there tomorrow with me to have a look at it?"

"The chances are better than excellent," he responded with a chuckle and then added, "you'll need an instructor to check you out in it and to update your license with a biennial flight review. I'd love to do that for you—run you through your paces."

"I'd hoped that you might."

Monday morning the cloud cover was gone, and Tucson wore its usual brilliant blue mantle and bright sun. Maddie picked up Jerry at his little stucco, and they caught the Interstate north. The Marana airport sat in the middle of a broad swath of cotton fields, just outside the sprawl on Tucson's northwest side. At this busy but uncontrolled airport (without an FAA tower or air traffic control service on-site), pilots communicate with each other directly on a unicom radio frequency to keep each other alerted about traffic. Sometimes it can be a bit hairy if several planes are in the pattern at the same time, but then it also can be confusing to have the interceding authority of an air traffic controller. On the whole, both Maddie and Jerry preferred small rural airports like Bisbee, or even Tombstone, where planes can come and go without traffic worries.

Maddie loved the little plane at first sight. Painted a basic white with red over blue markings, it looked much like Jerry's Skyhawk with its blue over red stripes. Jerry dutifully checked out the log books, glanced inside the fuselage through inspection holes, and even laughingly kicked the tires. As far as he could see, it was an eminently airworthy craft with no major damage in its flight history. They flew around in the pattern with Jerry flying left seat and with the owner in the back. Maddie got her hands on the right hand side controls.

"Once you get the hang of it, it stays with you, I guess," she said, eyes laughing with excitement as she maneuvered the little plane.

Since the first time Jerry and Sadie Hanning dropped out of the thunderstorm onto the landing strip at the Twisted K, Maddie had been having a recurring dream about flying. She was up in an airplane, alone and at the controls, but in her dream she could not make it fly straight and level. No matter how hard she tried she could not do it. The harder she tried in the dream the worse it became, and she always woke up feeling terrified that she was about to crash. Somehow her desire to fly again had mixed with her deep uncertainty about the future. She consoled herself that anyone would feel insecure with her husband dying from cancer. No doubt the Jungians would have a field day with the archetypes represented by those dreams—or maybe it was the Freudians with the key: flying as sex? She was relieved when it turned out that she *could* make the plane fly straight and level, and from that first moment in the air there was every reason to believe that she would even be able to manage the tricky bits, too, getting it off the ground and then back down again.

Maddie handed the now former owner of Cessna N8645L—Four-Five Lima—a cashier's check for the asking price and instantly became the new owner. She decided to retain the tie-down at the Marana airport, where, after lunch at the airport café—one of those places where weekend pilots go for their "$50 hamburgers"—Jerry began her brush-up flight training.

Jerry kept her in the pattern for a long time, making eight touch-and-goes. His count. She was too busy to keep track. They did "soft field" landings and cross wind landings on the alternative runway. Then they left the pattern to practice straight and level flight, turns about a point, stalls, 360 degree turns and 180 degree turns. Maddie loved hearing Jerry say, "That's great" and "You have no problem with that," as he did over and over.

At one point he cut the power and said, "You have just lost your engine," a standard exercise for student pilots and flight reviews. Forgetting the niceties of a square landing pattern with all of its legs intact, Maddie began a rounded pattern that brought her down cleanly in the middle of the landing strip. She might have decided to extend her approach more normally, but that would have been risky in a no-power situation. Instead, she made sure that she was over the runway, then she slowed down by raising the nose and put on full flaps to increase lift and reduce the stall speed of the Skyhawk. When the Cessna settled onto the runway, she had been at no risk at any time. Jerry was impressed with her performance, and he told her so.

After about two hours, Jerry said, "Let's not tire you out any more today. Tomorrow, we'll fly to Ryan and practice with the ATC controller, then to Tombstone to rescue my plane, and after that you can be on your own. Okay?"

Maddie felt a wave of pride wash over her. And she also felt excitement. It was like being a kid again in possession of a favorite new toy. Back on the ground and after the plane had been tied down, Jerry handed her a sheaf of papers.

"Here's some paperwork for you to do tonight." He flashed a big toothy grin at her. "Be sure to take your operating manual home with you for reference."

The next day went exactly according to Maddie's expectations. She flew with Jerry beside her from Marana to Ryan Field, then across Tucson and finally to Tombstone, reviewing navigation and cross country flying. It would not be accurate to say that she was glad to get Jerry out of her plane. She liked being with him. But Maddie could barely contain her excitement about flying solo again. There is nothing quite like it. In a small airplane you become really alone, and, in spite of the roar of the engine, it is a remarkably silent experience. You can turn off the radio and climb to nine or ten thousand feet, even cut back the power and glide—and be by yourself. This radical aloneness appealed to Maddie very much just then.

Having her new plane and flying it solo gave Maddie personal satisfaction that she had not known for many months, a sense that she had actually accomplished goals that mattered to her, that the future was more than death and grief. After flying around the ranch property and seeing what it looked like from the air, she settled Four-Five Lima down onto the dirt runway, feeling more at home at the Twisted K than she ever had before. It felt like *her* home, not just the place where she lived. Her new-found sense of ownership extended for the first time beyond the house and garden.

Many months spent totally absorbed in caring for a dying person had left Maddie little time or energy for anything else. A person gets out of the habit of meeting personal needs—or even knowing what those needs are. Who would not have experienced a vacuum after the end came? Maddie certainly had. Total absorption and then absolutely nothing! As soon as the funeral was over, with their friends and Art's kids back to their lives, there had been nothing for her *to do*, nothing to occupy her time. She had stared off into space, languishing without the least idea of what she wanted to do or what she *could* do. Maybe the worst part was that, though Maddie ached to be with other people, when she did have company, she found she had nothing to say to them and became anxious to get off by herself again. No doubt about it, she had the "restlesses" as Grandmother Baar used to say. Maddie just could not manage to get comfortable inside for long, and when she did, one of those unannounced waves of grief would come over her again. Without warning she would find huge tears sliding down her face. But that was before.

Now Maddie felt an enormous sense of well-being, with her new airplane, with the ranch, and with all of the parts of her life—so much better than feeling sorry for herself the way she had immediately after Art's death. But no matter how hard she tried, she was unable to take credit for her good fortune. It simply did not seem to Maddie as if she had done anything to justify the good things that were happening for her—that somehow she had earned it all by caring for Art all that time. But she could not see that life worked that way: that rewards and punishments were somehow meted out with an underlying sense of justice. Where was the justice for Art? His three kids? Besides, she had taken care of Art because she loved him.

Despite all the good things and her new sense of well-being, it was as if something was missing. Beneath all of the positive turn her life had taken, there was a haunting feeling of meaninglessness, superficiality, even shallowness. And Maddie hated shallowness more than just about anything else. She yearned for a life that had deeply rooted origins and matching experience. Her entire family consisted of divorced parents and some distant relatives she did not know. And she felt no particular ties, except ones of blood and genes, beyond her immediate circle—no profound sense of belonging to something larger than herself.

She kept coming back to her Jewish heritage. Even when her parents lived together, and that had lasted until she was ten, they never practiced any sort of religion, neither Jewish rituals in the home nor attendance at church or synagogue. Occasionally they went to a *bar mitzvah*, or a death would demand their attendance at a Christian or Jewish funeral or wedding. But if Maddie had at any time been obliged to defend or define either part of her religious heritage, such as it was, she would not have been able to do it in any convincing way, in any way at all, really. Nothing religious changed after her parents' break-up, though lots of other things changed. Deborah had borrowed money from her rather distant family to go into business, and the trip that generated that loan provided one of the few occasions when Maddie experienced a traditional Jewish Shabbat. Deborah's Uncle Joshua, Maddie's grandfather's brother, had the money in the family, and his traditional Jewish observances matched Maddie's grandfather's disdain of them. It would have been ungracious of Deborah to go to him for money and not be part of the weekly ritual. Anyhow, Deborah borrowed the money and opened her own women's clothing store—nice, expensive things—in Tucson.

Maddie's father, Thomas Stringfellow, her Christian side, worked for an international investment corporation and had lots of money himself, which he managed mostly to keep away from his ex-wife, Maddie's mother. But Charles did see to Maddie's education and flew her all over the world to see him. He was the one, also, who had paid for her flying lessons. Maddie hadn't seen him for over two years, but they maintained a lively e-mail correspondence; and at the time of Art's death, Charles had been very solicitous, but trapped in Saudi Arabia in the aftermath of the September 11 attacks. Thomas Stringfellow offered little help to his daughter in establishing her religious roots—or any other kind of roots for that matter. No doubt members of his extended family, like Deborah's Uncle Joshua, were religious. But Maddie did not know any of them.

Where does all of this leave me? Maddie asked herself. She had to admit that "cynical academic" was a label that came pretty close to the mark. If she had learned any one thing from Art's death, it was just how unsatisfying cynicism can be. You can't cuddle up in bed with cynicism. You cannot understand the finality or horror of death or deal with it in any very effective way through cynicism. Maddie found cynicism, perhaps especially the intellectual variety, to be ultimately arrogant, empty and lonely. Jerry's invitation to attend the book group in Tombstone, and her picking up on that suggestion, put the strangest ideas into her head, and she began asking questions that she had never actually asked before in her life. Questions about the meaning of her life and about life in general. Questions about God.

But what good are questions without some answers?

Answers. Where do you get them? How do you know them when you see them? What do you do with them when you have them? Maddie did not even have answers to these questions.

CHAPTER SEVEN

The First Week in Lent, II

The world is, to a degree at least, the way we imagine it. When we think it to be godless and soulless, it becomes for us precisely that…. Worldviews are not philosophies, theologies or even myths or tales about the origin of things. They are the bare-bones structure with which we think. They are the foundation of the house of our minds on which we erect symbols, myths, and systems of thought.
—Walter Wink

Jerry shook Hank Tucker's hand and received a quick embrace from Theresa. He had just finished tying down Three-Eight Bravo beside Hank's Bonanza. No question about it, he thought glancing around, the Rocking T Ranch had a comfortable, settled look about it. A row of mesquite trees along one side of the house and a tall, carefully tended oleander hedge on the other softened the otherwise rough desert landscape. The house's inviting facade had an unassuming air, despite its rambling expanse. "You two seem to be pretty much like any married couple," Jerry Hanning said to the newlywed Tuckers—though perhaps a bit more affectionate, he thought smilingly to himself.

Jerry had flown out of Tucson mid-afternoon on Friday for Cochise County and for Hank Tucker's Rocking T Ranch in the Sulphur Springs Valley east of Bisbee. Unlike the one at Maddie Gronek's Twisted K, Hank's landing strip was listed on air charts of the area as a private airport. The absence of large landmarks made the ranch hard to find from the air, but that also meant that there were fewer obstacles to worry about than at Maddie's place where Mule Mountains made it a tricky spot to land unless you knew the country well.

Jerry had Maddie Gronek on his mind. Time spent sharing the cockpit of Four-Five Lima had confirmed her importance to him. The empty Tombstone airport echoed with their laughter as he had signed her logbook with his endorsement, opened a bottle of soda and produced two glasses so they could happily toast the occasion. Now they were flying buddies, he thought. He even fantasized about them taking trips together in one of their planes, sharing the flying and doing some fun things together—a real friend, and his only one in Arizona. But Jerry also remembered what it had felt like to share a bed with her. What he was not clear about, though, was whether the sexual excitement he felt that night was about Maddie or only about his own emptiness and longing. It was probably better that they guard their friendship and steer clear of a return to those dangerous feelings.

"How do you like living on a ranch, Teresa?" Jerry asked.

"It's a little hard to be so far away from the store, but I promised Hank." Teresa gave her husband a little pat on the cheek. "I really do plan to work less and to let my employees do their jobs without my constant supervision," she said. "I think I'm going to love it here. We still have my house in Bisbee if it gets to feeling too lonely out here."

Whatever else this marriage brought Teresa Bustamante Tucker, it certainly gave her some distance from the work life that had occupied her for over a decade. Judging from her appearance, graceful and elegant as always, and her attitude, relaxed and natural, so far she found ranch living with a man who worshiped her entirely agreeable.

For his part, Hank knew how to unwind and relax. For him it did not matter that he lived in the same place where he worked. It had always been that way for him, growing up on the ranch and spending a lifetime surrounded by the timeless rhythms of the desert. He once said, "I could wake up blind from a coma and just by the smell of the air and the feel of the soil, tell what time of year it is." And Jerry believed it. Hank's natural instinct for the land and respect for it showed in everything he did. He had no need for fancy theologies to find the sacred deeply embedded in the earth and aloft in the sky. Indeed, his sense of God was in some ways very like the one held by the tribal peoples who had lived on this land for centuries. On his study wall, a portion of a poem by Chief Dan George, spoke eloquently,

> The beauty of the trees,
> the softness of the air,
> the fragrance of the grass,
> speaks to me.

The faintness of the stars,
the freshness of the morning,
the dewdrop on the flower,
speaks to me.

And my heart soars.

Hank lived, if not exactly off the land, certainly in concert with it. That meant that he did not push himself to act contrary to it. He never worked through the heat of the summer day and never expected his employees to either. "Respect" was probably the most important word in the English language for understanding and describing Hank Tucker. Everything he did, he did with respect. Every decision he made was respectful—honoring the essential integrity of all life and all living things. Hank was a deeply spiritual man.

But at least from some points of view, Hank had a blind spot. Even with his essential agreement with the Native American feel for the natural environment, he made a significant departure from their thinking about the land. There he became entirely Anglo. The issue was ownership, and Hank understood himself to be the *owner* of the Rocking T Ranch. That sense of proprietary right lay deep within his being. Three generations of Tuckers before him had lived and worked on this ranch. They had struggled with weather and drought, fought with competitors over the land, sometimes Mexicans—this was Pancho Villa territory, after all—and sometimes with Indian tribes. Cowboys and Indians was not historically an idle child's game in this part of the world. Miners and quick-rich exploiters might ravage the land they stole from the Indians, but men like Hank, even though their ancestors were no less thieves than the miners were, shared more with the peoples they dispossessed than they would ever have admitted. Caring for the land constituted a way of life in this desert. And Hank, with all his gentleness and wisdom, his kindness and integrity, his powerful personality and natural leadership, was a man of his place and time, or perhaps a generation earlier.

The big threat to the land at this time and in this place seemed to Hank and many other ranchers to come from irregular immigration from Mexico. According to the ranchers, immigrants opened gates and left them open, tore down fences when they wanted to get through, left a trail of plastic jugs and other garbage wherever they went and generally made a nuisance of themselves. They were, by this same argument, disrespectful and even disdainful of property rights and the hard work of generations of ranchers. It was part of the culture here and the lore of this generation that something must be done to resist these "locusts."

"They just have no respect," Hank said. "No respect for property rights. No respect for the land. No respect even for themselves to come traipsing through here to do the shit work at wages that Americans won't work for. They take jobs that Americans could do if *they* weren't there; they take food right out of the mouths of American families. They need to go back where they came from and work to make their own countries places of opportunity for their children."

To which Teresa would respond, "Never mind that the locusts are human beings trying to improve their lot in life! They are poor people. What can they do? If they try to form groups or parties, laws get passed against them. When they do show some strength and rise in rebellion, they become outlaws, living in the mountains, hunted by the army. Even the rebels have their hierarchies that keep the peasants from getting too much power or accumulating any kind of wealth. Everybody wants to keep them poor. Who can blame them if they want to come to this country where there seem to be opportunities?"

To which Hank would retort, in language he believed constituted the final word in such an argument, "No matter. They're breaking the law. We have the right to keep them out, and I mean to uphold the law."

"But why do *you* need to do that? Isn't that what the INS and the Border Patrol are for?" she would ask with a seemingly innocent expression on her face, as she goaded Hank.

Round and round the argument went, one that you could hear in hundreds of places throughout this border country. But Hank had the strength of numbers on his side, especially if you weighted the argument with factors of wealth, influence and power.

In many quarters the issue was as much one of racism as it was of economics. But not at the Rocking T. It is doubtful that Hank Tucker had a nakedly racist bone in his body—certainly nothing like Charlie Snow's bigoted opinions. Racism was not a part of Hank's connectedness with the land, his broad view of humanity and his sense of the relationship between all living things. For Hank the border shouted *politics*. He could not see why the sanctity of this land should be violated because the sick politics of Mexico or other countries made them unable or unwilling to care for and provide opportunities for their own people. His remarkably broad, conservative view in so many ways found its limitation in his immediate environment, his own land and what he believed was his sacred duty to protect it and care for it.

Jerry remained confused about the immigration problem on the border. The issues combined power of argument and place, the pathos of human stories and deeply rooted fears of the unknown "other." And he soon discovered that this invitation to spend the night at the Rocking T Ranch was about Hank attempting to "enlighten" him about ranch life and the problem of illegal immigrants, at least from the ranchers' point of view. Colin Hines, St. Peter's INS officer-parishioner, was there for dinner with his wife, Sharon. The other guests were neighbors of the Tuckers, but did not include Charlie and Margaret Snow, the other ranch couple who attended St Peter's.

Dinner that night trucked out a sumptuous affair of almost cliched ranch food: a great beef roast, charred on the outside and pink inside, beans laced with pork, baked squash and roasted potatoes, half a dozen different breads, and a variety of green vegetables—everything laid out on earthenware platters on an enormous side-board. Chilled beer, mostly Mexican imports—Dos Equis, Negra Modelo, Corona—and bottles of red wine sat on another serving table. The dining room table, rough and coarsely hewn on the sides and bottom and highly polished on the top, was laden with condiments and sparkling silver flatware. Above it hung an enormous Mexican pierced tin chandelier. The chairs, made of rough pieces of mesquite, were carved and lashed together with leather straps and lacing—*equipales*. On the wall hung a collection of beads, crosses and crucifixes, sombreros, tooled silver plaques and more— all from Mexico and collected by Hank's father.

The guests, six besides Jerry, were in some way connected to life in this remote corner of Arizona. One rancher named John Vargas—just turned seventy-five and recently widowed—was as adamant as Hank about the need to keep out the illegal immigrants. Sam and Sheila Abernathy, another ranch couple that had the same kind of longevity on the land as Hank's family, were less vocal about the Undocumented Aliens (UDAs) but went along with Hank and John. Hank's foreman, Alex Cloud, sat quietly most of the evening. Alex was a short, intense kind of man, wiry and charged with lots of energy. His hands, the most noticeable thing about him, rough and weathered, outsized the rest of his body. Jerry guessed his age at about forty, but later learned that Alex would never again see sixty. Alex was a sometime parishioner of St. Peter's. He later unraveled a small mystery for Jerry.

"Now that I see your 172, Father Jerry, I realize how it came to be near

Tombstone the other day when we had that close call," he said. "Sorry about that." There was nothing apologetic in his unwavering brown eyes.

"Ah, yes," Jerry responded. "I wondered about that. I thought it might be Hank's plane, but knew he was unlikely to be flying it with a brand new bride at home." He smiled at Teresa. "I think I saw you again the next week, last Sunday."

"This time it *was* me," Hank answered. "My turn."

"What on earth are you up to?" Jerry asked. "Running drugs?"

Alex laughed humorlessly. "Got to keep up our lifestyle somehow in this invasion of Illegals," he said. Jerry found that he did not like Alex Cloud.

"Actually, there's no mystery," said Hank. "We try to keep an eye on that part of the county."

"To give a hand to the INS," Alex finished. "Don't we, Colin?" Alex looked down at his rough, powerful hands.

Colin Hines nodded his head in the affirmative. "Yes, this way some of the ranchers, those with airplanes, have been helpful. Others…" His voice trailed off. Clearly there was more to the ranchers' "help" than he wanted to talk about just then.

"Colin doesn't like it when we round 'em up and detain 'em," John Vargas responded.

"We really don't do it all that much," Hank responded. "But *we* aren't really the problem. What do you say, Colin?"

"Not a *big* problem," the INS officer responded judiciously. Everyone knew that he would rather have the ranchers stay out of the border enforcement business entirely. "It's the others that cause most of the trouble."

"Others?" Jerry asked.

"The white supremacists," Teresa answered without batting an eye. "The sick ones who shoot people."

"You mean that actually happens?" Jerry asked, feeling foolishly naive the moment the words left his mouth.

There was silence around the table. Hank sat playing with his water glass. The others found their own ways to keep occupied.

"What else can you expect?" Teresa asked. "Colin and his people—with the Border Patrol and the entire American government behind them—build huge fences, walls of steel and concrete and turn the border area into a militarized zone." There was no laughing tone in her voice this time, and no sparkle in her blue eyes. "On both sides of the border there are more armed soldiers than there are jack rabbits. The Tohono O'odham people are barred from moving around in their own land just because it spans both sides of the border. Sometimes they are treated, at least on this side, as undocumented aliens in their own homes," she continued. "It's outrageous. And it's accomplishing nothing."

"I admit," said Colin, "that we haven't succeeded in stemming the flood, no matter how many thousands we catch, detain and send back."

"Detain!" Teresa let out the word like an expletive. "You mean imprison! How many more prisons is the INS going to build? How many more people will you separate from their families? You all know as well as I do," she looked around the table at everyone sitting there, "from a business point of view, we are increasingly part of a world-wide economy, the famous globalization. If we create the desire for goods, which move pretty freely these days—remember NAFTA?—how can we deny the opportunity for workers to follow those goods to where they can earn the money to purchase them? What a greedy bunch we all are!"

"My dear," Hank began gently, as he made a vain attempt not to belittle his bride's opinions nor to patronize her, "I agree with everything you have said. But in the meantime we have to protect our own property. What else can we do?" He actually raised his hands in a gesture of helplessness.

"Even when it perpetuates injustice?" she asked, sparks of anger now flashing in her eyes.

Sam Abernathy, who had been silent for most of the conversation, responded. "I'm afraid so. As unfair as it seems, ranchers like Hank and me have to see to our own responsibilities. We owe it to *our* families, to *our* workers and their families, even to our parents and grandparents who lived and struggled here for their whole lives. Shoot! It's our life, too."

"It's about a way of life, about values," Alex interjected. "I'm not a landowner myself, but my own roots are here, too. Everything we know and value in life is bound up with this here land and its traditions. It must be defended against these...people."

Hank gave Alex a sharp look, as if surprised by his vehemence, but Jerry thought he saw something more, something wary and anxious.

A long, uncomfortable silence took the place of verbal jousting. Finally Sheila Abernathy suggested that they all lighten up.

"I agree," Teresa concurred. "Let's move to the Arizona room for coffee."

Tense small talk continuing, the dinner party migrated to the next room, where rough open beams held up the white plastered ceiling. Red Mexican tile covered the floor and worn leather and wicker furniture was arranged into conversation areas. Jerry's relief was enormous as they moved way from the intensity of the dining room conversation into a room, and hopefully an attitude, of relaxed amiability. One sour note rang in his ear, though. Just as they were all leaving the dining room, Jerry heard Sam Abernathy say to Alex Cloud, "…your turn to keep an eye on the Santa Ritas. Be careful…and discreet."

CHAPTER EIGHT

The First Week in Lent, III

The heart needs to be opened. To use a favorite metaphor, spirituality is "for the hatching of the heart." To extend the metaphor, the heart is like an egg with a shell around it. If what is within is to live, the egg must hatch, the shell must break, the heart must open. If it does not, the life within dies and becomes foul-smelling and sulfuric.
—Marcus Borg

Flying away from the Rocking T late the next morning and making the short flight to Bisbee for his prearranged lunch date with Kate Becker, Jerry Hanning put border issues behind him. He also let go, for the moment, of pastoral concerns over St. Peter's. Even his friendship with Maddie Gronek was put on mental hold. Instead, he settled into the idea that he was about to have a lunch date with an attractive woman. He had not felt these feelings of anxious excitement since he had first met Marjory over a decade ago. Deep in his gut he felt uncertainty and insecurity—even a little panic. But it felt good, better certainly than the last two years of emotional wasteland, cocooned as he had been in his grief and self-pity.

The Bisbee Municipal Airport was as quiet as usual, and Three-Eight Bravo was quickly tied down. Jerry was soon on his bicycle riding happily away toward the Chili Pepper Café in downtown Bisbee, a fairly typical southwestern Mexican restaurant with a jungle of green hanging plants, all plastic, bright wall murals painted in a rough primitive style and beige plastic table cloths covering what was obviously a hodgepodge of different kinds, sizes and shapes of tables, no doubt as eclectic as the chrome, plastic and wooden chairs that stood around them. Along one wall ran a row of red vinyl-covered booths. Jerry had taken the booth farthest from the door. Kate arrived five minutes behind him.

Kate Becker appeared to be as coolly confident and relaxed as ever. Her fresh, crisply-ironed blouse and white slacks made her seem matter of fact—even businesslike. Pale hazel eyes, carefully and subtly outlined, were magnetic in their brilliance. Her liquid, graceful movements carried her across the floor to Jerry with an understated sensuality that caught the eye of all the men in the room, and most of the women. She came briefly into his arms, yieldingly and lingeringly, belying her appearance of cool distance.

"Hi," he said.

"Hi yourself," she said softly. "Sorry I'm late. But it's good to see you." Somehow they both knew, partly out of their mutual intentions and partly from the way that they read each other's body language, that a brief public embrace was no longer likely to be the limit of their intimacy. That promise lingered in the air. "What have you been doing all week?" she asked.

"Mostly flying and giving some flight instruction. One student was Maddie Gronek. You know, the ranch owner west of here." He took a breath. "And you?" The intensity of their eye contact denied the banality of their conversation, and powerful energy flowed across the table.

"Oh, fighting with the dean, listening to bitchy students who want an 'A' without doing anything—the usual. Also had a call from my mother. She's forever nagging me to go back to Chicago. Just doesn't understand what it is about being in this country that could possibly appeal to me."

"Has she ever been out to visit?" Jerry asked, beginning to feel ill at ease in the disconnect between the words and the reality of what was happening between them.

"Are you kidding? She thinks Skokie is a long way from home. I'm sorry to say that my family is pretty North Shore hoity-toity. They'll go east or to Europe—but Bisbee, Arizona? Give me a break!" Kate smiled with what Jerry was beginning to think of as her most seductive expression.

They talked more about families, about Sadie and her friends and their lives, and they had a pretty good lunch, lingering over iced teas. As Jerry went to pay the check, Kate asked, "What do you have this afternoon? Lots of appointments at church?"

"Not much," Jerry answered. "For once, I have a free afternoon—nothing but polishing the sermon a bit."

She stood very close beside him. "Then, I have a request—a favor—to ask," she said, looking serious.

"Sure. What'll it be?" Jerry felt a fleeting moment of excitement quickly replaced by a mild panic.

"Remember when you offered to take me flying? How about this afternoon? The weather seems perfect, and I haven't seen this country from the air."

"With pleasure," he answered, pleased and a little relieved.

And it *was* fun. They rode out to the airport in Kate's Escort, Jerry's little folding bicycle in the trunk. In twenty-five minutes they were in the air over Bisbee. Jerry liked the physical closeness in the front seats of the Skyhawk as their shoulders brushed and, occasionally, arms and elbows touched. They flew over the broad open area east of Bisbee and along the Sulphur Springs Valley.

"There's Hank Tucker's place," Jerry pointed out to her.

Kate looked with apparent interest at the collection of buildings and a large corral, where the sound of the plane spooked the horses into running. Then Jerry banked sharply west and climbed up to seven thousand feet, passing over Tombstone, where he pointed out the OK Corral, the County Court House, now a museum, and other sites. "And there's the airport over there." Jerry pointed to the single strip of tarmac with no buildings or any sign of life.

"I've been to Tombstone, of course," Kate said into her microphone. "But it looks different from the air, kind of like a child's toy-city Tombstone." Their eyes met as she spoke, and looking at her Jerry saw wisdom and sensitivity, question and invitation in her unblinking hazel orbs. Not for the first time, he felt excitement and awkwardness looking into them and, at that moment, he was glad that he could flee back into the details of flying as a distraction.

They climbed on up to nine thousand feet and flew back over Bisbee, this time looking at the town itself, nestled comfortably in the crevices and draws and along the hillsides of Mule Mountains. The enormous gouge of the open pit mine, unrelieved from the air by the charm of the town, looked like the blight on the land that it was. Jerry always marveled at how a few hundred feet of altitude told a very different kind of truth about a place than the one seen at ground level. Decorative distractions on buildings, the buildings themselves, and careful landscaping disappeared as you gained elevation and perspective. Instead of beauty and charm, which Bisbee admittedly had in great abundance from the ground, the town from the air looked to him like the scar on the natural beauty of the setting that it actually was, a monument both to greed and ingenuity. Jerry was unable to see one of those mines—and there are hundreds of them in Arizona—without mingled senses of outrage at the ugliness left in the wake of human rapaciousness and admiration at the perseverance and skill of the miners who had created them.

Mining carries an attitude of mind that is nearly as permanent a legacy as the mines themselves. Miners have a kind of ruthlessness, more refined and scientific today than was true a century ago, but the mind-set remains. Find the ore, dig it out of the ground, get it where it can be refined and when the richness is played out or the price goes down, abandon the site to nature's own resources and move on. Little inherent respect for the beauty and majesty of the natural setting exists in the hearts of miners, apparently even today. Governments make feeble efforts to enforce some restoration of the sites, but as far as the developers and miners are concerned, the earth is something to be exploited, not cared for. Like a conquering army's, their rule seems to be rape, burn and pillage—and then move on to do the same thing somewhere else. In the meantime, mining town culture combines danger and the dream of riches to create a prevailing attitude of risk and ruthlessness throughout much of the rural American West—indeed, wherever mining is a major occupation. Stories of rough living, noisy saloons, violence and women— women who are attracted by the men and the money—are all parts of the same ruthless, exploitative, brutal and get-rich-quick life of the mining camp. And these attitudes are as permanent a part of the Southern Arizona landscape as the mine scars themselves.

From Bisbee they headed west hugging the border, past Fort Huachuca and Libby Air Force Base and the civilian city of Sierra Vista, another tough-minded piece of the mind-set of Southern Arizona. The military presence has probably been felt in this border country ever since Spanish conquistadores and missionary priests first came north to conquer and settle the land. Anglo incursion has been no different in kind. The conquerors carried a disdain for the native peoples and an abiding arrogance that might made right. But Fort Huachuca, named for the mountain range skirting the fort to the west, is something else again. It was originally built as a frontier outpost to keep the native population under control and to protect the border, like many such places in the west, but with a difference. Fort Huachuca was a black—an African-American—post. Its personal history thus combined different levels of frontier racism, both by and against the occupants of the post. Although Fort Huachuca was no longer segregated, its history, like the abandoned mines, was a part of the underlying reality of this wild, harsh and beautiful land.

Near Fort Huachuca/Sierra Vista sits—or floats rather—one of the monuments of contemporary border racism, an enormous balloon, permanently located there to keep watch over that section of the border and the illegal immigrants crossing there. Drug smugglers also get caught in that net.

"That's really horrible," Kate said about the balloon, lightly resting her hand for a moment on Jerry's knee. "What a lot of effort they go to, just to keep people out!" Then she moved her hand away; and Jerry found himself wishing she had not.

From Sierra Vista Jerry and Kate made their way back to Bisbee just as the two wing tanks in Three-Eight Bravo were showing low. After arranging for the plane to be refilled with aviation fuel, Jerry piled into Kate's car to drive into Bisbee where she would drop him off at the church.

"Thanks for the ride, Jerry," she said from behind the wheel. "This country really is interesting, and you get a very different perspective from above."

"I've always thought so," Jerry answered. "It seems to cut away some of the pretense of regular life and leaves everything somehow open and vulnerable."

They rode quietly for a while. Then Kate asked, "Speaking of 'open and vulnerable,' can I risk that with you?"

Kate's question gave Jerry pause. "Sure," he said finally, with more confidence in his voice than he felt.

"Where do *we* go from here, Jerry?" she continued. "Personally, I mean. You and me."

Jerry felt a lump rise in his throat as he weighed the risks and the dangers inherent in that moment, in taking a chance with her. And there was much to think about. Would he declare his attraction to her only to find that she simply thought of him as her priest? Her question did not seem to imply that. Then there was his own grieving. Was he really ready for the kind of relationship that Kate Becker represented? She offered something more than two teenagers holding hands. Both of them were well beyond that. And what of his responsibility to her and to the church as her priest? That was not a small matter. The church these days took intimate relationships between clergy and their parishioners very seriously, seeing the pastoral relationship as a kind of sacred trust that must not be broken. And there was the "power" problem—can a relationship between a priest and a parishioner be one that is on an equal basis between two adults? On all sides these days the courts are filled with cases of sexual harassment and exploitation of positions of power for sex. And a sexual relationship was definitely where Jerry felt he and Kate were headed, at least in his mind they were. Yet, they were both single and available. Who could possibly object to them having a relationship?

Jerry found that his hands had gone cold, and his heart was beating so hard that he feared it must be audible. I was not that he had not been attracted to women parishioners before, because he certainly had been. Perhaps discovering potential sexual partners in just about any setting is one of the most natural responses of human beings to each other, the very substance of attraction itself. He could list half a dozen women over the years of his marriage to Marjory who became serious focuses of his fantasies. He let himself engage in harmless flirtations that never went beyond a few verbal quips, always knowing that under the right circumstances and given a suitable opportunity, that these flirtations could become dangerous. But that never did happen—he refused to let it happen. Somehow he always knew where to draw the line. It always felt like what it was, nothing more than harmless fun, the kind of sparring that people have always done.

But Jerry's attraction to Kate Becker was different, and Jerry knew that this—and she—was different. Their mutual availability could not be masked, even if they wanted to hide it from each other or themselves. Loneliness and neediness defined them both. If something happened between them, it might not be the love of their lives, but it would be more than a mere dalliance.

All of those thoughts passed through Jerry's mind in an instant, partly because he had already thought about all of them before. His response to her, however, came almost immediately, with only the slightest pause, but long enough for Kate to give him an inquiring look, and to feel acutely vulnerable herself, before shifting her attention back to the road.

"There's some pretty strong stuff between us, Kate," Jerry began. She seemed instantly relieved, but she waited to hear what else he had to say. Jerry realized that the next sentence out of his mouth had the power to end this right there or to move them irrevocably forward. The responsible, professional thing for Jerry to do was to hide behind his clerical collar, as it were, and to retreat into the safety of roles. But at that moment, he realized clearly that he did not want this conversation to end there and in that way. Instead, he leaped in, a step from which there likely would be no easy return. "And I want to explore that," he said as he reached out his hand and gently touched her shoulder.

Kate turned and flashed Jerry a smile and then said, simply, "Me too." At that moment, she stopped the car at a four-way stop, and Jerry took advantage of that opportunity to lean over toward her. She turned to face him. Their kiss was short, but packed with much: excitement, hope, risk, desire. All of those feelings were there. Jerry could see that tears had welled up in Kate's eyes, giving them a shine that only added to their depth. "Do you want to come to my place?" she asked.

"Right now?" he asked. She nodded. His heart was pounding and his hands went even colder with excitement and anticipation. "Very much."

Kate's home turned out to be a small, tidy stucco house in a newer suburb outside of Bisbee where a broad plain of green fields opened toward the border. Like all of the other similar houses in the development, it wore a hat of reddish brown terra cotta tiles over designer-crafted dormer windows and textured stucco walls painted a rich beige earth tone. A single car garage was attached to the house, the clean lines and fresh newness of which fit Jerry's image of Kate perfectly. New landscaping skirted the house and was designed to soften the harshness of the bare, dry soil and the angularity of the building. Young plants promised a rich ground cover of green leaves and purple, white, and orange flowers. Infant mesquites and palo verdes were nearly ready to break out in spring leaves and blossoms. Both Kate and the neighborhood have little past—at least ones known to Jerry.

Kate parked in the driveway. She and Jerry got out of the car and walked silently up to the front door, a pressed imitation of carved wood. She fumbled with her keys, opened the door and led him into an immaculate interior of soft earth-toned furniture. Jerry was filled with anxiety and conflicting emotions—all of the things that had run through his mind earlier. But now it was different, different because he was past the point where he could simply turn back. He knew what would happen when they were inside the tidy, little house. He felt helpless to stop it; he did not want to stop it.

Kate put her purse down on a small table in the entryway, softly clicked the door shut and turned the deadbolt, actions that carried with them a sense of finality and no turning back. Small Indian rugs, pottery, woven baskets, even a pole ladder leaned up against one of the walls, were warm and unmistakably southwestern. It all seemed too cute and cliched to Jerry at first, but then somehow the room blended into the moment in a way that became a new kind of reality for him right there in that place where his life was being remade. Jerry reached out and pulled Kate gently into his arms, reveling in her willingness, kissing her, gently at first then with mounting urgency, running his hands over her back, marveling at the promise of soft flesh beneath the tight white pants. She looked into Jerry's eyes, smiled an invitation and, taking him by the hand, led him up the curving staircase to the bedroom. Warm sun poured through a south-facing window to outline dark furniture against the very white room—carpet, wall paint, pillows and comforter all shades of white. Kate pulled lightly flowered heavy drapes over the window, leaving only a soft glow of bright sunlight.

Perhaps everyone's first love-making with a new partner combines intense excitement and discovery with acute self-consciousness. Jerry tried to communicate to Kate something more than the passion of a one-night stand, laying a foundation, he hoped, for something deeper, more lasting. But he could not escape feeling awkwardly insecure. He said to himself: what if I disappoint her in some way? What if I call her Marjory?—a silly worry, but one that crossed his mind. What if I am impotent? Guilt can sometimes bring that on, he knew. But his fleeting fears went unrealized. And Kate was sensitive to his internal conflict, understanding instinctively that this was not something that was simple for him—but wanting it to be. Needing him and…needing more than she could even express. They luxuriated in each other. Jerry found her to be softly willing, her slim body, pale and milky, gracefully formed in every way, and openly available—a vulnerability in her that surprised him. She found him considerate and gentle—exactly as she imagined that he would be. She was especially moved by his appreciative and grateful response to her light caresses and tender kisses.

That first hour in Kate's bed won the prize for the least complicated-feeling and most gently-intimate moment Jerry had experienced in years. Literally, years. It seemed, in some way that he would have found hard to explain at the time, as if they belonged to each other, right that they should touch each other, that they should lie naked in bed together, that they should share every kind of intimacy, physical and emotional. How could anybody object if they found something important in each other? How could any bishop get in the way of something as clearly positive as this new relationship? How could their feelings for each other be anything but okay with everyone? After a time of quiet, private exploration, they could share with the people at St. Peter's what they had found in each other. For the time being, though, he thought it would be better for them to keep their relationship to themselves rather than jerking other people around, Sadie in particular, with their personal lives and—as yet—immature passions. As it happened, Kate herself raised the issue of privacy as she drove Jerry to the church.

"It would be a good idea for us to keep this to ourselves for awhile, don't you think?" she asked.

"Yes, I think so, too," Jerry answered, relieved that she saw it that way and that he had not had to raise the issue himself.

At the church, following a furtive glance around, Kate gave Jerry a light kiss. "See you tonight?" she asked with that now-familiar invitation in her eyes.

"Doing anything after the group?" Jerry asked, smiling back to her unspoken invitation.

"Hope so," she said.

"Works for me." Jerry got out and shut the door.

He thought again about her need for secrecy with both relief and some disappointment, glad that they would not have to face immediately the issues surrounding a new relationship in the midst of a small town congregation. But he also had a conflicting desire to announce it from the rooftops. Life was good.

After the potluck supper was cleaned up at St. Peter's that evening and the dishwasher was humming and thumping away in the kitchen, Jerry Hanning launched the evening's discussion by reading a short passage summarizing Walter Wink's views that most—perhaps all—human societies were based upon the domination of one group of people by another group; sometimes the basis of domination was racial, sometimes it was gender; it was always political and economic. Violence was the means by which it was imposed and enforced.

Teresa Tucker was the first member of the group to put Wink's strong assertion into local terms. "This fits what is happening right here, makes it seem part of a larger picture maybe, but no less terrible for that," she said.

"I don't get what you mean," Sharon Hines stated simply—and perhaps a little defensively.

"The border problems," Teresa replied directly to her neighbor. "I've watched and felt the racial prejudice here all my life. And all the rest. That's what it's about: domination, power, control."

Jerry, alert to the reactions around him, saw or felt everyone stiffen, some visibly and others internally. The previously relaxed atmosphere hardened into tension. Teresa's perspective differed from that of everyone else around the table, and while her immediate family had lived north of the border for at least two generations, that did not change the fact of her proud Mexican heritage and the racism she must have experienced all her life. Charlie Snow's feelings were the most noticeable of all as a dark vein stood out in his forehead, and his neck and ears took on a deep red hue. Then he gave what could only be called a nearly-silent snarl of warning and menace; long afterwards Jerry could close his eyes and, remembering this moment, picture a Bengal tiger with Charlie's face emitting a mostly soundless, growling challenge.

Then Charlie said, very softly at first, but soon rising to a pitch of rage, "You bleeding hearts! What do you know about what goes on here? How can you understand how disgusting these people *are*? From your comfortable living rooms? You need to be with them, smell them, both the animal stink and the fear. No matter what we do…what Colin does…they keep coming, wave after wave, van after van loaded with their stinking bodies." He shook with emotion as he cast a disdainful look in Teresa's direction.

Margaret Snow, Charlie's wife, reached out her hand and rested it on his forearm, as if pulling him back from a precipice.

"The world," Charlie continued a little more calmly, "is filled with people who would take everything from those who have and destroy everything they have built. It would be like…like what the Huns did to the Roman Empire. Left it a ruin. The Illegals will do the same to us—if we let them. That's our choice. Allow everything we have built to be destroyed. Or stop them. Any way we can."

Jerry looked around the room as nearly everyone seemed suddenly very interested in the table in front of him or her, charting the exact texture of the Formica top or perhaps examining a scar from some past mishap. Teresa alone looked back at Charlie, an expression on her face that said something like, *he just doesn't get it*, or, *what world is he living in*, or, *this is why the problem is so bad*, or, *it's the same-old same-old*.

It was quiet for a long moment. Then Silas Ruhl—adjusting his glasses on the bridge of his long, straight nose—cleared his throat and pronounced, as if from on high, "They earn whatever happens to them. They take a chance. If they win, then they get some of what they went looking for. And they should; they have earned it. If they lose," he shrugged his shoulders, "then they pay the cost of their audacity." His gray eyes were piercing.

Silas's pronouncement was, if anything, even more shocking to Jerry than Charlie Snow's angry outburst. Jerry would never have tagged Silas as a man with such a fatalistic outlook. Compassion for anyone seemed entirely lacking in him. Illegal immigrants, ranchers, government officials were alike in their failure to attract Mr. Silas Ruhl's sympathy. For the first time, Jerry truly became interested in Silas Ruhl. Just what went on inside of him? What was his story? Why was he in the church at all with this outlook, one that seemed, at least on the surface, to be so entirely lacking a moral or compassionate grounding? Jerry resolved to get to know him and to uncover the source of what had in a moment become for him the mystery of Silas

Ruhl.

Then there was Charlie Snow. Where did all of that anger come from? What little Jerry knew of Charlie, a comparative newcomer himself to this part of the country, did not account for this kind of response to a band of immigrants. Perhaps his own status as Arizona johnny-come-lately was explanation enough, and he was acting out of his own sense of insecurity and feelings of non-acceptance. Or maybe it *was* simply about race.

The rest of the evening's discussion was largely lost in avoiding more of the intense emotional outbursts of the first few minutes. Charlie and Teresa remained underlying poles of tension: Charlie's apparently racially-inspired hatred and Teresa's relentless corrective. Jerry tried to steer the conversation away from that seemingly insoluble conflict, but they always came back to it: protecting one's own privileged life and property against a largely unknown other; and compassion for human beings whose share in the good life seems less than just and equitable. For Jerry, it was anything but a no-brainer to discover where he stood. Theoretically, there was no doubt in his mind that Charlie and his kind were not behaving out of anything but prejudice and narrow self-interest. But then Jerry had real trouble seeing that that was different for the UDAs, who seemed equally determined to pursue their own interests no matter what. Everyone in this drama seemed pretty self-serving to him. But as Jerry tried to shake off this cynical dismissal of the problem, one that would allow him to keep a neutral distance on the issue, he was becoming increasingly aware of the naked racism and the power differential that existed between, on the one hand, ranchers like Charlie and Hank and, on the other, the undocumented workers. And, to make it even more confusing, it all seemed connected somehow to the underlying conflict he was feeling in his new relationship with Kate Becker. Were they equals coming together out of mutual need and desire, or was Jerry taking advantage of his position in an exploitative way? Perhaps it was a sense of guilt that led him to connect these two very different kinds of issues. Kate was hardly a powerless victim, and he felt like anything but a powerful exploiter in a system of domination. The UDAs certainly did fit that description, but he did not think that his and Kate's relationship was unequal. But his uncertainty about the relationship made him uncomfortable, made it harder for him to find his way through the confusing tangle of feelings and motives on the border and within his own congregation.

But there was another side to his new relationship with Kate Becker, one less fraught with ambiguity. It felt emotionally and spiritually healthy to

Jerry to have something else in his life, *someone* else in his life, besides a pre-adolescent daughter and a small congregation of parishioners whom he saw only on weekends. Maddie Gronek was his only real friend in Arizona. Not even his few acquaintances in Tucson offered the dimensions that an intimate relationship right here and now could and did promise. Jerry felt like he had turned a corner in his grieving, was ready truly to be part of ordinary humanity again. Is there anything as exciting as a new love affair? Thoughts of Maddie Gronek passed through his mind. Once again, it seemed like no matter how strong his feelings were for her, and he had them for sure, they were more of the brotherly kind than the ones he felt for Kate Becker, particularly after this afternoon. He was not Maddie's brother, but he could certainly fill the role of brother and friend to her. There was no question about where his feelings for Kate Becker lay, and there was nothing whatever brotherly about them—nor, for that matter, priestly. Jerry looked forward to the weeks and months ahead getting to know Kate and being a normal, healthy adult again.

The book group session ended largely amicably, primarily because of Jerry's careful return time after time to the book and to the author's purpose and to his repeated efforts to steer the group away from its growing divisions. After saying goodnight to everyone except Kate, who lingered, Jerry went to the church office to make his regular evening phone call to Sadie—something he did without fail when he was away from her.

"How are you, sweetheart?" he asked.

"I'm okay, Daddy," she responded.

"Just okay?"

"Oh, you know, whatever."

"Anything interesting happen today?" he asked, wishing there was some way he could tell her all of what had happened to him since he last saw her. Soon she would need to know that he was seeing Kate, but not yet and not in detail. There are some things you just don't tell your nine-year-old daughter, no matter how badly you need to share something exciting that has happened in your life.

"There was something," she began, her disembodied voice becoming more animated. "Carmen and Lizzie—Elizabeth's 'Lizzie' now, you know—they heard from their mother, got a letter. She didn't give a return address, but Mrs. Lopez says it was mailed from there in Bisbee."

"Wow," Jerry exclaimed, meaning it. "What did she say?"

"Not much, really, except that she doesn't drink or use drugs any more.

That was why she went away." Jerry already knew the story of the girls' mother, an artistic type who had flirted with alcohol and drug use for years, but who, following the death of her husband in a motorcycle accident, had wandered away in a drug and alcohol-induced fog, seldom to be heard from—until now, apparently. Sadie continued in her enthusiastic way to chatter about Carmen and Elizabeth—Lizzie—and their new excitement, about their plans and hopes. Finally she asked, "Are you and Kate having coffee tonight?"

"Yes," Jerry answered simply. "Do you like her?"

"She's okay." Sadie appeared to think for a moment. "Yes, I guess I do. It'll be fun for all three of us to stay at her house." There was a pause, then, "Are you going to, you know…" Her question trailed off, but Jerry had a hunch about what she was going to ask: about exactly what was happening between him and Kate Becker. Where does a nine-year-old come to know so much about life? Jerry pretended not to get it.

"What's that?" he asked.

"Oh, you know…nothing."

In the background Jerry could hear the sounds of a TV and, suddenly, squeals from the other two girls, and, "The movie is starting." It sounded like Carmen's voice.

Jerry hurried and ended the conversation with the usual parental endearments, wished her a good movie and a good night and, with a final parental, "now don't stay up too late," hung up the phone. Kate was waiting for Jerry outside in her car.

"I think you should check in at the hotel, don't you think? Or they'll wonder where you are."

"I already did that and got the key so I could come in later without anyone being the wiser. Even took a shower, but somehow couldn't bring myself to shave."

"I'm glad you didn't. I like you in a beard." And she proved her words by reaching over and kissing him on his bristly cheek, then softly and invitingly on the lips.

"So let's go," Jerry said.

Their second love-making was if anything more passionate, though it began more slowly and deliberately. After a lingering kiss, Kate invited Jerry to sit down, struck fire to a dozen candles around the room, and disappeared into the kitchen. Two minutes later Jerry heard a cork "pop," the clink of glass against glass and some other friendly, busy sounds. He leaned back on the sofa, gave a deep sigh of contentment and stared absently into one of the candles, allowing its flame to warm his soul. He did not even notice Kate come into the room until she set a tray on the coffee table in front of him: cheese, crackers, a bottle of Pinot Noir and two crystal glasses. She sat down beside him and poured out the wine and handed a glass to Jerry.

"To us," she toasted. "Whatever that may mean."

"To us," he echoed, feeling not the least bit silly, despite the old cliche.

They touched their glasses together formally in the same corny way, sipped, tasted, sampled, and then drank with pleasure. It was as if their actions had been choreographed, and the final steps had them laughing together. Kate took off her glasses and leaned back.

"Contented?" Jerry asked.

"Very," she said.

From that moment they lost track of time. They sipped wine, nibbled at the cheese and crackers—and each other—and slowly began a careful exploration of each other's bodies. Finally, petted and teased in the flickering candlelight, comfortable with each other and confident in a sense at once familiar and new, they slowly undressed each other, and, for the second time that day, began a ritual older than human consciousness or memory: touching, kissing, tasting, uniting. Their shadows danced to the light of the candles. At last, a glow of satisfaction filling their bodies, they lay back on the floor surrounded by candles, arms and legs entwined. Jerry was nearly overcome by a sense of well-being. At that moment, nothing outside of that house or separate from the two of them mattered.

"When did you know this was going to happen?" she asked at last.

Jerry thought for a moment and then said, "I'm not sure I 'knew it' any time before about two o'clock this afternoon. But I've wanted you, probably from the first moment I met you. Consciously, I think last Tuesday would have to be the moment when I actually began to think that maybe we were a serious possibility—or maybe it was Hank and Teresa's wedding."

"First you had to get over that saint stuff, though, right?"

"You still seem pretty saint-like to me." Jerry rose up on one arm and made an exaggerated examination of her pale, smooth body, feet to head and couldn't resist leaning down and kissing one of her nipples. "Now that's saintliness."

"Some fine saint I am!" she said.

Jerry felt as if he were twenty again, only wiser and more appreciative.

"Let's talk awhile," she suggested. She pulled on her blouse and skirt. Jerry got dressed and settled down beside her on the sofa.

Jerry asked her why she was so quiet in the group. She answered, "Oh, I really don't have anything much to contribute, you know. I guess I'm pretty self-centered. I hope this doesn't shock you too much." Her hazel eyes danced in the candlelight, partly in playfulness, but there was also a seriousness in them. "Not that I haven't tried to get more politically correct opinions and values toward life. But I always come back to the same thing: what matters to me—what I value—is feeling good, being comfortable and secure, and having someone to love and be loved by. I like good food and wine. I even go to the Episcopal Church, no offense, because of the beauty of the language as much as anything. I'm not sure I have any very profound religious feelings."

"So St. Peter's suits you?" Jerry asked.

"It would suit me better if it had a fine organ and organist and a choir…and more people," she responded immediately. "But I like the priest better and better all the time."

Jerry ignored her last joking statement, in part because he did not know how to respond except to joke back, but that was not something he wanted to joke about. It brought back the conflicted feelings and the anxiety in the pit of his stomach that he had felt off and on throughout the day. He *was* a priest and she *was* a parishioner. There was no escaping that basic truth. "A Sunday silver-and-brass Episcopalian? You had me fooled," he responded instead, a bit disbelieving. "I could've sworn I've seen you working in the kitchen, cleaning up tables, preparing the church for services. Those hardly seem the occupation of someone as 'self-centered' as you describe yourself."

"Oh, I'm not without redeeming social value." She laughed. "I even help out at the local soup kitchen once a month. But do you honestly believe that *anybody* spends time and energy if they don't get something out of it themselves? Feelings of 'being a good person' or winning points in heaven? But, Jerry, you need to know this about me. I'm serious about placing a high value on my personal comfort and pleasure. On being safe. I'm an only child, and everybody knows that only children are selfish. Well, I'm selfish." She smiled broadly to soften her words. But Jerry understood the seriousness of what she said. He knew that he had just heard someone tell him as honestly as she possibly could exactly what motivated her life—or at least what she understood to be her motivations. But Jerry could not believe her—or did not choose to, at least not entirely.

"And I think everyone else in the world operates out of the same motives," Kate went on. "That, in a nutshell, explains the difference between rich and poor. There's nothing noble about poverty. It's mean and nasty. And it's dirty.

The poor don't choose to be poor, but they have lost in the competition of life. I don't intend ever to be poor. And I mean to have exactly what I want." She seemed thoughtful for a moment. "In a way Silas Ruhl and I have a lot in common."

Jerry tried to suppress these disturbing self-revelations over the next few days, but did not succeed entirely. There was a disconnect in who she said she was and who he experienced her to be. Those two pieces just did not match. There was much more he needed to learn about Kate Becker.

Jerry got back to his hotel room a little after two, slipping quietly in by a side door reserved for hotel guests. He sleep-walked through his Sunday obligations and the book group at Nellie Cashman's Café, feeling a mixture of elation and euphoria, guilt and uncertainty. He thought that Maddie could tell that there was something different about him, noticed her looking at him quizzically, but he just ducked her questions. By the time Jerry finished in Tombstone, his departure had become flight in more ways than one. He was desperate to get home and to have some time to reflect on everything that he had learned and done since he flew out of Ryan Field on Friday, two very full days earlier.

Jerry spent the next week in a state of nervous excitement, panic and fear. He paced the house, found it hard to concentrate on anything, talked to Kate on the phone half a dozen times, and generally behaved like a victim of a near-fatal affliction. He and Kate made the final arrangements for the three girls to stay at her house the next weekend—something that had seemed like a good idea at the time, but that now felt very restrictive. He managed to carry on with some flight instruction appointments he had and generally took care of the details of living as a single parent. Still, Jerry continued to puzzle over what Kate had said at her house and again as he was getting out of her car outside the Simmons House Hotel when she dropped him off.

"Oh, and Jerry, thanks for understanding about keeping us secret. That's really important to me."

CHAPTER NINE

The Second Week in Lent, I

*"...Our concept of God matters. It can make God seem credible or
incredible, plausible or highly improbable. It can also make God seem
distant or near, absent or present. How we conceptualize God also affects
our sense of what the Christian life is about. Is the Christian life about
believing, or is it about a relationship? Is it about believing in God as a
supernatural being separate from the universe or about a relationship to
the Spirit who is right here and all around us?"*
—Marcus Borg

Nellie Cashman's Café felt warm and welcoming when Maddie arrived
there Sunday afternoon, relieved to get in out of the cold, breezy day. Jerry
seemed glad to see her, but he looked tired, and he appeared to be a bit
distracted. He had no little girls with him this weekend, not even Sadie,
which Maddie found a little disappointing. She had been looking forward to
seeing her "little goat girl," as she joking called Sadie.

Maddie had gotten up that morning and read the "assigned" reading for
that day's book group, and it was only when it was too late that she thought
about going to church. She could not remember the last time such an idea
had entered her head. Even though she had had her default religion filter
carefully in place as she read, the book still must have had some effect on
her. The words had entered her brain, and she remembered the points the
author made, even outlined the chapter with her usual pencil scratches in the
margins. But the filter had mostly kept *what* the author had to say from
penetrating any deeper than that comfortable academic level of her brain.

She got herself a fresh cup of coffee, her third one of the day, and settled
in at the same table and with the same table mates as on the last Sunday:
Linda Jackson—whom Maddie thought of as a kind of a horsey woman in
her fifties—and her husband, Jack Jackson—whom Maddie identified in an

equally unflattering way as the roly-poly mayor of about the same age. Though she could not remember all of their names, nobody in the circle felt like a stranger. Happily, Jerry went around the group telling off each person's name, starting with the Nellies (what a good joke, Maddie thought), Brenda and Hanna. The stiff and humorless Curtains, Jillian and Curtis, were there, their two sons entertaining themselves in the corner. Sue-Sue Hawkins, one of those kindly elderly women whom Maddie always liked on instinct, sat at the same table. Jim and Lisa Brown sat by themselves at a table—more people Maddie found she liked instantly. Ike McWarder, his dog, Doc, at his feet, and the motorcycle rider from Bisbee, Cord, occupied the same table. Jerry settled in somewhat apart from the others and began a discussion about the characteristics of God centered on God's location—"out there" somewhere or "right here."

Maddie's mind began to wander, and she looked carefully at Jerry. There was no doubt about it, he seemed different than the last time she had seen him. Maybe it was his now almost two-week-old beard, but there was something distinctly haggard looking about him. Still, he seemed in good spirits. She wondered if it was her imagination or if something important had happened with him since she had last seen him on Wednesday at the empty Tombstone airport. Her thoughts continued to wander as she went deeper and deeper into herself, thoughts about what it would mean to let go of the pre-modern understanding of God as the *only* way to define spirituality and to discover another kind of spiritual life based upon a different concept of the sacred. Except for a brief time in France, she had not even thought that a spiritual life was something that mattered to her. Now she began to feel a kind of yearning—nameless, vague and unclear, to be sure—but a yearning nonetheless: for something more, something profound—or just "other." But not an other that would alienate her from the people around her, some kind of sacred reality that integrated her with all of life.

When the discussion ended, Cord walked up to where Maddie was sitting and said, shyly, "You and I seem to be the outsiders in this group."

"Yes," she responded. A combination of conflicting feelings were at war with each other inside of her. Something about Cord made her feel insecure and anxious. She did not want to seem to be ill-at-ease, but the more she tried to appear calm and relaxed, the more she felt just the opposite way. At the same time, she had an urge to be alone and to think about the discussion the group had just had. There was something profoundly disturbing about considering other concepts for God. An unfamiliarly hungry place inside of her rose up and made her almost a little queasy. She wanted to get alone, to reread today's chapter in the book and try to figure out how she could deal with her conflicting feelings.

"You live in Bisbee?" Maddie responded to Cord with a question after what felt to her like a long and awkward silence.

Cord smiled, knowingly, it seemed to Maddie, which succeeded in making her feel even more insecure with him, but still she was encouraged to try. What an odd reaction he seemed to create in people, at least in her, she thought.

"I do live in Bisbee," Cord answered. "You live on a ranch nearby don't you? And have your own airplane. I heard you talking with Father Jerry before we started today."

"Right on both counts. I'm a brand new aircraft owner, a 1979 Cessna, actually, and newly checked out in it after an eight-year hiatus from flying." Her confidence began to return.

"No shit," he said. Then, after a pause, continued, "How about us having coffee sometime? Maybe at the great espresso place around the corner from the Copper Queen. You know, where the main street in the upper town makes a jog. It's right there."

"I know the place," Maddie responded. "My husband and I—when he was alive," she added, "used to go there. It's a good place."

"Your, ah, husband...is dead?" he asked, the flirting smile vanishing from his face. "Is that recent?"

"A few months ago," Maddie responded, feeling an urge to talk with him about Art's death. "I'm going to be away for a few days. How about Friday afternoon?"

"Great. What time?"

"Ah...I don't know," she muttered indecisively. She appeared to have made all the decisions she had in her just then.

"How about four o'clock," he suggested, lifting her out of her dilemma.

"Sure," Maddie answered, relieved to have Cord resume the lead, something which, despite his apparent shyness, he seemed willing to do. "Four on Friday, then."

"So what happens at four on Friday?" It was Ike McWarder.

"A mysterious rendezvous with a dark lady," was Cord's quip as he put on his leather jacket and scooped up his motorcycle helmet off the floor, ready to leave. It was obvious that Cord warmed to the Tombstone shop owner. Ike seemed to have that effect on everyone—certainly he did on

Maddie.

"For coffee," Maddie hurried to add. "And I'm about as mysterious as...as...an old shoe."

Cord and Ike both smiled at her in a way that made her feel like anything but an old shoe. She suddenly felt much better.

Maddie drifted away as the group members continued to have light conversation among themselves. In a few minutes Cord's motorcycle started up with harsh, metallic revs and then moved off with the buzzing sound of a hive of Africanized bees. Maddie watched him until he was out of sight. Jerry finished talking with Jillian Curtain—someone Maddie instinctively did not like. She had overheard Jillian complaining about the book they were reading, its author and the Jesus Seminar scholars generally.

"Are you okay, Jerry?" she asked after Jillian drifted away. "You seem...distracted."

"Just a little problem I'm wrestling with—trying to figure out how to have a new relationship," he said softly. "Nothing I can't figure out, though, I think. Thanks for asking."

Now, what did he mean by that? A woman? What else could it be? She felt a pang of jealousy. Maddie certainly did have feelings for Jerry, but...somehow it still did not seem right that the two of them should have an intimate relationship, maybe a little like brother and sister, shades of incest, she thought chuckling to herself as she remembered Ash Wednesday night. Judging from his manner, whoever lived at the center of this new experience of Jerry's, the whole thing was not uncomplicated. Maddie wondered just where that left her. Clearly in the category of "friend," she concluded to herself. So she tried to quash her feelings of loss and hurt. She certainly had no claim on him. But she still felt something very like personal loss.

The next morning, after checking with the weather service and filing a flight plan with the FAA by phone, Maddie took off from the Twisted K for San Diego, a comfortable flight of just under four hours. She had long been looking forward to this time with Sharon, an old friend who taught at San Diego State, partly to get a sense from her about what it would be like to have a teaching job and now partly just to have an adventure in her new airplane—which she had flown daily since her check-out. Jerry had insisted on talking Maddie through her flight plan as a part of his check-out before certifying her. His agreement that Maddie knew, more or less, what she was doing was a great boost to her self-confidence. At one point she asked him, "So you're declaring me safe, then?"

She did not get the expected joking response. Instead, she got a very serious Jerry, the customary twinkle absent from his eyes. "Only you can determine that. You can fly the plane. Now it's about your decisions. You decide whether to be safe or not."

At that moment, the burden of her own safety in the air shifted squarely onto her own shoulders. All of a sudden, flying had nothing to do with Jerry judging her and her skills as a pilot, but was, rather, about her assuming responsibility for herself. It was a realization that clearly had much larger implications for her than just her flying. *She* decided about her own safety— and about her own risks. Art no longer intervened between Maddie and her life, and Jerry refused to assume that duty even for her flying. That one moment did more than any other single conversation she had ever had both to thrust her out into the world of concrete experience and within herself to an intensity of awareness that surprised her.

The flight to San Diego was uneventful and, at the same time, filled with great significance for Maddie. All of the planing went off exactly as intended. She used radio navigation to supplement dead reckoning and went from VOR station to VOR station, making one relief and refueling stop in Yuma, all without incident. Her check points materialized as expected. It was a letter perfect flight. At the same time, spending four hours each way utterly alone with little else to do but steer the airplane along the invisible VOR radials had a profound effect on Maddie. Her mind ranged over many things, about her expectations for this visit with her graduate school friend and her son, Jeff, age six. Sharon was a single mother who had never been married, one of those women who had made the decision to have a child, and so she had made it happen. Maddie really wanted to see what that was like for Sharon. Maddie herself continued to have an aching desire to have a child, something she'd had to put aside first because she and Art could not seem to conceive one and later his illness put that possibility out of the question. She would need to act on that desire very soon or put it aside forever. Still, she refused to have her life dominated by her biological clock ticking away. This was not something she was ready to decide right now.

But her flying time was not taken up exclusively by practical thoughts. Even more important to her just then, Maddie could not get out of her mind something that Marcus Borg had written in the book the study group was reading. "If God is not thought of," he wrote, "as a supernatural being separate from the universe, then the persuasive force of much of modern atheism vanishes." His alternative is an idea called, and not originally by him, "panentheism," that God is present in all things, all times and all places, but is more than that. God is both "right here" and more than "right here." That meant to Maddie that God, understood in the panentheistic way, was there in the plane with her on the way to San Diego, and yet was not held captive there by her. This God did not take charge of her being safe on that flight any more than Jerry would. Maddie's flight safety depended on her, but the sense that she was not alone in that plane or anywhere else she went, changed her outlook and opened a whole new way of looking at her life. She saw that her purported disbelief was actually a kind of feeble belief system, one that constantly failed her, as time after time she bargained with a God in whom she did not believe for something she wanted or wanted to have happen differently than the way it turned out. What was it that the Christian Bible said about putting God to the test? That was what her unsatisfying sort of faith had been about—constantly testing God. Would he step in and give her what she wanted? Would he bring her father and mother back together again? Would he wipe away Art's cancer? The answer to all of those questions was "no." And in her disappointment, she realized, she had concluded that God simply did not exist. But now, armed with a new sense of what the word "god" could mean, Maddie speculated about how such a changed idea of him might work. And then she asked herself, why "him" or "he" after all? It was another one of those tiny, rare insights that become life changing. Weaning herself away from the habitual use of the masculine pronoun for designating God, she decided, became an essential first step, a part of her rethinking the *being* of God. This was not about feminism or anti-patriarchy or any other correct or fashionable thinking; it was about moving on into another—a liberating—understanding of the sacred so that spiritual ideas might have credibility in her life.

Maddie's old ideas about God faded. God became "presence," "being," "creative energy" or any of the similar expressions that panentheism led her to, and thus also exited the "warrior king" or the "remote father" (a genuine metaphor for abandonment in her experience). In much the same way as Tucson disappeared into the distance behind her as she flew west, so also those old definitions of God gradually fell from her mind and a whole new spiritual world opened up before her. Maddie's time in San Diego continued to awaken her to the interior life that she had up until then largely ignored.

Observing Sharon with her little boy resumed Maddie's longing to have her own child. So powerful did the feeling become, that she found herself looking at men as if they were potential sperm donors in some kind of human

131

stud farm, wondering what their genetic make-up was like. It even became a joke with Sharon.

"What about that one?" Maddie asked behind her hand as they were walking across campus the second day she was there.

"Too blonde," Sharon responded in mock seriousness. "I think you need to stick to the Eastern European gene pool. Keep a purity of eye and hair color. You know, standards."

There were also serious conversations, with Maddie wanting to know what it was like to live as a single mother.

"It's tough sometimes," Sharon answered. "There's nobody to share the work and responsibility with—or, for that matter, the joys. You know, the first steps, or the scrapes and bruises. All things being equal, I would much rather have somebody in my life, a partner as it were, than going it alone. But I wouldn't trade having Jeff for anything. Besides, I know lots of women who do have husbands to go along with their children. Clearly it's a mixed blessing."

Maddie also went to class with Sharon one day as she taught medieval history to undergraduates. Afterwards they spent some time in a student coffee shop as Sharon chatted with her students and answered questions about an upcoming exam. Maddie even went to the library and checked on some resources that had been on her mind, confirming that, yes, she did think that there was a connection between the Cluniac monastic revival of the tenth and eleventh centuries and the papal Gregorian Reform in the eleventh century. This subject over which much medievalist ink had been spilled usually rested on the lineal connection, that the one came from the other, but, as always she saw them powerfully linked in something larger than a simple cause-and-effect relationship. Call it the general quickening of society in the eleventh century or whatever, but it is undeniable that something was happening that would flower in the twelfth and thirteenth centuries into a remarkable society able to achieve astonishing things—the great cathedrals, the universities of Europe, the redevelopment of town life and gradual emergence of a commercial middle class. The real subject, Maddie could suddenly see, was a spiritual one—about that same panentheistic god she had read about and whose postulated being seemed to be transforming her life. Broad strokes seemed to flow from Maddie's mental pen, but they struck her as the very strokes that she needed to draw. Both personally and professionally. The time had come for her to return to teaching, and it came in just the same way that her time for spiritual growth had come. For Maddie, studying history needed to become more than facts and dates. Medieval history had the capacity to invite the mind to soar, to see the big picture, to form relational understandings about the big questions in living—the perfect parallel, she thought, to her dawning spiritual awakening. More than anything she found that she wanted to nurture these dual pieces of herself. She resolved to start the wheels turning immediately toward finding a teaching job. Surely something would come up. She also resolved to pursue her own still-fragile spiritual birth. But as for that other kind of birth—of a child, her own child—about that she was still uncertain. Is that really something she wanted to risk? Sharon seemed very brave. Was *she* really as brave as that?

Maddie flew back to Bisbee from San Diego on Friday morning and was in the Audi headed for Tombstone within the hour. Before keeping her coffee date with Cord in Bisbee, she planned to have a late lunch at Nellie Cashman's and perhaps talk with Ike McWarder for awhile. There was something very companionable about Ike. Even though she barely knew him, she sensed in him a kindred spirit. His invitation to stop by anytime had felt genuine. Today felt like the right time.

Maddie downed one of the Nellies' yummy cheeseburgers (hold the fries!) and drank a sweet-tart fresh lemonade, all the while ruminating over her time in San Diego. In some quiet hours spent by herself, she had raided Sharon's bookcase for some classics of mysticism, skimming through Julian of Norwich's *Showings* and browsing *The Cloud of Unknowing*. Maddie saw dimensions in both fourteenth century books that she had not seen there before. She now read them as something more than someone else's dull, archaic religious ideas from a long time ago—which was how she had always seen them before. Now she experienced them as genuine and timeless insights she could relate to. And that reminded her of what she had already read in next week's chapter in the Tombstone discussion book about God. The author, Marcus Borg, had catalogued ways a person—such as those medieval mystics—encountered the sacred in everyday life, but in not-such-everyday ways. The section on mysticism—direct, unmediated experience of the holy—interested her most. Somehow the idea of mystical experience being available to everyone, even today, resonated with something deep inside of her. Sharon also had a collection of contemporary writings on mysticism that captured her attention for most of a day. New awareness grew as Maddie recognized that many of the mystical experiences described in those books had happened to her, and that for much of her life she had passed those experiences off as being part of a bad day, or her place on the menstrual cycle, or a nascent migraine, or anything other than what she now had begun to think they were—the sacred breaking into her everyday life. In her systematic, scholarly way, Maddie had begun excitedly to think about the ways she could identify such a God in her own experience. Instead of being the cynical academic that she had thought herself to be, maybe she was actually something of a mystic, but one who had denied her essential nature. Perhaps she had more in common with those fourteenth century mystics than she did with the medieval Scholastics or with the natural philosophers of Newtonian physics and the *philosophes* whom she had always assumed were her true spiritual and intellectual ancestors.

And Maddie had a sense that Ike McWarder was someone she could talk to about these things.

Flying across the open spaces of eastern California and western Arizona that morning, watching the ribbon of Interstate Eight snake along below her, Maddie had what she now recognized was a spiritual experience. This was something that had happened to her many times in many places when it was very quiet, or more accurately, when some kind of white noise—a room air conditioner, or, as on that day, the steady drone of an airplane engine—drowned out other sounds of life around her. Under those conditions Maddie often heard music that was not there for other people. She once asked Art if he could hear this distant-sounding music; he answered that he didn't hear any music and looked at her in a way that made her feel she was not quite right. She never asked him about it again. Maddie heard that same music on the way back from San Diego, and like always, she was unable to hear it well enough to identify anything in it or to find a melody, but she heard it all the same. With her dawning spiritual awareness, the music made her feel a wonderful sense of companionship, of not being alone, of somehow being loved and cared for. It was more of the same kind of feeling she had had on the flight out.

Maddie thanked the Nellies, paid for her lunch and walked down the boardwalk to Ike Clanton's Bead and Craft Shop, wondering as she went if she had the nerve to tell Ike about what was on her mind. But Maddie felt so different, so unlike the self she knew, and she had to talk with someone about it. Jerry Hanning was probably the obvious choice for a father confessor; she smiled at the thought. But Jerry did not seem available somehow. She realized that his seeming unavailability might only be coming out of her and that it was nothing more than her pique at his daring to have a relationship with someone else. But Maddie still felt that way. And those feelings and her instincts told her that Ike might very well be someone she could talk to. She found him sitting at a small table in a corner of the store, Doc Holiday at his feet.

"Hi, Ike," she said.

"Hi yer-seff," Ike called back. He had an array of beads in what looked like a fishing tackle box on the table in front of him. His hands moved quickly stringing beads and tying knots.

"What are you up to there?" Maddie asked.

"I'm a little 'barrassed to admit to it," he replied, "but since ya caught me in th' act, I might as well include you in ma surprise."

Maddie pulled off her cardigan in the warmth of the room and sat down in a chair across from him. Ike was probably about fifty-five or sixty, she thought, with graying and thinning brown hair. His round, clean-shaven face had a gentle quality to it that she realized was at once open and yet also carefully guarded. Ike's only secret was that he had no secrets.

"Actually, I'm makin' somethin' for everybody in our God group. It's called an Anglican Rosary. You know, like the kind the Catholics use for meditation?" Maddie nodded. Ike continued, "This is a little idea I picked up on the Internet. It has the same basic notion as the Roman one, but with diffr'nt symbols and stuff—and a good bit smaller."

Maddie picked up a completed rosary from a pile beside him and held it in her hand, letting the stones—beautiful, smooth, deep green—run through her fingers. Every so often there was a larger black bead, flanked on either side by tiny black ones. She counted seven of the green beads, then three small black, one large black and then three small ones again. The pattern repeated itself four times around the circle. Dangling at the end were two more large beads, separated by small ones and a medal on the very tip.

"What are the green stones?" Maddie asked.

"Jade. The black ones're onyx. D' ya like it?"

"Very much. And the medal?" She looked closely at it. "St. Francis. That's very cool." Maddie continued to let the beads slip through her fingers.

"Like I said, I'm makin' one for every member of the group, the only difference bein' the saint on the medal." He paused for a moment, then continued. "Th' idea's that we find unity in th' stones, but diversity an' personal identity in th' medals. D' ya think they'll like 'em?"

"Of course," she answered at once. "They're beautiful...and there's something—oh I don't know, settling, I guess—about holding them." Maddie put down the one she was holding and picked up another, as Ike continued putting beads on the string and tying knots. "St. Benedict," she identified, founder of the Benedictines, the major order of monastics in the Middle Ages—and still today, she imagined. On another rosary was St. Joseph the Worker. On another one was Julian of Norwich, the fourteenth century mystic whom Maddie had read and thought a lot about on her trip to San Diego, an English woman who had major visions of Christ. "Mother Julian," she muttered, wondering what made her use the title "Mother."

"D' ya like her?" Ike asked, a canny, perceptive look on his face.

"Actually, I've been thinking about her some this week."

"Then maybe she's th' one for ya after all?"

"Yes," she said. "Yes, yes. You have...no idea how attracted I am to her. Which is pretty surprising for a mostly-Jewish girl." Mostly Jewish? Is that what she was? Or at least is that how she thought of herself? And if so what did *that* mean? She realized that she was unsure exactly *who* she was.

"I thought Julian might be right for ya," Ike answered. "Sort of had ya in mind as I strung it."

Maddie wondered what he meant by that comment. Was she so transparent that, to everyone but herself, she seemed to be some kind of mystic type? Whatever a mystic type was. Maddie looked so startled, that Ike hurried to add, "Don't be alarmed. I sometimes have these little insights inta people. Not ESP 'zactly, but a kinda instinct." He laughed.

Maddie thought for a moment, then in a rush which surprised them both, she began to tell him about the spiritual awakening that dominated her thoughts right now. As she opened up to him, she began also to reveal to herself much that had lain dormant, the unsolved mysteries of her life.

"I've had, ah...odd...experiences," Maddie began. "Sometimes I feel weird out in nature. You know, the simple stuff: trees, flowers, sunsets, running water, stuff like that; it's like there's somebody there with me." Maddie looked hard at Ike to see if he thought she was crazy. Apparently not, at least from the expression on his face. "My husband Art's death gave me a reason to ask the God questions. And suddenly my whole life is taking on a different shape. I'm not sure what to make of it."

Ike sat very quiet with a kind of intensity in his eyes and a serious set to his face. He did not laugh her off the way she was afraid he might. "Being aware of your spiritual side can make you uncomfortable," he said. "Partly, it's about never quite being alone, never entirely private, which can be both comforting and threatening at the same time. At least that's what it feels like to me."

"Yes. Then you *do* know what I mean." They sat quietly for a moment, then Maddie continued, "Probably the most startling thing that has ever happened to me—I hope you don't mind if I talk to you about this stuff…"

"Of course not. Go on, the most startling thing that ever happened to you was…"

"…when I was sitting in a graduate seminar room with a beam of sunlight breaking through the window onto the table's oak top. The sunlight seemed to grow until…until the entire room was filled with light. Even though my eyes were stunned by the brilliance, I couldn't look away. It went on for several minutes, at first only the bright, warm light. Then it began to change colors, brilliant blues and yellows, deep reds and vivid purples. It was mesmerizing, Ike. And a little scary. I looked around, and nobody else seemed to see it. In fact, I'm sure they didn't. I thought there was something wrong with me, afraid that I might be very sick—a brain tumor or something. It's amazing what rationalization can do. I even went to the student health center, but they couldn't find anything wrong with me. That same thing never happened again, so I just passed it off…until now. Suddenly I have a different explanation. I don't know why this should happen to me, of all people, but I…I just think that it has." She rested her elbows on the table and put her chin in her hands. "Why?"

"There just may be *no* whys or wherefores," Ike responded. "It just was…and *is*, a continuin' part of your personal encounter with livin'."

"I guess so," Maddie said, thinking about the ecstacy she sometimes felt out in the desert, or in the squawking sound of the cactus wren, or the multi-voiced song of the mockingbird. Maddie had always understood these experiences as spiritual ones. She just had not connected that kind of spiritual experience with any sort of God.

"I think the voices are the spookiest things of all," Maddie continued, confidant now. "Voice, actually. Only one. I never have heard many voices, though I understand that some people do. Anyhow, I've heard a voice calling my name, and when I looked around there was no one there. I can't even say whether the voice I heard was male or female. It was too soft and indistinct to tell. But it was clearly there. And it happened several times, all at one period in my life, a time of great excitement—right after I started on my Ph.D. and I was teaching for the first time. Everything in my life seemed to work, and it felt great, truly one of the primo times of my life. I passed the voice off as nothing more than my imagination. But I never talked about it with anyone until now, never even acknowledged it clearly to myself until this week in San Diego."

Ike nodded and listened, all the time continuing to string the beads. He finished the rosary he had been working on, intent upon making the finishing touches, attaching the medal and then drawing the cord back through the dangling portion to tie it off.

They were silent a long time, then Ike looked up at Maddie and said very softly, "I thought we were kindred spirits."

"You don't think I'm crazy, then?"

"Only if I am too." The beading materials lay on the table in front of him, abandoned for the moment. "There are times when I feel so connected to…th' universe, God…whatever…that the exquisite sensation is almost painful."

"Did you have trouble connecting those feelings and experiences with God?"

"Trouble! Did I? Do I! But God is no longer a deity out there somewhere, at least not for me, but somethin' much more immediate, present even. Like what we've been reading in the Borg book."

"Yes. Yes, I know what you mean. As I was flying to San Diego, I had the strongest sense of God being there with me, not as a talisman protecting me from danger or anything like that, just there!"

Ike's eyes began to water. He didn't cry exactly, Maddie noticed, but she saw that his eyes did become very liquid. "Comes on ya all of a sudden, doesn't it?" he asked.

Maddie just nodded.

They sat there in silence for a time, one of the most companionable silences Maddie ever remembered experiencing. Finally, Ike tied a knot in the bead cord and began once again on another of the rosaries. Maddie continued to let her beads flow through her fingers, finding their distinct firmness and smooth surfaces both comforting and inviting.

"Do you ever actually go to church?" Maddie asked at last.

"Never!" he responded. "But that's another story."

Maddie looked at Ike with a questioning expression, but he just ignored the implied invitation to talk more about the mystery of his non-church-going.

"I'm not even nominally a Christian," Maddie continued when it was clear that Ike had no intention of completing his statement, "but I think I'll go this Sunday."

Ike looked at Maddie with a shrewd look on his wrinkled face. "What's in it for ya? Isn't th' god of church and synagogue that same old tyrant, the one of blood sacrifice an' judgment?"

"I...I don't know exactly. I just know that I need to go. Did you know that Mother Julian," she weighed the rosary stones in her hand, "lived most of her life as an anchorite, actually physically walled in beside a parish church? And even the name we know her by is that of the church, St. Julian's. Nobody knows her real name."

"Something like that," he said.

"I once visited the city of Norwich, wandered around in the cathedral and studied the carved stones and the vaulting. Incredible! Julian's cell was only about a half-hour's walk away, and I can't believe it, but I didn't even bother to go there. If she can be walled up in a church," Maddie continued, "the least I can do is go to one...now—just to experience it on my own new terms. Not that I have *never* gone, you know, but this is different." Another thought came over her. "By the way, which saint did you put on your rosary?"

"Oh, I haven't made mine yet. But it won't have a saint."

"Won't have a saint? Why not?"

"I'm more drawn to 'nother kind of symbol, one that comes fr'm Chartres Cathedral in France." He put down a medal in front of Maddie. On it she saw the twisting path of the labyrinth; she knew that Chartres was an important pilgrimage site and an example of medieval spiritual geometry, the art of connecting heaven and earth in stone and glass; the labyrinth was integral to its design. "The path of the labyrinth goes in t' its center and then back out ag'in," he continued. "No blind alleys or dead ends ta confuse or amuse ya, as in what people think of as a maze. This's ma prime metaphor ever since I left th' rat race for this life—here in Tombstone. Not a bad comparison, eh, rat race to labyrinth—the one crazy-makin', the other life-givin'."

They fell into companionable silence again. Ike went back to stringing the beads and tying knots. Then he said, suddenly, "I wonder if old Jerry's heart is strong 'nough to handle both of us in church at the same time? I think I'd like to go with ya."

As Maddie later told Jerry, "I will always believe that, at least at that moment, Doc understood every word that we said, because he suddenly looked up at Ike and let out a little bark."

"End of a dream?" Ike asked to this curious punctuation.

"I wonder?" Maddie asked.

Maddie's drive from Tombstone to Bisbee to keep her date with Cord was mostly dominated by her wishing she could find a way out of having to do it. There were many things on her mind just then, and none of them included having coffee with someone who was probably younger than she and probably pretty boring and self-centered. A macho type. Maddie continued to think about the conversation with Ike and remembering odd experiences in her past life. The twenty minutes melted away in no time. As she drove into Bisbee, she marveled once again on how utterly charming the old mining town remained, both gentrified and unspoiled—if such a thing were possible, perhaps because the artists' colony there oversaw the restoration of much of it. Neither the rusting mine equipment nor the abandoned buildings on the outskirts of the old town detracted from the charm she always found there. The enormous hole where a mountain had once stood, both eerie and appealing somehow, is a gigantic scar, but one that always moved her. It was as if somehow this astonishing excavation holds in its bowl the collected dreams and memories of the miners whose lives were lived extracting the copper, layer by layer, deeper and deeper into the mountain. For the first time, she noticed as she drove down the twisting road to the town below, how prominent the red brick Episcopal Church, St. Peter's, was from that angle. Art's funeral had been held there—only four months earlier? It seemed like a lifetime removed. And now Jerry worked there as the priest.

Cord met Maddie when she walked through the door of the Bisbee Coffee Company.

"I was afraid you wouldn't come," he said, standing politely and in stark contrast to the image that he—carefully, she suspected—tried to create.

"I said I would," she responded, unintentionally a bit curt. "I didn't see your bike outside."

"No need for it here," he said. "I only use it for going to Tucson, or the other towns around here. "Let's order coffee," he invited, gesturing toward the counter, behind which the coffee-making machinery and pastries and sandwich preparation area were somewhat haphazardly arranged.

The remainder of the Bisbee Coffee Company was a dizzying non-arrangement of wooden chairs and tables, stacks of newspapers and magazines, and, on the walls, large black-and-white photographs of Bisbee's heyday, its miners, ore cars, mules and serious-looking mining equipment. Beside the front door was a dispenser of the Bisbee *Observer*, the weekly newspaper. A handful of customers sat mostly alone reading newspapers in the large, single room. In the middle of the floor stood an antique ore car filled with burlap bags, presumably loaded with raw coffee beans. Maddie and Cord sat down at the table where Cord had been waiting.

"So," he began, "you were away for a few days?"

"I was. In San Diego. Visiting a graduate school friend."

"Graduate school? In what? Where'd you go?" Cord seemed a bit nervous as questions tumbled out one after another.

Maddie gave him a short oral curriculum vitae.

"History, huh? I liked history in college," he said. "I also did graduate school in California—Santa Barbara, though not for a Ph.D. I did an M.F.A., in sculpture, mostly."

"So, you're part of the artist crowd here in Bisbee?"

"What's it to ya?" he responded in a mocking imitation of a defensive artist dealing with a hostile local. He grinned broadly. They laughed together.

Maddie was surprised by herself. Far from being nervous or uncomfortable in Cord's presence as she had been on Sunday, she now felt confident and relaxed. And she found herself getting interested in him and in his work. Hmm, an artist? "What kind of sculpture do you do?" she asked.

"I've worked in lots of media, but right now I'm into metal. Most people probably think of me as either some kind of junk dealer—because most of my materials are old iron objects of various kinds, including auto parts—or else they see me as a welder. I guess in a sense, I'm both."

"I'd love to see your work," Maddie said, and she meant it. As it was turning out, Cord was not really the angry-young-man persona he had projected on Sundays in Tombstone. Instead, she found him charmingly innocent, almost naive, and very sweet. Apparently the act she had seen on Sundays was little more than a cover for a shy and introverted personality. My kind of person, Maddie thought.

"Sure, you can see my work," he said. "It's hard to miss, actually: great clumps of iron rusting away in the yard." He flashed at her what she was beginning to think of as his boyish grin. "But tell me about your airplane," he said, changing the subject from himself—an unusual characteristic in men of her acquaintance, she thought.

"Well, I've only had it a week, and I just have a couple hundred total flying hours myself. Just enough to be dangerous, as an old teacher of mine once said." Cord joined her in what she hoped was a self-deprecating smile. "Actually Jerry Hanning checked me out in it and certified me to prey upon the airways." They smiled again. Maddie found that she liked smiling with Cord. People had told her lately that she did not smile enough, but that she went around with a worried frown on her face. So, she smiled again…at Cord.

Maddie's reaction to Cord was very complex. He exuded a kind of earthy sexuality that she found very attractive, but it no longer seemed to make her nervous. Instead, she looked at him almost as a student or younger colleague, someone to guide and nurture. He seemed to raise a kind of a mothering instinct in her—or so she told herself. And she understood the potency of the sexy young man/mothering older woman combination. She was emphatically not ready for a younger man, not at thirty-six, so hard up for male attention that she needed to find a kid to mother who would also join her in her bed. No, this could remain in the safe-and-sound category of friends coming from very different places in their lives. She, the recent widow, would remain essentially untouched by this encounter, an extension of friendship and interest, she told herself.

"How do you like living in this border country?" Cord asked.

"I grew up in Tucson. It's home," Maddie responded.

"But it's different down here. Haven't you seen the roadblocks?"

Maddie thought about two Sundays before and the Border Patrol stop, about how dirty she felt, implicated somehow in what had happened on the road between Tombstone and St. David. "You mean the guards…and guns and all?" she asked. "We had an encounter with them a couple of weeks ago." She told him about the road block and how the experience had made real for her all the vans and INS green busses and white- and green-striped patrol cars she had seen on freeways around Tucson and Phoenix, sometimes stopped alongside the road checking out some vehicle or other. "I had always known what it was about, but it felt different somehow when it touched me and people I knew personally. It's all pretty crummy." Maddie tried to smile, but could not manage it. "You remember those two little girls and Jerry's daughter…at Nellie Cashman's that first Sunday? I think they were really frightened when the Border Patrol stopped us and questioned them. It made me feel guilty that something as racist as that could exist and me not be trying to do anything about it."

"Makes you mad doesn't it?"

"But how does a reasonable person respond?"

"Would you like to meet some people who are trying to do something?"

"Are you serious? Sure, why not?"

They sat quietly for a moment. Cord remained thoughtful. Maddie just sipped her coffee and looked around the room, realizing that she liked the Coffee Company, that she liked Bisbee and that she liked being there with Cord. For the first time in a year, Maddie felt comfortable and at ease someplace, just sitting there.

After an hour and a second round of coffee, Cord and Maddie left the Coffee Company and walked along one of the twisting, hilly Bisbee streets to Cord's combination studio and home, a fairly dilapidated looking house of about the same vintage as the others around it, all nearly a century old. Peeling lavender paint with faded brown trim rose to a low pitched roof covered with curling gray composition shingles. An old Ford pickup truck stood forlornly beside the house. As they walked up to the house, Cord began to act nervous and excited.

He was right; you could not miss his work. Massive amalgamations of iron and steel rose majestically, or squatted insensibly, or twisted in abrupt angles all around the house. They looked strong, forthright and a little frightening in their intensity and power. Maddie walked around the tangle of old appliance parts, auto fenders, chrome pieces and rusty implements, some formerly employed on farms and others used in deep mine shafts or gaping open pits. Cord had let the metal parts speak out of their individual histories inside the sculptures. In one, a rusting plow seemed to cut into and divide a hodgepodge of trash sending the cans and other unrecognizable rubble out into an elegant curve. Another one had an old bedspring apparently ready to throw the objects on top of it into the air—an old vacuum cleaner tank that said "Hoover" on the side, a small water heater, a piece of an oscillating fan, an old iron, and a jumble of other domestic appliance parts.

Cord was almost jumping up and down and pacing wildly beside Maddie as he described each piece and its components—and what it felt like to create it, or to see it now.

"And that one, I call 'Genesis,' because it's about beginnings, of something being created out of nothing," he said.

She could see what he meant. Out of the seemingly random pile of rubble on the ground, there emerged clearly recognizable figures, identifiable as life, but not as any particular kind of life, not "Adam and Eve" or even human necessarily, but life. The component parts of these life forms emerged out of discarded household objects—a toaster, an ancient baby carriage frame, wheels, a part of an iron bed frame and dozens of steel food cans of all sizes and shapes, mostly smashed flat.

"It makes me feel hopeful," Maddie said at last after walking around the piece and letting its parts and its whole settle on her. "It's as if I'm present at the beginning of creation, but a creation out of the rubble of our contemporary lives. And I can imagine all of the hope and desire and love that's to come." All of the trash, formed as it was, somehow captured exactly the way she had been feeling.

"Yes. Yes. You see it, then." He fairly danced before her eyes.

"And the way you use the pieces—continuing their former purpose into their new life!"

"Of course. What else could you do? They have an integrity. Hands have held them. They have labored or carried or beautified something, each in its own particular way. You can't turn them into something else. That would violate their...their being, their integrity." Cord's words came all in a rush. His excitement was magnetic.

But she felt uncomfortable with so much intensity. "Do you sell many pieces?" Maddie asked, relieving some of her tension.

"Some," he answered. "Mostly smaller ones. Once in a while one of the big ones catches the eye of some rich dude from Chicago or St. Louis. Sometimes—with the big ones—they even hire me to install them, expenses paid."

Maddie could feel his pleasure in her enthusiastic reaction. She began to think about something that would be just right in her central courtyard and garden at the Twisted K ranch house, wondering how "Genesis" would look there. She would have to think about it.

"Wanna meet those people I told you about? They're having a little wine. Just about now."

"Which people?"

"The ones who try to help the immigrants."

"That's right. Sure," Maddie said, but she felt a little uneasy at the thought.

Cord led back in the direction they had come, but he turned off before reaching the Coffee Company, walking past the road that led up the hill toward St. Peter's Church. He stopped, looked around and then stepped into a large, barn-like building with a faded advertizing sign painted on its side, something about Beech Nut Tobacco. Most of the weathered exterior of the building had no paint whatever, except for the faded sign. A stairway led up half a flight to a small landing of more unpainted wooden surface and to another door, one that was opened almost immediately to Cord's knock. Inside, the feel was entirely different; tiny, bright beams of light were strategically placed all around a cavernous artist's studio. Stacks of stretched canvases filled the corners, others, mostly already painted with Bisbee scenes, some including people, stood against every possible prop: doors, walls, legs of tripods, chairs—anywhere there was a space. One lay flat atop a table. Some of the best portrayed naked women in many different poses, most particularly ones of a strikingly beautiful Latina. The artist was good and very productive; the work in that room would more than fill a large gallery.

In one corner of the huge room, battered over-stuffed furniture stood around a low coffee table holding a visual cacophony of coffee cups, wine glasses, plates, bowls, a box of Wheaties on its side and apparently empty, and, Maddie thought, about a thousand Styrofoam cups, give or take a few hundred. There were three people in the room.

One, a beautiful Latina about Maddie's age, was immediately recognizable as one of the naked models. Her name was Ginger, for Virginia, and she lived in this studio with the artist whose work filled it so completely. Maddie recognized Virginia as one of those beautiful women who knew the power of her looks and used it, the kind of person Maddie had often been jealous of— or more accurately put, disliked. Maddie herself usually got described as "cute." God, it's awful being cute! But Maddie sensed deeper stuff in Ginger than just a pretty face and a matching figure. She thought that it might be worthwhile getting to know her.

Then there was the artist, Harold, an enormous man about forty. He looked like he should be playing for a professional football team. His dark, hooded eyes, both intense and threatening, were even more memorable than his size. His shaved head gave him a mildly dangerous look, not someone a person would quickly forget.

The third person, an elderly, frail-looking woman, had gray hair, with wildly escaping wisps and strands sticking or falling in all directions, but generally pulled into a bun at the back of her head. Harriet Lawson, Maddie soon learned, had been a part of the artist community in Bisbee for thirty years. The skin of her hands was rough and tough, the muscle beneath it hard and strong, as befit a potter, one whose work had the reputation of being the best in Bisbee.

Cord poured glasses of red wine both for himself and for Maddie from one of the bottles on a sideboard. The fine crystal of the glass rang with sparkling clarity when they touched them in an otherwise silent salute.

Maddie found that she liked each one of these people. There was something at once both arty and real about them. They discussed their work, and like any artisans or workers who produce goods with their hands, they talked about sales, materials and subjects. They also talked local and national politics, community issues and personalities. It was never dull. And Cord kept pouring the wine.

Eventually the conversation got around to illegal border crossings and desperate people trapped in a place and in circumstances they did not understand and were ill equipped to deal with. They patiently explained it all to her. The desperation of the undocumented people was matched by the cruelty of the coyotes who they paid to bring them into the States and the inflexibility of local vigilante groups, some of whom were white supremacists. As the story goes, it was the latter who were known to hunt the often thirsty and hungry people set afoot in the desert as some kind of prey. INS officials and border guards, far from having a single-minded purpose of turning back illegal immigrants, often found themselves caught between the desperation of the UDAs and the determination of the vigilantes. It was all a revelation to Maddie, who thought back to the guard who had interrogated the three little girls, clearly a decent person doing difficult work with as much compassion as possible.

Looking hard at Maddie and then seeking an affirmation from Cord—which he gave with a nod—Harriet said at last, "We have four people this time, a man, a young boy and two women, abandoned by their coyote somewhere in the San Pedro Riparian area." Everyone listened carefully. "Pablo has them hidden at the Place. They're hoping to get to Boston, where apparently there's a promise of the usual 'good jobs.'" Harriet made little quotation marks in the air with both hands. "Through a cousin, of course, who is already there. They have no money, no tickets to Boston. Nothing. None of them speaks English."

Maddie asked what she realized was a predictable question, "Wouldn't the best thing be for them to return to Mexico—or wherever?"

"They'd never make it," Cord answered patiently.

Ginger picked up the narrative in her soft, cultured voice. Maddie puzzled over her as she talked, realizing that there was something familiar about her and wondering if they had met before. "Their only chance is to move north with help," Ginger said, "or turn themselves in to the INS. They are far too frightened to do that." She put down her coffee cup. Maddie noticed that she was not drinking wine.

"There's a very hard edge to that fear," Harold rumbled. "Mexican and Central American families often frighten their children into behaving by scaring them with stories about uniformed men: soldiers and police. They tell the kids that if they don't behave the men with uniforms will get them, so they grow up with a fear of any official authority." Harold's previous amiability was absent as he instructed Maddie.

"It's one of their greatest fears," Cord added.

Maddie sat quietly mulling over what she had heard, sipping the wine, enjoying the company and finding herself getting caught up in their passion to help the immigrants.

They finally resolved that Harold would take these four people north over some back roads in his SUV—their usual method—and pass them on to some other people in Tucson.

"But that's so risky," Ginger stated emphatically, not without some fear in her voice. "He was almost caught the last time," she said to Maddie.

"It's still the best way we have," Harriet answered her. "The only way, really."

"On a first offense, all they do is confiscate the car," Harold responded to her.

"And that's not bad enough?" Ginger asked. "Besides, you might go to jail." She shook her head of luxurious long black hair

"Not for long." He grinned back at her. "Don't worry about it."

Maddie thought to herself what a nice man Harold Jenkins was.

"I don't like it," Ginger responded, her eyes flashing. "There must be another way that's not so dangerous."

"Thanks for caring." He smiled warmly at her. "I do appreciate it. But, still, I'd better go. About midnight, I guess."

"I'll let them know, then," Harriet said and got up and placed her glass carefully on the sideboard, a massive and ornate antique piece, no doubt a part of Bisbee for much longer than any of them had been alive. She pulled a cell phone out of a backpack resting against the side of her chair and punched some numbers into it. After a moment she began to speak into it, slowly and carefully in Spanish, too low for Maddie to hear the words. When the call had ended, she stood up. It was their unspoken signal to leave.

Goodbyes said, Cord and Maddie stepped outside into what had become a very dark night. Few and widely scattered lights provided little illumination for the narrow streets. They had not gone ten steps when Maddie tripped and almost fell. Cord reached out and took her hand to steady her, then, giving it a little squeeze, he continued to hold it as they walked on down the street. The contact felt good, companionable, to Maddie. She felt safe and comfortable in his company, and she liked holding his hand. She squeezed back, feeling rather than seeing him smile. She realized she was also smiling.

"How about some eggs?" Cord asked, just as they reached the fork that would lead either back to the Bisbee Coffee Company and her car or toward his house.

"Oh, yes. I'm starved—and I guess a little tipsy. Too much wine." She giggled a little. As they turned right toward Cord's house, Maddie shook off a momentary panic. What on earth was she afraid of?

They climbed the three steps onto Cord's front porch, where he kicked the bottom of the door then pushed. It opened with a squeak of protest. "Better than a key," he responded to Maddie's unspoken question. "Besides, the squeaking door is a great burglar alarm."

Cord reached for a switch and lights from strategically placed table lamps and indirect, high-intensity beams in the ceiling, aimed at various works of art, softly illuminated a tidy and comfortable room. Large expensive-looking and matching sofa, chair and love seat formed center pieces before a small, but beautifully tile-fronted fireplace. A fire was already laid in the grate. The room was richly adorned with metal sculptures, Cord's own, Maddie was certain, and also some stunning abstract paintings. There was also one of Harold's paintings of Ginger, nude as in the ones in the studio

"Harold?" she asked, gesturing toward the painting. "Or should I say, Ginger?"

Cord laughed. "A little of both, I guess. Or do I mean a lot?"

Maddie laughed back and continued, "She's really beautiful." Cord just nodded. "And so's this room beautiful," Maddie added with what she hoped was obvious sincerity; to herself she added, and what a surprise, too.

"Thanks."

"Can we have a fire?" There was a distinct chill in the air at Bisbee's more than five-thousand foot elevation.

"You may be disappointed there," he responded.

"Disappointed? How so?"

He stepped aside and reached beside the mantel. Suddenly the fire came fully alive.

"Gas," he said. "Much cleaner and easier than wood, even though it doesn't smell as good." The room filled with an instant and cheery light. There was also the promise of warmth soon to follow.

"I'm no fire snob," Maddie asserted, knowing it was only a half-truth.

"So let's get those eggs going."

She nodded and asked, "Need any help?" but knew the answer even before she asked the question.

"Not really, but I like company." Cord led the way through a small dining room, beautifully furnished with highly polished dark furniture that seemed perfectly to fit the house, almost as if it had been built around it. Maddie wondered if Cord was gay. Men she knew with this kind of taste were invariably gay.

Maddie awoke the next morning to the incessant sound of a ringing telephone. The sunlight streamed cheerfully into Cord's bedroom and added a warm glow to the one she already felt inside. The room, like all the rest of the house, had been decorated comfortably and expensively. There was a bright, geometrically-designed Navaho rug on the floor. On the walls hung an ensemble arrangement of black-and-white photographs of a city she didn't recognize: odd angles, battered buildings, cluttered alleys, traffic tangles. In its sum, the placement of the photos left the impression of a place of chaos and no little stress, an odd theme, she felt, for a bedroom.

Cord got up from the bed and walked out of the room to answer the phone, his hard, lean, naked body rippling with health and youth. Maddie looked forward eagerly for him to return so she could look at him again in all of his beauty—and to touch and be touched by him.

The night before, they had eaten scrambled eggs in front of the gas fire, sipping a light, white wine and nibbling for a long time on cheese and fruit and talking. In retrospect, Maddie felt that it was probably inevitable that they would sleep together, and the atmosphere certainly did nothing to diminish that inevitability. They never discussed having sex as the conclusion of the evening, nor did Cord seduce her—nor she him, for that matter. After a long period of silence, Cord had simply reached out his hand and took Maddie's own tiny one in it. She offered no resistance. They sat there for a while like teenage lovers, still chaste in their passions. Then he rose and pulled her up against him. They stood there very close together looking in each other's eyes. When they kissed, it was gentle, unrushed. Then he reached to the switch and flicked off the lights, so that the only illumination in the room came from the fire and the soft, distant glow from what Maddie knew must be the bedroom. Finally, Cord turned off the fire, and all that was left was the glow of light from the bedroom.

Without a word, Cord put his arm around Maddie's waist and walked her through the dining room into a short hallway and then into the bedroom. In one smooth motion he pulled down the covers, and then he dimmed the bedside lamp. This time their embrace was hard and their kisses, with a mounting urgency, hungry. Finally he pulled away and began taking off his clothes. Maddie followed, with an impatience that surprised herself. Then she could feel his hands ranging over her body and hers over his. She sat back on the bed with both of his hands in hers and pulled him down with her.

Making love with Cord was uncomplicated and wonderful for Maddie. What it may have lacked in emotional depth, it more than made up for in physical intensity. Maybe it was the only kind of sex she was ready for. Cord was a slow and deliberate lover, and gradually she felt their bodies blend with joy and pleasure. Afterwards, she realized that there had been something new in this sex for her. There was a kind of ethereal quality, almost an out-of-body experience, except, of course, that she was anything but out of touch with her body's responses. She felt peculiarly connected beyond herself, and even beyond Cord, to something else, some other dimension, timeless and absorbing. There was a moment when she saw the light from the bedside table grow eerily in intensity, not unlike that day in the seminar room years before when she had had such a powerful visual experience. But that was all there was, an intensification of the light, and nothing more that was visual. The physical sensations were, however, beyond mere pleasure, more exquisite, supernal.

She lay there that next morning in the glow of the morning sun, waiting impatiently for Cord to return from answering the phone. When he did come back into the room, though, he was wearing, to Maddie's disappointment, a robe he had picked up somewhere, probably in the bathroom. He was also wearing a very serious and worried expression.

"What's the matter?" she asked. Thoughts about a replay of last night vanished.

"Harold hasn't come home," he replied, grave and concerned, and then added, "it was Ginger. She's worried."

"What can we do?" Maddie asked. She got up, suddenly self-conscious about her nakedness, and began to dress, comforted to feel the lump and then the individual bead-shapes of her rosary in the pocket of her jeans.

"Last night was wonderful," he said quietly at last.

"For me too," she answered.

CHAPTER TEN

The Second Week in Lent, II

This year immigrants attempting to enter through the [Bisbee] area will encounter nearly 1000 Border Patrol agents based in Cochise County, a mile of new border wall at Bisbee and an array of horses, all-terrain motorcycles, portable observation towers, high-powered stadium lights, remote video and night vision cameras, and electronic sensing devices.
—Arizona Daily Star

Ginger Vega made the transition from sleep to full wakefulness with the alarming realization that she was alone in the big bed. It was just past eight o'clock, and the sun streamed through the tall studio windows. For a moment she luxuriated in its warmth and light, remembering that Harold had taken a load of UDAs into Tucson. Then she began to worry. Normally, it took Harold about six hours to make the back-roads run into Tucson and return to Bisbee by the direct route. He had now been gone eight. Two hours isn't normally much to worry about, especially for Harold Jenkins, whose idea of time was always a bit vague, but she started to worry anyway.

Life the way Ginger experienced it was scary. You don't grow up Mexican, at least not in Tucson, without knowing how uncertain living—just living— can be. And Ginger always felt that the horrible thing that happened to her just after her fifteenth birthday had as much to do with being Mexican as did with being female. A middle-aged Anglo man had caught her doing what her mother had always told her not to do, walking alone at night. He forced her into his car. In a vacant lot near the old, abandoned train station downtown, he hit her, ripped off her panties and forced himself into her. It hurt a lot. She would never forget his grunts and the rancid smell of his tobacco-and-beer breath. It was disgusting. He was disgusting. She could still smell that stench and feel revulsion just thinking about him. The last and almost the only thing he said to her was, "How's that, spic cunt?" just before he dumped her out of the car and drove away. Ginger never told anybody official about the rape, not even her mother. She was so relieved when her period came the next week; the flow of blood had felt like a purging, washing out what she had been unable to accomplish in hours of sitting in the bathtub and everything else she knew to do. Two years later, a Student Health Center counselor Ginger's freshman year at the University of Arizona helped her finally to work her way through some of that pain, leading her to find the inner resources she needed to survive and move ahead with her life.

In a curious kind of irony, the humiliation and torment she suffered from being raped may have saved her from the fate that so many of her friends suffered—getting pregnant, in some cases several times, before they were twenty. She could not face having sex again after that, until she was in college and knew better than to let herself be used the way some of her girlfriends had. But that said, there was no way she was going to thank the bastard who raped her. Ginger used to think about running into him somewhere in Tucson and wondered what she would do if she did. But she never did. The dreams about him finding her and repeating what he had done—doing it again and again—gradually faded. But she had never forgotten, and she knew she never would.

Meeting Joel Vega in her junior year and falling in love with him did more to make Ginger feel like a whole person again than anything else that intervened. His gentleness and patience gradually helped her to become a real participant in a sexual relationship, and he taught her to accept and find pleasure in her body again. Oddly enough, it was when she was first sleeping with Joel that Ginger found that she could go to Mass again. During the four years that had elapsed since the rape, she had not been able to go, but she felt soiled and unacceptable, especially to God, later realizing that what she had actually done was to substitute the Catholic Church for God. Something about the love that Ginger shared with Joel Vega brought that cleansing, even while they were living in a way that the Church, in its wisdom, condemned. So they went together to the Newman Center on campus a few times, and when they were married, the service was also there. The priest at her family parish had refused to marry them because they were living together. But even at the Newman Center, Ginger felt little other than judgment from the Church, and she never regained the rich sense of belonging that she had had as a child. From the time they stopped attending, she never went to Mass again until the day of Joel's funeral.

Joel and Ginger were married the year they graduated from the University of Arizona. Joel's degree was in music, Ginger's in art. He never would say just how many instruments he could play, always insisting that he was "just a piano player," but he filled in on organ at a number of churches, once participated in an early music concert on the harpsichord and occasionally had been known to play the flute.

Ginger's work was primarily in oils. She did like pastels some, and for a time she did a lot of pencil drawings, becoming adept at drawing caricatures and made pretty good money drawing them at the Fourth Avenue Street Fair twice a year in Tucson, even when she was pregnant and after the kids came. But she never had been very confident in her own ability. Sometimes she thought that the rape had undermined all of the self-confidence she might ever have had, even her artistic confidence, but mostly she tended to think of that as a cop out. She often would just tell herself to "suck it up" and get on with life. And she did occasionally like something she had done. Not often. Most of her canvases she painted over and over, telling herself that lots of painters had painted over their canvases—some many times.

There never was much money in the Vega household. In fact, Ginger was the primary bread winner throughout their marriage. Despite her insecurity as a painter, she was always confident as a model, and in all kinds of modeling jobs. This is how the Vegas lived. Ginger did lots of commercial work in Tucson and Phoenix, and, at two different times, was in some demand in LA. Probably the best, at least she thought it was the best, photo series she ever shot was for a maternity wear chain when she was six months pregnant for the first time. She never posed nude for magazines, though she was once invited to, but she did pose nude occasionally for artists like Harold Jenkins. Now that Ginger was almost thirty-five, she was proud that Harold still wanted to paint her, but that could not last much longer, she told herself.

Finding Harold—or, more accurately, being found by him—was one of the greatest strokes of luck in Ginger's life. After Joel died in that freak motorcycle accident—almost two years before—she went into a big decline. She and Joel had always had a lot of alcohol and pot around. Ginger had stayed away from the coke. But after Joel's death, booze and coke were how she coped. At first she neglected everything—fixing meals, doing the laundry, even the simplest things to care for her two children fell by the wayside. Finally, in a rare clear-headed moment she realized that she was only hurting her kids by her behavior and inability to cope. She left them with her parents and took a modeling job in LA, then another one, and another one after that. At first she called home to talk to her mother and father and to the kids, but the calls soon became too painful. So she drank and smoked and sniffed. She lost some weight, which ironically made her even more in demand as a model. Everything she earned went on drugs and drink.

During the thirteen months Ginger spent in LA she did sleep with a couple of men, a handful of times. Sex just didn't give her what she was looking for. It only reminded her of Joel and how much she had lost. It seemed better to her just to stay anesthetized, to feel nothing. And then along came Harold Jenkins.

Harold said that he fell in love with Ginger the first time he saw her, and he said that it broke his heart to see her doing what she was doing to herself. In a process that Ginger never will entirely understand, he persuaded her to go back with him to Bisbee and to pose for a series of nudes. She had no other jobs lined up. Ginger had become pretty unreliable by then, and her life was beginning to take some seriously negative turns. So she said, "What the hell," and went with him. Partly, she wanted to get back to Arizona and see her kids again—even though she knew that she was not yet ready to let them risk actually being with her. All they needed right then was her back in their lives, she had thought.

Going to Bisbee with Harold was not a romantic adventure. They had not slept together when they left LA, and she was not even attracted to him. In the studio, they slept in beds separated by screens for months. Ginger posed and Harold painted. She even began, with Harold's encouragement, to paint too. And little by little—and she understood that it was because of Harold's gentleness—she became clean and sober. There were no dramatic withdrawal scenes or wrenching occasions when she fell off the wagon. Harold encouraged her to go to AA meetings, and even went along with her for a while. Eventually she went on her own. In tiny stages, she began to purge the grief and pain she was carrying. One night, probably more out of gratitude than anything else, Ginger got up in the middle of the night and got into Harold's bed with him. She had been there ever since. They made love occasionally, but never with great passion. Ginger just did not share the love Harold felt for her, and great passion can never be one-sided.

One of the reasons Harold was such a good model for the recovering Ginger was because of his great dedication to his work. He made a good living selling his paintings and was productive far beyond his ability actually to sell what he painted. Second only to his work, Harold was committed to helping stranded Mexican and Central American workers find their way north. When Ginger met him, he had already been part of the Bisbee group for several years, and she quickly fell right in with them. The main problem for the UDAs, she found, was the way they were dumped by the people they had paid to get them north, mostly in the desert and often not far from Bisbee. There was much altruism in the Bisbee group's sometimes risky efforts, but Ginger would admit that there was a lot of adventure in it, too. It brought the thrill of doing something illegal and dangerous together with the conviction that it also was the right thing to do. Usually Harold drove the UDAs from Bisbee to Tucson. Sometimes Ginger went along. But lately it had been getting more difficult, especially since the terrorist attacks on New York and Washington. The Border Patrol covered all the main roads. The ranchers watched the back ones, rough dirt tracks mostly. Harold had even seen a small red and white airplane that seemed to patrol the area around Bisbee, looking for them especially, he thought.

And now he was late. Where could Harold possibly be?

Ginger's first thought was to call Cord. It was obvious that she had gotten him out of bed. Alone? She doubted it. That woman, Maddie, was a little older than Cord, probably about her own age, she thought—and very cute in a pert, petite, sassy kind of way. Ginger wondered if Harold would like to paint her. No doubt about it, his genius was painting nude women. Ginger often wondered how she would do with that traditional subject matter? Probably not her style, she usually concluded.

Cord answered the phone with a kind of growl, "Yeah?

"It's me, Virginia, Ginger. Harold hasn't gotten back yet. He has never been this late."

"Do you want me to come over and wait with you?" he asked.

"Would you?"

He said he would be over in a few minutes. Ginger said she would fix breakfast and asked how many there would be.

"Three of us, I guess."

Ginger just laughed.

Maddie shared a knowing glance with Ginger when she and Cord arrived at Harold's studio half an hour later. Ginger fixed eggs and toast and strong coffee. They sat, mostly without talking. Ginger busied herself around the studio, straightening it up—fussing, really. Finally she called the number in Tucson where they had expected Harold to go.

"They don't know what's happened to him," Ginger said after hanging up the phone. "He never showed up."

"God!" Cord exclaimed. "What do we do now?"

"Go look for him?" Maddie asked, bristling with energy. "Do you know what route he was going to take?"

"There are several possibilities, all in the same area," Cord said.

"It would take all day…and more," Ginger added.

Maddie solved the problem. "Let's go in my airplane. We can be in the air in less than an hour and can search quickly that way."

She was right. Ginger put call forwarding from the phone in the studio to her cell phone, and they left immediately. It took less than the hour Maddie promised before they were taking off on her private runway.

"I'm not crazy about flying in small planes," Ginger said. "But it feels too important for us to find Harold for me to be squeamish." Looks like the fair Maddie has lots of bucks, Ginger added to herself.

"What is your best guess about the route Harold would have chosen?" Maddie asked. She looked over her shoulder at Ginger in the back seat, who adjusted the tiny microphone in front of her mouth the way Maddie had shown her before she answered.

"He tries to stick with seldom used dirt roads. I think he would first go along the San Pedro River then skirt south around Miller Peak and north past Huachuca Peak to Canelo, Elgin and Sonoita, then a short way along Arizona highway eighty-three." She put the road map she had been reading down onto her lap. "I know he says that's about the riskiest stretch of road. There's always a danger of running into the Border Patrol on eighty-three, and there's a fairly new roadblock a few miles north of Sonoita. He has to do some creative, nearly-cross country driving on very poor back roads. Then he strikes out on a gravel road across the Santa Ritas, passing north of Madiera Canyon and on another gravel road to Sahuarita, slipping into Tucson from there."

Maddie steered the plane carefully along that route, checking with a sectional chart from time to time, while both Cord, in the seat beside her, and Ginger in the back searched the route below them. Maddie pointed out landmarks along the way and followed ribbons of gravel road. Cord used a small but powerful pair of binoculars Maddie had in the plane to scan the landscape on both sides of the Skyhawk. Ginger concentrated on the road below and its immediate environment. The harsh wildness of this country, its inhospitable topography, craggy mountains and the spiny vegetation that she knew was down there made her very uncomfortable. But it also surprised her how deceptively smooth and safe-looking it seemed from the air. Ginger said a little prayer that the plane's engine would keep running.

They must have guessed Harold's route pretty close to right, because after they had been searching for about ninety minutes they spotted his SUV lying on its side in the bottom of a ravine a few miles west of Highway eighty-three beside the gravel road through the Santa Rita Mountains in the Coronado National Forest. There was no doubt that this was Harold's car, because he had the name and address of his and Harriet's Bisbee gallery, "Pots and Paint" on the side. The name was clearly visible to Cord using binoculars on the upper side of the battered car as they flew over it. It looked as if it had rolled over many times.

"Do you see any sign of anyone there?" Maddie asked. Ginger was too stunned to speak. Cord grunted a negative as Maddie made a steep turn to pass over it yet again. This time Ginger saw the crumpled form of a person lying about a hundred yards from the SUV. She saw no one else.

"There's someone," Cord yelled, pointing toward the same person Ginger had just seen. "But it's not Harold." They made another pass over the SUV, even closer this time, the closeness and the steep turn making Ginger very nervous. There was nothing else to see.

Maddie abruptly pulled up the nose of the plane and added full power as it strained to gain altitude in a tight, climbing circle. She adjusted the radio, and Cord and Ginger heard her call, "Tucson approach, this is Cessna 8645 Lima, I've spotted a wrecked SUV in a wash in the Santa Ritas northeast of Madeira Canyon. There's at least one person lying on the ground. Four-five Lima."

"State your position again, Four-Five Lima."

"Tucson approach, I'm about seven miles south south-west of Mt. Fagan. Four-Five Lima."

"I copy, Four-Five Lima. Are you okay to stay in the area for a few minutes?"

"Roger. Four-Five Lima."

Maddie continued to circle over the wrecked SUV, though now they were high enough that it was hard to see the details they had seen before. Round and round they circled, none of them saying anything. Abruptly the radio crackled in Ginger's ear with the voice of the ATC controller. Not for them, but for another aircraft inbound into Tucson International, but startling, still. Silence again. Once more the controller broke into the quiet. Another pilot responded. Then the silence resumed. Finally Ginger heard the disembodied voice call, "Cessna Four-Five Lima?"

"Roger, Tucson. Four-Five Lima," Maddie responded into her mike.

"A highway patrol trooper is on his way from Green Valley. Thanks for your help, Four-Five Lima."

"We'll stay in the area, Tucson, until the trooper arrives. Four-Five Lima."

"Roger, Four-Five Lima."

It wasn't very long before a tiny speck on the road below them, moving fast, began to leave a dust cloud in its wake. The trooper. A second vehicle followed less than a mile behind the first one, probably a paramedic unit, Ginger concluded correctly. Four-Five Lima continued to circle over the wrecked car. It startled Ginger when Maddie cut the power, still in the tight circle, and began once again to lose altitude. Ginger would swear that she could see the spines on a saguaro cactus as they made one side of the turn very close to the hillside. That was an exaggeration, but they *were* close. There was still no movement on the ground. The sick feeling in Ginger's stomach just then had little to do with the flying and a great deal more to do with her fear about what had happened to Harold and his passengers. She imagined broken bones, lots of pain, long months of recovery. The up side that occurred to Ginger was that she would have a chance to repay Harold for all of his kindness to her. She would be able to take care of him.

At last, the trooper pulled up on the road above the crippled SUV. They saw him stop and look at the ground, then step back and look again. Then he slipped back into his car. A red paramedic vehicle pulled up beside the patrol car. A moment later the trooper was out again, this time slipping and sliding down the ravine to the wreck with two paramedics right behind him with a stretcher. Just as they reached Harold's SUV, the controller called Maddie again, "Four-Five Lima, I have a relay from the Highway Patrol for you."

"Roger, Tucson," Maddie said into the mike. "Four-Five Lima."

"The trooper says to thank you and asks you to call the Highway Patrol when you get to a phone."

The three of them were back at the studio again in just over an hour. Cord fixed some sandwiches, trying to get Ginger to eat something, but he could have spared himself the trouble. None of them felt like eating. Maddie called the Highway Patrol on her cell phone as she had been instructed and gave her name and address. Cord insisted that they give the police no more information than was absolutely necessary.

"There doesn't need to be any obvious connection between the plane that spotted the SUV and Harold's friends in Bisbee waiting to hear what happened to him," he said. "That would be hard to explain. There's no point in implicating ourselves in what they will know he was doing."

Cord was right, so they waited to hear something. The minutes dragged.

For something to do, Ginger asked Maddie if she minded posing for a little drawing. Maddie said she was flattered to be asked. Ginger settled Maddie in a comfortable chair, and in a few quick strokes made a quick caricature of her as Amelia Earhart and handed it to her.

"Wow," Maddie said. "That's speedy. And it's good." She paused and studied it thoughtfully for a long moment and then said, "I remember…there was a woman who did caricatures at the Street Fair in Tucson."

"That could have been me. I did them for several years."

"From what I heard, it was always a toss up whether the men—or women for that matter—were more interested in being drawn or in having an excuse to stare at the artist. Now I know what they meant."

"Now who's being flattered?" Ginger asked. They laughed together. It was the first light moment they had shared. "Okay if I do something more serious?" Ginger asked getting fresh drawing paper and pencils.

"I'm still flattered that you want to draw me."

"Why flattered? You're a great subject. Harold must be aching to paint you in the altogether." Ginger grinned. She could be mistaken, but she thought she saw Maddie blush. Then it occurred to Ginger to think to herself, if he's still alive, that is. But she could not say it aloud. Ginger started to get that sick feeling in her stomach again. "Harold really is a fine painter of the nude body," she added aloud.

"I've seen some that he did of you. You're right."

Ginger began a serious drawing of Maddie as Maddie continued, "Tell me about yourself. I know you lived in Tucson."

As Ginger drew, she told Maddie the superficial details of her life, about Joel's death and how it had led her into a terrible time. Then Maddie told Ginger about Art's death.

"I'm so sorry, Maddie," Ginger said, continuing to warm to her, realizing that she had felt—jealousy? competition? At least a little cold toward her.

"I guess the preparation I got during Art's illness really did make a difference for me." Maddie said. "It must have been horrible for you to have it happen so suddenly."

"It was." They sat silently for a time, the scrape of the pencil on paper making the only sounds. Cord sat pensively in a corner.

"Do you have kids?" Ginger asked finally. "I have two." She thought of her children with a pang of sadness and regret. Surely I must be getting my life together enough that I can soon see them again, she thought to herself.

"No. No children, I'm sorry to say," Maddie replied.

The doorbell rang. Ginger went to see who it was and found a young Cochise County sheriff's deputy standing at the door. She had seen him around Bisbee. He probably lived there. The dis-ease in her stomach turned to a dull ache.

"Yes, officer?" Ginger asked

"I have some bad news for you. Ms. Vega? May I come in?"

Harold's car had apparently been run off the road, and all but one of the people in it, including Harold, had been killed. A young boy about ten was in a Tucson hospital and had confirmed that a dark blue or purple SUV had forced them off the road in the Santa Ritas.

Harold dead? Ginger could not believe it. She started to cry, gradually becoming hysterical as the poor young officer became flustered and uncomfortable and soon excused himself. Ginger was unable later to remember all the details that followed, but she did recall Maddie putting her arm around her and sitting with her on the sofa for a long time and then insisting on taking her back to the ranch with her. Ginger later asked herself what she would have done had it not been for Maddie.

CHAPTER ELEVEN

The Third Sunday in Lent

"I suggest 'Spirit' as a root image...[for] God. It leads to an image of the Christian life that stresses relationship, intimacy and belonging.... [S]in remains. Only now the emphasis is not on sin as a violation of God's laws but on sin as betrayal of relationship and absence of compassion."
—Marcus Borg

"The hell, you say!" Jerry heard Hank Tucker explode. The Sulphur Springs Valley rancher was in St. Peter's kitchen with Charlie Snow cleaning up after Saturday evening's potluck supper. Charlie's response was inaudible, but that was when Jerry first noticed a pronounced smirk on Charlie's face, an expression he wore for the rest of the evening. For his part, Hank became uncharacteristically quiet and thoughtful, even troubled. His moderation and seasoned—though partisan—judgment was missing from the group discussion. Instead, he sat both distracted and uncommunicative. There was one moment when Jerry thought that whatever was troubling Hank would boil over into angry words, but Hank held his tongue with what looked like great restraint.

Kate was reading from Wink's book, making a point she wanted to make, "Jesus challenged the Domination System of his day right where it affected men and women in the routine of their lives...His words still challenge the manifestations of the Domination System today." She put down the book and continued, "This is what I mean."

"No question about it," Jerry added. "He is saying that the message of Jesus was not just about his own day, but about all times—a critique of human society always and everywhere."

Jerry felt Kate's foot touch his under the table and linger there for just a moment. Everyone else in the room no doubt connected the smile that lit up her face with the reading. Jerry alone knew better.

Suddenly Charlie Snow let out a disgusted "pshaw!" and said, "This is such a bunch of crap. Well it is," he said to his wife who had put a restraining hand on his forearm. "You know it is. This is what is wrong with such a lot of do-gooder Christianity these days. Nobody has the nerve to stand up for what's right. And when someone does, the bleeding hearts start wringing their hands."

"What are you talking about, Charlie Snow?" Mrs. Findlay asked impatiently from behind thick glasses that served to magnify her intensity; a vision of generations of students coming under that unblinking gaze hovered over the table. "Are you still talking about the UDAs? What about the people who rob *them*? I read the other day that over near Naco, there is a regular gang that preys on the Illegals, takes everything they have—even their shoes—and leaves them to die in the desert."

But Charlie did not back down before her withering gaze. Instead he risked even more. "Take all the whining and moaning about the carload of wet backs and the Bisbee guy that went off the road in the Santa Ritas. Someone ran them off the road, they say. Serves 'em right, it seems to me." He sat back, the smirk again on his face.

"What's that about?" Jerry asked. "I must have missed something." He had no inkling at that moment what Charlie was talking about.

Bobby Hurschberger filled them all in. "A carload of Mexican workers, including a kid, was found today in a ravine in the Santa Ritas. Though the police want to talk to one of the passengers—the ten-year-old boy who was in the car—before they will know for certain, it looks from the evidence as if another vehicle ran it off the road. Everybody else is dead, including the Bisbee artist whose car it was."

"Deliberately ran it off the road?" Jerry asked.

Mrs. Findlay shrugged. "They don't know yet for sure."

"Serves 'em right, all of 'em," Charlie muttered. "Even better, I hear that the military is now sending some if its helicopters to help patrol the Douglas-Naco corridor where so many of them get across the line. That should really make a difference."

It was to the credit of the other members of the group that expressions of shock and horror lingered on their faces at Charlie's outburst. Hank Tucker had seemed to go white. Jerry could not believe what he had heard: Charlie had actually condoned—no, applauded—the violent deaths of a carload of people. It was at that moment that Jerry remembered Hank's and Charlie's altercation at the dishwasher. He was certain *that* conversation, Charlie's outburst and Hank's odd behavior were all connected.

Jerry found himself suddenly overcome by a hurricane of feelings and images. Coming at once and on several different levels, they left him no pastoral distance from the conversation, especially from the ugliness of Charlie Snow. At one moment in the midst of Charlie's outbursts, Jerry actually had an impression of Charlie as some kind of devil—or, more accurately, like someone possessed by something evil. In some quarters even today—and for most of the past twenty centuries—such an awareness of an evil presence would be taken very seriously by Christian clergy. But Jerry's theology did not work that way. At least it never had before. He did not believe in demonic possession, or at least that was what he told himself, any more than he did in personified evil, in Satan. So how else would he describe what he saw in Charlie Snow? Jerry found himself confronted by something primitive and ugly; "evil" was the only word he knew to describe what he experienced. This was not "the Powers" as Walter Wink identifies them, abstractions or disembodied structural flaws. In Jerry's imagination, he could almost see a grinning devil gleaming out of Charlie Snow. It would not have been inconsistent with the moment if he had seen a yellow glow coming from Charlie's eyes. He did *not* see that, but he half expected to. And it gave him the willies. Perhaps Jerry saw nothing more than a kind of psychic extension of Charlie's ego, but that is, after all, only another grammar for the same phenomenon. Something ugly was happening inside Charlie Snow, and the wickedness of it filled Jerry's consciousness.

At the same time Jerry's senses were heightened to the surroundings of the room in a deeply negative way. Most of the time he was able to ignore the somewhat battered appearance of St. Peter's parish hall. The worn tables and rickety folding chairs, yellowed linoleum floor with decades of built-up wax and chemically plastered dirt, especially in corners, paint that had not been bright and fresh in at least two decades—and that was badly marred from being scraped by tables and chairs—and light fixtures that cast uneven illumination through a generation of dust and cobwebs. It suddenly all looked so tawdry. Why hadn't Jerry seen this before? He knew the room really did not look *that* bad. What had changed in him to make his senses so acute?

Breaking through all of that ugliness, both of Charlie Snow's vituperation and the squalor of the room, was what suddenly seemed to Jerry to be the cool—icy—beauty of Kate Becker. He was acutely aware of her presence, and the contrast with Charlie Snow was marked. While Charlie seemed to radiate evil and the room felt to Jerry as if he were looking through a window that had accumulated a generation's build-up of dirt and grime, Kate glowed for him with a quiet, cool radiance, like the light of a flourescent tube shining brightly and harshly in a room that was dull and unlovely—and was made no more beautiful by the icy radiance. Jerry remembered both times they had made love. A mental vision of her lean, white body beckoned to him. Each time they touched, sometimes by accident and sometimes on purpose, he felt the thrill of excitement. At times it was more than his senses could tolerate. Intense, cool beauty and horrifying, dark ugliness—both at the same time! How could a person stand it when beauty, surrounded by evil and ugliness, appeared to be so cold?

Jerry's mind swirled with images and his body was intense with feelings; still he was hit with more. Sadie came into the room from where she and the Lopez granddaughters had been watching TV and playing games as they had done two weeks before. At once a hollow, gut wrenching fear washed over Jerry. A premonition? A normal parental worry in that heightened state of senses? He did not know, nor did he take time to try to analyze his feelings. It was all he could do at that moment to feel them and to contain their power.

"Yes, Sweetheart," Jerry said to her, pulling her to him for a hug whose intensity surprised her.

Sadie looked questioningly at her father. "Daddy, we're hungry," she said after a moment. "Are there any snacks?"

In response, Mrs. Findlay lifted her cavernous handbag onto the table, and, rummaging noisily, pulled out three Snickers bars. Had she been prepared for such an eventuality? That certainly showed another side of Elspeth Findlay. "Will these do, young lady?" She smiled beatifically, the opposite of the expression she had cast at Charlie Snow earlier.

"Oh, yes. Thanks," Sadie answered. She took the candy bars and ran back into the TV room. The door slammed. Everyone laughed. The tension in the room abated somewhat, and Jerry moved past his internal turmoil, for the moment anyway.

Sunday morning's sky wore a face of tiny, puffy white clouds drifting lazily across a blue foundation, unmarred by the brown soot coughed out of the internal combustion engine in cities—a gift of small town, rural Arizona. Crisp March air clung to Jerry's body with a cloak of freshness. It was one of those moments when it felt good to be alive. Just walking from the Simmons House to St. Peter's, accompanied by the much-varied song of a mockingbird, was pleasure itself. Then seeing Kate Becker, who arrived early at church with the three chattering girls in tow, added to the morning's brightness. Kate and Jerry had time and opportunity in the church sacristy for a quick kiss, exactly what they had had time and privacy for the night before. It had been with a sense of regret that Jerry had gone all by himself back to the Simmons House for the night while Sadie and her friends went off to Kate's house.

"I have a couple of free days mid-week," Kate said. "Are you busy? Maybe we could go somewhere? Or you could just come here and spend some time?" Her smile, radiant and seductive, was not very saintly—at least not in the commonly understood sense of the word "saint."

Jerry felt a stir of excitement and anticipation. "Sure. Let me talk with Carmen and Lizzie's grandmother—see if Sadie can stay with them. I'll come down on Tuesday morning. What do you want to do?"

"I don't know. We'll think of something." She smiled in what Jerry thought was a delightfully wicked way. He grinned self-consciously.

"What are *you* smiling about?" she asked.

"I'll bet you can guess," he answered, falling naturally enough into the role of private lover.

"Yes," she breathed, managing to be at once provocative and matter-of-fact.

Jerry glanced at his watch, almost time for church to begin. He went directly into the vesting room and threw on an alb and stole. The morning's acolytes, all from Tombstone—Justin and Joel Curtain and Hanna-Nellie Silver, her straight back even straighter than usual as she prepared to carry the cross down the aisle—had already vested and appeared ready. The usher was also from Tombstone, Jim Brown; he had one hand on the bell rope, ready to give the signal to Bobby Hurschberger, who doubled as volunteer parish musician, to start the processional hymn on the battered old piano, which despite errors, he played with energy.

Jerry was in for a surprise that morning. All of the members of the Tombstone God Group sat patiently in the congregation waiting for the service to begin. That included Mayor Jack Jackson *and* his wife, Linda, a surprise in itself. Jerry was even more surprised to see Maddie Gronek and Cord sitting rather uncomfortably, he thought, at the back of the church. Beside them, and even more surprising yet, sat the proprietor of Ike Clanton's Bead Shop, Ike McWarder. The only member of the Tombstone flock missing this morning it seemed was Doc Holiday.

The three girls sat with Sue-Sue Hawkins in her favorite pew, and Kate

Becker sat next to Sadie on the center aisle. Sue-Sue had already recruited the three girls to help her with a special coffee hour gift to the congregation that she had planned for this morning—rich, dark coffee, fresh squeezed orange juice from the tree of one of the Browns' grown children in Tucson and great fresh, homemade donuts from Nellie Cashman's. It was a gift from the Tombstone contingent to the Bisbee portion of the congregation. Counting other regulars, the Bisbee book group members and the usual visitors, the small church fairly bustled with activity.

The congregation sang the familiar Lenten hymn, "Forty Days and Forty Nights" for the processional. And Jerry was surprised by the singing this morning, even stunned by the strong deep voices coming from Jack Jackson, Ike and Cord. He might have closed his eyes and imagined himself in a much larger church, towering organ pipes resonating, choir singing soaring descants—an experience of the church he had not had for almost three years. And then Jerry realized that St. Peter's, with no organ and only a piano, no choir, and a small congregation—fifty-two that morning—still carried the life of the church in all its power as they sang their hearts out. The divisions in the parish—Tombstone vs. Bisbee, Hank Tucker vs. Charlie Snow—seemed more remote than ever before. Jerry felt euphoric.

The difference was not in the surroundings, even though it *was* a good Sunday. The difference was with him—or *in* him. Whatever Jerry had experienced the night before—certainly some kind of spiritual in-breaking into his consciousness—continued to resonate in him this morning, but rather than carrying a mantle of evil, now he had a nearly overpowering sense of well-being. When Jerry administered communion wafers at the altar rail and pressed the bread into the palms of the recipients' hands, it was with an intimate sense of who each person was and how each one's story was unique. And he loved them. This was the first time in years that he had had this once-familiar sensation in a congregation on a Sunday morning, something that used to happen to him all the time. It was like feeling connected at some primitive level with each person and through them to the source of all life. He had no doubt about God's existence that morning, whoever or whatever God might be. It felt wonderful to have that confirmed anew.

Jerry also carried with him the gospel passage that he had read that morning in the service, especially the final verse. Jesus is telling a parable about a man who planted a fig tree that does not produce figs, threatening to rip it from the ground. The man's gardener suggests instead, "Sir, let it alone for one more year, until I dig around it and put manure on it. If it bears fruit next year, well and good; but if not, you can cut it down." Jerry had an abiding sense, right there and then in the chancel of St. Peter's Church in Bisbee, Arizona, the third Sunday in Lent, that the fig tree would produce figs the next year, and, given an opportunity and some tending, that human beings, all human beings, were as salvageable as the fig tree. Jerry himself had been the recipient of such a grace. He had thought of himself as primarily the gardener, when all along he had been the fig tree.

Nor was that the end of this extraordinary morning's experience. When everyone had received communion, Jerry stepped behind the altar and looked out at the congregation. They had finished singing the communion hymn, "Deck Thyself, My Soul, With Gladness," and some of the people were sitting, some were kneeling on the kneelers. Others stood to say the post communion prayer, "Eternal God, Heavenly Father…" And Jerry could see in their eyes and in their body language, that he was not the only person who felt something different and intense this morning.

That knowledge was confirmed at the front door after the service as Jerry greeted people on their way out to the coffee hour put on by Sue-Sue Hawkins, the Tombstone contingent and their three young assistants. Instead of hand-shakes, Jerry repeatedly received warm hugs from people he knew only slightly. And that warm feeling did not stop with him. He noticed a marked warming of everyone toward everyone else: people hugging each other, touching as they talked, smiling, laughing, eating doughnuts and drinking coffee. Not even the distinctions between Bisbee and Tombstone seemed important. Whatever had happened to Jerry was not limited to him alone, but had spread to this small congregation in this arty former mining town, better known for its saloons and history of labor/management struggles than for religious feeling. What had begun for Jerry in an ugly heightened awareness in the parish hall of St. Peter's Church in Bisbee on Saturday night had, by something truly miraculous, been transformed and scattered far abroad this morning. He did not begin to understand it.

Bobby Hurschberger seemed mildly disappointed after the service when Jerry thanked him for his offer to take them all to the airport. "There really is more room for three girls and me in Kate's car than in your Chevy," he said.

Running his hand through tousled white hair, Bobby give Jerry an inquiring look and quietly knowing smile. Jerry wondered just how secret his and Kate's little secret really was. Stories about lack of privacy in a small town came back to him. Considering the fact that all congregations are, by definition, small towns themselves, it must be doubly true that there really are no secrets in small town congregations. At that moment it frankly did not matter to Jerry Hanning.

There were more surprises waiting for Jerry in Tombstone that afternoon. After a quick and perfect flying experience for Jerry's passengers, he set the Skyhawk down at the abandoned Tombstone airport. The surface of the runway was fast deteriorating, and the windsock was in tatters. Unless someone made some efforts to maintain the airport, it would soon be unusable, Jerry thought. He made a mental note to do his part to keep up the landing strip by getting a windsock from the flying shop at Ryan Field. There was no sign of Hank Tucker's Bonanza or any other airplane that afternoon. Jim Brown was waiting to hustle the four of them to Nellie Cashman's in his Buick and gave the girls big, warm welcoming hugs—almost as if he had not seen them for weeks rather than minutes. No surprises there for Jerry.

The euphoric mood of the morning continued into the afternoon book group. They laughed a lot, especially about Ike McWarder's appearance in church. Brenda-Nellie, her round face shaking with mirth, poked good fun at him. "So, Ike, what got into you this morning…to venture into dangerous foreign territory, that is? And such a fine tenor. You and Jack and Cord could go on the stage as a trio." Everyone laughed with her, even Ike, who cleared his throat and brought out a mysterious paper bag that had stood at his feet.

"I guess it was thinkin' about all of you that led me t'take such a dangerous step as actually t'go inta that church place." Without pause, Ike changed the subject. "And I've got a little gift fer each of ya." He reached into the bag and began distributing small leather pouches tied together with draw-strings at the top. Each one had someone's name attached. "In each of the bags," he said, "is what's called an Anglican Rosary. I've an instruction sheet for ya." He gestured toward a stack of papers beside him on the table. "The beads're all the same, but the medals're diff'rent—specially picked. I've also got somethin' fer the kids, too." He handed one to each of the five—two Curtain boys, one Hanning girl and two Vega girls—all of whom were sitting together playing a game with a deck of cards. Sounds of pleasure and packages opening came from them as they looked at their wrist beads, strung on elastic cord in the contemporary Buddhist style. "They'll bring ya luck," he said.

Jerry weighed his own bag in his hand, feeling the texture of the leather and the beads inside.

"Can we open them one at a time?" asked Lisa Brown. "So we can hear what each medal is."

"Of course," Jerry answered. Ike nodded that that would be okay. "Shall I begin?" Jerry proposed as he opened the leather bag and poured the green and black beads and shiny medal of St. Peter into his hand. The medal was a good choice for Jerry, he thought. Peter, the chief of the apostles, but the one who never quite got it right, the one who denied Jesus, the one who seemed just a little oafish at times—exactly how Jerry felt recently. Yes, it was a good choice for him, the vicar of St. Peter's Church. He liked the feel of the beads in his hand.

The Curtains were next. Jillian, clearly delighted at the selection made for her, the Blessed Virgin Mary, smiled as if she really were the mother of Christ. Curtis, likewise, was happy with his rosary selection as John the Baptist. Jerry gave Ike a sharp look and saw in his twinkling eye, that, true to form, there was a private joke in this selection: the stern Baptist for Curtis and the pedestal-dwelling Mary for Jillian. Jerry caught the joke, but happily the Curtains did not. If anyone else got it, they didn't let on.

Jack Jackson's medal was of St. Benedict, founder of the Benedictines, an appropriate choice for the mayor since the Benedictine Rule places leadership in the hands of the elected Abbot. Linda Jackson received a medal of St. Mary of Bethany, the one who sat at Jesus' feet while her sister, Martha, served in the kitchen.

The Browns were well identified, Jim with St. Joseph the Worker, and Lisa, a noted animal lover, with St. Francis of Assisi. Brenda-Nellie had a medal of the Celtic goddess-saint, Bridget of Kildaire and Brenda's partner, Hanna, one of Hildegard of Bingen, the twelfth century abbess who was such a rich role model for late-twentieth century women. Ike himself had a medal of the labyrinth at Chartres Cathedral, a choice that said more about Ike and his spirituality than perhaps even he realized. The labyrinth was *the* image of the twists and turns of life as one moves inevitably toward the center. The return to the world again to live within it is equally certain. Cord, the artist, had a medal of Renaissance Florentine fresco painter, Fra Angelico. The only one that did not make obvious sense to Jerry was the selection of Julian of Norwich, a late medieval mystic, for Maddie Gronek. He wondered just what that could possibly mean. One thing was for sure. Those "saintly" designations of Ike McWarder's for this group would stick, at least in Jerry's mind they would.

CHAPTER TWELVE

The Third Week in Lent

How
Do I
Listen to others?
As if everyone were my master
Speaking to me
His
Cherished
Last
Words.
—Hafiz

Jerry Hanning called Ginger Vega on Monday afternoon. She was surprised and a little flustered to hear from him.

"This is Father Hanning. Maddie Gronek asked me to call. I'm the Episcopal priest in Bisbee."

"Yes, Father. This is Virginia Vega. I…I'm glad you called. Actually, we have met. I attended a wedding a few weeks ago, and we spoke briefly at the reception."

"Were you with a large man with a shaved head?"

"Yes, that's right. He's the one who has…has died," Ginger responded uncomfortably.

"I'm so very sorry."

"Thank you. I'm so glad you're willing to do a service for Harold."

"Don't think anything of it. But it *would* help me if I can get some information from you—for the service tomorrow."

"Cer-certainly. What can I tell you, ah, Father?"

"First, will there be any relatives present?" he asked.

"No. They're all in Seattle, and Harold's body is already being shipped to them."

"And you, were you and...Harold...living together?"

Ginger felt herself bristle inside, all the old motifs of judgment and self-accusation brimming up from her adolescence."So what?" she said, not quite believing her own rudeness. But what business was it of his?

"I didn't mean anything by the question," he said. "I just didn't want to make a faux pas."

"Sorry, I didn't mean to be rude."

"No offense taken," he said. "Will there be any music in the service?"

Ginger was glad to have him move away from what, for her when confronting the Church, was a very touchy subject, her domestic arrangements. Why did priests always focus on sex? No doubt a product of celibacy. But Episcopal clergy weren't celibate were they?

"Yes, one of Harold's friends is a guitarist and singer. He's going to do two songs."

"Is there anything in particular you would like me to say or to do?"

"I don't think so. What can you say about Harold? You only met him the one time."

"How would it be if I invited other people to share memories of him?"

"You're willing to do that?" She was surprised. That was something she had never seen before.

"Of course. This is about helping you and Harold's other friends deal with your loss. It's not about me." There was something very soothing and supportive about Father Jerry's voice and manner. Ginger found that she actually looked forward to meeting him again.

The days that followed Harold Jenkins' death had been a blur for Ginger. Harriet Lawson, the potter and Harold's partner in the Pots and Paint Gallery took over most of the other details. She closed up the gallery and her studio to make the arrangements, breaking the news to the family, engaging a funeral home to receive the body from the police and to ship it to Seattle for burial. Harold had just made out a will, perhaps with a premonition that something was going to happen to him. In it he left Harriet his share of the gallery and Ginger the free-and-clear studio and its contents. There was no money to speak of—Harold did not believe in bank accounts—but much of his work was in the studio ready for sale. So Harold's death did not leave Ginger without a place to live. But it did mean that she was going to have to begin to generate some income, initially arranging for gallery shows of Harold's work, then getting seriously to work herself. As recently as three months before, that thought would have terrified her, but by now she was ready to take care of herself again.

Ginger grieved Harold's death, but it was not a revisiting of what had happened to her when Joel was killed. She did not start drinking or drugging again. In an odd way, this shock left her more confident and resilient than before it happened. Partly her burning anger at whoever had killed Harold and those innocent people in the SUV sustained her. The studio was great and she was glad to have it, but the real legacy that Harold left Ginger, even in death—perhaps especially in death—was a restored self. As soon as the immediate crisis was over and all of the details were handled, she would go back to Tucson and be reunited with her family. Then she would rebuild the details of her life—right there in Bisbee.

Ginger had done a thorough cleaning and reorganization of the studio for the memorial service and had hung most of Harold's recent work on the walls. Five nude portraits, including two of her, were the best of the lot, though some others were, she thought, very good. An excellent arrangement of individual Bisbee houses hung on one wall. She counted a total of forty-one completed paintings, and five incomplete ones. There were six of Ginger's own work, which she left stacked in a corner. She had decided that the first thing she would do as she got back to work was to show Harold's finished canvases. Then she would figure out what to do with the unfinished ones. It would not be the same as the artist completing his own work, but she thought she might try to finish them herself as a way to say goodbye to Harold and to thank him for everything he had done for her. He had saved her life, of that she had no doubt.

The gathering was set for eleven o'clock, but people began to arrive about ten-thirty, bringing food and drinks in festal proportions. Some also brought folding chairs. They laid out food on tables and counter tops and organized the chairs with the paintings as a kind of focus. Ginger had not thought of the two paintings of her as being in any way inappropriate or embarrassing until the priest walked through the door with Maddie Gronek. In all fairness to him, Ginger thought later, it was impossible not to look at the paintings of her, both from the way the room was organized and because of the power they carried—the product of Harold's work. But Ginger suddenly felt exposed, almost ashamed.

No! she thought. She was not going to let him do this to her, shame her. By the time she worked her way through the crowd to Jerry Hanning, he was standing in front of one of the paintings of her, a pose that Ginger always had thought was the best of the series, and he was studying it carefully and quietly, comparing it to the other one of her. It had always seemed to Ginger that this particular picture had caught something very true about the person she is, and revealed much about the essential person of the painter as well. It was loving without being unduly erotic, and it was honest without dwelling on blemishes. In the picture, Ginger was looking over one shoulder with an expression of inquiry, even curiosity, in her eyes. One breast was fully exposed from the side, but the other one was entirely absent from the canvas. Just above the exposed hip were the tell-tale stretch marks of pregnancy. Standing there watching the priest study that picture made Ginger feel stripped bare in more ways than in the physical fact of the nudity. It was as if her entire life were exposed, along with her body, to his scrutiny. She did not like it one bit.

"Like what you see?" Ginger said sharply to Jerry Hanning. Having him stare at that picture made her very angry.

"This is...breathtaking," he said. Jerry turned and looked at Ginger, smiled knowingly, she thought, and continued, "And you're Virginia Vega. I remember." Above the black shirt and white clerical collar was a face that surprised her, even on a second seeing. She saw a full, though not quite mature, beard and also clear, penetrating blue eyes. On top of his head was a shock of brown hair, lighter than the very dark beard, unruly curls going where they wanted. Compassion and empathy radiated from a surprisingly rugged exterior. There was nothing mocking or judgmental in the way he looked at her. Suddenly she felt at once totally attended to and special in that moment, but she could not shake her old resentment toward feeling judged and unclean by the church and by the clergy.

"Right!" she snapped, more sharply than she intended. Jerry Hanning's expression did not change. He reached out a hand and gently touched her arm.

"I'm very sorry for your loss. Maddie told me how you found the crash in her Cessna and radioed it in. Of course it has all been on the news. I...I...think I admire what Harold was trying to do, though don't report me to the Border Patrol for that." He smiled with what struck Ginger as great warmth. "Actually, I'm a little unsure about it all—all the border issues. Guess I'm just a little too new here to have a very confident opinion. I gather there's no word yet about who caused it." In a smooth flow of words, he managed to put Ginger at ease. She felt that there was no way she could entirely trust him, but she resolved at least to back off.

"Will this be okay? Or do you want to rearrange the room?" she asked, finally feeling a little less on edge with the priest.

"This's just fine. It's clear that you arranged it so that Harold's best work was the focus of the space. That's the way it should be." He paused for just a moment, then said very calmly and quietly, "He must have loved you very much. It shows." He half-turned and made a gesture at the picture beside him. Her view became obscured by a fresh flow of tears—for Harold? For herself? She hardly knew.

At that moment Maddie Gronek stepped beside Ginger and put her arm around her, lending her a kind of strength that seemed to flow from the one body to the other. Ginger shook her head and wiped the tears from her eyes.

"Shall we begin?" Ginger asked. Jerry nodded in the affirmative and raised up a small black book he held in his hand. "Everyone, let's get started," Ginger said in a loud voice. Immediately the crowded room quieted down. "This is Father Jerry Hanning. He's going to lead the service for Harold." She sat down beside Maddie and Cord.

Ginger looked on as if from a great distance, not quite present, but still there. Jerry took charge. First he kissed the cross on a white stole he carried with his prayer book and put it around his neck. Then he stepped over to Anthony, one of Harold's friends, who held a guitar in his hands, and conferred quietly with him. When Jerry turned back to the assembled friends of Harold Jenkins, he had a seriousness on his face that said, "What we are doing here is important." He began the service by reading, "I am resurrection and I am life, says the Lord..."

Ginger was surprised at how quickly the service went: formal prayers, a reading from the Gospel of John, some very moving music and a series of short personal testimonials. Ginger did not say anything. Instead, she just sat there thinking about Harold (and Joel), trying to get a handle on the ups and downs of living. How does a person understand the unexpected shifts and changes? The unearned reward? The undeserved punishment? The fact of sudden death? She struggled, but could find no meaning in it. It was at this point as, listening with one ear and also caught in her own reflections, Ginger heard Jerry begin his short homily as a conclusion to the individual remembrances of Harold's friends.

"Don't spend a lot of time trying to figure out what God was up to in the sudden, tragic death of Harold Jenkins," he began. "That was not God's doing, not a part of some sacred plan beyond Harold's or our knowing. No, his death was the senseless and brutal act of some person, not an act of God.

It was the result of something courageous, though illegal, that Harold was doing.

"Where was God in this, then? you might ask. Indeed, where is God at times like this? For that matter, where was God when Jesus was being crucified on the cross? This is our clue to understanding the role of the Holy One in the center of our sometimes shattered lives. God is in the same place for Harold as that Sacred Presence was for Jesus, the same place that the same Holy Life is for us today as we grieve for Harold Jenkins. God is in the redemption of the acts committed by people and by the natural processes of creation."

Ginger watched Jerry look long, and, she thought, lovingly, at Maddie Gronek. There was something very strong between them, she thought. Then Jerry looked directly at her, caught her eye and seemed to look right through and beyond all of the events of her life into some very deep place where the person she really was resided.

"God is about redeeming all of creation," he continued, "of making wonderful things emerge from pain and loss, opening paths for us to a new life. The loss doesn't become any less awful. It just becomes more bearable in the face of new possibilities. God raised Jesus from the dead—whatever we are to understand by that statement. God also raises us from our loss and our deaths, all of the many deaths we encounter day in and day out.

"As for Harold, why should we expect anything less for him now, any less than what God promises us all?"

Jerry stood there quietly for a moment, then nodded to Anthony, who began to strum chords and then sang out in his clear tenor voice the words of "Amazing Grace." Ginger was surprised. Everyone seemed to be surprised by this choice. By the time he finished, the tears gave way to smiles, smiles through tears. It was as if God had somehow stepped right in at that very moment and redeemed the pain for everyone present.

For Ginger, the redemption that Father Jerry spoke of came partly in the form of an idea, a way they could continue what Harold was doing when he was killed without running the same risks that he ran—risks that certainly were not going to become less any time soon. They were not going to stop having desperate people marooned on their doorsteps. Ginger looked at Maddie and wondered if she would agree to what she had in mind.

Following Harold Jenkins's service, Jerry went back to the church to change. Excitement built about meeting Kate Becker, whom he had called on his cell phone to alert that he would be with her shortly. Now they could pick up their interrupted personal lives as planned. "I Can't wait," he said just before breaking the connection and jumping on his bike for the ten minute ride.

But what happened next quickly dampened his enthusiasm.

"Hi," he said, bubbling with energy and life, as he stepped inside the front door. Kate's response to his kiss was perfunctory and carried no noticeable passion. Inside, Jerry told her about the funeral as he processed the experience and began to unwind. He also filled her in on what he had learned about Harold Jenkins. "Nothing could be farther from the truth," he said, "than what Charlie Snow implied the other night. This man was no coyote. He was part of a group that picks up people who have been abandoned in the desert and tries to get them somewhere to safety."

"Why don't they just turn those people in to the INS or the Border Patrol?" she asked, but he had the distinct impression that she was actually making a statement.

"Those poor people don't want to be locked up in jail."

"Then they should stay home where they belong."

What on earth had gotten into her? She was both argumentative and judgmental. Jerry was perplexed and decided to get off this hot topic onto something more personal where he hoped there would be less unpleasant heat and maybe some of the pleasant kind that he remembered so well.

"Anyhow, I have been thinking about us. It's time I had a talk with the bishop," Jerry said. "You know, let him know that I'm seeing someone in my congregation. Bishops can get pretty squirrely about relationships between clergy and their parishioners, especially when they don't know about it."

"Jerry," she began.

But Kate was interrupted by the ringing of Jerry's cell phone. He looked at the digital read-out and recognized the number as one with the 694 prefix that identified the University Medical Center in Tucson. "This is a hospital call. I think I'd better get it."

"Of course," Kate said, appearing slightly relieved. What an odd reaction, he thought looking inquiringly at her as she turned her eyes away. He quickly answered the phone.

"Father Jerry. Thank God," he heard. "This's Lisa Brown. We were on our way from Tombstone to Tucson…partly to drop off your new chair. Something's happened to Jim. They're talking about surgery. I…I'm still not sure what has happened. I…I'm really scared."

"Relax, Lisa," Jerry said, trying to calm Lisa Brown's obvious agitation, but not succeeding. "What's happened?" His concern for her and for Jim Brown became mixed in with his mounting distress over what appeared to be a very different Kate Becker. There was definitely something wrong, in both places.

"As I said, we were on our way to Tucson—to do some shopping and…and everything, you know, to visit the kids and all—when Jim collapsed in pain. Chest and arm pain. We were just getting off the freeway onto Kino Parkway. Thank God I was driving. I took him straight to the emergency room at Kino County Hospital. You know, it's right there. *They* had him transported to UMC in an ambulance. Anyhow, nobody's saying very much, and I'm all alone. I can't reach any of the kids who live in town and the ones from Phoenix can't get here for awhile. I guess it was a heart attack. Where are you? Can you come over?"

Jerry could tell that Kate was following the conversation. He looked at her with the obvious question in his eyes, and she nodded, yes.

"Of course I can. I'm in Bisbee, but I can be there in a little over an hour. Where are you?"

"I'm in the cardiac intensive care unit. I think they're going to operate on him real soon."

"I'll be right there, Lisa. Don't you worry, now. Jim's in good health and has a great attitude. And that's one of the best heart hospitals in the country." Jerry sounded more confident than he felt. "I'll see you as soon as I can get there." He hung up the phone and asked Kate, "Can you get me to the airport real fast?"

"Yes," she said, a weak smile on her face. "What's happened? Who is it?"

"One of the parishioners from over in Tombstone, Jim Brown. I think you know him. He's an usher. It sounds like a heart attack."

She nodded her head. "I heard something about surgery."

"By-pass, I imagine. Probably just stabilizing him first. That's the usual thing."

"I was just about to ask you a favor—and disappoint you too, I'm afraid," she said. "Some things have changed—just this morning—and I have to go to Chicago for a few days. Some business I have to take care of…family stuff."

"Is somebody sick?" he asked.

"No, not exactly. But I do need to go. I have a flight from Tucson to Chicago, and I would appreciate a lift."

"Sure. No problem. Glad to have the company—especially yours." But his disappointment was bitter and sat heavily on his heart.

Getting to the airport and then aloft occupied them both. They had flown for half an hour in an increasingly uncomfortable silence, the only sound coming from the Cessna's engine as it pulled them through glass-smooth air, when, finally, Kate spoke into her head set microphone, "There's some things that I think I need to tell you before I leave." The engine noise was all Jerry heard for what seemed like a long time. Then she continued, "I really didn't mean to leave it so long, but with you planning to talk to the bishop, now I can't wait any longer."

"What's that?" Jerry asked, adjusting himself in his seat and sitting up slightly—just out of habit.

"I haven't lied to you, Jerry, but I also haven't exactly told you the full truth. Remember the other day when I told you that I'm a pleasure seeker?"

"Yes." Jerry felt his stomach begin to tighten and his breathing become shallow.

"That was only partly accurate. You see, I have a very bad history with relationships. I've had a lot of boyfriends, though mostly only one at a time. Actually, I've been married three times and divorced twice."

That revelation was a shock for Jerry, but one from which he quickly recovered. "And the third marriage?"

"That's the other part of the problem. I'm still married, Jerry. To number three. He won't give me a divorce. He's afraid...I don't know what he's afraid of, but he won't do it. We've been separated for three years, and I asked him again last month. It's the same answer. No. He won't even discuss it."

Jerry was stunned. All of a sudden, what had been two single adults harmlessly exploring a relationship that had every promise of being a lasting one, now became a married woman and her priest having a secret affair. He felt his whole life change in a moment, as if a steel prison door had slammed shut on his life. Now he understood Kate's desire to keep their relationship secret. Immediately Jerry shifted into denial.

"There must be something we can do!" he exclaimed.

"I don't know what it would be. I've been ready to file myself half a dozen times. I've even wished that he would die."

"What if I called him? Maybe even went to visit?"

"He would laugh in your face. Say something like he hopes you find me a good piece of ass." Jerry was surprised by the depth of her bitterness. "I'm really so very sorry, Jerry."

Jerry's mind was in turmoil. There had to be something they could do, some way to salvage what they had, to appeal to her husband, some alternative. But Jerry knew he was kidding himself. Outside, the roar of the aircraft engine continued, and over the radio another pilot called Tucson approach control. Finally, Jerry broke into the monotony with, "Then, we can just keep our relationship secret," knowing as soon as he had said it that he did not mean it.

"You know that isn't going to work," she said.

Jerry was struck by her calm acceptance. It even made him a little angry. How could she just go for this? They had to fight it somehow. He would resign his job. Nothing mattered at that moment, but only their fragile, new relationship. His face developed a fixed, determined expression.

In a gentle, compassionate way Kate reached out her hand and touched his cheek. She said, "I'm really very sorry, you know. I should've known better from the start, should never have let this happen."

Now Jerry understood her reticence and aloof distance ever since he had arrived at her house. She had already made the decision to do this, to tell him the full truth. Did it mean the end of their relationship? He could see no other possibility. Was that it then? One day. Nothing but a one-night stand, after all. He stole a glance at her. There was a set to her jaw that convinced him that she was determined and serious. Jerry thought about meeting with the bishop—and that was even more important now than ever. Somehow he had to explain himself to him in terms both of them would understand. Yes, it would be a very different meeting with the bishop than Jerry had expected to have.

Jerry dropped Kate off at Tucson International and then, without even turning off the engine or kissing each other goodbye, he was back in the air to make the short hop to Ryan Field for his car and to drive to the hospital for Jim and Lisa Brown. Landing at TIA and then flying to Ryan Field for his car so he could drive to UMC all felt sickeningly reminiscent of the day Art Gronek died. Any thoughts of a future with Kate Becker had just died as certainly as Art Gronek had done last Thanksgiving weekend.

As it happened, Jim Brown had emergency double by-pass surgery on the two arteries that were almost entirely blocked. Lisa was her strong, capable self and held up like a trooper until Jim was out of surgery before she broke down and cried.

The next couple of days Jerry spent a lot of time with Lisa and with Jim.

He met their children and grandchildren in and around the hospital, and Jim seemed at first well on the road to recovery. Jerry was dogged in pastoring the Brown family through their crisis, and that gave Jerry some consolation for the rest of what was happening in his life. Inside, he was a mess. He missed Kate and what he had hoped they would have together, and now knew could never have happened. He felt guilty about a relationship that should never have started in the first place, and he felt anger towards Kate for not being straight with him. But all things being equal, he should have known better than to get involved with a parishioner, no matter how innocent it may have seemed. But it all became even worse when, two days after they said goodbye at Tucson International, he got a phone call from her.

"Jerry?" He heard her distant and coldly unemotional voice say over the phone.

"Yes," he answered. "Kate? Where are you?"

"I'm still in Chicago. Going to be here for awhile—until the end of the week," said the remote voice that claimed to be Kate Becker. "Jerry, my husband wants me to come back and try it again—our marriage. I've decided to do it. As soon as the semester is over, I'm leaving Bisbee for good and coming back to Chicago."

Tidal waves of emotion hit Jerry one after another—shock, anger, bitterness, hopelessness. And then, oddly, came relief. Partly the relief came in the realization that there was nothing else he could do but accept what she had said. He had had some time to think about it, and he had to admit to himself that he was not particularly surprised. There was no future that he could see for their relationship. And it would be easier for everyone—especially for him—if she simply were no longer there.

In the midst of looking after Jim and Lisa Brown, Jerry realized that his short, intense time with Kate Becker and the power of his spiritual awareness the weekend before were connected. They were of a piece. The emotional power of a new intimate relationship and a heightened sensitivity to the spiritual dimension, both the ugliness of evil and the beauty of something new, were tightly intertwined. The gift that Kate had given Jerry was that in important ways he was alive again. And Jerry realized that this new life, following years of grief and depression, was still available to him, with or without Kate Becker.

CHAPTER THIRTEEN

The Fourth Week in Lent

Unprotected by prayer, our social activism runs the danger of becoming self-justifying good works. As our inner resources atrophy, the wells of love run dry, and we are slowly changed in the likeness of the beast.
—Walter Wink

The ringing of the phone was a welcome interruption to the barren quiet of the Bisbee studio. "Ah...is this...ah...Harold Jenkins' home?" the tentative male voice asked.

"Are you a friend of his?" Ginger cautiously asked back, not wanting to rush right into the bad news of Harold's death if the caller did not already know what had happened...or give any information away to a telemarketer.

"I never met him," answered the voice on the phone. "And I know about his death. I'm really sorry for your loss," he said, relieving her of the former worry, and then quickly disposed of the latter. "I'm Brother Joey Warnock at Holy Trinity Monastery. That's in St. David." Ginger could barely hear him, he spoke so quietly. "I'm sorry if I seem rude, but may I ask who you are?"

"I'm Virginia Vega. I worked with Harold. Is there something I can do for you?"

"I...I have a...problem." He paused for so long that Ginger began to wonder of he was still on the line. "Can I count on your...discretion?" he asked at last.

"Of course."

"There are some people here...from Mexico, Guatemala actually, who are...desperate. I wonder...since Harold...ah...helped...people, is there...ah, someone...I can call to help them?"

"Well, I'm not sure. That's not a part of Harold's life that I knew much about," she lied. There was no way Ginger was going to commit herself to anything to a stranger on the phone. She had read enough adventure novels to know that much.

"Of course, you don't know me, do you? I had thought about that. But you do know Father Hanning? From the, ah, funeral?" She admitted that she did, slightly. "If you wouldn't mind calling him," Brother Joey continued, "and then…ah…this is a lot to ask, but if you could come by the monastery to talk with me, I can explain the problem. I can't leave, you know. And I'm breaking all the rules helping these people, anyhow. I'm just a novice, you see, and I…I could be made to leave if anybody found out. I think the prior and…everyone…agree with me, but they—the whole community—are all firm that nobody here must be involved, especially in anything illegal."

"Is there a number where I can call you?" Ginger asked, as noncommital as she could be.

"Not really. But I can call you back later, say, six o'clock tonight? I'll have a little time then."

As soon as he hung up, Ginger called Maddie at the Twisted K. "Well, it's happened. More stranded people," she said to Maddie as soon as she answered, and then Ginger told her about the call from Brother Joey.

"And you want Jerry Hanning's phone number in Tucson," Maddie concluded.

"Yes."

"Do you want me to go with you to St. David? You don't have a car, do you?"

"You're right, I don't. I just thought I could borrow Harriet's…or something. Are you sure you're ready for this?" Ginger was feeling a little guilty about dragging her new friend into doing something as dangerous as this might become and to which Maddie had already agreed.

"Of course. Call Jerry, and then get back to me."

There was no answer at Jerry's home, so Ginger called the cell number Maddie had given her.

"Hello. Jerry Hanning speaking," he answered.

"Yes, Father Jerry. This is Virginia Vega."

"Oh, hello Virginia. It's good to hear from you. How are you?" His voice was warm and good natured.

"I'm okay," she answered. Once again, Ginger felt that same vague hostility rise in her. She fell back on a stiff formality. "The reason I called was because I got a phone call a little earlier from a Brother Joey Warnock—at a monastery in St. David. He said you knew him."

"That's right," he said. "What's up with Brother Joey?"

"He's trying to do something for some people he knows."

"Illegal immigrants?"

"Yes."

"And you want to know whether or not to trust him?"

"Yes."

"I know Brother Joey only very slightly, but I think he can be trusted. At least I doubt he would be a shill for the government...or the ranchers." Jerry told her about his one encounter with Brother Joey and Joey's stowing water and food in the desert. "But are you really sure you want to get involved...in all of that trouble, that is? Anything I can do to help?"

"Not right now." Ginger ignored his question about being involved with the immigrants. "I may go over to the monastery and talk to him." She did not even hint of Maddie's involvement.

"I'm sure it'll be fine—at least the conversation part. But I still think..."

"By the way, where is it, the monastery, that is?" she interrupted his return to offering unwanted free advice.

"You can't miss it. It's just south of St. David on the main road from Tombstone. On the west side of the highway."

"Thanks."

"Sure. If there's anything..."

"I'll let you know. Thanks." She hung up, realizing that once more she had been sharp with him. "I've got to get over this," she muttered to herself, thinking that he was a very nice man—for a priest.

Ginger asked herself for the fiftieth time why she wanted to help the immigrants. She cared about their plight, but while her motives included a revulsion against racism, her desire to aid them had little to do with Hispanic racial solidarity. She was appalled by the cruelty and inhumane treatment UDAs received at the hands of coyotes, ranchers and government officials on both sides of the border, but she did not feel herself to be some kind of crusader. Nor did she think of helping them as part of some great adventure, as she had before Harold's death. Actually her motives were simple and straight forward: she cared about the people, and she wanted to honor the memory of Harold Jenkins.

Brother Joey called for the second time promptly at six o'clock. Ginger and Maddie were waiting nervously to hear from him, both of them feeling on edge and uncertain about the road on which they were embarking. Half an hour after his call they pulled up beneath the monastery's fifty foot-high cross to find one lone man sitting waiting for them in the early dark.

"Virginia?" he asked when they got out of the car.

"Brother Joey?" He nodded in response.

Brother Joey had two young Guatemalans hidden down by the San Pedro—a brother and a sister. They had been abandoned by the coyote to whom they had given all their money and had no idea how either to go on or back the way they had come. Apparently, there was nowhere to go back to. They had a cousin in Denver and some vague idea that if they could only get there, they would be okay.

"I think we can help these two kids," Maddie said at last. "Do you know the abandoned airport just south of Tombstone?"

"Not really," Brother Joey answered.

"It's a little over three miles outside town. On the road to Bisbee," Ginger explained to him.

"Can you get them there by dawn?" Maddie asked.

"No problem," he said. "There's a sympathetic winter visitor down the road who would be willing to help, I think." Ginger knew there was a mobile home park less than a mile from the monastery where people often spent the winter away from the cold northern climate.

Maddie remembered that the way to the Tombstone airport from St. David passed through the same roadblock where she and Jerry and the three girls had been stopped a couple of weeks before and reminded Brother Joey of it.

"It should be okay," he said. "Cars are rarely stopped going south!" He laughed. "Going *toward* the border!" Ginger and Maddie nervously joined in his amusement at the irony of the situation.

"Then here's what you do." Maddie continued with the instructions, "Three miles the other side of Tombstone, but before you come to the airport, there's a road that breaks off to the east headed for McNeill. Davis Road it's called. Turn left there and go about a mile, maybe a little more. There's a dirt track that goes south right to the eastern end of the runway. It's not the entrance to the airport, just an extra access road." Brother Joey was nodding furiously and taking notes in a small spiral notebook. "Take them in there, off the road, and have them wait by the windsock, well hidden in the brush. It's at the mid-point of the runway—as far away from either road as you can get. You know what a windsock is?"

"Yes. We have one here for when Father Jerry comes to visit. He scares all the neighbors who think he's crashed." He giggled this time. It seemed doubtful that giggling was Brother Joey's normal response to people thinking an airplane had crashed. This much direct involvement with people—especially with women—must be radically outside the experience of the young novice, Ginger thought.

"Right," Maddie answered, also sounding nervous. "Just have them there and in hiding before dawn. I will be there in my plane as soon after sunrise as possible."

He nodded.

"And be sure to tell them that they're being picked up in a small airplane," Ginger added. "We wouldn't want them to be surprised." Maddie flashed Ginger a quick, toothy grin, knowing her reticence about flying. Ginger realized just how close she had come to feel to Maddie. It looked as if she had made a new friend out of all the turmoil around Harold's death. "I'll be there to translate for them," Ginger added.

"You're coming along?" Maddie asked, somewhat surprised.

"Of course," Ginger answered. "I wouldn't dream of having you go alone." That was actually the first moment that she knew it herself, and Ginger was probably more surprised by the realization than Maddie was. But it had been Ginger's idea, after all, that had gotten Maddie into it. The least she could do was to go along. Maddie suggested that Ginger spend the night at her place so they could be up and in the air by dawn.

"The earlier the better for picking up our passengers," she said. Ginger agreed.

They stayed up late that night at the Twisted K ranch house talking and laughing; it made Ginger feel like a kid again. She could not remember the last time she had done that with a girl friend—or for that matter, since she had had that kind of girlfriend at all. They talked about the deep losses each had recently experienced; their common experience of the deaths of loved ones deepened the growing bond between them. It was also natural that they should talk about the acquaintances they had in common: Cord and Jerry Hanning.

Maddie started off a round of laughter when she said, "Actually I've slept with both of them. In the last month."

That kind of bed-hopping did not fit with who Ginger understood Maddie to be, especially as she had hinted about some important spiritual things that were happening to her and how Maddie—at least part Jewish and not even baptized—had gone to church on Sunday. In spite of herself, Ginger could not help letting the old anti-sex religion bias creep in, no matter how offensive she had always found it to be. But being religious or spiritual—whatever that was—just did not fit in her mind with sexuality. And what was the priest doing sleeping with a woman? She gave herself a mental shake. Then Maddie told her about the night she and Jerry had slept in the same bed, but without having sex. The situation struck them as funny in an ironic way, both of them laughing hard at the absurdity of it in the retelling, tears rolling down their cheeks. Then Maddie switched to Cord—and became very serious.

"I just don't know where that's going, where it can possibly go. I'm older than he is, and I know that I'm rebounding from Art's death. I'm afraid that I'm using him, and it really can't go on much longer. But he does make me feel so much more alive. And that's exactly what I needed to feel—alive again. I can't imagine how that can be bad," she said.

"Of course it isn't," Ginger answered. "Besides, Cord acts like your trained puppy. Believe me, that's good for him. He's been a pretty cool customer with the ladies. It's good to see him fall. Enjoy," she said, giving Maddie her blessing. "But what about Jerry Hanning? What is his story? I have a hunch that he is more to you than you have admitted."

"I'm not sure," Maddie began. "Actually, I've known him pretty well—aside from our night together in bed." She laughed again. "He was really there for Art and me during the months before Art's death. I definitely am attracted to him, and I can tell that it's mutual. He has helped me with my plane and getting me flying again. But there really hasn't been anything romantic between us—except what almost happened that night—even though I have sometimes thought that there might be. Could be. Right now I think he has someone else in Bisbee. I guess it's a good thing for me that I have Cord."

"Who is she?" Ginger asked, realizing that this news bothered her, priests were not supposed to have girlfriends, were they? Clearly, she had some adjustments to make in her own thinking.

"I really don't know," Maddie said. "There's someone in the congregation I wondered about. And I could tell that Jerry was troubled about what's happening, but also excited and distracted. His daughter and her two friends stayed with the woman this last Sunday."

They shifted away from Jerry Hanning and onto the future.

"I'm going to start looking for a teaching job, here in Arizona if possible," Maddie said.

"What *I* want has become pretty simple," Ginger said. "I want to paint, even do caricatures again for tourists. But I think I've had it with modeling. Perhaps some local stuff if someone wants to paint me, but no more LA or even Phoenix. And I want to have my two daughters with me. I miss them so much!" She could feel the tears streaming down her face as she confessed this to Maddie. "I wonder if my kids can forgive me for abandoning them the way I did."

Maddie was thoughtful for a moment, and she smiled slightly and asked, "What are their names? Your daughters."

"Carmen and Elizabeth," Ginger answered, only to have Maddie's face give a quizzical look back at her and then to see her delicate features break into a wide grin.

"Was your maiden name Lopez?" Maddie asked.

That surprised her. "How did you know?"

"I know your daughters; in fact I saw them on Sunday at church here in Bisbee." She smiled again. "Your parents, of course that's who they are. It all fits. They live next door to Jerry Hanning in Tucson and your girls are pretty much inseparable from his nine-year-old daughter, Sadie. They often come with him in his plane to do his weekend sessions. They're the ones who stayed with Jerry's girlfriend in Bisbee last weekend."

Ginger sat there stunned. "You've got to be kidding," she said at last. But she knew that Maddie was not joking. Then she got really excited. "How are they? Have they grown? But you would have no way of knowing that, would you? Do they seem happy? Do they miss me?"

"What a lot of questions." Maddie smiled at her. "They seem great. I know they miss you a lot. But I also know that they think you'll be with them very soon. You recently wrote a letter, I think."

"Yes. I said I would be home soon."

"I know," she said. "Carmen read it to me."

Ginger could not believe her ears. How could this be happening? "Do you think they will be okay if I suddenly reappear on the scene?" she asked.

"Are *you* ready?" Maddie asked her back.

"I think I am. I think I can finally trust myself to be with them again." And she knew it was true as soon as she said it. First pain and then joy swept over her, both feelings exquisite in their intensities.

"Any way I can help?" Maddie asked.

And that was when Ginger really lost it. The tears flowed, and she knew how desperately she wanted to see her daughters, to be with them, to be their mom again in the day-in-day-out way she had been before. What had happened to her? She had been a good and loving mother. Then she had gone completely haywire. Could they ever forgive her?

Ginger got very little sleep that night. The combination of excitement over the prospect of seeing Carmen and Elizabeth and being with them again and the anticipation of the dawn rendezvous had her too keyed up to sleep. When she did finally drift off, she awoke feeling refreshed and as filled with energy as she ever had done in her life.

Not long after waking, Four-Five Lima took off from the Twisted K ranch while it was still dark, Refugio, the ranch foreman, providing runway lights with a pickup truck. They landed at the abandoned Tombstone airport just after dawn and taxied to the tattered windsock. It was so worn—in shreds really—that it was impossible to see it from the air in that light. But Maddie's guess on wind direction was correct, and the landing was no problem—not even for her perpetually nervous companion. The passengers, a brother and sister in their late teens, were named Hector and Maria; they were waiting as planned. Maddie had expected them to be timid getting into the small airplane, but found them quietly willing. Ginger helped them into the cramped back seats and showed them their seatbelts. She barely contained a giggle at the thought of herself as a kind of flight attendant obeying FAA rules about seats and belts. Maddie remained in the Cessna with the engine running. During the two or three minutes they were stopped by the windsock, not a single car passed by the lonely Tombstone airport on either road. Then they were taxiing back to the end of the runway. In another minute they were airborne—somewhat laboriously, with the combination of a very full plane and high altitude—and banking sharply to the right, flying directly over Tombstone as they gained altitude and headed northwest. The entire flight took about an hour. They beat their contacts, who were to pick up the passengers at the Marana airport Coffee Shop, by twenty minutes; they were on their second cups of coffee by the time they arrived. Hector and Maria nervously waited throughout for some kind of disaster to befall them. None did. The contacts soon had the young Guatemalans on their way toward Phoenix.

Ginger and Maddie were elated by their experience, one which had been both exciting and dangerous, and yet at the same time they were filled with the sense that they had done something important for two strangers whose need was desperate. Ginger was sure that Harold would have been proud of what they had done. For her part, Maddie felt useful in ways she seldom had before. Could they be blamed for thinking the sun shone brighter, the sky gleamed bluer and the desert glowed fresher? Helping the two Guatemalans had been exciting and filled with rewards, not the least of which was the profuse thanks from the young brother and sister.

And Ginger was going to see Carmen and Elizabeth within days, rather than weeks or months.

Maddie had a conviction that some very new things were on the horizon for her. Despite all of the losses they had suffered between the two of them, life looked bright. The future was something to look forward to with real anticipation.

It was two days later, when a carpenter's concerto—the sounds of creating what would soon become three bedrooms and a bathroom in a corner of Ginger's Bisbee studio—provided the soundtrack for the excited voice of Harriet Lawson, proprietor of Pots and Paint, with some very good news. To Ginger's surprise and delight, two of Harold's paintings (at double the price he had been getting) and one of her own water colors had sold that very morning. But that was only one of the reasons Harriet had stopped. Three UDAs, two Salvadorans and one Mexican, had been stranded outside Bisbee and had been picked up by one of their group. One of the Salvadorans was a pregnant woman named Marta who was desperate to get to Phoenix where her sister was waiting for her. Marta was anxious for her baby's birth to be documented in a Phoenix hospital—any Arizona hospital, really—so that it would have U.S. citizenship. "They're at the Place as usual," Harriet said.

The usual plan for dealing with the UDAs was for them to be passed on north as quickly as possible. In the meantime, one of the abandoned Phelps-Dodge mine buildings—the Place they called it—had been commandeered to keep their guests out of sight. The building, well outside Old Bisbee on the road to Douglas, was a storage shed housing old mining equipment. One of the Bisbee group, an electrician in a former life, had brought in power for a small hot plate and a tiny but effective space heater. A few blankets and a stash of canned food made the Place, if not exactly homey, at least serviceable. Happily, through some management error, a small restroom still had water supplied to its sink and toilet. The group's own combination lock on a side door provided security and it also meant that both uninvited visitors and security guards would not find an unlocked door, except when it was actually occupied. Even then it was made to look as if it were locked. Bisbee residents stayed away from the shed themselves so that no local person was seen coming and going, and their guests were always instructed to stay put once they were inside. A prepaid cell phone in the shed provided a communications link. Calls to the cell were always made on public phones so that there would be no possibility of tracing them back to one of the group. Ginger loved the

189

cloak and dagger stuff.

Ginger quickly called Maddie to make arrangements for the pick-up and transfer. "Hi," she said. "Harriet's here. We have some more friends arriving. Can you get together with them?"

Maddie quickly picked up on Ginger's meaning and purpose. "Already? Sure," she said with a grin. "I'm coming into town this evening to have dinner with Cord at his place," she said. "Why don't I stop by and see you first, say around five?"

"That's great," Ginger answered. "Oh, and by the way, two of Harold's oils and one of my watercolors have sold. I'm so excited." She beamed at Harriet.

"Terrific." Maddie changed the subject abruptly, and asked, "What about your daughters? Have you talked to them yet? Figured out what you're going to do?"

"I'm a wimp, I guess. I haven't had the nerve. Funny isn't it? I'm afraid of my own children." Ginger told Maddie about the construction going on in the studio to make rooms for her and the two girls, and then she asked Maddie's opinion, "What do you think, should I just show up in Tucson, or should I call them first—kind of warn them about what's going on?"

"Hmm." Maddie paused thoughtfully. "What do *you* want to do?"

"If I were in their shoes, I might want a little warning."

"Sounds to me like you already have a plan," Maddie said, laughing.

"I guess you're right. What am I waiting for?"

"Just what I was wondering. I'll see you about five."

Ginger hung up the receiver. She and Harriet chatted for few minutes, planning the pick-up and arranging to have more pictures framed for showing, and then Harriet went back to her studio. Ginger was left with the crashing sounds of the workmen behind opaque plastic sheeting intended to keep out the dirt, if not the noise, from the rest of the studio. The phone didn't exactly sit there glowing threateningly, but it might as well have done for how she felt. Finally Ginger pushed the familiar sequence of buttons and listened to the musical beeps.

"Hi, Mama," she said into the receiver when Margaret Lopez picked it up and gave her cheery hello.

"Virginia. I've been thinking about you all day. Is there anything...more...wrong?"

"No. Nothing wrong. In fact, everything's really good."

"And the funeral went okay? Your father and I really would have been glad to come, but I understood your need to deal with it yourself."

"It was fine. A priest—not a Catholic one—did it for us. Oh, of course you know Father Jerry, don't you? I forgot."

"Yes, Isn't it a small world? I read the story about it in the paper. It must have galled you to be called the 'live-in girlfriend.'"

"It was the truth, Mama," she said, instantly aware of that defensive tone she did not seem able to keep from her voice these days.

"I didn't mean anything by it."

"I know, Mama. Anyhow, I'm great! Now. But, I've been thinking that it's time for me to see Carmen and Elizabeth. What do you think?"

"If you feel ready," Margaret Lopez said.

"Oh, I am, Mama. I'm really doing okay. Besides, Harold left me his studio and I'm having it remodeled. So there'll be room for the girls. I'll stay on in Bisbee and really get into my own work again."

There was a long pause while Margaret Lopez adjusted to this new direction in her daughter's life and to the implications it held for her two granddaughters—and for herself. "I would hate for you and the girls to be *that* far away, but it really might be the best thing for all of you." She paused. "You know, I've really loved having Carmen and Lizzy with us, but my prayer has always been for you to be okay and for the three of you to be together again."

When Ginger called back later and spoke first with Elizabeth and then with Carmen, they were understandably very excited to hear from her.

"So, what do you think," Ginger asked Carmen, "do you want to come and see my place in Bisbee and spend the weekend with me?"

"You mean it?" she asked, excitedly. "Mommy wants us to spend the weekend with her," Carmen said away from the receiver to Lizzie.

The squealing of the two girls told Ginger that in spite of everything, they would be okay. She promised to pick Carmen and Lizzie up on Saturday morning and to bring them back with her to Bisbee to see the studio. They would sort of camp out there that night in the construction rubble. Ginger didn't know who was more excited, but she thought that it was probably her. She also thought they treated her with a bit of caution. Well, that was understandable, it would take them some time entirely to trust her again—or for her to trust herself, for that matter.

Harriet made the arrangements with their most recent group of stranded immigrants, and Ginger went with her to pick them up, well before dawn on

Saturday morning, and drive them directly to the Tombstone airport. Marta, the pregnant girl, was very frightened, but also very determined—and very relieved that Ginger was able to speak with her in Spanish.

"What is it like in Phoenix?" Marta asked.

"It's a very big city. Not like here," Ginger answered.

"Are there many police there? Will it always be dangerous for me and for my baby?"

"You will be much safer there," Ginger said and told her about Phoenix's large Spanish-speaking population and how she would melt into so many other people. Marta talked about her sister and her family. Through her fear and uncertainty about what lay ahead and the experience of being left in the desert in the company of two young men that she did not know, there was still a steely determination that nothing was going to get in the way of her child's future. Marta told Ginger that she assumed that her husband was dead. It had been six months since he had made his way north to prepare a way for her, but no trace or word had come from him since he left. She had paid the coyote everything she had saved to give her baby a new life, only to be abandoned in the desert. Now, she was not at all certain what these North Americanos were up to in helping them. And she was very uncertain about flying in a small airplane.

"I'm pretty nervous about flying, too," Ginger told her. "But the woman pilot is very good and very careful. It will be fine, and it is the safest way to get you to Phoenix."

"A woman!" Marta was quiet for a moment. "Well maybe that's okay, then. But won't you come with me," she said. "I know I would not be so frightened if you were there.

"I would be happy to go with you, but there isn't room in the airplane. It only holds four people, including the pilot."

Marta was clearly very frightened, but that look of firm determination returned. Ginger found herself liking and admiring this young woman. Suddenly her plight and her future became very important to Ginger.

When the car pulled up at the western edge of the lonely airport just before dawn, it felt kind of spooky. In the distance the yelping of a coyote— the four-legged variety—added to the ominous emptiness. A slight breeze blew across the creosote and Joshua tree landscape. Scattered spindly ocotillo bushes stood like giant upside-down spiders against the lightening dawn. The runway stretched out before them, a heavy black ribbon, marred by weeds and bushes here and there, but straight and eerie in the dawn's light. Ginger tried to imagine Maddie in a few minutes appearing out of nowhere in her small plane and finding this spot, miraculously coaxing the Cessna down onto the rough runway and then flying off again with her passengers, this time to a small airport somewhere on the western fringe of metropolitan Phoenix.

Harriet kept the car running while Ginger gave final instructions to the three very nervous people. "Just walk down the runway. Be sure to hide in the bushes if another car comes. About halfway to the other end, you'll see a pole with a kind of flag on top of it. It's called a windsock."

"I know what that is," the young Mexican man responded. Pablo was eighteen, just a bit cocky, but very protective of Marta, Ginger was relieved to discover. The other man, very thin and nervous seeming, never said a word.

"Good. Just wait there. Remain hidden in the brush until the plane comes to a stop. Just in case, make sure that the big numbers written on its side say, '8645 L.' If any other airplane stops, just stay hidden."

"Won't you come and wait with me? I know I would be less frightened if you waited with me," Marta said.

Ginger looked at Harriet. She shrugged and nodded slightly in the affirmative. "I'll come back for you at the entrance," Harriet said. "Can't sit here that long."

"Okay, Marta," Ginger said. "I'll wait with you. Let's go then."

Ginger and the three immigrants got out of the car, and Harriet quickly drove back to the main road and on toward Tombstone.

The four solitary people walked silently through the dark pre-dawn, each feeling very alone in spite of the others. Ginger kept hearing sounds of animals and birds moving through the bushes. The thought of coyotes and wolves kept creeping into her mind. Then came the haunting sound of a solitary owl, perhaps looking for its breakfast. Even though Ginger knew they had nothing to fear from the owl, still its lonely "hoot" made her feel painfully vulnerable in the middle of that empty runway. She moved toward the edge and the protecting brush, only to hear the scurry of some small animal, whose size took on enormous proportions in her imagination. That did nothing to make her feel any better. Either there was the open vulnerability of the runway or the unknowns of the desert floor. Some choice! Some help she was to Marta! Then it occurred to Ginger how terrifying this whole experience must be for the girl—young, pregnant and nearing her delivery date, practically alone in the world, and here in what was for her a hostile foreign country where people were trying to catch her. Now there was the immediate unknown of the airplane.

Finally they reached the windsock at the halfway point of the runway. It was still tattered and battered, and Ginger knew that once again Maddie would have trouble seeing it. They sat down on the ground and out of sight. Ginger's skin crawled as she sat there imagining all kinds of horrors. God alone knew what terrible desert creatures crawled around there. No one said anything. They settled in to wait. Even the air became very still, the windsock above their heads hanging in limp shreds. Gradually the pale light of dawn began to appear in the east. Then in the distance came the unmistakable sound of a small plane's engine, the steady drone incongruous in this otherwise empty desert morning. Then another sound competed with the aircraft engine as a truck passed on the Bisbee-Tombstone road, its lights casting a brilliant glow as it disappeared behind low hills. After its noise had receded, the sound of the plane was also gone and the stillness of the morning resumed. Must not have been Maddie Gronek's plane, Ginger thought. But that gave her something else to worry about. If it wasn't Maddie, then who was it? She imagined all sorts of things—the Border Patrol? The military?

Marta stirred beside her, and she reached out a hand and touched the girl's shoulder reassuringly. She wondered to herself just who this reassurance was intended to serve—Marta or herself. A car passed by on the highway, its lights looking faded in the growing dawn. And then there was the sound of another aircraft engine. This time it grew louder and louder. Ginger could see its navigation lights blinking in the brightening sky. The plane was quite low now, coming closer and closer to where they waited. Then it passed overhead in a roar and a stirring of the air. Maddie—surely it *was* Maddie— must have been no more than a few hundred feet off the ground. Ginger watched as the plane banked steeply and lined up on the runway. In a moment it was down and taxiing toward where they waited. It was an impressive landing, as smooth and steady as an airliner. Marta looked at Ginger and smiled bravely, but nervously.

Ginger helped all three of Maddie's passengers into the plane, assisting Marta into her seatbelt next to Maddie. In a moment they pulled away, and Ginger stood alone waving to Marta. She felt strangely sad and yet elated at the girl's departure, her hair and clothes blowing and flapping furiously in the blast of air behind the taxiing Four-Five Lima. And then the Skyhawk was finally airborne and gradually gained altitude as it turned toward Tombstone.

Ginger felt very much alone in the still-dim light of early dawn. Even the birds and the small animals in the brush had become quiet, perhaps frightened by the airplane noise. Then she heard, breaking through the silence, the sound of another plane overhead coming directly toward her. She stopped walking to listen and to look, at first thinking Maddie was coming back. But then she glanced toward Tombstone and could still see the retreating plane's blinking lights. In another moment, a red and white airplane was circling very low over the empty Tombstone airport—empty, that is, except for Ginger. She thought at first that it might land, but instead, it just circled the airport— once and then a second time. She felt naked and exposed standing there at the side of the runway with only a creosote bush as protection. The craft came so close to her that she could see the silhouette of the pilot clearly. Finally, the plane banked sharply to the east, and, as Ginger stood transfixed watching it, vanished into the light of the rising sun. Shaking with fear and exhaustion, and in the let-down after the adrenalin rush she had felt watching Marta and her companions being spirited away, Ginger resumed her interrupted walk in the chill morning air back along the side of the landing strip toward the entrance, pulling her light coat around her as she went. But there was no hurry as Harriet's car had not yet appeared. She sat down on a large rock beside the dusty airport entrance road and waited, watching the sun, dancing red and orange over thin, high scattered clouds as it came up over the desert mountains. It seemed like a very long time before Harriet finally arrived twenty minutes later. Ginger smiled with relief and began to get into the car when another vehicle, a white and green Border Patrol Blazer with full emergency lighting on the roof, pulled off the main road into the airport entrance. Ginger watched from the front seat beside Harriet as it came to a stop.

"Oh, my God," Ginger said to Harriet.

Two uniformed guards got out of the Blazer, one on each side of Harriet's car. They were intense in their watchfulness. One of them had his hand resting on the sidearm on his belt. The man on Ginger's side of the car, a very handsome Latino, took one look at Ginger and smiled broadly. She thought at first he was going to come on to her. That look would have scared her out there in that lonely place if Harriet had not been beside her. Then she realized that the look was not so much a leer as it was a gloat. It was as if he said, "Gotcha."

"Kind of early to be out here isn't it?" the guard asked Ginger in Spanish.

"The best time of the day," Ginger responded, also in Spanish without even thinking about it.

He smiled again and said, "I think you both had better come with us."

Then it dawned on Ginger. He thought she was a UDA and that Harriet was her coyote, or at least a contact. It was time to put an end to that kind of thinking. Black hair, dark eyes and olive skin was enough! Talk about "racial profiling!" She switched into her best, university-educated English.

"Why precisely should we go anywhere with you? Is there any reason why two adult women should not be out here watching the sunrise?"

He looked a little startled. She watched him make a mental gear shift.

"Perhaps I should see some ID," he said.

His partner made a gesture toward Harriet and said, "You, too, Ma'am."

Ginger fished into her purse for her wallet as Harriet quickly found hers and handed it over. Ginger pulled out her Arizona driver's license, some credit cards, a library card and an old UA student photograph ID that she still carried for nostalgic reasons. The Border Patrol guard studied each one carefully and looked at her in the apparently intense way that people do when they are trying to get something right—and are feeling just a bit foolish.

"Sorry," he said. "But we received a report about an airplane taking off from here a little while ago. Can't be too careful, you know. It's our job."

Ginger said nothing, just put her possessions back in the wallet and the wallet into her purse.

Harriet said, "If that's all, we'd like to be on our way to breakfast."

"Yes, that's fine," said the guard on her side of the car, looking purposefully into the back seat of the car. "Have a nice day."

The guard beside Ginger just nodded as Harriet pulled away.

"Let's get out of here," Ginger said to Harriet as she began to laugh uncontrollably, hysterically.

Ginger's internal glow grew as the old white four-wheel-drive Subaru Maddie had lent her sped into Tucson along Interstate 10 later that same morning. It all felt so familiar, the same old landmarks and streets. And then she was in her old neighborhood: seventy-five-year-old stuccos interspersed with newer houses, usually brick and mostly from the 1960s. Some of the yards were well tended and manicured. Others looked as if neither a hoe nor a shovel had been put to them in years. That was Tucson. It really felt like home.

Her parents' house was one of the red-brick bungalows, book-ended by a nineteen thirties stucco on either side. Ginger wondered which one was Jerry

Hanning's. She could see that Papa had been busy in the yard. The dazzling revelry of a yard full of yellow Arizona poppies, chaotic in their spread, was bordered by well-trimmed shrubs and desert plants. She knew that as soon as the poppy season was over that new bedding plants, especially zinnias, would begin to appear under her father's sure hand. Ginger and her sister, Lucy, always teased Papa that he just could not root out the landscaper that was native to his Mexican blood, which was pretty funny, since he was nearing retirement as a pediatrician. Dr. Charles (or, if you knew him well, Carlos) Lopez usually joked back that when he did retire, he was going to go out and find an old Chevy pick-up and load it down with just the right landscaping tools and go into business. The irony was that Ginger could not imagine anything that would make him happier than puttering around in desert yards and gardens—so long as he had some children around to keep him young. He loved his work and he loved his gardening.

Mama was as surprising to some people as Papa was. Her career as a Spanish literature professor at the University of Arizona had ended with early retirement two years before Ginger crashed and ran away from the horror of Joel's death. A beauty who had not succumbed to the spreading flesh syndrome that besets many women when they reach their sixties, Mama was a petite little bundle of energy who had raised two daughters while following her own career. It was a good thing that she had taken early retirement, considering that Ginger saddled her, and Papa, with her two daughters for a year. A wave of guilt spread over her, but she shook it off quickly. This was not the time to look back.

Ginger was ready to be with her girls again, could begin to trust herself with their upbringing, perhaps in ways she could never have done before. The phrase "sadder and wiser" was probably true about her. But that was not quite the right way to describe who she had become. There was an underlying sadness, perhaps, but the truth was more complex than that. Ginger felt as if she had grown up. Her emotions were on the surface in ways they had never been before—certainly not since before the rape when she was fifteen which had shut down her feelings before she'd ever had a chance really to discover them. And now these newly recovered feelings were the emotions of a mature woman, not of an immature girl.

Ginger and Margaret Lopez talked over coffee as they waited for Carmen and Elizabeth to get home from their soccer practice. Papa always took them for it. Ginger became more and more excited the longer she waited. When the girls finally arrived and saw their mother, they squealed as one and ran to her, enfolding her in their little arms and burying their heads into her stomach. Ginger's heart pounded and tears filled her eyes. Still she pushed back and looked at them and then pulled them to her again, over and over. She could not get enough of looking at her girls, or touching them, or holding them.

CHAPTER FOURTEEN

Mid Lent

Now there is rejoicing in heaven; for you were lost, and are found; you were dead, and are now alive in Christ Jesus.
—Book of Common Prayer

Recent events had made Jerry Hanning feel like some kind of innocent. His blazing new romance had turned into a pile of cold ashes in only a week, leaving behind it both emptiness and guilt over having had an affair with a married parishioner. No matter how innocent his intentions may have been, those were the facts. Kate Becker *was* married and she *was* a parishioner. Jerry's distress grew daily over his need to speak to the bishop and what such a conversation might mean for his future. He felt vulnerable in the current climate of very real concern about sexually predatory clergy. He wanted very badly to feel good about all that had happened with Kate, but he could not get out of his head the fear that he had used her inappropriately—not that she had been unwilling. Far from it. But still, the taboo was a serious one, and one that existed for very good reasons. Clergy simply could not treat their parishioners like objects to meet their own personal needs, sexual or otherwise. It was not, for Jerry, an issue of having sex. It *was* one of having sex with someone who should have been off limits. But, then, who *was* off limits and who was within them? What was a legitimate relationship for clergy and what wasn't? He knew that in some ways, he deserved to be removed from the Bisbee church as its vicar. But he very badly did not want that to happen. He liked it there and was beginning to develop some very good relationships in the congregation.

Theological discussion proved impossible Saturday evening in the St. Peter's book group. There was too much excitement over the NCAA basketball tournament that was in full swing. The local favorite University of Arizona team had won its second game and would now be moving forward toward the play-offs; memories of the recent national championship were still fresh. So the evening was filled with good-natured fun, but it was not particularly productive, at least as far as the agenda was concerned. Some bottles of wine materialized, and they talked about basketball and sports, parish life and hopes—and avoided their intense discussion topics of previous weeks. When they finished and were ready to leave, Jerry was glad of an earlier invitation to stay at Hank and Teresa Tucker's home in town—Teresa's family home, actually—rather than he and Sadie just going to the Simmons House Hotel as usual. That would have seemed pretty lonely now for Jerry. Having had Kate Becker in his life, however short a time it had been, had given him a sense of belonging to someone and having had something to look forward to. Now all that was left was a hotel room and a lonely night. That had seemed for a time to work okay for him and for Sadie, but no longer—for either one of them.

So Jerry and Sadie went with Hank and Teresa after the group's meeting. Teresa's Bisbee house, nineteen-twenties charm and period feel with warm wood and slightly fussy Victorian decor, at first seemed incongruous in Bisbee. But the more he thought about it, the more Jerry realized that it suited Teresa down to the smallest spoon-back chair. Elegant, understated—and capable of making a person feel pretty uncomfortable on occasion. In fact, that was an accurate description of Teresa herself. She had the ability to cut to the heart of disputes, say difficult things when she thought they needed to be said, and make a person feel uncomfortable about shoddy, unexamined opinions on important subjects. Hank admitted to Jerry that Teresa had suggested that he talk with his priest, hence this evening's invitation. A grumpy Sadie—who had made no bones about preferring to be with friends than hanging out with a "bunch of old people"—was settled into bed. Hank led Jerry into the book-lined living room, poured huge Jim Beams, neat, for both of them, put on a Billie Holiday CD and told Jerry that he was having a change of heart over illegal immigration and about personally being a vigilante, but he worried that his changing opinion was primarily out of disdain for Charlie Snow.

"But he's the crumbiest little turd I've ever known," Hank exclaimed. "It's people like him that give ranchers in the Sulphur Springs Valley a bad name. In fact, it's people like him that give *people* a bad name."

Jerry had laughed out loud and then tried to resume a more serious expression.

"I don't know what first clued me in to him. Maybe it's his so-called sense of humor, which consists of saying the word 'fuck'—no offense, Father, and talking about tits and ass. Now, I'm not unmoved by feminine beauty and I'm not a prude, but on Charlie's tongue references to the fair sex are just crude. Not even Mrs. Findlay and the other older ladies escape Charlie's snide comments. There is something distinctly *not* funny in imagining how low *her* bosoms droop."

Jerry had smiled behind his hand.

"And he's so damn cruel." Hank was steaming. "I once saw him beat a month-old calf with a broken piece of fence post for nothing more serious than its being too slow going where he wanted it to go. Another time I saw him twist a beast's ear until it bled. He laughed. Laughed! Shoot!"

Hank gathered himself and continued. "And he doesn't treat his ranch hands much better. If he dared, he would probably try to beat them, too. At least he's smart enough to know that too much of that with his men would end up with him getting the crap beat out of him. Maybe calling him a crumby little turd is too good for him," Hank had snorted.

Jerry failed at trying to come up with moderating words.

"Yeah, then there's his callous attitude toward the death of our portrait painter, Harold Jenkins. This is too much, even for Charlie. He actually said they got what they deserved. Got what they deserved! Can you believe that? You should have heard what he said to me in the church kitchen last week."

Jerry remembered how, after a heated conversation with Charlie Snow, Hank had been thoroughly subdued for the rest of the evening.

"'So,' Charlie says, Hank continued, "'how about those wet-backs and their Bisbee buddy? Got theirs, didn't they?'

"'How's that?' I ask him, but knew I shouldn't have, knew I was about to have to listen to him prattle on and on in his whiny way about something.

"'I guess one of *our* people got them,' Charlie says.

"The way he said *our* meant that he saw me as one of his cohorts. 'Got *who*? One of *our* people? What are you talking about Charlie?' I ask.

"'Caught a car load trying to get through on a dirt road over the Santa Ritas into Green Valley. Ran the assholes right off the road, he did,' Charlie says.

"'Charlie Snow, what the hell are you talking about?' I ask. It was all I could do to stop from wiping the supercilious smile off his nasty little face. So he tells me the horrible story of a carload of Illegals being run off the road, their car rolling over many times into the bottom of a wash. We learned later, remember, that the police described this as one more in a string of deliberate acts of violence against the Illegals. Apparently Charlie was in it up to his big ears, though I doubt that he had the guts actually to do anything himself. The thing that makes me so mad, besides the nastiness of the cold blooded act itself, was Charlie's suggestion that somehow the culprits were *my* people, too.

"'And guess who it was that did it?' he asks me, still grinning like the moron he is.

"'Just a damn minute, Charlie Snow,' I says. I could feel the blood running to my face. I gave myself a mental shake, trying not to lose control. So I says, 'Are you saying that you know who it was that ran those people off the road?' Charlie just grinned, and I swear he giggled a little.

"'I don't want to hear one damn thing from you—not about this, or anything else.' I says. 'You're a sick person!' But what Charlie had said made me very uncomfortable. It had never occurred to me before, but these people are likely to be ones I know. After all, I do know most of the ranching families in Cochise County." Hank got up and began to pace back and forth in the huge kitchen.

"That night I just sat there thinking about what Charlie had said, imagining those poor people inside that car as it rolled over and over until it came to a stop at the bottom of that wash. I even imagined someone driving away, proud of what he had done. When I saw the story later that night on the news, it was even more horrible than I imagined. Only one of them still alive! The driver, a law breaker certainly, was not a coyote but was somebody I actually knew, someone who had painted our wedding portrait—and done a fine job of it, too—and came with his girlfriend to our wedding. That night I dreamed I was being chased by the devil, who was going to kill me," Hank added. "The devil looked just like Charlie Snow." He took a deep breath.

This last comment made Jerry feel very uncomfortable as he remembered his vision that same night and how he had imagined Charlie as a personification of evil.

"Anyhow, I no longer see the Illegals in the same light," Hank continued. "So am I just reacting to Charlie Snow?"

"I doubt that," Jerry had responded. There was no way Hank Tucker would make a fundamental shift on principle over something as petty as a personal dislike.

"But," Hank had continued, "I just don't have the stomach for it any more. I'm not sure that we were ever right doing what we did. Oh, Charlie may certainly have had some reverse influence on me. Kind of like raising my consciousness, so to speak. But, there are just too many things going on around here that I don't understand—and flat out don't like. My neighbors, like Charlie, are becoming pretty crazy over it all. And I don't like all the armed men all over the county. It feels like I'm living in a police state."

Jerry looked at his senior warden over the rim of his whiskey glass. Billy Holiday was singing ironically about how a good man was hard to find. "The question is, just what do you intend to do about your changing opinions?" Jerry asked. They looked at each other long and hard. A new song began, "Speak Low When You Speak Love."

Hank laughed and said, "I guess Billie has it right. Maybe I need to begin to speak low but firmly about all of this. I'm not about to go on a campaign against my neighbors, mind. But I also don't feel good being part of it anymore. For one thing, I *can* begin to cast a blind eye toward anyone who crosses my land." A long silence had intervened, then he had added, "But I really want to *do something* to make this better." He put down his glass and looked almost fierce in his determination. "But what can I *do*?"

"Don't you know the governor?" Jerry asked. "And about everybody else who is anybody in Republican politics in this state?"

"I guess I do," Hank said somewhat pensively. "Even a few Democrats— besides you, that is." He grinned.

"The way everything has gotten tighter and, I gather, even more intense around the border since September Eleventh, voices like yours are needed to argue for clear and compassionate thinking. Why don't you throw your political weight around a bit? Maybe the solution to the illegal entering is to find ways of making it legal."

"You're right," Hank said, becoming very thoughtful. "I've been thinking along those same lines. The answer is to work out some orderly way to bring in the labor that so many farmers and contractors seem to want and need— without putting the workers' lives in danger, cutting them off from their families, creating border incidents…and tromping all over our land here." Hank rubbed his chin, picked up his glass, and took a full swallow of the whiskey. "By damn, that's something to think about. Thanks, Jerry."

Kate Becker was back in church the next morning. She came in a little late, just after Jerry had come to the conclusion that she would not be there. He wondered if she had planned it that way to avoid awkwardness. He had just begun the Kyrie, "Lord have mercy."

"Christ have mercy," the congregation responded.

"Lord have mercy," Jerry continued. "The Lord be with you."

"And also with you."

"Let us pray." Jerry read the collect for the Fifth Sunday in Lent.

Kate had just slipped into her usual spot and settled down onto her knees. Then she looked up at Jerry. Their eyes met. He thought that she might be crying, but he could not be sure. Jerry felt like he had been stabbed in the chest with a knife.

The congregation sat for the readings and the psalm. Everyone stood for the Sequence Hymn and then the Gospel, the story of the raising of Lazarus, and Jerry began the sermon. He was talking about the many ways in which people can serve and care for each other in the way Jesus loved Lazarus and his sisters, Martha and Mary. But his mind wandered. He realized how true that same statement was for him, how many ways that people had cared for him in the course of his life. And in that moment he knew the truth of what Fr. Benedict had said to him—that in a deep sense, he and Kate had been loving catalysts for each other, the occasion for each of them to move out of being emotionally stuck. She had been led to a decision to go back home and try to make some sense out of her marriage and her trouble having lasting relationships. Jerry moved out of grieving, sorry-for-himself alienation, and into the crisp fresh air of a renewed life. They had received nurturing from each other in exactly the ways they needed it, and now they could each move on. Whatever happened with the bishop, he now felt that he had a different perspective on the whole wonderfully painful interlude—and felt better about it, less guilty of some kind of abuse. He only hoped that Kate felt the same way.

Jerry walked down the center aisle continuing the sermon, one of the ways he liked to preach. As he went by pew after pew, he reached out and touched the shoulders of some of those sitting on the aisle as he told stories of people caring deeply about each other, some of them right there at St. Peter's and using the preaching opportunity subtly to encourage new relationships between the two factions—Bisbee and Tombstone—in the St. Peter's congregation. When he came to Kate Becker, he touched her shoulder and gave her a little smile. She smiled back. He finished the sermon and returned to the chancel for the rest of the service.

Jerry now felt confident that there would be little discomfort or awkwardness when he and Kate saw each other. When she came through the line at the door following the service, they hugged briefly and warmly.

Kate said, softly, "Thanks, Jerry."

He nodded and squeezed her arm. His heart was thumping, but it was okay—okay for both of them, he thought. Despite the sadness and loss, much warmth still existed between them.

CHAPTER FIFTEEN

The Fifth Sunday in Lent

The Christian life involves a journey inward (the hatching of the heart) and a journey outward. Our journey outward as followers of Jesus, as advocates of the dream of God, as the church, calls us to be a community of compassion and the leaven of compassion in the world.
—Marcus Borg

Maddie was scheduled to pick up stranded immigrants for the third time early that next Sunday morning, and the details were pretty much the same as on the first two flights. Her two passengers would, as before, be waiting at the Tombstone airport where she would arrive shortly after dawn. Cord would be waiting there with them and would fly along with Maddie as Ginger had done the first time.

"You really must be very careful," Ginger had said to her the night before on the phone. Maddie could hear the happy sounds in the background as Carmen and Lizzie explored their mother's studio home. "There is something going on here. I can just feel it. You know, the Border Patrol showing up the way they did the last time."

"Cord and I have a plan," Maddie answered. "He'll carry a cell phone, and I'll have my ranch pager set to vibrate in my shirt pocket. If there's any reason why I shouldn't land, Cord'll push the one button on the phone that calls the pager. I'll just fly away…into the sunrise." She laughed.

Ginger joined Maddie in a mirthless laugh of her own, one carrying little conviction. "I'm sorry, but I just can't shake the feeling that you're in danger," she said finally. "But I *do* feel better knowing Cord will be with you."

Maddie was also relieved that Cord would be with her, but that relief did not replace her gnawing concern about her relationship with him. Just where *was* this going? Maddie had asked herself that question ever since their first time together. Even though he excited her sexually, Maddie knew she was not in love with him. Long term? She did not think so. The shallowness of her commitment was inscribed in a conversation they had had early on.

"This is very embarrassing," Maddie had said, "but regardless of my brand new and wonderful familiarity with your body, I don't even know your name." She had caressed Cord's hard, bare stomach as they had lain in bed the day after finding Harold Jenkins' crashed car. "What kind of a wanton have I become?" She had laughed again. It was clear that she did not feel embarrassed. She felt good, very good.

They had just made love in a curiously thoughtful and, at least for Maddie, especially nurturing way, allowing the sorrow and nightmare of that weekend's events to flow out of them. And then it had suddenly occurred to her how little she knew about this man, including his name.

Cord had leaned over and lightly kissed her on the lips.

"My name is no great mystery," he said. "A bit of a mouthful, that's all. Jennings Albert Cording, III. You see why I prefer 'Cord'?"

Maddie laughed. "I'll bet there's some murky family history there," she said.

"You guessed it. Partly it's that family history that brought me here. Believe me, Bisbee, Arizona, is both literally and figuratively about as far from Boston and the Cordings as it could be."

But as Maddie found out over the next few days, this image of Cord as the young rebel fleeing parental domination was really a joke, even a pose which he enjoyed striking. Cord's parents were both lawyers in large East Coast firms. Both of their fathers before them had been lawyers, recently retired, and Maddie got the impression that several generations before them were also members of the Massachusetts Bar. As an eldest child, Cord assumed that he would continue the family tradition. And he had tried, but his heart was not in it. There seemed to have been no particular family crisis over his decision to pursue art, and he was able to support himself with the proceeds of a family trust in his name. His parents had even been to Bisbee to visit, declaring it "charming in a wild-west sort of way."

But while she liked getting to know Cord and did enjoy his company, Maddie found that when she was away from him, she did not really miss him. She was not jealous of him. She did not worry about him. In fact, she realized that she hardly thought about him at all. It just felt good to be in someone's company. She struggled with a sense of guilt over it being so soon, less than five months, after Art's death. How could she have become sexually involved already? And that made her suspicious of her feelings—

and her motives—in the relationship with Cord. He clearly cared for her and treated her at one moment like a visiting dignitary, at another like a china doll, and at another like a sensuous bundle of nerve ends laid out for him to play like a well-tuned musical instrument. And he played her well and thoughtfully. But Maddie knew this was an interlude for her—a temporary stop along the way—the way to where?—nothing more. She resolved to break it off with Cord without letting it go on any longer.

Maddie also found herself at odd moments (lots of odd moments) asking herself some new questions that seemed both very different from and yet, strangely, also connected to the ones she had about her relationship with Cord. These were questions about meaning: Where were the meaningful places in her life? Who was God, for that matter? What did the word "god" even mean? What did it mean to be a Jew? How did her Jewish heritage fit in with the things that were happening in her life? Just what was her life about? For the first time, Maddie realized that she had missed something important by her parents' disconnect from religion. An entire cultural world seemed to be missing from her life.

Being Jewish had always held an emotional primacy with her, perhaps because she had always identified more with her mother than with her father. Maddie had just always accepted that Judaism was her heritage—a piece of the matrilineal descent that she knew was a part of the ancient faith. And she went through periods of intense pride and satisfaction in that heritage. But she still did not know what it meant to be a Jew.

And, then, what did it mean to be a Christian? Was that only about believing that Jesus was the Jewish Messiah? She was unable to see what that contention had to do with any contemporary Christians she knew. There were the "Jeeeezus" Christians, the ones who talked about how they were saved and that "Jeeeezus" was their personal savior. Those were not the Christians that she related to. More her speed were the ones like Jerry Hanning, Ike McWarder (insofar as he could be called a "Christian"), Ginger, and, yes, even Cord. But none of these seemed to care one way or the other about whether or not Jesus was the Jewish Messiah. All of the Christian people she knew were looking for meaning, were searching—not for a Messiah so much as for a spiritual focus. Her experience of Jews was that they were not so much looking for something as they were trying to be faithful to something. She liked the idea of being faithful, of following prescribed rituals and practices. A piece of her felt a hunger for that kind of connection. But Maddie was more like her Christian friends, because she was searching, too. But her Jewish roots had to become a part of her search, along with the journey, as Jerry Hanning put it, with her Christian friends in Bisbee and Tombstone who, like herself, were looking for an ill-defined something that would help explain their lives and give them personal definition.

Maddie was very glad that she and Jerry had not had sex the night they spent in the same bed together. It meant that, even though the sexual tension between them remained, the barriers to his being her friend were much less than they would otherwise have been. The day of Harold Jenkins' funeral, while Harold's friends were talking among themselves, she and Jerry had had a few minutes for a conversation that became very important to her.

"You know, Jerry," Maddie had said, "some interesting things have been happening for me." They were standing in front of some of Harold's paintings, to which Jerry's attention seemed to wander—to the one of Ginger's erotic beauty, certainly, but also to one of an elderly man sitting in front of one of the saloons in Brewer's Gulch and another of a battered Victorian house. "Hey, remember me? Earth to Jerry," Maddie said.

Jerry seemed a bit embarrassed. "Sorry. But these pictures really are very good," he said. "And I don't just mean the one of Ginger." He laughed self-consciously. "Looking at them helps me to unwind from the service, I guess."

For some reason Maddie had found herself being very annoyed with him just then. For his apparent distraction? She had been unsure just why. She had been tempted to drop the subject entirely, but she really did need to talk to him about what was happening with her.

"There are some spiritual things happening with me," she reluctantly resumed. "I feel like a new person, or, rather, a *different* person."

"You mean like Ike McWarder identifying you with Julian of Norwich?"

"Exactly. I've been…um…having…actually, realized I have always had…experiences. What our book calls 'mystical.' Anyhow, I've got this need to explore my spiritual life, in my roots, you know. Wherever. But I really don't know where to start."

"What do you want to do?" Jerry asked. He looked directly into her eyes. And that gave her a very strange sensation. It felt to Maddie as if she had a constriction in her throat. She looked away.

"I want to be, what do you call it, led?" she asked. "But it's hard to let go of the idea of having a destination, some kind of a goal to be working toward. With a clear goal, I could map out the route, kind of like flying cross country. This is not what I'm used to."

Jerry looked at Maddie with a kind of wisdom that she had forgotten he had, except perhaps instinctively, and maybe that was why she had needed to talk to him. His concentration now seemed fully on her. He said, "Probably the hardest part of following a spiritual path, as you say, is letting go of the goal and simply getting into the experience, walking the path." He ran his fingers through his hair in an oddly focused kind of way. "Especially since having goals and pursuing them is also important for spiritual wholeness. It's a dilemma I struggle with constantly. There's a principle, put particularly well in Hinduism, I think, that goes something like, 'disassociate yourself from the fruits of your action.' By letting go of the results, it's easier to get into the experience. But I wonder if that's always desirable?

"There's a story about a medieval pilgrim who comes upon stone masons working on a building. The pilgrim asks the first mason, 'What are you doing?' The mason answers, 'Chipping stone.' He asks the second mason, 'What are *you* doing?' The second mason replies, 'I'm earning wages so I can support my family.' When he asks the third mason the same question, the answer is, 'I'm building a great cathedral.' Which one has the right answer?"

Maddie sucked on a finger for a moment, "Well, I guess it's supposed to be the third mason—building a great cathedral. But...but that doesn't seem quite right." She laughed. "This is a parable worthy of Jesus." She reached out her hand and lay it gently on his chest for a moment.

It was Jerry's turn to feel a lump in his throat. "High praise," he managed to say. "But the story is not original with me. I like it because it feels true." He was thoughtful for a moment. "Can't the first and second masons also appreciate the building as it goes up? And doesn't the third mason also support himself and his family? And maybe all three can take pleasure in chipping the stone. For that matter, what if the pilgrim had come on another day, would he have gotten identical answers from his three masons? Sometimes the right answer is that there is no right answer."

Jerry's little parable and its rejection of exclusive truth had helped Maddie to give herself permission to explore, to sample, really to try it all. She could be part of a Christian community in Bisbee at what she was thinking of as "our" small church and with people she was coming to love. And she could pursue her Jewish heritage. She had no family observances in which to participate, no Shebat to celebrate. But she could and did find out when Sabbath services were held at a Reformed congregation in Tucson. At least she knew enough about contemporary Judaism to know that the Reformed tradition was likely to be the one that would best suit her. She was very excited by all the possibilities laid out before her, but she was also a little scared by them. There was no doubt that experience as a Jew was part of her immediate future.

Maddie was up that Sunday morning at five o'clock, dressed to go to church later in Bisbee, and had some toast and coffee. Despite the ordinariness of the preparations, she felt an uneasiness in the pit of her stomach that was different from the excitement she had felt on the two previous flights. Probably that only came from Ginger's fears, she told herself. But still, she was more than half expecting to get a call from Cord telling her that something had gone wrong and that they would not be going this morning. Maddie was pacing nervously when Refugio knocked at the door and, shaking his head at what she was up to, told her that he was ready with the truck to give her some light on the runway.

"You must be very careful," he said. "Some of these people—the ones who come in from Mexico—are not very nice. I don't like to think of you being alone with some of them." As usual Refugio was being protective of her.

"Thanks for caring. But one of my Bisbee friends is going to be with me this morning." They walked together to the runway. Refugio just shook his head.

Maddie finished preparations and started up the Skyhawk, which was reluctant in the crisp morning air. It would catch and then sputter to a stop. She feared it would not start at all. Once again she twisted and pulled out the priming valve, let the fuel run into it and pushed it home. Then she did it again, and a third time. Finally, the engine caught and kept turning with a confident roar. The left-side door banged shut in the rush of air that washed back from the propeller. Maddie went through the check list as the engine warmed. Oil pressure okay. Running and landing lights on for take-off. Transponder tested and on, set for altitude. Radio on and set to the Sierra Vista/Libby Air Force Base frequency. Gyros set. Altimeter set to the approximate ranch altitude of 4350 feet. There was not a cloud in the sky. The stars and moon, despite the false dawn appearing in the east, were astonishingly brilliant. Maddie reveled in the throb of the engine and the star-studded night sky, a dazzling display away from the light pollution of city life. Everything checked out. There was a gentle breeze blowing almost exactly in line with the runway. Conditions could not be better.

The one thing that always worried Maddie taking off in this minimal light from the ranch strip was the possibility of a small animal running across the runway. She had long since resolved that she must not swerve or take any other evasive action should a rabbit cross her path. That was too vulnerable a moment to take chances. The rabbits would have to take theirs.

With everything ready, she ran up the engine and checked the magnetos and the carburetor heat. Everything was fine. Then she pushed in the throttle, feet still firmly on the brakes, to raise the rpms, and only then did she begin the run to get up speed for lift off from the dirt strip. As always, she was relieved that no rabbits decided to make the dash in front of her, though, as usual, at least one ran alongside the speeding aircraft. She edged the nose wheel off the ground and the airspeed picked up quickly, the wheels bouncing over the uneven surface, small pebbles clattering against the Skyhawk's undercarriage. And then with a smoothness and steadiness that always gave her a little exhilaration, Four-Five Lima was airborne and climbing rapidly in the fresh, cool morning air. Maddie quickly made a left turn and headed away from Tombstone and toward the Bisbee airport, skirting west of Mule Mountains. The second she was in the air she knew that the Cessna would be tracked by the radar at Libby Air Force Base, and indeed, she needed to call in and let them know who she was.

"Libby, this is Cessna Four-Five Lima squawking VFR," she checked to make sure the transponder showed 1200, "out of ranch base doing touch-and-gos at Bisbee and then Tombstone and west to Tucson."

"Roger, Four-Five Lima. Traffic quiet this morning, ma'am."

"Thank you, sir. Four-Five Lima." That should cover what I'm up to, she thought.

Her mind ranged back over the previous day as she continued to sort what it had been like to attend Shebat, Sabbath morning services at the temple in Tucson. There was something both familiar and yet strange in the experience. With the exception of the religious symbols and men wearing yarmulkes, it was visually much like attending a large Episcopal service in a nineteen fifties brick building: pews, a raised area, a bit more like a stage than in most Episcopal churches she had attended with Art, but still a raised central focus. It was very musical, again, not unlike some sung services she had attended in the Episcopal Church. The Rabbi and cantor both had extraordinarily fine singing voices—much better than any priests she had heard conducting church services. Torah was read ritually, psalms were sung. All in all it quite shocked her to discover how similar it all was.

But the differences were equally startling. The use of Hebrew, the worship book's movement from right to left (at least in the book if not actually on the pages themselves), and the very different character of the music. Rhythms, harmonies and melodies all were strangely exotic and "foreign" sounding, Middle Eastern. For some reason, she had thought that it would sound more familiar to her. There was also something different in the pace of the liturgy. The only word she could find to describe her experience of it was "frenetic." An energy seemed to flow in a compelling kind of way that moved from one reading or prayer to another, never quite seeming jumbled, but also just slightly ahead of her comfort level. It lacked the stately quality of the Episcopal liturgy, but more than made up for that in the way she felt drawn in—even as confused as she often felt—and almost driven toward the next part. She found herself shaking with exhaustion and exhilaration at the end of the service. In Maddie's imagination, it felt like coming home to a place that she knew should feel familiar, but was not, to a place that resonated deep within herself, and yet had more to do with her lizard brain than any conscious memory she had. Could just having "Jewish blood" create that kind of response in her? Did she carry some archetypal folk memory that transcended her experience, even that of her parents? All she knew was that she had to sort out the jumble of feelings that she felt, that she had to get out of there as quickly as possible, and that she absolutely had to go back. Indeed, she could not wait for next Saturday. Maddie had slipped out immediately after the service ended and practically fled to her car. Yet as she drove away she could not take her eyes off the building, feeling a mounting sense of loss as she drove away. But that was yesterday.

Maddie flew the short few miles to the Bisbee airport that Sunday morning just as dawn was breaking, made a quick touch-and-go at the quiet strip and then circled around the east side of Mule Mountains and the town of Bisbee, hugging the ground as closely as possible. She reached Tombstone just as there was light enough to land on the rough, unmarked surface of the runway, flying low over the windsock, which, to her surprise, was brand new. What a difference from the tattered, virtually invisible old sock that had fluttered largely uselessly the last time she was there. Jerry Hanning? She thought it probably was his doing.

The pager under her jacket remained still.

She banked the Cessna sharply to the left and came around, more or less at pattern altitude, to line up on the west end of the runway. In Maddie's previous experience, wind direction at this strip had been mostly from the western quadrant. But instead of landing toward the west as on those earlier occasions, and hence toward the main highway running between Tombstone and Bisbee, she came in low over the highway and set four-five Lima down on the western half of the strip, making what felt like a thoroughly natural taxi to the spot beside the windsock where her passengers would be waiting. Maddie felt certain that any casual passersby would think nothing of her brief stop at that point before turning around and heading back toward the western end of the runway again to begin the take-off run. At least that was the way she had planned it. But that was not what happened.

There was a scrambling of bodies to disengage from creosote bushes and desert broom, Cord leading the way. A second and then a third body materialized. And then, a small, but undeniably fourth person trailed close behind one of the others.

"What's up?" Maddie shouted over the idling engine to Cord when he opened the passenger-side door. "I count four people and I can only take three."

"I know. They didn't let us know about the kid. I'll stay behind and walk into Tombstone. I can hang out with Ike or the Nellies until time for church, maybe pick up a ride with one of them. You'll be back by then, won't you?"

"No problem," she answered, but felt uneasy about that decision.

One by one Maddie's passengers got into the plane, a woman and the child in the back seats and the man was just getting in when a very noisy and fast moving car pulled off the highway with a squeal of tires on the pavement that was audible even over the sound of the slowly turning aircraft engine. If the motor noise helped to obscure the car's sound, nothing impaired the look of the dust cloud rising behind the speeding vehicle. Maddie watched it bump as it left the roadway, practically jump the cattle guard, and cross the unpaved area between the drive and the runway.

"I think you'd better get in," she yelled at Cord. "I don't like the looks of this."

Cord agreed, gesturing to the man and pushing him to get in the back of the plane with the woman and the child. He was a large man, nearly two-hundred pounds, and it would have been a squeeze even without two people already in the back, but they managed it somehow and created a pile of packed humanity. The Skyhawk was very definitely overloaded, including nearly full gas tanks; the altitude was over 4700 feet which demanded even more of the small craft in breaking loose from the ground. There was no way Maddie dared to go down the runway in the direction of the speeding car, an apparent SUV, to regain the full length of the runway for takeoff. Instead, she would have to take off, overloaded, at moderately high altitude and with only half of the uneven runway for her use. Maddie later thought that she should have been thoroughly scared. But instead, she was exhilarated. Adrenaline can be a heady drug.

The Cessna was already moving at full throttle even before Cord got his door shut. Maddie pulled back on the yoke to rotate the nose wheel off the surface, but it was still too soon, and she had to let it continue on the rough surface, always risky for the fragile wheel. The second try worked, and the nose cleared the surface. Their speed began to increase. Maddie remembered at that moment to put on full flaps to increase lift and reduce the stall speed.

"They're getting closer," Cord shouted, still not in a headset with microphone.

Maddie looked down at the speed. Still not high enough to take off. She checked all the instruments and adjustments with a kind of calm deliberation. There was nothing more she could do to make the plane reach flying speed a moment sooner than it was ready. And now she saw that she had another problem. The end of the runway was only fifty yards ahead. Either she had to chance it soon and pull back on the wheel, risking the danger of stalling, or stop right now and face whatever consequences there were from the people in the SUV. Maddie remembered in an instant the deaths of Harold Jenkins and his carload of UDAs. There seemed to be no real choice. At the last possible moment, she eased back on the yoke and felt the wheels leave the runway, only to hear, almost immediately, the sickening bleat of the stall alarm. She eased forward on the yoke to level out the wings, and she could feel the Cessna's wheels brushing the tops of creosote bushes. The stall alarm stopped as the speed increased and the plane began a gradual, complaining climb.

Dead ahead was one of the most unfortunate features of the Tombstone airport, a ring of hills that was unforgiving to low-flying aircraft. It was clear that they would not have enough altitude to clear them straight ahead with the weight the plane carried. Maddie had no choice but to circle around the airport while gaining altitude. She began a slow banking turn to the left in the direction of Tombstone, about five miles away now. It was as if she had decided to stay in a left hand traffic pattern to come around for a touch-and-go.

"Do you have to go so close to them?" Cord asked into his microphone.

"Not really much choice," she said. "Besides, there isn't anything they can do about us now. I think we are even far enough away in this faint light that they probably can't read the registration numbers." To reenforce that visual obscurity she banked slightly to the right, away from the runway, making the numbers painted on the side of four-five Lima even harder for people on the ground to see. It was at just that moment that a hole opened up in the plexiglass windscreen beside and in front of where Maddie's left hand held the Cessna's wheel. At the same time, another hole appeared on Cord's side.

"Shit!" he exclaimed. "They're shooting at us."

"Let's get the hell out of here," Maddie muttered. She banked the plane sharply to the right despite the closeness of the low hills in front of them. Spider web cracks ran out from both holes made by the passing bullet. Fortunately the plexiglass held together rather than shattering as glass would have done. The hills loomed ahead as she made a further bank to the right, paralleling the range of hills toward the even higher ones directly to the east. But by now they had laboriously gained enough altitude that she could finally turn once more to the left toward Tombstone and ultimately Tucson.

"What are they doing?" Maddie asked.

Cord released his seatbelt and knelt on the seat over the top of her to look back at the runway. But he still could not see much and reached down to the side pocket and pulled out Maddie's small binoculars. Bouncing back up onto his knees, he looked down over her once again.

"They're going back down the runway toward the highway." He was quiet for a moment. "Now they're on the road headed for Tombstone." It was clear to both of them that they were on an intersecting course with the SUV. If Maddie maintained her present heading they would cross over the highway just as it entered Tombstone; their antagonists would be in a perfect position to take another shot at them if they wanted to.

"No such luck, you creeps," Maddie mumbled as she banked to the right again, making a wide circuit around the one-time home of Doc Holiday and Wyatt Earp, giving these contemporary bad guys no more chances to shoot at them. Cord reached over, touched her arm and gave it a little squeeze.

"That was damn close," he said.

"How are our passengers?" Maddie asked, remembering for the first time since she had begun the take-off run that they had human beings in the back of the airplane, probably frightened ones.

Once again, Cord was on his knees, his headset off, looking back. He reached out and touched each of them in what looked to Maddie like a kind and reassuring gesture. A wave of warmth passed over her for Cord, only to be replaced almost immediately with her earlier resolve to end it with him, for his own good if not for hers. Then she noticed that her hands were shaking and tears were beginning to fill her eyes. Whoever heard of a crying pilot? Maddie realized just how shaken she was in the aftermath of that terrifying takeoff. At the same time, she felt overcome with relief and thankfulness that Cord was on the Skyhawk, that their passengers were safely away with them, imagining what might have happened had she left any of them on the ground. The Cessna's windscreen showed just how risky leaving someone on the ground might have been.

The entire congregation was standing outside in front of St. Peter's Church after the Sunday service, sipping coffee and eating coffee cake, joking about this odd Lenten bounty of fat and sugar, when Ginger said to Jerry, "I would love to keep Sadie with me while you go to Tombstone for the book group, and then all of you," she gestured to Cord and Maddie, "can come over for an early supper before you have to get back."

"Sounds like a winner to me," Jerry answered. "That okay with you, Sweetheart?" he asked Sadie.

"That's cool," she said right back to him.

Ginger smiled in her warm, open way. Maddie watched Jerry's face as it went from a slightly puzzled expression to one that showed a thoroughly male reaction to a beautiful woman. Maddie could have been mistaken, but she thought she saw Ginger's expression carry just the slightest hint of self-consciousness. They were flirting with each other. Perhaps they didn't even really know it. She could not help but wonder if the future had something in store for these two single parents whose lives already seemed destined to connect. A wave of jealousy swept over Maddie as she wondered just what it was that she wanted to have happen here.

"I still can't believe that you are Carmen and Lizzie's mother," Jerry was saying to Ginger.

Ginger just smiled back at him.

That Sunday's book group session was different for Maddie than the previous ones had been. First of all, the conversation was particularly lively about applying the abstract principles of spirituality to everyday life. And this was the part of Christianity that Maddie found most appealing, especially the book's insistence that compassion was the natural result of any genuine religious feeling. While Judaism certainly has much to say about social responsibility and Jews were deeply involved in compassionate works, its main contemporary focus seemed to her to be inward toward the preservation of its own community, with good reason, and on faithfulness to the tradition. Christianity, at least in the ideal sense, seemed to demand that the faithful put their religious convictions on the line through direct action and that compassion was the foundation of all action—or so Borg says in his book. Maddie suspected that if a person were to scratch the surface of any religion, that same "compassion" would appear. Throughout the session Ike's rosaries and the designations they made for each group member were an important sub-text.

Jerry guided the conversation toward ways a life anchored in a faith system could be manifested in the world. There were some predictable responses. Jillian Curtain was at once the most predictable and, at the same time, oddly surprising.

"Well," Jillian said. "The most compassionate thing anyone can do for another human being is to bring them to the Lord Jesus. He is, after all, 'the way, the truth and the life,'" she said, quoting the Bible simplistically as usual. "He forgives all our sins." The words were vintage Jillian, but the body language and manner were less confident, more tentative than sure.

"Yes, of course," said Brenda-Nellie, letting her rosary beads and medal of St. Bridget run through her fingers. She was clearly exercising much restraint in her response to the Blessed Virgin Mary-Jillian Curtain. "But really, Jillian, don't you think a hungry person needs first to be fed and cared for before dragging Jesus into it. Or maybe—and I'll admit I may have a biased view as the operator of a restaurant—feeding people really *is* about Jesus, with or without the preaching, maybe especially *without*." Her concluding exhale showed just how close to the end of her patience with Jillian she had come.

"Nothing is more important than knowing Jesus," Jillian retorted. Brenda-Nellie-Bridget just rolled her eyes. The funny thing was that this typically Jillian statement did not seem to carry the same blind conviction as it had before.

"I've been thinking about all of this lately," Maddie said. "I have a burning need to know more about Jesus *and* about the faith of my mother's Jewish family. But I don't see why those things aren't compatible. Jesus *was* a Jew, after all. There must be a way to understand the two faiths without having to reject the one or the other—Judaism as having gone wrong the way Christians have thought for centuries or castigating Christianity as persecutor of the Jews."

"It's even worse than that," said Jerry. "John's Gospel especially accuses the Jews of being responsible for Jesus's death, demonizing 'the Jews' in dozens of places. We have to begin by remaking our traditional language about God if we are to achieve any kind of reconciliation between different faiths."

Ike McWarder cleared his throat and began on a subject that seemed to matter to him very deeply. "I've been thinkin' about the prayers we use, as well as Bible passages. They're pretty exclusive. There's a lotta talk about Christian unity and bringin' people of the *Christian* faith under 'God's grace and love.' That was pretty progressive thinking thirty years ago—that Episcopalians, Roman Catholics, Evangelical Protestants and Unitarians might sit down together, eat together, maybe even worship together. 'Course, they're still miles away from that even now."

Maddie noticed that Ike's usual dialect speak was gradually slipping away.

"But even that becomes the most outrageously narrow thinking in a world that's come to be unified by transportation, communication, international corporations, the marketplace, the computer and the Internet—on and on. It's ludicrous to continue to pretend that the best we can aspire to in religious dialogue's tryin' to get past the Vatican's refusal to admit that other Christians have a right to exist.

"The real conversation has to be between Christians and Muslims—especially after Nine Eleven," he continued, "and between Jews and Buddhists, Hindus and native peoples—and every combination of them all! I think that, at least for me, rather than sayin' that 'Jesus is *the* way *the* truth and *the* life,' we need to put more energy into discovering how the message of Jesus about God speaks to all people and not just to those of us who call ourselves 'Christians.' It can't be about proselytizing, but about how Christ speaks to Hindus, Buddha to Christians, Chief Seattle to Muslims, Mohammed to Hindus. And so forth and so on. Granted, we are a long way away from anything remotely like that kind of dialogue. But it's that to which we must aspire."

There was a long moment of silence. Facial expressions around the room were a real study. Maddie could see resistance battling with thoughtfulness on Jillian and Curtis Curtain's faces. The Nellies were, each in her own way, deeply moved. Maddie expected to see a light bulb come on over Linda Jackson's head. Jack was the perfect politician, inscrutable. She watched Cord begin to do that fidgety dancing-in-place thing that he does when he gets excited about an idea. Jerry, like Jack Jackson, was largely unmoved on the surface. It made Maddie realize how much like a politician a priest had to be.

Gradually the group moved on and away from this intensity as they talked at length about outreach projects that a church can do and the responsibility that individuals have to be active in their faith in some way. This part of the conversation made the absences of Jim and Lisa Brown—the model worker-servant Christians—particularly noticeable. Jim was still in the hospital in Tucson recovering from emergency heart surgery, and Lisa was there looking after him. But there was no doubt in anyone's mind that Joseph the Worker-Jim and St. Francis-Lisa would be back at their compassionate work in short order.

Maddie came to a strong personal insight from this conversation, feeling herself to be an embodiment of that interfaith conversation Ike had spoken of. It was a dialogue that was going on in her head: Christian? Jew? An amalgamation of the two? Something else entirely? She knew as never before just how important such a conversation was to her.

"Let me get this straight," Jerry said. They were at Ginger's studio in Bisbee, just over an hour after the book group ended in Tombstone. "You were picking up undocumented immigrants? And taking them where? I still can't get over how bold you've become," he said, focusing his attention on Maddie. "And I just can't believe that someone would actually shoot at you for that."

"Well they damn well did." Cord was sitting on a tattered sofa with his feet on an old oak desk chair. He paused to let his words sink in. "And you know, we should have followed them, at least gotten their license plate number," he insisted.

"You're probably right, but just then I had had quite enough of that SUV and whoever was in it," Maddie said.

"I can't blame you." Cord's reply was immediate. "What gets into people to do stuff like that? Fanaticism? Greed? What? I just don't get it." Cord's outrage did him credit.

"What do you think, Ginger? Jerry?" Maddie asked. "Maybe there *is* something we can do—should do."

"We need to find someone to replace that windshield," Cord said, bringing Maddie back to the present.

"That's no problem," said Jerry. "There's a mechanic at Ryan Field who can order the parts and then make the installation. But I'm more concerned about the way the holes got there. You're absolutely certain it was intentional?"

"Don't forget Harold," Ginger inserted.

"We take them different places," Maddie answered one of Jerry's incredulous barrage of questions.

Jerry seemed to make a decision. "I just don't think these people, whoever they are, should be allowed to get away with something like this," he said and paused. "I have an idea. First thing, though, is to report to the police that someone took a shot at your airplane." Jerry looked at Maddie very intently. Suddenly Jerry was her flying instructor again. "You don't have to say you were picking up passengers at Tombstone. After all, Libby ATC already has on record that you were doing touch-and-gos at Bisbee and Tombstone. Just report it as if it was some drunken cowboy taking pot shots first thing in the morning."

Maddie agreed, and they spent the rest of the evening working out a plan for Jerry to help in identifying those people in the SUV who shoot at airplanes.

CHAPTER SIXTEEN

The Fifth Week in Lent

"O Almighty God, who alone canst order the unruly wills and affections of sinful men: Grant unto thy people that they may love the thing which thou commandest, and desire that which thou dost promise; that so, among the sundry and manifold changes of the world, our hearts may surely there be fixed where true joys are to be found.
—Book of Common Prayer

After Maddie and Cord left, Jerry Hanning and Ginger Vega stood in the Bisbee studio as they had done two weeks earlier on the day of Harold Jenkins's funeral. Harold's paintings, including one of Ginger, formed a backdrop as on that previous occasion. Jerry had already shed his clericals in favor of shorts and a polo shirt on the unseasonably warm Sunday afternoon. Ginger was in jeans and a red tee-shirt that had "U of A, Sweet Sixteen" and a graphic of a fierce, scrappy wildcat, the Arizona mascot, emblazoned on it.

"Are you still surprised to find out that I'm Carmen and Lizzie's mother?" she asked.

"Oh, not as much so as you might think. Carmen really does look like you."

"Thanks. It's great to be with them again. I guess I hadn't even realized how much I missed them! But they're fine. And they certainly have formed an attachment to you and to Sadie." They glanced together over where the three girls were playing interior decorator in the corner of the studio.

"I want my walls pale yellow," Lizzie said.

"I like yellow," Sadie answered her.

"Don't you think blue would be good in my room?" Carmen asked.

"Blue...?"

Jerry returned his attention to Ginger. "How are *you* doing?" he asked her.

"Oh, I'm okay." She bit her lower lip for a moment, then continued, "More than okay, really. It's surprising isn't it? The way life deals out contradictory hands? Harold dies so horribly, and yet out of all that awful stuff comes a new life for me that's beginning to include my girls again, having my own place to live, even a growing sense of purpose in my life. That's just what you said at Harold's service isn't it? About the ugliness of life being redeemed, and we find ourselves being led in surprising new directions?"

"My goodness, you *were* paying attention," Jerry said with a small laugh.

"Of course I was," Ginger responded a little sharply. Then she realized that he was joking, was even a little embarrassed, and her face retreated into one of her wide smiles. Her dark eyes shined. "Sorry for being so touchy," she said. "Anyhow," she continued, serious again, "I'm seeing things very differently right now. I've always been pretty controlling about my life. Wanted to know where I was going. What the future looked like. Things like that. Now, I'm just kind of...willing, you know. I have ambitions, but they seem more about today and tomorrow than about next month or next year." She stopped short. "I'm kind of laying myself bare, aren't I?"

Jerry couldn't resist looking over her left shoulder at her portrait. Her eyes followed his, and a dark blush rose on her cheeks.

"Damn," she said. "I've got to do something about that thing." Then she laughed.

An hour later as Ginger left Sadie and Jerry and her own two daughters at the Bisbee airport for them all to go back to Tucson, she suddenly became very shy and then said to Jerry, "Thanks so much for giving them a ride back to Tucson." Then she smiled. "Do you have plans for tomorrow evening? To watch basketball? The NCAA. An Arizona fan here, you might have guessed." She pulled out the shoulders of her tee shirt with each hand and drew his attention to the Arizona logo on the front.

"No plans," he said. "But it'd be fun to watch some basketball."

"Why don't you come over to Mom and Dad's place and watch with us. I'm sure the three girls will be together anyhow, and I know Mom and Dad would love to have you."

"I'd like that," he said—and meant it.

Jerry and the three girls took off for Tucson with the sun only just above the horizon and directly in their eyes as they turned west. Gold, purple and orange danced across clouds suspended above jagged peaks in a sky that looked like an impressionist painting, but instead was the real thing. On the right, the Catalina range had bright pink ridges and dark purple crevices where the setting sun fell into shadow. Jerry felt good, and his spirit seemed to be radiating the colors of the sunset like an emotional slide projector. He flipped the toggle switch for the Cessna's navigation lights as they passed across the Tucson sprawl in the Old Pueblo's growing dusk.

The basketball party at the Lopezes' the next night was a great success. Sadie and Ginger's two girls were in and out of the Lopez's living room preparing a dance to a pop hit for the adults. Their carefully worked-out choreography and dress-up costumes had a kind of charming innocence that always touched Jerry. Margaret and Carlos Lopez were, as always, good company, joking lightly and comfortably with each other in ways that only people who have lived together respectfully for nearly forty years can do. Jerry discovered that Ginger was bright and funny. When the game was over, sadly without a happy result for Arizona fans, Margaret brought out steaming plates of Chili Colorado, beans and rice and flour tortillas. Jerry finished his second Corona of the evening and a third helping of red chili—with a spreading glow of contentment. Ginger invited him to step outside for some air.

They walked into the dark night, stars twinkling in the sky, the sounds of the city around them. Car engines revving and roaring, a police siren screamed in the distance, a dog barked at some real or imagined challenge to his domain. And Jerry was powerfully aware of Ginger's warm presence and delicately sweet scent. Who would not have been? Then she abruptly changed the mood.

"I got a call from Cord. There is a young Mexican couple with a baby marooned in Bisbee. Maddie wants to pick them up Wednesday morning. She wants to know if you're ready to, how did you put it, 'fly recon'?"

"Of course," Jerry said. "Will you come with me?" he continued impulsively.

Ginger paused thoughtfully and then said, "I'm not a great flyer. But, if you want me to, sure, I'll come."

"I do want you to. Besides, I need someone to help me—a 'spotter,' so to speak. Will Carmen and Lizzie be staying here?"

"For now at least. I don't think I want to take them out of school before the end of the year. Besides, I'm not sure they're ready to go with me. I think that means I'll be going back and forth a lot." She paused for a moment. "Maybe I can hitch a ride with you some weekends."

"With pleasure," he said.

Jerry had to think long and hard about what seemed to be happening with

Ginger Vega. Was this one of the old, "here we go again" things? Was he about to jump from one inappropriate relationship into another one—if, indeed any kind of relationship were likely to result from this new friendship. Was Ginger Vega a parishioner or wasn't she? Technically, the answer was no. She was not even an Episcopalian. Morally, he was not so sure. Just where were the boundaries in his building a new relationship? How did priests—anybody, for that matter—meet people and form relationships of any kind except through their work and among their neighbors and the parents of their children's friends? Was Ginger off limits or not? Then he thought about Maddie—and for a moment he felt an intense dislike for Cord. Where, if she were available, did she fit into the complicated web of church/real life relationships. She was not even a baptized Christian. Did that make her "fair game"? But, there was no doubt that Jerry had been a pastor to her—and to Art—and they were also friends, important friends to each other, and that was entirely separate from his work life as a priest. It was a hopelessly complicated morass. Perhaps, now that he wanted a long-term intimate relationship again, one was denied to him in order that he might pursue his vocation. Did that mean that the Roman church and its celibacy of the clergy had the right idea? He did not think so. Then what? He still had to work that out.

A little later Jerry talked with Maddie on the phone—something that had become almost a daily habit with them.

"You know, I went to the Temple service on Saturday," she said.

"Uh-huh."

"Then to church on Sunday in Bisbee. I'm a little confused. If you can believe it, I'm confused that I don't feel more confused—if that makes any sense—or at least more conflicted over it than I am. My brain tells me I should just pick one of them—church or Temple—and go with it. But the rest of me is excited and wants to be both places, church *and* synagogue."

"I see no reason why you shouldn't do both," he answered.

They talked some more about her experience at the Reformed temple, then shifted to her next flight of stranded immigrants on Wednesday morning and their plan to follow any vigilantes who might show up. Finally, he went on to tell her about his evening, watching basketball and being with Ginger and her family.

"Hmm. You and Ginger, huh?" Maddie asked cynically. "I watched you drooling over her portrait and saw the two of you flirting with each other yesterday."

Flirting? Had they been flirting?

Jerry lifted off from Ryan Field in the still darkness of that blustery Wednesday morning to pick up his "spotter," Virginia Vega, in Bisbee, and be in place as agreed before Maddie arrived at the deserted Tombstone landing strip just after dawn. The sky was still shrouded in total darkness. Signs of the beginnings of a major spring storm were all around him and becoming increasingly evident as the sky began eventually to brighten with the new day. Heavy, small dark cumulus clouds competed with high stratus ones to dominate the normal blue of the southwestern sky. Winds were unpredictable and unruly, nearly calm at one moment, powerful and gusty the next. The brightening sky had a diffused light in that peculiar way a gray overcast has of at once softening the intensity of the sun while spreading its deflected light with an indirect, shadow-less glow. Any new weather system can be tricky for flying; today's bore watching.

Throughout the solitary part of the flight Jerry ruminated about the pain and alienation that he saw all around him in that border country. He knew that one way or another, it had always been that way. It did not matter whether the antagonists were Apaches and the cavalry, Pancho Villa and the Mexican government, ranchers and Native Americans, miners and mine owners, ranchers and undocumented aliens—somehow it was always the same. Poor people struggled against the wealthy, haves against have nots, enfranchised against disenfranchised. All the struggle, the violence, and even the underlying hope for a new life on this continuing frontier seemed to come to the same result: alienation and loss of hope. No matter how hard decent people worked to change things, the inequality and poverty remained. It makes a person ask, why bother, why care? And yet, Jerry realized that the grace is in the struggle, in the bothering, in the striving. Perhaps Jesus was right that need would always exist, that the perfect society would never be built—if for no other reason than it is essential to our humanity that we should have to care for one another. "God! Here I am preaching to myself," Jerry said aloud.

Ginger was waiting when Jerry landed on the broad Bisbee landing strip. She looked a bit apprehensive, even grim, as she unsmilingly got into Five-Eight Bravo. With what seemed to be a slight shudder, she took his right arm in her hand and pressed her head against his shoulder. He had forgotten that she really did not like to fly.

"Sorry," she shouted over the noise of the engine into his headset-covered ear.

Jerry pointed at the other head set resting above the instrument panel, already connected and ready for her. She put on the unbecoming appliance and began again.

"I really am sorry that I'm so wimpy about flying. Something about it just terrifies me. I'm better once I get going." She attempted a brave smile.

Jerry reached out his arm and gave her a short reassuring hug.

Within minutes they had climbed above Mule Mountains and continued to gain altitude until the Skyhawk reached nine thousand feet. The sun was only just beginning to cast its cloud-diffused light across the rough landscape, and occasional bumps from the weather system kept Ginger worrying. Nine thousand feet gave the Skyhawk over four thousand feet of air between it and the Tombstone airport. Jerry and Ginger would make a broad, lazy circle over the vacant strip, both of them watching for any signs of movement near the runway. Ginger had Maddie's powerful binoculars which she used to sweep the ground below them. If they saw anyone, they would call it off and Maddie would fly away without ever coming near. Then Jerry and Ginger would continue to circle until the car got tired of waiting and left. They would follow it, get its license plate number and see where it went. In that scenario, a car would come back for the immigrants.

Jerry adjusted the radio to 122.5, an unused frequency in this area, and called Maddie. "This is five-eight Bravo. Come in Four-Five Lima. Are you there, Maddie?" There was no response. Jerry continued to circle. "Any sign of life down there? Lights? Anything?" he asked Ginger..

"Not so much as a gecko with a headlight," Ginger quipped.

"You must be feeling better."

"I'm okay. It's always like this. The fear goes away once I'm actually in the air. Though, I *could* do with a few less bumps."

"Sorry."

They flew through the blustery morning air for a few minutes without speaking. An occasional car drove by on Highway Eighty below them, but none stopped at the airport. The sun's light came, alternately deflecting off the cloud cover and then breaking through to bathe the desert in bright rays.

"I wonder what's happened to Maddie?" Jerry asked.

"Wait a minute," Ginger said suddenly. I think there *is* something down there." She pointed to a spot just off the main highway, but away from the airport entrance road. "The sun," she said. "See. It's reflecting off something."

"I do see," Jerry said. There was no doubt about it, the sun's rays were hitting an object, perhaps a car's windshield, and sending a beam of light that hit Five-Eight Bravo exactly where it circled. Then it was gone as the sun slipped once more behind the cloud cover. Jerry circled slowly over that point, far enough away from it so their engine noise would not be too loud, and in a sharp right bank so Ginger could get a good look with her binoculars.

"There's no doubt about it," she said. "There's a car down there. Friend or foe, I wonder?"

"What're the chances of it being a friend?"

"I get your point."

"Four-Five Lima, this is Five-Eight Bravo. Come in, Maddie."

This time there was a response. "Hi Jerry, we're on our way. Sorry I'm late, but I must have gotten a touch of flu. It cost me my breakfast a few minutes ago. I think I'm okay now. Should be there any minute."

"Sorry to hear about the flu. We do have a problem, a visitor," he answered. There was a long minute of silence. Then the disembodied voice of Maddie Gronek broke in again.

"I was afraid we might." Another silent moment passed. "Seen anything of our friends?"

"Nothing," Jerry responded. "Are you sure they're there?"

"Pretty sure. They're desperate to get to Tucson. Their baby is sick, and they're scared."

Jerry mulled over this new piece of information for a moment. Perhaps they no longer had an option. He pushed down the call button. "Then you think we need to go ahead, and not abort?" he asked.

"Affirmative."

"How about Plan B, then?" Jerry asked.

"I didn't know we had a Plan B."

"We didn't until right now. Just a minute. Ginger, look in the binoculars. Can you see the windsock? Which direction is it pointing?"

"Generally to the west."

The wind was coming from the east, at least for the moment. No doubt that would change as the storm came closer. But an east wind served him very well just then.

"Is it standing straight out?"

"Mostly."

"That's good." He pushed his microphone call button. "Maddie, you'll be landing toward the east. I'll touch down first—try to create a diversion. Is Cord with you?"

"Affirmative."

"Be sure he gets that family on quickly. Then get out of there. Didn't you say you began your run from the windsock last time?"

"Yes," she said.

"There's a steady breeze coming from the east, so you shouldn't have too much trouble. Just come in right over me. I'm going to land downwind and give our visitor something to think about."

Downwind landings are tricky, primarily because the ground speed is greater than it would normally be landing into the wind. A ten knot tail wind, which is what Jerry estimated there was, would add ten knots to the ground speed. A conventional landing into the wind would have the opposite effect, reducing the ground speed by ten. In effect they would be landing twenty knots faster this way than landing conventionally. On a rough, neglected field like the one at Tombstone, that was potentially serious. Ten knots was doable, though Jerry would have to make a soft field landing, keeping the power on to hold the vulnerable nose wheel well clear of the ground while braking to slow down. That would also mean that if he managed to set it down just right, they would come up to the waiting vehicle very fast, exactly what he had in mind.

Jerry pulled on the carburetor heat and cut the throttle down to a bare idle.

"Oh, my God," Ginger gasped.

"It's okay," he said, reaching out and touching her knee. "We need to lose altitude and be as quiet as possible. Keep an eye open for Maddie's plane. She should be coming from the west side of Mule Mountains any second now."

Jerry continued to circle, ever tighter, right over the center point of the runway.

"Where are you Four-Five Lima? Three-Eight Bravo."

"Just coming into the pattern on the forty-five, making right traffic," she said. "Four-Five Lima.

Jerry imagined the invisible rectangle with the runway as one of the long sides and looked where Maddie should be. Sure enough her navigation lights were clearly visible at about one-thousand feet—pattern altitude. Any observer who knew anything about aircraft would see her doing exactly what she should be doing. With a little luck Jerry's Skyhawk would be a complete surprise for them. Poor Ginger, he thought to himself as a sharp gust jolted the gliding Cessna, knowing what the next few minutes would probably feel like to her.

"There she is," said Ginger, pointing toward the left.

Jerry continued the rapid descent, planning the power-off circle to touch down just about opposite the windsock going the opposite direction from the one Maddie would soon be using to land, except that she would be needing to touch down very close to the end of the runway, right where Jerry's Cessna would be sitting in about a minute.

"Maddie, I'm going to touch down at a little west of the windsock and taxi fast toward the upwind end. Give you that diversion I promised."

"Roger."

"Here we go."

Jerry cross-controlled the plane with opposite aileron and rudder pressure to slip the plane down the last two hundred feet, applied full flaps and brought the craft's airspeed to just above stall. Still, the brush and cactus along the sides of the runway were passing by much too fast for his comfort. The Cessna settled roughly onto the broken tarmac, and then Jerry added some power to keep the nose off the ground while still braking to stop the Skyhawk before it ran out of runway. He had planned it just about right and, stomping hard on the left brake, it came to a skidding, turning stop at the very end of the runway. The waiting car was now clearly visible about fifty feet away across an open area, but nestled under a sparse, lonely mesquite tree. Jerry hoped the top soil right there was as loose and dusty as he remembered. Brakes firmly locked under his toes, Jerry revved the engine to two thousand rpms, and then turned and looked back. Sure enough, a great cloud of dust and sand totally covered the waiting car.

"Ginger, keep a close eye on them in case the car starts to move." Jerry continued to feel the revs of the tight, recently rebuilt Continental engine. He felt just a little sorry for whoever was getting the business end of this dust cloud. If they did not have windows tightly closed, there was even some danger for their eyes. Too bad for them! Creeps!

With a final engine roar, Jerry heard and then saw Maddie's plane go over their heads and settle on the runway twenty-five yards from where they sat. The roar must have been a final adjustment on altitude as she cleared them with very few feet to spare.

"You sure make a lot of dust, Five-Eight Bravo," she said.

"And you cut it pretty close, Four-Five Lima."

Jerry and Ginger sat there and watched as the other Skyhawk slowed and stopped beside the windsock. Movement beside the plane suggested that Cord was out, probably even before the roll had stopped. Jerry picked up the binoculars and saw him hustle some other people into the plane. Fortunately, they were ready and waiting. And scared to death, he imagined. He doubted Maddie was stopped on the ground more than two minutes—a total of not more than three minutes elapsing since he had touched down. He thought that whoever was in the car was clueless about what they were up to. There was no way they could see.

As Maddie began her roll down the runway, Jerry let go of five-eight Bravo's brakes and pushed the throttle in the final inch to full.

"Now get going, Maddie," he said into the mike, then to Ginger, "you okay?"

"Surprisingly, yes," she said.

Jerry looked over at Ginger and there was a broad smile on her face. Her eyes were dancing with excitement. Well before they reached the windsock and in advance of Maddie's takeoff as fully loaded as she was, Five-Eight Bravo was airborne. Jerry kept waiting for the other Cessna to lift off the ground. Maddie waited to the last possible moment, and he saw her get precariously close to the vegetation before she gradually, and then more quickly, gained altitude. She was away. She's incredible, Jerry thought. "Get on out of here, Four-Five Lima," he said.

"Roger, skipper," Maddie laughed—shades of dozens of World War II movies. Jerry would have bet there was just an edge of hysteria in that laugh.

"Now, back to plan A," Jerry said to Ginger, grinning widely.

Jerry banked Five-Eight Bravo to the right, away from the Tombstone airport, climbing rapidly in the cool morning air and riding the headwind and some naturally appearing early thermal updrafts. But Jerry did not fly away. Instead, he returned the plane to its circling pattern, climbing toward the old altitude of nine thousand feet.

"Can you see them? The car?" Jerry asked Ginger, looking at the altimeter. They were just passing seventy-five hundred feet.

"Not right...yes, there it is. It's just leaving the airport drive and turning toward Bisbee."

"Can you see the make, the license plate number?" Jerry glanced at Ginger as she peered intently into the binoculars.

"It's an SUV, an older one, I think. It says 'Ram' in big white letters on the side," she answered.

"A Dodge?"

"It's very dirty, but I think it's a kind of muddy-blue color. I could mix it up in oils and get it pretty close."

"What about the license plate?" Jerry asked.

"Really can't see it—at least to read it. As I said, the whole car is covered with mud and dust." She laughed. "We may have contributed some of that."

Jerry leveled the plane off at nine-thousand feet, high enough that the driver below them would not necessarily be aware of them keeping track of him, and they would be able to stay above him and not lose him in Mule Mountains as he drove into Bisbee.

"What's happening, Five-Eight Bravo?" It was Maddie.

"We're keeping an eye on the car, an SUV," Jerry said into the mic. "Ginger says it's an old Dodge, kind of a muddy blue. That sound familiar? From last time?"

"Could be," Cord broke into the conversation. "Probably the same one. You sure stopped them with that dust storm."

"Unless they're just early morning citizens. Anyhow, we'll follow along and try to find out who they are, or where they live…or something."

Maddie broke in with, "Be careful. Don't forget how nasty these people can get."

"Right."

Jerry and Ginger followed the SUV into Bisbee with no difficulty, circling lazily from time to time to keep from outdistancing it. Following the car became tougher when the driver reached Mule Mountains and very hard as it joined the twisting streets and growing traffic of early morning Bisbee.

"I've lost it," Ginger said. "I took my eyes off it for a moment to look around…and…and then it was gone."

"Then maybe this is it," Jerry said.

"But we don't know any more than we did before—not even that they actually live in Bisbee."

"We can look for the car. It's not a very big town, after all. And there can't be that many muddy blue old Dodge SUVs."

Jerry continued to circle and gain altitude. Ginger was searching the ground with the binoculars when suddenly she gave a deep sigh. "There they are," she said. "They must've stopped somewhere, but now they're at the Douglas Road intersection…and they're taking it. For some reason, I'm relieved that they're not from Bisbee—'our fair city.'"

"It makes more sense that they would be from Douglas, or more likely the Sulphur Springs Valley, than Bisbee," Jerry said, but saying it filled him with foreboding. He thought about Hank Tucker. He doubted that Hank would be involved in something like this, especially with his recent change of heart.

Charlie Snow then? Was this something that he might have done? He was sorry to admit to himself that it was possible.

They distantly followed the SUV along Highway Eighty all the way to the outlying areas of Douglas, past Cochise Community College's main campus. It turned north on highway 191. At the intersection of Double Adobe Road it pulled over beside half a dozen parked cars. Someone got out of the SUV and got into a white pickup truck. It pulled away. The SUV continued along and then turned back west into the Sulphur Springs Valley. The white pickup headed toward Douglas.

"Can you get the license plate number on the pick-up?" Jerry asked Ginger.

"Yes, I think so. No mud," she said, scrambling for a pencil and pad of paper in the passenger's side pocket of Five-Eight Bravo. She balanced the binoculars in one hand and the pencil and pad in the other on her lap. "Got it," she said scribbling on the pad.

"Now, let's see where the SUV's going," Jerry said.

The Ram's destination turned out to be one that made Jerry very unhappy. There was no mistaking Hank Tucker's ranch and his red and white Bonanza sitting beside the landing strip. If it wasn't Hank in the SUV, and Jerry could not imagine that it could be, then it must be one of his men or one of his neighbors. He banked the airplane sharply and headed back to Bisbee to wait for Maddie and Cord to return.

The return of that Dodge Ram to Hank Tucker's ranch raised a problem in Jerry's mind that had been lurking just beneath the surface of his conscious thoughts. What business did he, a priest, have playing sleuth? Why did he feel that it was not only his right but his duty to follow and, if possible, help to have arrested people who were at some level defending their own property? This was not out of some abstract desire to be a good citizen, nor was it about revenge. It was much more complicated than either one of those motives. In a way his personal explanation, he thought, was embedded in the meaning behind the archaic words of the traditional collect for the fifth Sunday of Lent, the very one he had read that Sunday. While allowing that God, and God alone, can provide the human motivation for living ethically and decently, as the church has always taught, all the same there is the moral obligation to seek to live in concert with the sacred—that is to say, with a higher standard than one's own immediate pleasure or gratification. Only in living with such an elevated moral purpose could one find peace, joy, and fulfillment in living. Resisting the evil perpetrated against other human beings could not help but be a part of living with a higher moral purpose. Shooting at airplanes was evil. Persecuting poor people, even if they did enter the country in violation of the law, was also evil. A system which favored one group of people over another one for no other reason than where they were living when their mothers gave birth to them, or the color of their skin, or the language that they spoke—such a system was also evil. That kind of system had to be resisted. Jerry had to be a part of that resistance.

Such a moral imperative, though, raised the question in him of just what kind of resistance that means. While Jerry could understand how some people feel justified resorting to violent means in resisting oppression, he was personally drawn to nonviolence as advocated by Martin Luther King, Jr., or Mahatma Gandhi. But both violence—which is contrary to everything that Jerry believed Christianity stood for—and nonviolence call for more activism than Jerry felt comfortable with. Jerry was not at his core an activist. He saw himself more as a facilitator, one who confronts the hard questions and points to directions, a consciousness raiser. At least that had always been his role in the past. Perhaps that was before he felt personally touched by injustice and large-scale wrong-doing. When someone took a shot at Madeline Gronek's airplane with human beings on board—with Maddie on board!—the whole question of illegal immigration, national laws that enforce and reenforce an international policy of inequality, morally indefensible by any Christian standard, it became very personal. In some way that Jerry did not entirely understand, that single act converted his theoretical and theological opposition to the immorality of life in this border county into a personal campaign, particularly against the vigilantes, but more importantly in favor of the poor people whose lives were so at risk. He was determined to be counted in the campaign against such inequality, perhaps even at the political level helping to change the law and to take a moral stand against what he saw as injustice.

Why was this the catalyst Jerry needed when news reports of violence and bloodshed against defenseless people seeking only a better life for themselves and their families had not had that effect on him? What made this different than the deaths of Harold Jenkins and his passengers? After all, nobody had actually been hurt in Maddie Gronek's Skyhawk. Jerry found that he really could not definitively answer those questions. But this *was* different. He suspected that there were many factors that contributed to his changing commitment: some of them as deeply personal and emotional as the reawakening that came from being with Kate Becker; some as profoundly disturbing as having faced the death of someone he loved very much…and grieved fully. Even his role as a single parent must be making a contribution. And Maddie Gronek was his friend! But in the end, he could not get past that fussy, old-fashioned collect for the fifth Sunday in Lent. This "sinful man" has had his "will and affections" ordered by the God who created him in the first place. Who else could he be, but the person he had been created and formed to become? The whole concept of God seemed more real to Jerry Hanning at that moment than, perhaps, at any other time in his life.

CHAPTER SEVENTEEN

The Fifth Week in Lent

At the center of the Biblical understanding of salvation is a relationship with God in the present, whose gifts are freedom, joy, peace and love and whose fruits are compassion and justice.
—Marcus Borg

"I still feel so guilty," Ginger Vega said to Jerry Hanning. "You know, about abandoning my girls for more than a year." They were back in Five-Eight Bravo on their way to Tucson later on Wednesday afternoon. Maddie and Cord had returned from delivering their passengers without further adventure, and Ginger was on her way to her parents' home to spend the rest of the week in Tucson. "If I'd been stronger…more the way you were, perhaps I could have done the right thing," she continued.

"The right thing?" Jerry asked. "What makes you think there's a right thing, a right way for a person to act when someone dies…or…or any something horrible happens? I'm certainly no model! I've been among the walking dead for nearly three years. People react to crisis the way they react, and then they have to deal with what they've done and move on."

"But I was so self-indulgent."

"Yes, I guess you were. But now what?"

At first Ginger was shocked that Jerry actually agreed with her self-judgment, and her initial reaction was that she needed to defend herself. Then she realized that all he had done was acknowledge the truth. The one she had said herself. Ginger had expected Jerry to disagree with her, to tell her that she really had not been the idiot that she knew she had been. His refusal to talk her back into denial opened up the rest of the conversation.

After a long silence, she continued, "You know, I used drugs and drank a lot. I probably would have killed myself if it hadn't been for Harold. Poor Harold." She told Jerry about how he had found her in LA and brought her back to Bisbee, took care of her, and introduced her to AA.

"Have you worked the steps?" he asked. "Made your apologies?"

"Some of them."

"How about Carmen and Lizzie? Have you made your apologies to them?"

"They're kids. They know I love them," Ginger responded defensively.

"But I don't think they know that you're sorry…about the time you spent away from them. Maybe they're *the* most important people for you to seek forgiveness from."

Damn, Ginger thought. He was right, of course. But she did not like hearing it, not one bit she didn't.

They flew silently again. Finally Jerry said, "Enough of the tough subjects! What do you say that we gather up our daughters and the five of us go out to dinner tonight?"

"I would like that," she said, favoring Jerry with one of her warm, inviting smiles.

As it turned out, Ginger and Jerry and their three girls spent a lot of time together that week, beginning with going out to dinner at a gourmet burger place that same evening. It was the perfect choice—noisy, crowded…and full of life. Nobody cared if they had three kids who might make a lot of noise. While they were waiting to be seated, they wandered around the strip mall next to the restaurant, looked in windows while the three girls teased each other and ran ahead and then back again.

"A herd of wild creatures," Ginger said.

"The wildest," Jerry agreed. He looked at her and grinned. She had a sudden flash that in this man there was little artifice. He really was what he seemed to be, someone who liked people and had experienced a great deal of personal pain. It was all there in his face, even covered as it was in his new beard, and unmasked in his eyes: a rich sense of humor, a touch of insecurity, but solid in a very clear sense of who he was, hopeful and generous, optimistic and hurt.

Ginger took his arm in her hand and pressed her head against his shoulder for the second time that day. This time it was not about the fear of flying, but about a very real contentment, not a sensation she had felt a lot these last few years. She wondered if there might be a future somewhere down the road for the two of them. What a thought! And him a priest. They walked quietly for awhile.

Something was happening to Ginger that she liked, but that she did not understand. The purpose of her life had always been to take care of herself.

And everything considered, she once thought that she had done it pretty well. It didn't take a genius, either, to figure out that the second sixteen years of her life had been about coming to understand and accept the first sixteen, not that she was particularly unusual in that.

Much of what she had to cope with was paradoxical. Middle class *and* Latina! Most of the people she knew were either the one or the other, and only rarely both at the same time. Sometimes that was so lonely that she almost wished she could just be like the other Mexican girls her age, get a job in fast food, get pregnant and marry some macho jerk. But those were only the desperate times. She never wanted anything even remotely like that, not in her darkest, most painful moments, and that is a cliche about Latina teens that is not true anyhow—kind of like her father being a landscaper; there were lots of stereotypes in her personal history. Dark skin, hair and eyes—not the usual standard of beauty in America—*and* the ability to live off her looks as well as to manipulate people with them! Something she admitted to doing. The fact of racism, on the short end of the stick, and the kind of appearance that is always being commented on by men most likely to discriminate on the basis of race—macho Anglo creeps—is very ironic if you think about it. And she thought about it. Ginger could not honestly remember a time when she did not turn redneck heads, or any other kind of heads for that matter. These are the twin paradoxes of her life, middle class and Latina, dark skinned and attractive to Anglos, leaving her neither inside nor exactly outside any part of the life around her. So she learned to take care of herself.

Or at least Ginger thought that she had. The problem was that if she were honest with herself about it, she had not especially thrived looking out for number one. It had taken her years to process the fear and the other effects of the rape—the insecurity, self-loathing and blame. Attempting to cope with that pain by becoming beautiful, remote and untouchable had served to keep Ginger disconnected from the people around her. And that compounded the circumstances of her growing up as neither the one nor the other. Nor was it really who she was, denying as it did the exuberance that was essential to her nature. This false sense of self had left her so disconnected internally that her effectiveness in any part of her life had been severely handicapped, and that included her growth as an artist. Instead of growing up emotionally, she traded on her looks—a much less risky proposition. Though she had to work hard at selecting makeup and clothing carefully and constantly watching what she ate. Even Ginger's role as a parent suffered from her personal disjunction. She had, from her own point of view, done only a fair job as a mother until she faced the crisis of Joel's death—and it was a terrible crisis, to be sure. Her personal reserves were so low at that time that all she could do when tragedy hit was to run. And she ran.

But now everything appeared to be different. Decisions were easier, mostly, she realized, because she was not so afraid of them any more. She found that she genuinely liked the people she was around. All of them. It was easier to be with her parents than ever before in her life. And she suddenly found her own parenthood almost simple and natural, as if someone had given her a brain transplant. She could understand the role better than she ever had before. She had new friends. Ginger had always before had acquaintances, but now she actually was forming friendships. With both men and women.

"We'd better get back to the restaurant or we'll lose our place," Jerry said. They rounded up the three girls and made their way inside where they ate burgers, fries and sodas, and laughed at almost everything.

After dinner the five of them went back to Jerry's place and watched a movie on the VCR, popped popcorn and drank more soda. It would have sounded pretty dull to Ginger in the telling, but she did not know when she had had a better evening.

The next day, after the girls had gone to school, Ginger took Jerry to meet a childhood friend of hers, Jorge Casias, one of the most decent men she had ever known. Jorge worked as a tile setter, mostly in Tucson. His business ranged from solo work when it was slow to running large crews doing several jobs at once when it was busy. He unabashedly hired both documented and undocumented workers. He always said that he was mainly interested in the quality of their work, their willingness and reliability. Ginger and Jerry got to one of Jorge's current jobs just before lunch time.

"Hey, Ginger, you gorgeous thing. Where have you been? I haven't seen you since…since…"

"Since Joel's funeral. I know. It's okay. I had a rough time, but I'm better now. Much better." Jorge looked questioningly at Jerry. "Jorge, I'd like you to meet my friend, Father Jerry Hanning. He's a priest in the Episcopal Church."

Jorge extended his hand to Jerry. They shook hands, then he gave Ginger a quick firm hug.

"Are you looking to have some tile work done?" Jorge asked.

"Not at the moment," Jerry answered, "but I've got a kitchen and an

Arizona Room that I've been thinking about redoing. What kinds of tile do you do?"

"Anything, really. Saltillo, any ceramic, marble—Italian, Spanish. We do it all."

"Actually, Jorge," Ginger intervened, "we came to see you about the illegal immigrants that you and the other tradesmen hire."

"What do you want to know, Ginger?" he asked cautiously.

"Just describe the situation for Father Jerry. He's trying to learn about what's actually happening—as opposed to what the papers say is coming down."

"Well...Illegals are big in all the trades," Jorge said. "They learn to do their work in Mexico, and then come here and try to make some money. You name it, and undocumented men are in it. Tile, stucco, carpentry, cement, paint. All of it. The building boom in Arizona would collapse in a minute if it weren't for these Mexican and Salvadoran workers, mostly Mexicans. 'Course there're lots of unskilled ones, too."

"How does it work? How do you connect with them?" Jerry asked.

"That's easy, really," Jorge began. "You know, we're all related." He looked at Ginger, and they both laughed at the cliched stereotype. "Cousins contact cousins. If I need a couple of guys, I just make a call or two and before you know it, there they are. Usually, I don't know them, but I'm told to look for someone waiting on a particular street corner wearing a red tee shirt or something. I try to help them when I can, and I pay the ones without papers the same amount as workers with papers. Actually, my wife wouldn't let me get away with anything less."

"How *is* Carla?" Ginger asked.

"She's great. All three kids are in school now and she's back at teaching, fourth grade at the moment. She loves it."

"Not all the UDAs are as fortunate as to work for you, are they?" Jerry asked, probing to see if the abuse stories he had heard were true.

Jorge was thoughtful for a moment. Finally, he asked, "Do you have a little time?"

Ginger said yes for both of them.

"Then let's go for a ride."

They went outside and climbed into Jorge's big white Ford pickup. It was absolutely spotless. Same old Jorge, Ginger thought. Most work vehicles were trashed, beat-up and old. Not Jorge's.

They drove south into a warehouse and industrial district. Weathered old buildings and fenced yards stacked with heavy machinery, building materials and junk were scattered throughout the area in a neglected looking disarray. Jorge pulled up in front of one of the more dilapidated-looking ones and gestured that they should get out.

"What's here?" Jerry asked.

"You'll see," Jorge answered.

They went through a door. Inside was a cavernous space devoid of interior walls. Steel pipes held up the girders that supported the roof. All around the outer walls were beds and cardboard boxes, presumably containing personal items. In the center of the floor some rickety card tables and worn folding chairs gave a kind of a homey touch, pitiful in its barrenness.

"What's this place?" Ginger asked.

"It's kind of a work exchange. The Illegals live here and are sent out to any work that comes along—usually at much less than the going rate for documented workers. They eat whatever they're given—usually day-old bread, tortillas, beans and occasional meat, usually bologna. They're mostly too frightened to do anything about it."

"This's horrible," Jerry said, looking around.

"Some of us do what we can to break this system. I don't know. We just don't accomplish too much."

"The immigration laws have to be changed," Ginger said.

"Good luck," Jorge said with an air of disgust and looked hard at Jerry. "The people who make so much money off their labor—contractors, builders, developers, mortgage companies, bankers, tradesmen like me—are not going to put up with that. Don't hold your breath for the laws to change any time soon—maybe ever."

Jorge returned them to Jerry's car, and Ginger and Jerry went back to Jerry's place where they made sandwiches and a fresh pot of coffee and talked until the girls got home from school. It was hard to shake the morning's experience.

At one point Jerry, looking quite despondent, said, "Everything seems so futile—all the efforts and the risks that you and Maddie have gone to, Harold's death...everything! And yet they remain desperate to get here, put up with horrid conditions. I just don't get it—how people can use each other this way."

"I know what you mean, Jerry," Ginger said. "I try not to think too much about the big picture. I just focus in on what is right in front of me. Do what I can where I am."

"I know you're right. But it just doesn't seem like enough somehow. Just not enough."

Later that same afternoon Ginger, Jerry and the three girls drove to Ryan Field in the Lopezes' minivan to pick up Maddie and her stepson, Sean, who had just arrived to spend his spring vacation with Maddie, something she had been looking forward to ever since she got back from France. A mechanic at Ryan was going to install a used windshield in Four-Five Lima while it was there.

Sean Gronek showed every sign of being a great kid, perhaps a little shy, but thoughtful and gentle. He had a mop of black hair, large permanent teeth, and clear, unwavering dark eyes that looked directly back at you when he spoke. He was very charming telling the girls about how much fun he had had flying, first in a big plane and then with Maddie in hers. In return, the girls shared their flying adventures with him. It felt good to Ginger to put a boy, especially such a good-natured one, into the mix with the three girls. He and Sadie already knew each other, perhaps that helped.

That night they all went out to dinner, this time to a Mexican restaurant, but like the night before, a noisy, family kind of place. Ginger could not help noticing the way Jerry and Maddie tended to look at each other with the kind of intensity that suggested that nobody else was there for them at that moment. And yet, their conversation was carefully very neutral; there was no flirting. It got annoying after awhile watching them being so careful not to show each other—or anyone else—where their true feelings were. Ginger wondered if they were even aware of those feelings themselves.

Ginger had had thoughts about becoming more personally involved with Jerry once she felt ready, but she increasingly became convinced that they did not work as a couple. In the end, she thought of him as a friend, as a priest even—a unique combination in her experience. Maybe she could not get past the idea that priests were supposed to be celibate. No matter how much she rationalized it, deep inside she had been formed with a religious bias against sex that she was far from ready to let go of—no matter how much she would have like to do so. Maybe she even needed Jerry as a priest. It was so hard to know. But no bells rang for her and Jerry. And they clearly rang for he and Maddie—even though they did not seem to hear them at the moment.

"Where's Cord?" Ginger asked Maddie when everyone else was occupied with a story Jerry was telling the kids.

"Oh, I broke that off. Wednesday after that last flight," Maddie answered.

"Really." Ginger was not particularly surprised.

"It didn't seem like Sean needed to meet him. Besides, I just haven't felt good about going on with Cord, all the while knowing that there really isn't a future. And there *are* some other things going on with me," she answered a little mysteriously. "Tell you later."

"How'd Cord take it?" Ginger asked.

"Pretty well. Said he wasn't surprised. He got a little mad, though. Can't blame him really, can you?"

"No I guess not."

After dinner they all went back again to Jerry's place, and as it turned out, for a conversation none of them was likely ever to forget.

Sean, who had seemed particularly quiet after dinner, was the spark plug. "I've been thinking," he began. "Like, every one of us in this room, you know, has had somebody real important to us, like, die."

"Everybody dies, Sean, so everyone knows someone sooner or later who has died," Maddie said.

"No, I'm serious, dude. Like, every one of us—a father, a mother, a husband, a wife. That's heavy. I have lots of friends. Like, that hasn't happened to them. "

"Makes us kind of the same," Sadie said.

"Dude!" said Sean.

"How come people have to die?" Lizzie asked in all innocence.

"Yeah, how come? How come? It isn't fair," Carmen and Sadie said, more or less together.

Everyone looked at Jerry, maybe because he was a priest, or perhaps because he was The Man. Either explanation made Ginger a little angry, even at herself, who also looked to Jerry. But Jerry did not launch into some lengthy sermon filled with Bible quotes and reference to sources, nor did he come off like some know-it-all father figure. He smiled, leaned back in his new rocking chair—the one made by parishioner Jim Brown—and asked all the rest of them what they thought—just as if he really did not have the answers.

At first Ginger suspected him of being patronizing. But pretty soon she saw that he only wanted to get out of the way of what could (and did) become an important conversation. They moved quickly past statements of outrage and unfair! and started to talk about how they felt. None of them clammed up either out of fear or shyness. Their mutual losses somehow must have made even the youngest child, Ginger's Lizzie, feel safe. Maddie started to cry and pretty soon all of them followed suit, even Jerry, which surprised everyone else in the room, except perhaps Sadie.

"I've been so lonely without Marjorie," Jerry said quietly.

Maddie mirrored that with vivid memories of her husband Art's long illness and her feeling of helplessness throughout that time to do anything, no matter how hard she tried. "I really don't know which is worse," she said. "The waiting for him to die or the loneliness since he has been gone. Oh, it's the loneliness," she answered herself immediately. "The knowing that he'll never be there again. It's still awful." She reached out and hugged Sean to her, sharing with the boy their common loss.

Ginger made a valiant effort to honor Harold Jenkins's recent death. And Harold *had* mattered to her, but she soon had to confess that "his death just wasn't the same as with Joel. I guess you all know that. I was really fond of Harold and grateful for everything he did for me. But it was different with Joel. I know that no one will ever take his place, not entirely."

But Ginger missed some of the conversation after that as she remembered what life had come to be like for her just before she met Harold. She had been working on a fashion shoot for a sports clothing catalogue. It was Friday afternoon, and she was broke. After the shoot, for which she was almost an hour late, she had spoken to the producer, a slimy Anglo with very white teeth and bad skin who always dressed in garish, often leather, clothes with lots of gold chains. She always thought he looked like a pimp, thinking it was a joke. It was no joke. He had responded to her demand for money with, "A bit short are you, Sweetheart?"

"Yeah," she had answered. "This is my first job in a couple of weeks."

"Can't help you, I'm afraid. You know the rules." He had seemed thoughtful for a moment, then added, "But I know a guy whose in town just for the weekend. He's looking for a date for tonight. He would pay a thousand bucks for a beautiful girl like you to keep him company."

"A thousand for one date?" Ginger had asked. "What does he have in mind?" She was becoming suspicious.

"Some kind of public event that includes dinner. Should I call and tell him you'll do it?"

She did not even pause. "Sure, why not?" she asked.

Ginger was staying with a girlfriend at the time. Her "date" had picked her up in a cab just after seven. He was an average looking guy in his mid-fifties. A bit overweight and pretty self-conscious. They went to an expensive restaurant just off Sunset Strip and had dinner with some business associates of his. Ginger never did figure out what the business was. She really couldn't care less. There were about twenty people in the party. Ginger's date was very attentive in a leering kind of way, but there had been lots to drink and the food was good. It was clear that he was proud of her and the way she looked. She was unimpressed.

Ginger drank a lot at dinner. Afterwards when they were back in a taxi, the date said, "I picked up some new coke. You wanna hit?"

Ginger did very much want that, and she gave him her best smile.

They had ridden to his hotel, silently took the elevator to his floor and walked down the elegant hallway to his suite. He let them in with the electronic key card. As good as his word, he quickly prepared the white powder trails for each of them. It was an instant high, and Ginger could still remember how good it felt, as if her entire body had come alive with new energy and strength. This was one of the hardest memories for her to erase in recovery—how very good she felt right then. How good it always felt to get high.

Then the memories had become less pleasant. The date kissed her and began to caress her body hungrily. Ginger just closed her eyes and let herself slip into a kind of semi-dream state. She wished later that she could say that she did not remember having sex with him, but she did remember—knew that she always would. She felt nothing but perhaps a little thankful for the wine and the coke. Afterwards, he was very pleasant and friendly.

"I'll be back in LA in a couple a months," he said. "Maybe we can do this again." Once more he gave her a kind of leering smile as he passed her a white hotel envelope. "I've already given your...agent...his, uh, commission." He gently pushed her out the door with, "You should have no trouble downstairs getting a cab."

Ginger knew that nobody would believe her if she said that it was not until she was walking away from that hotel room that it really dawned on her what had just happened. She had not simply had sex with a date, but she had become a prostitute and had just turned her first trick, a rich one, at that.

Another thing she will never forget about that night was throwing up in the elevator on the way down. She could not stand what had become of her. She stumbled out of the hotel without a thought to the discovery of the mess she had left in the elevator or the person who would have to clean it up. Once she got out of the hotel she walked and then ran down the street. How could this happen? What had brought her to this? She was still shaking by the time she was finally calm enough to flag down a cab. The final indignity of that evening was when she had to break open the envelope for the money to pay the cabby. Her "date" had thoughtfully included five twenties along with nine one-hundred dollar bills, anticipating that she would not be able to pay for the cab otherwise. She sat there in the cab wondering if that was standard procedure. Her nearly-hysterical laughter at the thought must have startled the poor driver.

Ginger had met Harold the next week. And she was more than ready to find another way to live.

She shook her head and came back to the present. Listening to the adults that evening in Jerry Hanning's living room was deeply touching, but it was the children who really broke everyone's heart. There is something about a kid talking about their daddy or their mommy who has died that is a sure thing to bring on the tears. Sadie was the one with the longest experience of loss, and so she appeared to have processed it better, certainly than Sean, whose loss was still so fresh. But Sadie said something else that really got everyone's attention, particularly Jerry's.

"You know," she said. "I just don't remember my mommy very well. I…I sometimes think I should, but I just don't. No matter how hard I try." She began to sob.

Jerry pulled her to himself and cradled her. "It's okay, Sweetie," he said. "Sometimes I have trouble remembering her too."

The adults forgave him that little lie, because it was clear that he remembered everything about her, and not a day passed that he did not think about her. That was also true for Ginger with Joel, and with Maddie about Art.

Carmen had remained pretty quiet, so much so that Ginger had started to wonder what was going on with her. But finally she said in a sad little voice, "I only wanted a chance to say goodbye. Why wouldn't God let me say goodbye?"

This one time, Jerry stepped in with a priestly comment, and Ginger was glad that he did. "I don't think it's too late to say goodbye, do you?" he asked.

Carmen was still for a moment, all of them watching her. Then she said, "If he's in heaven it is. Where is heaven anyhow?"

"I think heaven's lots of places. Maybe even right here," Jerry said as he reached over to Carmen and tapped her gently on the chest. "Maybe you don't need to say goodbye to your daddy there."

Ginger wanted to hug him.

They put the three girls to bed at Jerry's house under Margaret Lopez's care, and Ginger rode with Jerry to take Maddie and Sean to her mother's house in the foothills of the Catalinas. It wasn't far, only about fifteen minutes each way. On the way back Ginger and Jerry analyzed the evening and agreed that it was amazing the way the kids had all opened up.

"And do you think you've exorcized your personal ghosts?" Ginger asked him. "Both of them?"

"What do you mean by 'both of them'?" he asked, avoiding her meaning.

"I know about Marjorie, you talked about her tonight, but Maddie told me that you had someone in Bisbee."

"There *was* someone briefly, you know, the woman the three girls spent that one night with, but that's over now." He let a short silence grow up between them. Had he left it there the openness would have ended right then. But he went on, turning the car west on Grant Road for the final leg home. "Actually, I learned that she's married, has been separated from her husband for a couple of years, and was trying to get a divorce. The result of my romantic efforts is that she's going back to her husband." He chuckled briefly. There was no bitterness in his voice, nor could she hear regrets.

"Wow," was her involuntary response, and then, "as Sean might put it, 'that's heavy, dude.'" They laughed together self-consciously.

"Actually," he continued, "I think we helped each other, Kate and I. That's her name, Kate. Both of us had some big blocks in the relationship department." He told Ginger about a brief contact they had had in church Sunday and how everything seemed to fall into place for them. Ginger was amazed at his openness with her, wondering at the evening and at the circumstances that had thrown them together and seemed to be making them friends.

Back at Jerry's house, they sat in the car for a moment finishing their conversation, then they got out and walked up on his front porch. Ginger could see her mother through the front window, sitting with a book in her lap. For some reason the porch light was out, but the light streaming through the window was enough that Ginger and Jerry could see each other clearly, yet it was dark enough that it felt almost as if they were the only two people in the world right then. It seemed natural that they should kiss, and they did. It was nice enough, but still no bells rang for her. Neither was that solitary kiss followed by urgency or fumbling with clothing. It was like a kiss shared by a brother and a sister.

Ginger puzzled over her tepid response to Jerry Hanning, wondering if she was just responding to the priest, not her ideal image of an available male at the best of times, and not to the man himself. The best way she had ever found to sort out her feelings about someone or something and to understand what was happening with her was to draw or paint the person or place she wondered about. For her this was pretty much the way it is when some people write in a journal, kind of like a letting go of the conscious mind so that the unconscious can conjure up images by pouring them out in words, or in Ginger's case, in line, texture, shading and, sometimes, color. And those drawings were easy to interpret; the overall tone of the drawing or painting tended to convey the underlying meaning.

That Saturday evening back in her Bisbee studio, Ginger began a drawing of Jerry Hanning. Even in a few quick pencil strokes, Ginger began to see a very clear Jerry emerge, at least who he was for her. Just for kicks she put on his clerical collar, and she realized that that was an essential element of him for her. As his face emerged, she knew that she had him on some kind of pedestal, a very lonely pedestal for him, she suspected. Then just for fun she made a couple of quick erasures and added a figure of Maddie with the two of them looking into each other's eyes. This was how she saw both of them. Together.

But if the drawing said something about her two friends, it also said a lot about her. It spoke of her need for stability, for a connection with religion, for a life ordered by predictable pieces. It also said that she wanted someone in her life. Only she had no idea who that someone could possibly be.

Sadie, who was spending the night at Ginger's studio with Carmen and Lizzie, came up to Ginger and watched as she was finishing the drawing. "Cool," she said. She stood quietly, reflectively, and then asked, "Does my daddy love Maddie?"

Ginger did not know what to say to her. Did he? She certainly did not know. But Sadie certainly saw in the drawing what Ginger had put there. And Jerry Hanning was not a neutral subject for Ginger. She cared about him, and she cared about Maddie. Was she just projecting her own needs onto them?

"Why do you ask that, Sadie?" Ginger asked.

"I don't know. I just got the idea from your picture of them. I think it would be pretty cool if he did. I really need a mom, you know."

Hearing that made Ginger feel sad for the vulnerable little girl. And sad for her own fatherless girls. And sad for herself.

The more Ginger thought about Jerry Hanning and Maddie Gronek and the drawing she had done of them that Saturday evening, the more she realized how lonely she felt. But Ginger did not want just to fall into another relationship in which she defined herself by someone else, as she had done with Joel and even with Harold. Ginger knew that she had to define herself by herself if she were to continue to be the kind of person she had, in such a comparatively short acquaintance, come to like, even to respect. When a new relationship came along, she would be ready for it. Or she would not have one.

Ginger put the drawing of Maddie Gronek and Jerry Hanning in the corner of the studio, its face to the wall.

CHAPTER EIGHTEEN

Palm Sunday

...People can and do change, and their change can make a fundamental difference. We must pray for our enemies, because God is already at work in their depths stirring up the desire to be just.
—Walter Wink

Jillian Curtain sat in Father Jerry Hanning's church office looking highly agitated, repeatedly pulling locks of hair behind her ears, making needless adjustments to her clothing and minutely scrutinizing first one hand and then the other. "I...I don't know where to start...or what to say," she began.

It was Saturday, the day before Palm Sunday, and Jerry had more than enough on his plate already getting ready for Holy Week. "What is it, Jillian?" Jerry asked, attentive to her and her distress, but also feeling his own burdens.

"I've...I've been seeing...another man," Jillian finally managed to say. "Here in Bisbee. We're...having an affair. There, I've said it."

Jerry tried to hide his surprise, but an admission by her that she had just murdered someone would have been nearly as unexpected as this uncharacteristic announcement had been. "You seem very upset by this," he answered her, feeling utterly inadequate in that hollow response. Suddenly the busy preparations then going on in the church for Palm Sunday seemed both remote and unimportant.

Jerry had arrived at St. Peter's late that morning, with a jumble of details laid out before him, service planning and sermon preparation heading the list. A heady atmosphere of excitement filled the church, and volunteers vacuumed and mopped, put up decorative touches in the sanctuary, polished the brass and silver and straightened hymnals and prayer books in the pews. Mrs. Findlay seemed everywhere present, the anticipation of a church repeatedly stuffed with people more than justifying all the work and effort of the Holy Week octave. Jerry had small-talked his way through the bustle of activity, taking care of a number of small details, and finally had made his way to the office.

He had just begun on his sermon when Jillian Curtain had arrived for her appointment. She had been a bit breathless and in a swirl of tense vibrations and uneasy body language. Jerry had wondered, right up until she finally blurted it out, what "the Blessed Virgin Mary"—he had smiled again at Ike McWarder's joke at Jillian's expense—could possibly want of him, especially at this time of the year when there was so much else going on. The two of them had not, after all, made much of a pastoral connection. She was much too fundamentalist in her thinking to relate to what for her must have seemed like Jerry's shockingly liberal theology, and she was apparently too rigid to change easily. But as the two of them had settled down on either side of the small coffee table in the church office, Jerry had noticed something different about her. He had always thought of Jillian as mousy and controlling—especially with herself—someone almost without gentleness or warmth. He had never before thought of her as pretty or even especially feminine, but today, despite her nervousness, she was suddenly both of those things. There was a kind of presence to her that was new and vulnerably uncertain. Her words had tumbled out one after another as she struggled to come to the point, and her eyes filled with tears.

"Oh, Father, it's really terrible, what I've done. I know it is," she said. "I just don't know what to do."

Jerry thought for a moment. "Do you want to do a sacramental confession?"

"No. That's alright. Really. That's kind of a Catholic thing isn't it?"

Jerry had begun to answer that confession was part of their tradition as well, but she was uninterested in this or any other theological fine-point, and she had gone right ahead with what she was she needed to say.

"This is not something that fits my values," she concluded, "or it never used to. Curtis and the boys would be very hurt if they found out. And I don't want to hurt them. I…I think it would be terrible, really. But I'm…so…happy. Frightened, but really happy, too. And sometimes it hurts. I don't know why it should hurt to be happy. I…I just don't know what to do."

"Do you want to be with this other man?" Jerry asked, as he thought about the Curtain family dynamics—at least as he had observed them. There was a hard edge to Jillian's relationship with Curtis, and an awkward tension seemed to hover over them. Even the two boys reflected the tension between their parents with humorlessness and over-serious attitudes. The effects of this affair were undeniably liberating for her. What of Curtis and the children?

"I'm so happy when I'm with him. I don't know what's happening to me. Ja…this man," she corrected herself, "is not the first one I have thought of in this way. But," she hastened to add, "this is the first time I've actually done anything. To be truthful, I had a little crush on you when you first came here." She flashed him an awkward and embarrassed smile.

"I'm flattered," Jerry answered, but tried to move the conversation back on track. "Have you been unhappy with Curtis?"

"Oh, yes, I guess I have. Yes! And it makes my skin crawl just to be with him. I'm always afraid that he will…you know, want to make love. But he never does anymore. What's happening to me?" she asked again. "What about my Christian values? I really believed that this is a wrong thing to do. I still do, I guess. But how can it be bad when I feel so good? I…I just don't know what to do!" The tears were now streaming down her face.

"How long has this been going on?"

"Not long. A couple of weeks. We've, ah, been together five, no six, times. I don't know what to do. I can't help it. I'm so excited. I know I shouldn't be…but, but, I feel so much more…alive. That's it. I feel more alive."

"It's very exciting having a new relationship with someone. But that doesn't suddenly end an old one. Curtis is still there in the middle, isn't he? Just how long have the two of you been married?"

"Almost fifteen years." She answered quickly, as if she were glad to have something simple to say, something that didn't ask anything of her, something that didn't cost her a new anxiety. "You must think I'm pretty terrible."

"Of course not," Jerry answered. "But you seem to be pretty down on yourself." He drew her back to the subject. There was no point in avoiding the truth about what was happening here. She was having an affair, and she thought she should feel terrible about it, but she didn't, and for that, if not for the affair itself, she felt guilty. Jerry thought about his own short-lived romance with Kate Becker. It wasn't the same, he knew, but it did help him to understand some of how Jillian felt—dishonest, furtive and very excited.

Finally, Jillian escaped from the church like a junior high schoolgirl leaving the principal's office, agreeing to see Jerry again on Good Friday after the noon service. Jerry knew there was no easy resolution for Jillian, but he had suggested that she use the deep emotional and theological themes of Holy Week to help her to get through her personal crisis: the Joy of Palm Sunday's triumphal entry into the holy city, Jerusalem; celebration, loss and betrayal on Maundy Thursday; pain and death on Good Friday—in her case, it meant the death of her old life with husband and family or of the exciting new one she had found with this other man; the depression and hopelessness of Holy Saturday; and finally the joy of resurrection on Easter Day, a remade life beyond the old one that had been left behind. Jillian was going to have to make some hard decisions, and there would be loss no matter which way she jumped. She would either lose the comfort of a fifteen-year marriage and a stable family life—which Jerry would have said that she valued above all else—or she would have to say goodbye to this new man with whom she had found so much excitement and joy. This was a dilemma that was no less painful by its being so familiar. It was the price she would have to pay for allowing passion and hope into a life that had become tedious and despairing. Only time would tell if it would all be worth it.

Jerry wanted to do what little he could for this woman, even though she was someone whom he had not particularly liked—at least before this happened. Now, Jerry was touched by her dilemma, by the humanness in her inability to resist the temptation of an affair, particularly from inside an apparently stifling marriage. If what he had already seen was any indication of the ways Jillian would be changing, it may be the best thing that had ever happened to her. Jerry had a hunch that this personal crisis—and it would bring much pain—would leave her a warmer and kinder person, more tolerant of human frailty in the end, no matter how it came out.

Jerry scrambled to get through all of his planning details and to get to the last session that night of the St. Peter's discussion on *The Powers That Be*. Already the Holy Week themes, including a small taste of the new life of resurrection, seemed to have been played out among the group's members. After the discussion, they chatted, shared little hopes and dreams, and lingered around the table. Everyone was reluctant to see the group come to an end. Even Charlie Snow and Hank Tucker appeared to have called at least a temporary truce. Kate Becker's absence was a loss they all felt, but Jerry missed her especially and felt a pang of guilt at her abrupt departure. Like Jillian Curtain, Jerry needed to experience the new life that Easter promised.

Jerry felt as if he had hardly slept that night before he was up seeing to final details for the complex Palm Sunday service. The altar guild had created a towering passageway down the central aisle of the church by fixing some eight foot long palm branches brought in from Tucson to pews on either side. The tips of the branches leaned inward and created the feel of a Gothic cloister, secure and protected, through which the procession passed amidst celebration and many Hosannas. Fan palms from the tree in Jerry's back yard decorated the altar and reredos, and a basket of crosses made from folded palm fronds were blessed and distributed to the nearly one-hundred people in attendance. Parts of the Passion Gospel text were read dramatically by members of the two Lenten study groups, symbolic of a new kind of unity that Jerry hoped would emerge within the two major contingents of the parish. Sadie, Carmen and Lizzy were the acolytes in the service. And Jerry could not help but be moved by the presence in church that morning of so many people whom he had come to count as friends. Maddie and stepson, Sean Gronek, the Tuckers, Ike McWarder, Ginger Vega, the Browns and the Nellies—Brenda-St. Bridget Litz and Hanna-Hildegard of Bingen Silver. Despite it being overshadowed by the coming commemoration of Christ's passion, this morning's triumphal entry theme carried many feelings of celebration.

The coffee hour afterwards was abuzz with talk about the invitation from the Tuckers to the whole congregation for an Easter Sunday barbeque at the Rocking T Ranch right after church next week. It was a handsome and grand gesture on their part.

Jim Brown, newly released from the hospital following his heart bypass surgery, was warmly greeted by just about everyone. He had doctor's orders to take it easy and to stay put at home for at least a week. Church did not count in that prohibition, or so Jim decided. His recuperative regime of rest, gentle exercise, no strenuous or stressful work, and no driving the car was clearly spelled out. He knuckled under and stayed home rather than going to the Tombstone book group meeting that afternoon at Nellie Cashman's. But everyone else was there as the discussion ended amidst high spirits, good feelings toward each other, a reluctance to see the group dissolve, and some very fresh ideas about God.

Jerry took Jillian Curtain aside as the group was dispersing. "You and Curtis seem pretty tense with each other," he said. "What have you told him?"

"Nothing, but he knows something's wrong," she replied.

"It's pretty hard to hide something as important as that."

"Father Jerry, I just don't know what to do. I'm really torn, you know."

"I do know. Let's just meet at the church on Friday as we agreed. One o'clock. That okay? Give yourself some time to sort it all out. You can call me in the meantime if you need to." He gave her a card with his phone numbers on it. He was under no illusions that Jillian would have solved anything by Friday, but he knew she would need to talk.

"Thanks." Jillian reached out and gave Jerry a quick, warm hug, something very unlike her usual distant handshakes.

But Palm Sunday had not yet run its course for Jerry Hanning. His Skyhawk carried its first illegal cargo that same evening. This new part of his already complicated weekend had come up when he dropped Sadie off at Ginger's studio Saturday morning. Maddie and Sean, had picked them up at the Bisbee airport.

"What are we going to do with the two stranded men who are waiting at the Place?" Ginger asked Jerry and Maddie. All four children were watching the plumber who had come in to work on Ginger's remodeling project.

"I guess I'll have to pick them up," Maddie had said.

"I don't think so," Jerry answered. "You've taken enough chances for now. And I think you're being watched."

"Jerry's right," Ginger inserted.

"Isn't there one of the others who could drive them to Tucson?" Maddie asked.

"That's a real problem." Ginger's distress showed on her face. "The Border Patrol has the roads so tightly watched that it's become very dangerous. I feel so bad about it, but I'm afraid we're just going to have to leave these poor men in the desert to fend for themselves. Maybe we could just urge them to turn themselves in."

"They'd never agree to that," Maddie concluded knowingly.

"I'm sure you're right. But I think we can deal with this pair," Jerry said. "If you'll drive the three girls to Tucson," he said to Ginger, "I'll take the two UDAs in my plane late tomorrow afternoon. Nobody will think twice about me flying out of the Tombstone airport on Sunday afternoon. All we have to do is get the passengers there."

"Don't worry about that," Ginger had said. "Harriet can make sure they're on time, probably going that roundabout route through McNeil and then west right up to the airport from behind. You're sure about this?"

"I'm sure," Jerry had said.

Changing subjects, Ginger asked, "Are you going to come over to the studio after your book group Sunday afternoon? I will have Sadie with me again, won't I?"

"Yes and thanks. Sadie has made it clear," he smiled, "that she will be with you and your girls." He paused briefly and then looked toward Maddie, who was standing beside him, and asked, "Can you give me a ride to Ginger's place tomorrow afternoon? I'll just leave Three-Eight Bravo at the Tombstone airport, ready for me and my passengers."

"I'm not so sure I *will* give you a ride," Maddie answered Jerry in mock anger, "the way you're cutting into my smuggling business!" She smiled engagingly...or at least it struck Jerry as thoroughly winsome.

Ginger's expression watching Jerry and Maddie talk was not unlike that of a matchmaker planning her moves, first looking at the one and then the other and then back again. Indeed, the two of them were gazing hungrily at each other, wanting to touch or caress, but not daring to do either. Maddie's dark hair and eyes—which seemed to shine this morning—and Jerry's now well-trimmed beard and clear blue eyes somehow just seemed to fit.

Later that afternoon Jerry picked up two Mexican laborers, Pablo and Memo, who reached the Tombstone airport well ahead of him. Memo, who spoke pretty good English, and Pablo, who did not, had been abandoned by their coyote and were left desperate to get to Tucson where cousins had promises of jobs. It was the usual story. They were mostly quiet and very polite. All Jerry had to do was stop beside the windsock as he taxied to the opposite end of the landing strip for take off, open the door and let them in the plane, finish the taxi to the east end of the runway, and fly to Tucson as usual. This pattern hardly deviated from Jerry's usual routine. And it all went without incident.

The flight itself was so uneventful that Jerry's mind tended to wander, thinking about many things, especially Maddie Gronek, not anything in particular about her, just thinking about her. Oh, he wondered how her visit with Sean was going. Did the boy's visit bring back thoughts of Art, making the time difficult for her? And he wondered what had happened to Cord, who was inexplicably missing both from church and from the final session of the book group that afternoon. Jerry was glad the younger man had not been there; for some reason Jerry continued not to like Cord, and he prided himself on never harboring a dislike against anyone. Mostly, though, he just thought about Maddie.

Jerry did have some passing thoughts about what he was doing right then, rescuing stranded immigrants—acts that were clearly illegal but ones that also somehow felt to him like the right thing to do. This was a new experience for Jerry Hanning. He had never before felt so deeply about a cause—or caught up in one—that stepping outside the law in pursuit of it had seemed justified. He remembered how critical he had been toward the sixties generation for its draft resistance, demonstrations and public flaunting of the law. Indeed, his whole generation had at its core a revulsion towards the one that preceded it, a rejection of what he had always referred to as that "activist stuff." And so Jerry had been what he thought of as a cool observer of public life, believing in the rule of law, thinking that an orderly pursuit of justice through the legal system was the only acceptable course to take to right wrongs. And he still believed in working through the system in order to change it. His advice to Hank Tucker had been sincere, and he thought that Hank should use his influence and connections to change the official response toward the worker-immigrants. The real solution to the dilemma of trying to live and work in that border country—short of the utopian desire to end all inequality of wealth and power—had to be in a new government attitude and, for Jerry, a more humane response to human suffering. In the meantime, he found himself doing something he had always abhorred, taking illegal action in support of some cause. He was uncomfortable with it, but he could not see what else he could do.

Jerry landed at Ryan Field with his two passengers well past sunset. They did what they could to help him secure the plane once they were on the ground, pushing it into place and leaving it secured for the night. He found their gratitude—at least in part to be back on the ground, he thought wryly—very touching. Memo just kept saying, "Thank you, Mister Jerry. Thank you, man." He walked them to Wings, the airport restaurant, shook hands with them and said goodbye. He could not remember when he had last felt so useful and as appreciated as he did at that moment.

Jerry lifted off from Ryan Field early the next morning to fly to Hank Tucker's place in the Sulphur Springs Valley. It was Monday of Holy Week, and with Palm Sunday behind him, Jerry had a short window of opportunity in this busy week—time to try and solve the mystery of the muddy SUV, the one that he had followed back from the Tombstone airport to the Rocking T Ranch. He had just made a right turn in the traffic pattern and was preparing to depart from Ryan Tower's control.

"Permission to change frequency to TIA. Five-Eight Bravo," he called to the air traffic controller.

"Permission granted, Father. Have a good day."

At that moment the Skyhawk's engine began to sputter and cough. Airspeed and altitude began to slip. No doubt about it, the plane was losing power and would soon be in serious trouble unless Jerry found the source of the problem and found it immediately.

"Ryan Tower, Five-Eight Bravo. I'm having a problem here. If I didn't know better, I'd say I was out of fuel. Both gauges are showing empty."

"Are you okay, Five-Eight Bravo?" asked the Ryan controller.

"No Ryan, I'm not okay. The engine is out. Five-Eight Bravo." Jerry adopted a "best" glide attitude. "Request permission to make an emergency landing on runway Three-Three. Five-Eight Bravo."

"Permission granted, Five-Eight Bravo. I'll clear the space. Good luck, Five-Eight Bravo." Jerry heard the controller's announcement to the other aircraft in the area, but hardly registered it.

The seldom used landing strip, Three-Three, lay at near-right angles with Runway Six/Two-Four, the two ends of the main and parallel runways. Three-Three was much closer to Jerry than runway Six where he had just taken off. His had barely enough altitude to reach Three-Three, let alone to go around to Six. Jerry made his first turn immediately, setting a glide pattern at eighty miles per hour. The silence was eerie.

Jerry followed all of the prescribed emergency procedures: a close eye on the speed and the altitude, magnetos off, the now-useless fuel flow valve in the "off" position, and 10 degrees of flaps set. His mind was racing. How could the Skyhawk possibly be out of gas? He had made a visual check on both of the wing tanks, and both were full. At least they had been fifteen minutes ago. Jerry began the final turn, adding another ten degrees of flaps, and then a final ten, letting the Skyhawk sink in, barely above stalling speed over runway Three-Three. A strong cross wind from the right forced him to crab to the right to remain lined up with the runway. He fought the wheel and used lots of right rudder. Five-Eight Bravo settled smoothly on the landing strip just about where runway Three-Three intersects runway Six-Right.

"Pretty impressive, Five-Eight Bravo. Everything okay?"

"Just great, Ryan Tower," he said a little bitingly. "But thanks for asking. Can you send somebody to give me a hand with this thing? Nick at Triangle, if he's free. Five-Eight Bravo." Jerry opened the door, pulled off his headset, and jumped out. He could not remember when it had felt so good to put his feet on the ground.

Twenty minutes later, his Skyhawk having been towed to Triangle Air Service's hanger, Jerry stood with part-owner and mechanic, Nick Foreman. Nick had been doing the routine maintenance on Five-Eight Bravo since Jerry came to Tucson.

"So what do you think, Nick?" Jerry asked. "Some kind of leak?"

"Some kind, all right. Look here." He pointed under the cowling at a loose copper tube with its fitting obviously unattached. "That's your left fuel line. And here, there's the right one." He pointed at a second copper tube. "You just left forty gallons of aviation fuel down Six-Right and over the good folks who have the misfortune to live east of this airport."

"But, how on earth do the fuel lines come to be loose? How does something like that happen?"

"It doesn't just happen," the mechanic continued. "I would blame myself as your mechanic, except that I haven't put wrench one to this bird in almost a year except to change the oil. If the lines had held a few more days, I would have done your Annual and you would have been okay. Is there somebody who doesn't like you?" He laughed nervously.

"Apparently so," said Jerry noncommital and unwilling to explore the possibilities with Nick. "Any problem fixing it?"

"None at all, at least nothing that a half-inch open-end wrench won't cure. Give me ten minutes and you're back in the air—if you have the nerve for it." He paused for a moment. "Don't you think you should call the cops?"

"Tell you what, Nick." Jerry ignored the mechanic's question. "Do you have time to do the Annual right away?"

"I guess I do. There was a cancellation this morning."

"Then give it a good once-over. See if something else has come loose in the vibration." Nick just looked hard at him.

Jerry did not like to think that he was frightened away from flying his plane, but at least it seemed fair enough to take a couple of days to get over what had happened. It had shaken him. Jerry called Hank Tucker and told him that the conversation he had asked Hank for would have to wait. But he was unable to bring himself to tell Hank why he wanted to talk to him and, now, why he had had to cancel it. No matter how hard he tried, Jerry could not evade the conclusion that what had happened to Five-Eight Bravo was not an accident, that it was not just something that happens. Would somebody actually sabotage his airplane? And if so, who could it have been? Nick had no explanation for how those fuel lines came to be loose—both of them. If someone had loosened them, then that someone accepted the risk that Jerry would be killed. And what if he had had the three girls with him as he often did? Would whoever loosed those fuel lines also be willing to have them be killed?

A warning? Perhaps that was what it was. It certainly got Jerry's attention. And what about Maddie? Jerry thought that he had better warn her. He punched in the numbers.

"Hi," he said into the phone when Maddie answered. "How's the visit going with Sean?"

"Great," she answered. "He's a terrific kid."

"I think so too. He sure launched us on quite a conversation last week, didn't he?" Jerry remembered the emotion-laden conversation about the deaths of people close to them.

"It was amazing. I think we all felt much better after it. Any chance we can get together some more while he's here?"

"Absolutely." Jerry paused. "Anyhow, the reason I called," he continued, reluctantly coming to the point, "is that I think somebody loosened the fuel lines on my 172." He told her what had happened. "It must have something to do with flying the immigrants and our little double-teaming operation. I think you'd better be careful, too," he concluded.

"God!" She seemed stunned. "That's pretty scary. You okay?"

"I'm fine."

A long silence sat heavily on them. Finally, Maddie continued. "Ah…it would be hard for someone to come in here at the Twisted K and mess with my plane. But thanks for the warning. I'll ask Refugio to have a careful look under the cowling—and I'll be extra cautious in my pre-flights."

Jerry felt a stab of fear in his stomach when he thought about Maddie being at risk. "We really do have to figure out who is running people off the road, shooting at airplanes and maybe even sabotaging them," he said, "no matter if my suspicions about my plane are right or wrong."

"Where *does* that stand, identifying the bad guys?"

"On hold for now. I was going to fly to Hank Tucker's ranch today to talk with him about the SUV that Ginger and I followed to his place. That's what I was doing when I had the emergency landing at Ryan."

"Isn't he—Hank Tucker—one of the vigilantes?"

"He has been, but I doubt he'd be part of anything like this. In fact, he's had a change of heart."

"You're sure?"

"As sure as I can be."

"Anyhow, I'm going down early on Thursday to talk to him about the SUV—all of it. I still haven't heard about the license plate on the pickup truck. I guess this seems pretty low priority for my friend at the Arizona Department of Transportation."

"I suppose so, unless you're prepared to tell the guy at ADOT why you want it. And that raises a bunch more questions, ones we aren't ready to raise…or answer, for that matter. Just what did you tell him?"

"Only that I had a pastoral concern—not entirely a lie, considering the connection to the Rocking T and Hank Tucker." Jerry paused and took a deep breath. "You know," he said, "there's something else I wanted to talk to you about…to tell you, actually."

"Yes. What is it, Jerry?" He thought he could hear an odd tension in her voice.

"You know that I had been seeing someone in Bisbee."

"I gathered that." Her voice was emotionless.

"Well, that's off now. For good. Has been for a couple of weeks, actually. Sorry I haven't mentioned it—or her, really—before now."

Their receivers both went dead in their ears. Then as one they said, "Are you still there?" They laughed together.

"Now, I've got to talk to the bishop…about having had a relationship with a parishioner," Jerry added.

"Is that a problem?"

"It could be. And I'm worried about it."

Thursday morning Jerry was off early on a day heavy with unknowns, including a lunch date with Kate Becker right after some straight talk with Hank Tucker. It seemed as if this was Jerry Hanning's week for difficult conversations. On Tuesday, he had driven to the cathedral in Phoenix for a reaffirmation of ordination vows, an annual event in Holy Week, and a luncheon with the other clergy. Afterwards he talked with the bishop about Kate Becker.

"So let me see if I have this right, then, Jerry," the bishop had said. "You've had a short affair with a woman in the parish whom you thought was divorced, but who was only separated from her husband?"

"That's right," Jerry answered simply, refusing to embellish the story, especially about his one-time hopes and dreams for the relationship. "I always knew I should have talked with you first…as she and I began having coffee and talking. But…but it just went farther and faster than I expected."

The bishop laughed knowingly and settled back in the leather chair behind his broad, cluttered desk. "Yes, that's the way those things happen, isn't it?"

Jerry just nodded, but was feeling better.

"Frankly," the bishop continued, "I'm glad you're no longer sleep-walking. I'd sort of hoped that something good would happen for you as you got back to your ministry, that you'd find someone to share your life with." He paused for a moment. "But this is a bit more complicated than I'd bargained for.

There's no doubt that I share some of the responsibility with you. You were very vulnerable, and I knew it. I'm making no moral judgments here. It's clear that you behaved in good faith. But I'm going to have to think about what, if any, pastoral response I need to make as your bishop—and hers. You'll hear from me after Easter."

In less than an hour after Jerry began his taxi at Ryan Field that Thursday morning, he was on the ground at Hank Tucker's Rocking T Ranch and parking Five-Eight Bravo next to Hank's Bonanza. Talking with Hank promised to be difficult, but he could not avoid doing it—any more than he could have ducked telling the bishop about Kate Becker.

Beside the Rocking T's landing strip, sat a cluster of ranch buildings and vehicles in an open yard, the center of which was filled with a simple ramada made of rough-hewn timbers and saguaro cactus ribs. Several pick-up trucks and sedans, including the Lexus Hank usually drove, sat unceremoniously in the dusty dirt yard beside the ramada. So also did the SUV, or at least Jerry assumed that it was the same one—a dark smokey-blue Dodge Ram, slightly battered and scratched, but very deadly looking. At least that's how it looked to Jerry just then. This must surely be the same one, minus the mud. Ranch hands began to gather, curious about the plane that had landed. Hank and Teresa stood at the front door of the ranch house, hand-in-hand, still the newlyweds.

"Hi, Tuckers," Jerry called as he came close to them.

"Hi, yourself," Teresa responded.

"Coffee?" was Hank's one-word greeting.

"Hot and strong."

"You got it."

A gray tabby cat scurried under the SUV as Jerry walked past. Teresa gave him a warm hug, and Hank extended his hand as they walked inside the house and straight into the old-fashioned kitchen. The sun streamed in through east windows framed with crisp blue and white checked curtains. Smells of freshly baked muffins and coffee—two of the best smells in the world— filled the air as they gathered at an ancient round kitchen table, one very like the one that Jerry's grandmother had had in her kitchen. The chairs, as old as the table, were hard and straight and yet surprisingly comfortable in their contour-molded, pressed-back design. Coffee was poured, and plates of blueberry muffins and butter appeared in the center of the table. The moment was packed both with pleasure and with dread. Jerry liked Hank and Teresa Tucker, but he had to be straight with Hank about what had been happening to Maddie and to him and their airplanes and get to the bottom of where Hank fit in it all. Jerry did not like to think that Hank was a part of this sinister side to the rancher vigilantes.

"So what's this 'brain picking' you want to do?" Hank asked, smiling.

Jerry didn't smile. "Well, I have to admit that it's a bit touchier and more important than I'd led you to believe."

"What's the problem, Jerry, or is it 'Father Hanning'? Am I being senior warden?"

"No, not that." Jerry flashed a quick grin. "And this really isn't about you either, at least not directly." At least I hope it isn't, he thought to himself. After a moment's reflection he launched directly into the story he had to tell, "I'm part of a group based in Bisbee—a pretty recent member, actually—that has been helping stranded Undocumented Aliens."

Hank looked at his priest very hard, sternly even, then his face broke out into a broad smile and he gave out one of his low, rumbling laughs that seemed to originate deep in his belly. "Didn't I tell you, Teresa? That Jerry was involved somehow?" He laughed again.

"I can't tell you how pleased I am to hear it, Father," Teresa said.

"Anyhow," Jerry continued, relieved, at least on that score, "I'm so glad that you aren't disappointed or angry. I know, Hank, that your opinion on the UDAs—at least until recently—has been pretty negative." He told them the full story beginning with Harold Jenkins's death and the difficulties they had had with apparent vigilantes. When he finished with the story about following the SUV back to this ranch, the very one that Jerry thought was sitting right now outside the door, Hank was sitting on the edge of his chair taking in every word Jerry said. Finally, Hank cleared his throat. It was his turn for confession.

"When the two women were busted at the Tombstone Airport by the Border Patrol, I was the one who turned them in. I was making one of the flights Alex and I used to do to check for UDAs and people helping them. That was the last one of those flights I made. I told you last week that I've had a change of heart about all of that. But I'm shocked that someone has been shooting at private aircraft, no matter what the reason."

"I have a hunch," Jerry inserted, feeling better and better about Hank, "that it's the same people who killed Harold Jenkins and his passengers by running them off the road in the Santa Ritas. Maybe that's what's making them increasingly bold, or maybe scared and desperate. Anyhow, the latest thing is that it looks like somebody loosened the fuel lines on my Skyhawk

Monday. It was pretty hairy. That's why I canceled on you."

"You mean to say that you think someone messed with your plane? Sabotaged it?"

"I'm not sure, and I can't prove anything. But it *is* suspicious. Besides, I did take two laborers from Tombstone to Tucson Sunday evening. What I think is that somebody is giving me a not-so-friendly warning."

"God!" Hank exhaled through his teeth.

"Now the question is, who owns the SUV that's sitting outside? That's our main link to these people—at least right now it is."

"That's simple. I do," Hank answered. "It's fifteen years old or so, not really an SUV, you know. It's older than that, but it has the biggest engine on the place. It goes!"

"Who drives it?"

"That's a problem, 'cause just about everybody on this ranch does. Anyone could have driven it—any one of the hands, even their family members, Alex, either of us," he gestured toward Teresa. "Even the neighbors. John Vargas down the road has borrowed it from time to time. The keys are always left in it. Sorry I can't be more help."

"Any idea at all who might have had it early last Wednesday morning?"

Hank thought for a minute and then responded, "None whatever, I'm afraid. But I'll ask around. Its doubtful I'll learn much. Maybe between now and Sunday I can find out something. We can talk at the barbeque after church."

Jerry left the Rocking T with mixed feelings of relief and disappointment: relief that Hank was not implicated in vigilante violence and that the rancher was okay with what Jerry had been doing; and disappointment that the SUV led no further. Now, it looked as if the only solid lead that remained was the ID of the pickup truck driven last Wednesday by the SUV's passenger.

Kate Becker was already sitting at a table in the Copper Queen's coffee shop when Jerry arrived. Their greetings were subdued. "Hi," Jerry said.

"Hello." She remained seated. Kate looked as ironed, cool and together as she always did.

"You look terrific," Jerry said.

"You look pretty good yourself," she answered. There was a kind of distant look in her hazel eyes.

Jerry was ill at ease, unsure what he felt just then: a sad yearning, a fleeting moment of anxiety—hope or fear, he wasn't sure which—that she might want to rekindle their relationship.

Kate reached out and touched Jerry's hand. He felt himself tense and wondered if he had communicated that ambivalence and uncertainty to her. It seemed he had.

"Sorry, but I really don't have designs upon you," she said. "At least none that I intend to act on." She took her hand away.

"I didn't mean to look so awkward, but I guess I can't hide what's going on inside," Jerry spoke as honestly as he knew how.

"I know. I'm pretty tense too," she said. "But I wanted you to understand what's going on with me. That just felt important. Thanks for coming."

Jerry nodded, still awkward, but relieved after all that this meeting was really about closure, not some attempt to drag their affair on. They both ordered iced tea, and Jerry picked up his menu and began looking at it. Someone laughed in the bar on the other side of the lobby. Jerry could hear an occasional word or two of conversation from the handful of other diners scattered around the single room. He smelled odors of frying foods coming from the kitchen. The teas arrived. The silence had begun to be painful.

"I'm glad you called," Jerry said, "but, is this a pastoral visit or an awkward conversation between former lovers?" He smiled.

"I don't think we have a choice there. We are former lovers, after all." She smiled back in a gently teasing way. "And this certainly *is* awkward!"

Jerry laughed and relaxed even more.

The silence and the awkwardness resumed. Kate continued, "I really do care about you, Jerry, and I loved the time we spent together—all of it." She smiled again. "But I saw James, my husband, when I was home. It was hard to avoid, actually, and I realized that I still felt some pretty strong things for him. And all of a sudden, I got it. I had done the same thing with him that I had done in other relationships I have had, both married and unmarried ones. When it gets tough, I leave. For once I finally accepted the truth of my own behavior. I used to think that I had made bad choices in men. Now I know that the problem was me, not just them, and partly I finally get it…because of you. There was no way I could turn you into anything but what you are, a good and decent man. I guess the others were decent, too, in their own way. Jimmy especially. He has really stuck with me. Won't call it quits. I even told him about you—not who you are or that you're a priest or anything, but that you exist as a part of my life. He said that it hurt—hurt! Imagine that! That he would actually admit something like that to me! He said he had missed me very much and had wished every day—a prayer by any other name?—

that I would return to him.

"Well, anyhow, we spent a couple of days and nights together, and we talked a lot. I can't say that I felt the great passion that we had at first. But it was very comfortable and…and I liked it. I really want to try again with him."

"I'm happy for you," Jerry said as he slipped on his pastoral mask, "and I wish you the best," not sure that he meant what he said. "But you really don't owe me an explanation." Then he let the mask fall. "Knowing you and feeling something for someone again was very good for me too—still is. You were very important for me. You still are."

"And you are for me," she said. "I don't think any of this could have happened for me without you." She reached out and laid her hand on his. This time he did not flinch or stiffen. Her smile showed that she understood that.

"One other thing," he said. "I had a talk with the bishop on Tuesday. He wasn't real happy with me, and he was concerned about you. I think he knows I'm not some kind of predator. And I think he understood. But I gave him your name and phone number. Hope you don't mind."

"Of course I don't mind. Do you want *me* to call him?"

"Thanks for the offer, but I've put the ball in his court." Jerry felt a warmth and fondness for this woman who had been so vulnerable with him and who had meant so much to his new life. But he knew with a certainty he had seldom before experienced that this was the right course for both of them.

Kate smiled at Jerry as if she knew exactly what he was thinking—or perhaps was feeling similar things herself.

CHAPTER NINETEEN

Maundy Thursday

May God be merciful to us and bless us,
Show us the light of his countenance, and come to us.
—Psalm 67

Maddie decided to attend the Maundy Thursday service at St. Peter's. While she had made the choice to be in Bisbee and not at the Passover service in Tucson, a part of her thought about being at Temple. Still, she knew she was where she wanted to be just then, and that was with her Bisbee and Tombstone friends. She made a point of getting to St. Peter's well before anyone else arrived—just before sunset—so she could sit quietly and alone in the church and think about everything that had been going on in her life. Jerry had been busy getting ready for the evening's service and so she had the place to herself. And Maddie had a lot to think about. She thought about Cord and how sorry she was for the pain she had caused him, but she knew that she could not continue to see him.

"Cord, you know this isn't working for me?" she had said the week before, moved to act by Sean's expected arrival.

"Yeah, I know. I can tell," he answered, thinking about how unresponsive and distracted she had become.

They had been sitting in her car outside Cord's place for several minutes, mostly in awkward silence. Dinner in a hotel restaurant just outside Bisbee had been the same, a tense meal filled with long silences and occasional, stilted conversation.

"You're very sweet, and I *am* fond of you. But I guess the timing just isn't quite right for us," she continued.

"Shit! The timing's just fine for *me*." He sat there staring morosely ahead and then, amidst unmistakably hostile body language, got out of the car and, looking back, said, bitterly, "Have a great life." He slammed the door.

Maddie sat there a moment, wondering if she should go after him and then decided not to, realizing that she had taken the right course. Nothing would be gained by prolonging the agony of bringing this to an end, despite her urge to smooth everything over and make it "all better again." Maddie spent the next few days depressed and guilt-laden. But that was a week ago, and she knew that it had been an important decision for her to make. She was glad she had made it.

She sat there in St. Peter's looking around the interior of the old church, nine decades of people's hopes and needs settling heavily and yet reassuringly all around her. She sensed memories of prayers echoing silently off the wooden beams and across the pews. She imagined weddings, baptisms, confirmations, anniversaries, and the collected grief of families at the funerals of loved ones—all silently filling the cracks and crevices and layering down emotions like a laquer of beeswax on the dark wood. She remembered Art's funeral in that same place. Her heart was warmed by the late afternoon sun flooding through the murky stained-glass windows and spilling across a single bouquet of mums and white carnations sitting on a small table. A bowl, water pitcher and fluffy, white towels sat ready for the service's ritual foot washing. She thought about the conflict she felt between being there and the powerful sense of connection she experienced the two times she had attended Sabbath services in Tucson.

And Maddie knew there was something different about her. She knew that deep inside her much that was new and filled with promise had been stirring now for over a month. Nor did she need the pregnancy test she had taken the day before or a doctor's confirmation which she expected to get the next day. She already knew the truth about what was happening to her body. After years of trying and hoping, Maddie was finally pregnant. She was so excited that, despite the awkwardness of the circumstances of her pregnancy, she could barely contain her need to announce it to the world. Dust mites danced across the beams of sunlight in the empty church as if they were a troupe of angels performing a delicate, graceful ballet in celebration of her new and wonderful secret.

Maddie also thought about Sadie and Ginger's two girls and of her step-children, Sean, and his twin sisters, and she wondered what their lives would be like, touched as they all had been by the childhood loss of a parent and forced to grow up before their time, wise and yet so very vulnerable. And what of her baby? What tragedies and joys would help form him or her? What role would Cord play in the baby's life? Did she even want him to know about it? Perhaps she should just go away and have her child quietly and leave the ranch in Refugio's care. But was that fair to either the child or to Cord? She simply was not yet ready to decide about that. Life seemed so pungent, so fecund, so risky. The earthy, paradoxical quality of the Christian Church's most revered metaphors flashed through her mind: vines, branches and pruning sheers; shepherds and single sheep lost from the herd; bridesmaids trimming their lamps for expectant bridegrooms; lost coins and buried treasure with finders risking all to possess them; lepers and social outcasts coming to dinners and wedding feasts. Everywhere she looked she saw paradox, contradiction, rejection of conventional thinking, messiness.

She felt deeply the powerful images of this climactic week in Lent, the comradery and bonhomie of the Last Supper ritual that was about to be reenacted—the perfect climax to her experience with the book group in Tombstone—and dread over the horror of Good Friday, dark with foreboding and threat. She realized how these great symbolic occasions, frozen in the timelessness of the church's liturgy, so closely paralleled her own experience of living, and fit so well with the contradictions of Jesus's message: warm fellowship and death, deep despair and soaring joy.

Another set of complimentary images and metaphors came to her from her Jewish side. How could she escape those Passover themes? Why would she want to? She experienced deeply the release from bondage and the invitation to enter the Promised Land that forms the centerpiece of the Exodus story. For the first time in her life, Maddie truly understood what Passover was about...and what Easter was about. She began to know what had moved Jews and Christians so deeply over the centuries: how Jews were bound to their own kind by the Passover promise of delivery all through the centuries of the Diaspora; how Christians survived the horrors symbolized in Good Friday with the promise of Easter. She looked around the darkening interior of the church, its exposed dark-beamed ceiling giving a feeling of loftiness that the small building really did not possess. Her gaze fell on the baptismal font near the front door of the church. Images of water: the parting of the Red Sea and baptism in the Jordan River, they both seemed of a piece. The metaphors worked for her. All of them, in an instant with no real warning, they just worked.

Following the Maundy Thursday service, Maddie and Jerry walked to Ginger's studio where Sean had been waiting for her. "This is a conversation I've been waiting to have with you," she said kind of mysteriously, taking

Jerry's arm and sending a jolt of memory through him about walking with Kate Becker along this same street and having *her* take his arm. It felt so familiar, so filled with promise, but so confusing. "Well, anyhow," she continued. "First of all, I want you to know that my relationship with Cord has been…pretty important…and, oh, you know…it's been…"

"Sexual?"

"Yes," she said simply. "Anyhow, I've thought from the beginning that it was very temporary, but…"

As Maddie said these things to Jerry, the hesitancy and her reluctance to speak left him with an uneasy feeling. There was even a kind of pain in his stomach. What was going on here? Are they going to live together? It's much too soon after Art's death. He tried to adopt a pastoral attitude. Then he thought about Cord's uncharacteristic absence on Sunday and again that evening, and for some reason felt reassured and encouraged by that disappearance.

"What I've realized," she continued, "is that in some ways it should never have happened in the first place." Maddie glanced over at Jerry. "Not that it hasn't been good for me—and for him, I think. But I'm just not in love with him, and it feels like I need to clear up things in my life that…just…don't feel like a good fit. Know what I mean?" It was all she could do right then to keep from telling Jerry that she was pregnant. But she decided to go slowly and to wait until she was certain—or at least had outside confirmation. She was as certain as any woman could be.

"Sure. I know just what you mean," Jerry answered feeling unaccountably very relieved. "That was how I felt about my relationship with Kate Becker. Kate and I might have had some real potential as a couple under other circumstances, but we had to adjust to the circumstances we had." Apparently something like this was true for Maddie and Cord. "So what about Cord, then?" he asked.

"I've had the 'I only want to be friends' conversation with him."

"Yes. How did he take it?"

"He was angry."

Jerry felt both relief and happiness at what Maddie had just told him. The longer they walked together, the higher both of their spirits became. Maddie was relieved, feeling that in some way her friend, Jerry, had been restored to her. Jerry, for his part, experienced elation far exceeding the few words she had spoken.

Ginger let them into the studio amidst stacks of construction debris that filled one entire end of the enormous space. New rooms were clearly emerging out of the wreckage. Ginger had been giving Sean some drawing lessons, and the boy clearly seemed to have some real talent for drawing.

"That's great, Sean," Jerry said, looking at a pencil drawing of a street scene. "But, of course, you have a fine teacher."

"She's cool," Sean answered, blushing lightly and clearly flattered by this adult attention.

"I'd like to have it framed and put it up at the ranch," Maddie added. "Would that be okay?"

"Sure." Sean beamed and took a deep breath, obviously feeling shy and vulnerable. Finally, he changed the subject. "Have you seen the great things *she's* been doing?" he asked gesturing toward Ginger.

"Not now, Sean. Help me get the food to the table. We're ready to eat." Ginger pulled a towel she had draped over her shoulder into her hands and wiped them, then let it fall onto the kitchen counter.

After dinner, Sean and the three adults had settled back into the conversation area.

"I wish the girls were here," the boy said suddenly. "It's, like, lonely without them."

"It is," Jerry agreed.

"But they'll be here all weekend."

Jerry was scheduled to pick the three girls up and bring them back in the Skyhawk on Saturday for Easter. "But weren't you going to show us some pictures?" he asked.

"Oh, no," Ginger demurred. "Not much is finished yet."

"Not true," said Sean, jumping up. He ran over to a stack of canvases in the corner and picked up the first one. It was, true to Ginger's disclaimer, unfinished—a painting of an elderly woman sitting outside a house in Brewery Gulch. It was more abstract than Harold's Bisbee scenes, and it carried a kind of power that made the solitary figure come alive—even unfinished as it was. Then Sean picked up another picture. This one was of a house surrounded by gigantic metal sculptures.

"Cord's place and his work," Maddie explained to Jerry. "That's really good, Ginger," she said.

"But here's my favorite," Sean said, picking up what looked like a very large pad of drawing paper. He held it up for their examination. It was the pencil drawing of Jerry in a clerical collar and Maddie, looking at each other with intensity and passion.

"Oh, Sean, you weren't supposed to show that one." Ginger turned from him to Maddie and Jerry. "I was just fooling around a bit from memory the other evening."

"Sadie told me about this," Jerry said. "But she really didn't do it justice. I didn't get it that we were both in the same picture." Jerry looked over at Maddie. She looked uneasy, which was exactly how he felt. There was no doubt that Ginger had projected a tender intimacy onto their likenesses. Truth as she saw it? A prediction? Neither Maddie nor Jerry paid a lot of attention to the other paintings Sean showed them after that. Neither of them could set aside the mental image of that drawing or the implications it carried

Maddie and Jerry drove back to the Twisted K together that same night with Sean sound asleep in the back seat. Memories of last Ash Wednesday when, lonely and needy, they had spent the night together, loomed up between them, haunting them, and yet offering a new future. So also did Ginger's drawing. Jerry carried the sleeping Sean to his bedroom and helped Maddie get him into bed. What little was left of the evening was filled with little silences, furtive glances at each other and an accidental touch or two. When the anxious evening passed, it ended for them in the cloistered courtyard of the Twisted K ranch house outside the bedroom doors. They shared a lingering kiss standing there. Maddie rested her hand on Jerry's face for a long moment, making him vividly aware for the first time of just how tiny and dainty her hands were, and then she pulled away.

"I think Ginger knew something that neither of us had figured out," she said looking directly at him.

Jerry nodded and said, "Uh-huh." He reached out to her again and cradled her in his arms.

"But let's go slow. Okay?" she continued.

It was hard for Jerry to say anything. He just muttered, "Okay."

"And I promise not to wake you in the middle of the night." She grinned in the half-light.

They kissed again and then, reluctantly, but with unspoken mutual agreement, parted for the night.

Maddie did something the next day, Good Friday, that felt a little weird to her—in fact, it felt a lot weird. She had just gotten back to the Twisted K ranch after dropping Jerry at St. Peter's and keeping a short appointment with her doctor in Bisbee. She was pressed into this strange and uncharacteristic behavior by Jerry leaning over to her and saying before he got out of the car, "How about a date, just the two of us, on Monday, say? We can have dinner and see a movie. You up for that?"

"Yes, of course. Did you expect any other answer, you dummy?" Maddie responded playfully.

"Well, I had my plans, designs even. But, it wouldn't be the first time my hopes have been dashed," Jerry responded and grinned.

"Watch it, Buster," she snapped back, laughing and knowing that he meant their night together, back in what seemed to have been another life. Only a month ago?

Jerry laughed, a flash of white teeth peeking out of the underbrush of his bearded face, which Maddie had not been able to resist reaching out and touching lightly.

Later that morning, the doctor confirmed what Maddie already knew. She was thirty-seven years old, widowed and freshly into her first trimester. What was it about that total package that filled her with such joy? She ought to feel embarrassed, maybe even humiliated. But joy was what she felt.

So now it was time for Maddie to go on with that weird thing she just had to do, weird, but also necessary as a symbolic transition. Back at the ranch, she walked out into the stand of black oaks where Art's ashes had been scattered. This was only the second time she had been there since the day of his funeral. The first time was the week she returned to the ranch after having been in France. That day she had simply sat there quietly and wept, having a catharsis that she had not expected. It was hard to explain, but now it seemed important to her to be with Art for a few minutes, whatever "being with him" might mean. Her time with Cord had not initially felt terribly important, not something that compelled her to share with Art, however absurd such a "sharing" might be. But now, both the baby and newly acknowledged feelings for Jerry Hanning were important, so important that somehow she had to include Art in what both of them seemed to represent for her future.

It seemed very foolish and superstitious to be out there in that grove of black oaks. Maddie knew Art wasn't in the soil or in the trees. Still, it was right somehow that she should go out there and "talk" with him. So she did. Maddie sat on a sun-bleached tree stump and told Art right out loud everything in her mind. She told him about her time in Paris, about flying, about going to Temple, about the now-defunct affair with Cord; and she told him about the baby, tears of joy filling her eyes as she did so. She also told him about her real and growing feelings for Jerry Hanning. Maddie had heard of widows going to the graves of their husbands to ask "permission" to begin a new romance or to get married again, always thinking that it was stupid. And now, here she was doing something very like that, and it did not feel "stupid" at all. Weird, yes, but not stupid, fearing that if someone came upon her out there in that grove of trees talking out loud all alone, they would bundle her off to the little men in the white coats. She just sat there, the dry wind whistling down the draw, dust and sand blowing all around her, and talked and talked.

She heard no voices and saw no apparitions. But inside, Maddie felt that Art had heard her. She could not explain it, even to herself, except to say that it seemed to be so. And it was okay. It was all okay.

CHAPTER TWENTY

Good Friday

Loving our enemies may seem impossible, yet it can be done. At no point is the inrush of divine grace so immediately and concretely perceptible as in those moments when we let go of our hatred and relax into God's love. No miracle is so awesome, so necessary, and so frequent.
—Walter Wink

Virginia Lopez Vega grew up attending St Mary's Catholic Church in Tucson on Sundays and went to its K through 8 school during the week. Both parish church and school were staunch defenders of Catholic orthodoxy and ritual. When Palm Sunday came, ushering in as it did Holy Week each year, she had reveled in the rich symbolism and experienced deeply all of the powerful themes of the day and the week it began—all pointing toward the wonder of Easter.

Ginger could not remember exactly when Easter had become more for her than beauty and rich sensual experiences of bright, frilly dresses, well-dressed boys in white shirts and dark ties and trousers, trumpets and choirs and rumbling organ bass notes. But she did experience a time in adolescence when the story of Jesus's Passion and Resurrection became so profoundly true for her that she would cry tears of sorrow, beginning with the reading of the Passion Gospel on Palm Sunday, continuing with most of the Holy Week services and ending with tears of joy on Easter Sunday. No other memory of Ginger's childhood was as filled with joy as that year's glorious Easter Sunday morning.

The next year, Ginger managed only Palm Sunday and Easter, and neither one moved her very much. What had intervened, of course, was being raped. Her sense of uncleanness so profoundly debased her sense of God's being a loving presence in her life, that she was robbed of every joy of her childhood faith.

This year Ginger decided that it was time for her to try Holy Week again. At a deep, unconscious level she was hoping to recapture those old childlike feelings, even though consciously she knew that that was unlikely to happen. More realistically, she wanted to share with Carmen and Lizzie the mysteries of Holy Week that had meant so much to her as a child. So they attended the Palm Sunday service at St. Peter's in Bisbee. It was not the Catholic Church, and that was definitely a mixed blessing for her. She did not feel as judged and demeaned by the small church and its priest—her friend—as she had done in her home parish, but she still was not sure that the experience was exactly real or that there was any acceptable alternative to the church of her childhood. Still, she resolved to finish out the week with Jerry and St. Peter's: Maundy Thursday; Good Friday, perhaps the toughest service of the year emotionally—especially for someone who had recently experienced the deaths of loved ones; and, of course Easter Sunday. Jerry seemed to have become her priest. Did this mean that she had become an Episcopalian? She had no opinion on that subject.

Palm Sunday was fine for Ginger, a bit smaller in scale than what she had grown up with to say the least, but all of the familiar themes were there. Ginger liked Jerry's sermon. But, then, she was going to appreciate St. Peter's that Sunday no matter what happened. She was ready to be part of a church again; she was also open to having the priest as a friend. She amazed herself.

Though her intentions were good, Ginger missed the Maundy Thursday service after all. There was a problem with the construction on her studio, a complication about the inspection, and she had to meet with the "main guy." To have called him a "general contractor" would have been to exaggerate his actual role and importance, but he did have some influence over the other workers. Little by little the work was getting done, but it was clearly going to take much longer than she had been promised.

Ginger did keep her resolve to go to St. Peter's Good Friday service. The warm day seemed to suit the commemoration of Christ's passion. A harsh, dry southwest wind created a dirty brown sky; dust and dirt blew, swirling and seeping into every crevice. Nothing escaped its harsh blast. From the time Ginger got up, through her attempts to work while carpenters and sheet rockers ripped and hammered, and especially as she walked to the church, she had a growing sense of foreboding. The forlorn sound of loose boards banging against each other on a frame house and a street sign twisting and shuddering in the sandy blast compounded her uneasy somatic sense. Ginger told herself repeatedly that these intense feelings of foreboding were all her imagination, that it was only the horrible day, that it was just her old anxiety over being in church and being judged there, that it was the horrible theme of Good Friday. Instead of brooding nervously, she changed the focus of her thoughts to a story she had just read in the newspaper about one-hundred-twenty-two immigrants being rounded up and detained by the Border Patrol just a few miles east of Douglas. She thought about the little boy in the story who had wandered off and was finally located by a squad of guards. Mingled rage and relief helped replace her own uneasiness.

Walking up the front steps of the church reminded Ginger of the first time she had been there, a wedding that Jerry had conducted for a local rancher and a Bisbee store owner—the Tuckers. She had been with Harold that night. Memories of him swept over her, sad, thankful memories for his gentleness and generosity. How much her world had changed since that night!

The trees around St. Peter's were coming into leaf and softened the red brick of the building even as the wind bent and shook them and as gusts brought fresh clouds of dust swirling over it. Her feeling of dread came back as soon she walked inside. Ginger looked at her watch; she was about twenty minutes early. Jerry had said that this was one of the biggest services of the year at St. Peter's. He said something about the people here being so deep in "fall/redemption" theology that Good Friday rivaled Easter Sunday in importance to them. Ginger knew no alternative to fall and redemption and wondered what he had meant by the comment.

Ginger walked cautiously, even fearfully, into the darkened church. People were already sitting in some of the pews. She made the sign of the cross and genuflected as she entered one, kneeling long enough to say a Hail Mary and an Our Father—a habit from her childhood. Then she sat down. An anxious feeling, deeply disturbing and fearful, settled on her as she sat there quietly trying to get into a spirit of humility and peace. Instead, she became increasingly agitated. Closing her eyes and trying to focus inwardly, she started every time she heard a sound. A door opened. A pew squeaked. A kneeler hit the floor with a muffled bang. In the distance someone laughed. It was one of the longest twenty minutes of Ginger's life.

Finally, Jerry Hanning entered, surveyed the congregation, smiled at a pretty blonde woman just across the aisle—that must be Kate, she thought, and then he looked at her. Their eyes met just for an instant. Suddenly Ginger felt better. Jerry knelt and led the congregation, also on its knees, in a period of silent prayer. Ginger endured. Finally Jerry rose and began the service.

"Let us pray," he said.

Somewhere in the prayer that followed Jerry described the assembled congregation as "a family." But Ginger did not feel like she belonged to any sort of family, at least not at that time and in that place. She wanted to flee, but knew that she could not. She listened to the reader drone on and on over a reading from Genesis. It was the one about Abraham's willingness to sacrifice his son, Jacob—not Ginger's favorite Bible story at the best of times. She thought about the little immigrant boy she had read about, the one rescued by the Border Patrol the day before. What kind of a parent would have put his little boy at risk that way in the first place? What kind of a God would demand the sacrifice of a man's son? That lesson was followed, as on Palm Sunday, with a reading of the Passion Gospel. But while on Sunday that had been the version from Matthew, Good Friday, Jerry had said, is always from John. Ginger shuddered as she listened to the dramatic rendition, glad that her Jewish friend, Maddie, had been spared what it said, as she heard—really heard—for the first time the anti-Semitism it contained. It blamed the Jews for the death of Jesus. Repeatedly it is "the Jews" who are the villains. She found herself being embarrassed and angered by what she was hearing. This was racism, clearly and unambiguously, right in the heart of the Christian message. Why had she never heard this before? Why hadn't she realized what it meant, what its implications were? How many people had read and listened to that passage over and over and, like her, had simply thought it represented biblical truth, not some horrible perversion of God's hope for creation and the people of the world.

Ginger's excuse was that she had stopped attending church and had forgotten this kind of message before she was old enough to perceive what it was saying. In the meantime, she had internalized the anti-Jewish sentiment, and she had also absorbed the underlying assumptions: that people could be judged on the basis of their race, or religion, or, for that matter, by implication, their gender. She had not even picked up on it when that kind of racism was being directed toward her. It had never occurred to her that such feelings were inherent in this unfortunate passage of Holy Scripture. No wonder racism was so prevalent with that kind of religious authority behind it.

Ginger looked around the still-darkened and mostly-filled church and simply endured the experience: an endless list of prayers; people prostrating themselves at the foot of a rugged cross; and the singing of maudlin hymns like "Were you there when they crucified my Lord?" accompanied on an old piano. Even communion, which she received, did little to alleviate what was for her, frankly, the horror of the service. She kept her head down, avoided eye contact, and remained solitarily within herself. She guessed that the service must have been effective, since its presumed goal was to drive a person into some deep, interior, grieving space. But the service also had the result of making Ginger, by the time it had ended, ready to flee. The church was still in darkness. Almost all the worshipers were still sitting in their pews, or, more likely, were on their knees. Absolutely the only thing Ginger wanted was to get out of that church and go home. She was utterly unprepared for anything personal and important to happen to her there that day.

And then it happened. Ginger had her head self-consciously bowed, her arms clasped over her chest, and she was taking short, quick steps as she hurried down the central aisle toward the door. Then she looked up and her eyes were drawn magnetically to a man sitting in the last pew. He looked like he must have been about sixty, maybe one-hundred and sixty pounds, strong arms and broad shoulders; large weathered hands rested on the pew-back in front of him. His face was tanned and lined, clearly somebody who spent a lot of time out-of-doors. On his face there was a kind of beatific smile and he showed no sign of recognition when their eyes met. As Ginger looked at him, she knew. There was no mistake. Flashes of being dragged into that car. The night dark in the same kind of threatening and horrible way that St Peter's Church was today, on Good Friday. Once more she could smell the beer and tobacco breath. She felt the pain as he forced himself into her. She heard his demeaning obscenity. Tears streaming down her face, Ginger ran from the church, the accumulation of sixteen years of humiliation and pain bursting upon her, threatening to break her heart, to explode her brain.

Of all places to see *him* after all these years! A church—and on Good Friday! As Ginger started to think—and that took her a good many minutes— she understood that the reason she had never encountered him in Tucson was that he wasn't even from Tucson, but from Bisbee, or somewhere near by. Maybe he was a rancher…or something.

By the time she got a hold on herself, she had partly walked and partly ran almost to the Copper Queen Hotel. She stopped, shook her head slightly, and turned around and walked deliberately and resolutely back to the church, only to find that the people were all leaving. She brushed past a fierce-looking old man and went inside, the hand of fear gripping her stomach at the thought that at any moment she would come face to face with *him* again. But he was gone. For the second time that day, Ginger ran out of St. Peter's church, this time not in flight, but in a desperate need to find him, to confront him, to do, what? She did not know what she would have done had he been there.

But he was gone.

Ginger sat down on a convenient bench and pulled her light sweater around her, cold in spite of the warm day. The wind continued to blow and rage as before, but Ginger hardly noticed. There were no tears in her eyes now, no searing pain in her chest—only anger inflamed her, a burning rage at what he had done to her. That she had let him and his ugliness so effect her life. That, after all this time, she had let him escape. And Ginger had to talk to somebody. To Jerry.

Jillian Curtain waited after the Good Friday service until everyone else had left the church before joining Jerry on the front pew. She seemed more than usually quiet and reticent as she sat down beside Jerry. He wondered what the service with its heavy emphasis on penitence and guilt had been like for her. She had put up a good show of participating, while her body language shouted resistance and dread. Kate Becker, flashing him a solitary and rather sad smile, had exited the church walking tall and dignified. Ginger Vega, like Jillian, had also apparently been uncomfortable in the service and seemed to flee the church as soon as it was over. Jerry wondered what was going on with Ginger.

"How are you, Jillian?" Jerry asked. His mood was mellow and subdued in the aftermath of the powerful liturgy. He had neither judgments nor solutions for Jillian's dilemma, but he was prepared to help her any way he could. She was uncertain of herself and ill at ease. Was that because of his presence in his priestly garb and role? Or was it because of the church itself with all of its signals about inadequacy and missing the mark?

Jerry was painfully aware of the way in which the church and its clergy, especially when they are in clerical collars, can trigger guilty responses in people. How did we get it so wrong, he asked himself, if the church can conjure up feelings of guilt in people without doing or saying anything. Jesus worked among the "outcasts and sinners" of his own time, eating and living with them, regardless of the prohibiting taboos, and yet the church has acted as if the only people welcome at *its* banquet table are those without flaws. Not for the first time, Jerry wondered how he—how the Church!—could act to defuse those knee-jerk responses. Perhaps learning to be truly welcoming was a first step. It is a tragic irony, that the people who most needed the ministrations of the church and its clergy were the ones least likely to seek it out or benefit from it—because they did not feel welcomed. Rather, they felt judged and condemned.

"I…I saw *him* yesterday," Jillian said. "I meant to tell him that it was over. But…but I couldn't. What *am* I going to do. I just don't know!"

"What do you want to do? Deep inside, in your tender heart?"

Jillian thought for a long time, and then she began to cry, softly and gently but with apparent decision.

"I'm so sad," she said. "We had been so certain—Curtis and me—so full of confidence. And now? I…In some way it seems like there's no going back—at least to where we were."

Jerry sat there feeling closer to Jillian than he had ever thought possible, wishing there was a way he could smooth out the road ahead for her. He reached over and put his arm around her and held her close…for a long time. Finally her resistance melted and she gently rested her head on his shoulder. Jerry began the words of the "Our Father," and she joined in. "Just don't forget that I'm here for you," he said finally. "All of you." He reached over and touched her forearm lightly, wishing he could soften her pain by giving her a rule or a commandment as one might a child. Perhaps it would help if he could just say to her, "Go back to your husband, woman! Do your duty by him!" But that was too simple, and he had no sense it would be right in any case. He did not say it. He did not fall into the usual pattern of judgment, condemnation and requirement.

Jillian left and Jerry went into the church office and picked up a message waiting on his cell phone. He dialed the number and got straight through to Bruce Fallon at ADOT.

"I finally have that name for you," Bruce said. "Sorry it took me so long."

"Shoot," Jerry said.

"The Chevy pick-up truck is registered to C and M Snow."

"Thanks, Bruce. It's a member of my parish, as I had thought it might be. I really appreciate the favor. I owe you one."

"No problem, Jerry. Have a great Easter."

"You too," he rang off.

Charlie Snow! Now what?

Jerry heard a noise at the door and looked up to see Ginger Vega standing there. "Hi. I thought you had gone already," he said.

Ginger's eyes looked hunted and wary, and her face—almost unlovely— had a fierceness that Jerry had never seen on it before. She was clearly dealing with very strong emotions, feelings he found it hard to identify in church on Good Friday. Was this a return to her old anti-clerical, anti-church feelings? Perhaps it was about the church after all.

"I have something I need to talk to you about, Jerry. Can we have lunch? You do eat on Good Friday?" she asked in a rush. She did not seem hostile toward him, just very serious.

"Of course I do. And I'm starved. There's the little sandwich place just down from the old Phelps-Dodge general office. That okay?"

"Sure. Anything."

They bowed their heads against the wind and blowing dust and sand and finally ducked into the Sirloin Tip. Jerry wondered if last night was what this was about. Was she embarrassed by the implications of her drawing of him and Maddie? No, that did not fit with how she looked just now.

They took their seats at a window table and placed their order. Drinks and sandwiches came as they talked about their daughters and what a nasty day it was outside. They even laughed some, in a tense, awkward kind of way. Then, Ginger's voice softened, and she became serious.

"It was very hard for me to be in that service today. It…it felt like I was fighting against all of my most primitive instincts and desires just to be sitting there."

"I thought something was going on with you. Do you think it was about death?" Jerry asked, still without any clear idea of what was happening with her. "Death, its ugliness and finality, is really what Good Friday is about—at least on the human level it is. And you've certainly had your share of death in your life."

"I suppose you're right. But…it didn't so much feel like grief. It felt more like fear."

"Tell me about it, about the feelings you experienced."

"I had the scariest premonition I've ever had. On the way to church I had a sense of foreboding. Probably just the wind, I thought. It was so nasty and dusty and all. The closer I got to the church the worse I felt. And then sitting there waiting for the service to begin, it was…it was all I could do to stay. I had no sense of praying, no feeling of peace. I didn't feel like I belonged."

"Do you think that's about it not being a Catholic church?" he asked.

"I thought about that at the time, but I know that's not it. Oh, maybe a little. But there was more than that. I think it brought back some old feelings—and something that's kind of spooky, really—that I had thought were safely buried away."

Ginger lowered her voice even more to barely above a whisper, looking around to be sure she was not overheard, "When I was fifteen," she said, "I was walking alone after dark—something I'd promised my mother I wouldn't do. An older man, an Anglo, dragged me into his car, took me to a deserted parking lot and raped me."

Jerry was stunned. He knew that this kind of thing happened all the time. And this was not the first time that a woman had talked to him about being raped, but he never got over how terrible it was and how devastating it must be to have your body violated in that way. Also, for the second time in a few minutes he found himself deeply moved by another person's pain. It was small consolation for those who were hurting, but for Jerry, his reaction marked his having become fully present to other people again. About that, at least, he rejoiced.

Ginger went on to tell him about the years it had taken her to get over that one horrible half-hour and go on with her life. Jerry felt her pain as if it were his own as she told about what had happened to her. She also confessed to him about how, despite her being a life-long Catholic, being in church had become impossible for her after that, how she had always felt judged and unclean there. Jerry thought about his own reflections earlier. Here was a poignant example of what he had felt to be true.

"God! That must have been horrible for you. I guess a man can never fully appreciate what that would be like for a woman. What did you do afterwards? Did you report it? Was the jerk ever caught?"

"No, I never did report it. I was too humiliated. I got some counseling in college…and Joel helped. Helped a lot. But…but I guess I've never really gotten over it." Ginger leaned over the table toward Jerry with a look on her face that combined anger, hatred and disgust. "And now, today—and this is what makes all the rest, the premonition and everything, so scary—I saw *him* again…today, the same man, for the first time since it happened. There is no doubt about it; I would know him anywhere. He was sitting right there in the church, on the back row."

Jerry was stunned, shocked by everything he had heard, but mostly he was horrified that Ginger should find this man in his church. *His* church. The one where he had pastoral responsibility. The one where he had become so fond of so many people. He thought quickly. Who had been sitting on the rear pew? The only men on the back row were Charlie Snow and Alex Cloud sitting side-by-side. Either one of them fit her description as a small, powerfully built man. Jerry felt sick—and angry—and both at the same time. Charlie Snow. What kind of a sick guy is he? And what about Alex Cloud? Why not him?

"I know there's nothing I can do to him now," Ginger continued. "I checked several years ago when I went on a real vengeance campaign." She smiled bitterly and ironically. "There's a seven-year statute of limitations on rape in Arizona, though there's a move to repeal it, particularly with the possibility of DNA evidence. Still," her lovely face had a hard, firm set to it, "at least I want to confront him, maybe publicly, and make him squirm a little."

Jerry was thoughtful, trying to understand, to make connections as he thought about Charlie Snow and Alex Cloud—one of them, both of them. "Tell me something. Does it seem to you that what happened was as much about your being Mexican as it was about your gender?"

"Yes. Absolutely." The fierce expression returned to her face. "And it was the racism part that compounded it. I know that rape's always about hate and power. Maybe not so much about sex at all. Not only was I subjected to *that* man's power, but it also happened because I had brown skin. He demeaned me in...in...so many ways."

"Well," Jerry began, "I have some information for you that I think, oddly enough, is probably relevant. The pick-up truck whose license number you got last week from the air—you remember?"

She nodded. "Of course I remember."

"It belongs to a member of this parish, someone with outspoken racist opinions—anti-Latino ones. *He* was sitting on the back pew. The other man sitting beside him works at the ranch where we followed the SUV. Your description of the attacker could fit either one of them—compact and muscular, strong...and with a desire to hurt Mexican people. I have a hunch that in some kind of sick, odd way 'what goes around comes around.' The same person who hurt you years ago is in this vigilante trouble, too." It occurred to Jerry how painfully ironic it was that after so many years, Ginger's recent loss was likely connected to the same man whose violence had already had such a profound impact on her life.

"The problem is," Jerry continued, "we don't have any evidence. Really, I'm just speculating about this. I think I'd like to talk with Hank Tucker about it, though. You remember him from his wedding a few weeks ago? Come with me—or rather," Jerry grinned in a sheepish way, "give me a lift there? Can't fly in this wind. While we're there we might be able to check out one of the men in church today."

"Absolutely," she said with determination.

"There he is now," Hank said to Ginger, gesturing toward Alex Cloud as he walked across the open yard in front of the Tuckers' ranch house. Jerry and Ginger had driven straight to the Rocking T Ranch. They stood with Hank beside one of the front windows at the Tucker home. The high-powered, old SUV sat threateningly outside beside some other ranch vehicles.

"That's him. No doubt about it," Ginger said. Jerry reached out and touched her shoulder and could feel her shaking.

"Damn him," Hank said through his teeth. "I knew he was pretty hard and had some strong negative opinions, but I never guessed it could go as far as…as all of this." He made a sweeping gesture with his arm. "I'm very sorry, my dear," he said to Ginger. She just smiled faintly and leaned gently against Jerry. Alex disappeared from view. "Let's go, then," Hank continued, stuffing his broad straw hat on his head.

The three of them piled into the old SUV and drove together to Bisbee— about a twenty minute drive—to the Cochise Country Sheriff's Office, where Hank was expected. Calling from his ranch, Hank had said to a deputy friend of his, "You have any way of identifying the car that was used a few weeks ago in the Santa Ritas. You know, to force the artist and his Illegals off the road?"

"Sort of," the Deputy had answered. "We got a fine set of pictures of the tire tracks. Problem, though, is that we prob'ly can't do much more than eliminate cars that *didn't* do it. Looks like a brand new set a Firestone's. Why d'ya ask, Hank?"

"I've got me a suspicion about one of my ranch vehicles. Okay if I bring it by for you to look at it?"

They pulled up outside the Bisbee office of the Cochise County Sheriff. Jerry and Ginger waited outside in the car while Hank went inside the office. They sat silently, Jerry feeling calm, but tense. Ginger, on the contrary, held in check a mounting sense of excitement and anticipation, mingled with waves of righteous anger. Hank was back almost immediately with his deputy friend carrying what proved to be a blown up black and white photograph of a tire tread, and it took neither a forensics expert nor a genius to see that it was the tread of a tire that was identical to the new-looking tires on Hank's ranch SUV.

"Sure could'a been this car, alright," said the deputy. "But there's prob'ly a hundred more sets of these tires—just in Cochise County. Why'd you think it might be this one?"

"Just a suspicion," Hank answered. "Nothing more than that."

The deputy shook his head. "Can't go very far with suspicions—least not these days. The lawyers don't leave much wiggle room for law enforcement.

Sheriff says to let us know if you get anything more. He's real interested." The deputy went back in the building, and Hank returned to the driver's seat of the SUV.

"Now what?" Hank asked.

Jerry helped Ginger back into the rear seat of the SUV, got in himself and slammed the passenger's side door. "I don't know, Hank," he said. "Any ideas?" He turned and looked at Ginger inquiringly.

"None," she answered. Suddenly the excitement she had been feeling evaporated, and a dark mood of frustration and loss took its place. What now, indeed? Ginger knew—she knew!—that Alex Cloud, the man who had raped her, was also the one who was responsible for Harold's death and the deaths of those other people who rode with him. "I know it's him. But I don't know what to do about it." The hatred inside of her burned with an intensity that shocked her.

"Well *I* do," Hank said emphatically. "I don't have to *prove* anything to fire his ass and throw him off my property. That much I *can* do."

They sat quietly for a moment. Then Hank started up the car and revved its powerful engine. The sound had a mildly threatening tone. It was like a powerful force that had been enlisted in a wicked purpose. Jerry tried to shake off the feeling that the car itself was evil in some primitive way, but he could not. He was glad to get out of the SUV when they got back to Hank's ranch. Jerry also noticed that Hank make a special point of doing something that he *could* do just then: he removed the keys from the SUV and stuck them emphatically into his pocket.

"Now to find Alex," Hank said with a firm, thin-lipped and determined expression on his lean face.

"Just a minute, Hank," Jerry interrupted. "I don't have a plan, at least not yet I don't, but why not hold off for a few days with Alex. Let's keep him where we can find him—see what happens."

Hank grumbled something about "filthy rapist murderer," but agreed, "For a couple a days, then. But no more. I want him out of here."

It was as if Ginger's hair had drooped and her clothing, with a life of its own, had sagged. Ginger looked as discouraged as she felt. Jerry could not match her discouragement, but he had his own distress over Alex Cloud, and especially the way in which Alex and Charlie Snow were clearly connected.

But Maddie was a marked contrast to both Jerry and Ginger when they gathered at Ginger's studio for an early pizza supper. She could not remember when she had been as fundamentally and essentially excited as she felt just then. Knowing that the seed of new life was sprouting within her, an experience that she had almost—*almost*, but not quite—accepted would never happen to her, was the miracle of creation that she had always associated with the spring of the year, this very time of year, with Passover, with Easter. Long before she had ever thought of herself as a real Jew or as a potential Christian, she had loved the bunnies and chicks, the eggs and other signs of new life at Passover-Easter time. What had always seemed incongruous to her as a part of the Christian faith—an adoration of gestation adopted by them from other peoples—now made perfect sense to her. The joy of new life and the moon-cycle dated, annual Resurrection celebration—the Christian Passover—now seemed to fit perfectly together. Rebirth matched to birth. Was she jumping the gun feeling the way she did on Good Friday, the day of Jesus's death? Well, so be it. She had much to celebrate.

"Why the long faces?" Maddie asked.

"Ginger's had a very upsetting day," Jerry said, pulling Maddie to him and giving her a short embrace. He told her about everything that had happened to them since they had last seen each other just before noon.

"You actually saw *him*—twice! God!" Maddie said to Ginger, an expression of incredulity on her face. "You're sure?"

"I'm sure. And I'm just as certain that he is the same one who killed Harold and shot at your plane." Ginger's mouth formed a firm, thin line.

"I think she's probably right," Jerry added. "And I'll bet he's also the one who sabotaged my 172."

"My God," Maddie said again, quietly this time. "What are we going to do about it? About him?"

"I don't see anything we can do," Ginger said. "That's just the problem. There's absolutely nothing we can prove. It's my word against his about," she lowered her voice, "what he did to me." She glanced toward Sean who was busy in a corner of the studio with a drawing he had left unfinished. "And that's way past the statute of limitations. The rest is just circumstance and conjecture."

"Then we need to find some way to force him to trip himself up," Maddie said. "There must be something we can do—like set him up in some way." Her brow wrinkled with a little pensive frown. "Surely we can come up with *something*." But no matter how much they tossed it around, no ideas came. It was discouraging.

Later in her Audi, as she and Jerry were leaving for the airport for Jerry to fly back to Tucson in the now-calm evening air, Maddie said to him, "Jerry,

I have something important to tell you." Dusk was fast approaching.

"Shoot," he said, suddenly in a lighter mood than he had felt all afternoon. He reached over toward her and lightly, gently, but lingeringly, embraced her. It made his heart race to touch her.

Maddie's heart was already pounding, partly from her excitement and joy over what she had to tell him and partly because she was afraid of what his reaction would be to her, perhaps shocking, news. "Jerry," she began, "what I have to say is very important to me. But I'm afraid it's going to be hard for you to hear." A silence grew up between them, one that felt to both of them later to have been an ominous one. "My doctor's appointment today," she continued. "You remember?"

"Yes," he said. "Is something wrong?"

"Wrong? No. Nothing is wrong. Just the opposite. For me anyhow." She paused, reflectively, then continued. "You know how disappointed Frank and I were about not having a child all the years we were married?" She put up a hand to stop an anticipated response to her question. "Well, now it has happened for me. With Cord—though he doesn't know it…at least not yet. But, Jerry, the doctor confirmed it today. I'm definitely pregnant."

Jerry was shocked, just the way Maddie had feared he would be. He had no words. He even lacked thoughts. "Ah, well, I mean…that is…ah…that's great, Maddie. This is something that you really…ah…want, then?"

Maddie started the car. They drove in silence. Finally, she said, "I know this complicates things for us—our relationship that never has quite gotten started somehow. But, Jerry, I cannot tell you how excited this makes me feel, how important this baby is for me."

Jerry's mind raced. The more he thought about Maddie, pregnant and happy about it, the more he could relate to her feelings of elation. He could even share that excitement. Theoretically. At least in his head, he could. But it was different in his gut. Something angry and alien there seemed to take him over. He felt a primitive revulsion to the child—even to Maddie. What was happening here? It humiliated him to admit those feelings even to himself. He tried not to let his anger and abhorrence show. He wanted to shout, to strike out in all directions at once. The silence lengthened.

"It's getting dark," he said finally in a carefully controlled voice as they pulled into the Bisbee airport's parking lot. "I'd better get on out of here while I still can. See you on Sunday," he said, each word tumbling out after the ones before it, but feeling as if they came from a great distance. Jerry hated to see the pained expression on Maddie's face. But there was nothing he could do about that right then. He had to get out of there, had to get home, had to be alone.

CHAPTER TWENTY-ONE

Holy Saturday

*O God, Creator of heaven and earth: Grant that, as the crucified body of
your dear Son was laid in the tomb and rested on this holy Sabbath, so we
may await with him the coming of the third day, and rise with him to
newness of life.*
—The Book of Common Prayer

Maddie had an idea. Maybe she was the one to think of something simply
because she was less personally involved with Charlie Snow and Alex Cloud
than Hank Tucker, Jerry Hanning or Ginger Vega. Jerry, after all, had pastoral
relationships with the two men, especially with Charlie Snow, and Ginger's
motives for seeking justice against Alex Cloud were enormous. Hank Tucker
was too close to his foreman to be an aloof third party. Even Hank's disdain
of Charlie Snow made him too highly motivated for objectivity. But Maddie's
connection to both men was about as remote as it could be and still be
motivated to act at all. So far as she knew, she had never seen Alex Cloud,
and Charlie Snow occupied only a vague corner in her memory: a man sitting
on a church pew next to a sweet-looking, slightly pudgy, middle-aged woman.
But Maddie was still anxious for justice. And her motivation was as
impersonal as "doing the right thing" and making two bad guys pay for what
they had done—especially to friends of hers. But this was also personal. In
her wildest dreams, Maddie had never imagined that it might happen, but
she had been shot at in her airplane, and she found that she did not like that
experience one bit. Perhaps her comparative objectivity and her astonishment
that someone might want to shoot at her gave Maddie a certain clarity of
mind. In any case, she did have an idea.

"Ginger?" Maddie said into the phone.

"Hi."

"You busy? Have you talked to Jerry today?"

"No…to both questions."

"Okay if I come by?"

"Wish you would. I'm pretty low."

"What's the matter?"

"Same old stuff. The whole thing. It's so damned depressing. I know that creep's going to get away with…with everything."

"Try not to think that way. Actually, I've got an idea. That's what I want to talk to you about. See you soon." She pushed the "off" button on the cordless phone and punched in Jerry Hanning's number for the tenth time that day. She had been trying to call him since the first thing in the morning, but there had never been an answer. She had tried his cell with the same result. At first she had worried that something was wrong. Then she finally accepted what she feared was true: that he was so upset and angry about the news of her pregnancy that he would not even take her call. She replayed over and over in her mind the brief exchange when she had told him her news, and she kept coming back to the sad conclusion that having a child, the one thing that life had always denied her, seemed destined to cost her the friendship, perhaps even more than friendship, she valued most in the world. Jerry's rejection hurt a lot.

Maddie's day had started miserably. The wind was blowing so steadily and fiercely that it had been a wretchedness just doing her morning chores, feeding the dogs and goats and letting water run into the half-barrel the animals shared. Not even the scarf she used to cover her face could keep out the sting of blowing sand and the grittiness of the dust in her mouth. The loneliness of the ranch came even clearer to her as she realized that Sean would be leaving the next day and she would be entirely on her own again. Only Refugio Mendez, his wife, the changing faces of his pair of helpers and an occasional visit by the Mendez children and grandchildren would relieve her loneliness; she had never felt really a part of their lives. Worst of all were her feelings of loss about Jerry Hanning. How could she have expected him to respond any differently? How could he help but think badly of her—pregnant before her husband had been dead six months? It was hard enough for her not to let those negative buttons get pushed in her own brain; why should she expect him to feel otherwise or to share her excitement? She told herself that she would meet someone else; after all she had loved Art to distraction, and then along came Jerry. It would hurt, and she would be lonely. But it would pass. The pain always passed. At the lowest point of the morning she asked herself the inevitable question: should she terminate the pregnancy? Her answer to herself was emphatic and immediate. Under no circumstances could she imagine that she would do that with this child. As far as Maddie was concerned she carried a sacred gift that was hers to nurture and to care for.

It was not as if Maddie had a doctrinaire attitude toward abortion. Just the opposite. She firmly believed in a woman's right to end an unwanted pregnancy. And she also believed with equal vehemence that a woman had the right to choose *not* to terminate a pregnancy. She wanted this child and felt that this new life was one of the ways in which her redemption from Art's long illness and death was being worked. No, she was thrilled about the baby, absolutely thrilled. It was hard for her not to go around with a silly grin on her face all day long. But it was still a rotten day.

Maddie picked up the phone and tried one more time to reach Jerry Hanning. Once again the cheery recorded message came on, "This is Jerry Hanning. Leave me a message." This time, Maddie decided to leave more than her previous, "This is Maddie. Call me back." After the mechanical beep, she said, "Jerry. I think you must be pretty angry at me. I'm sorry. I really am. This is not what I had planned—had even dreamed any more could happen. But it's important that I talk to you. I think I have an idea of how we might catch our villains in the act." She hung up and sat morosely. In spite of herself, she was letting the windy day and Jerry Hanning undermine her happiness.

Jerry and the weather were only a part of what troubled Maddie Gronek that Saturday. There remained the question of Cord. What was she was going to do about him—tell him about the baby or simply go away and keep it to herself, at least for now? If her relationship with Jerry Hanning was over before it got started, then why not just leave Cochise County and have her baby somewhere else? Tucson perhaps. This was *her* experience. Why not keep it to herself? Looming over these personal worries and the rotten day was the helplessness she felt imagining that those two men, Alex Cloud and Charlie Snow, might get away with their wicked deeds.

Wicked deeds! Listen to her. What kind of moralistic idiot was she becoming? But she still did not want them to get away with what they had done. She had looked at the clock—almost ten—and then ran for the bathroom a second time that morning where she lost what was left of her breakfast. That was when she had gotten the idea—hanging unceremoniously over the toilet. "Of course," she muttered aloud. "It might work." Then she called Ginger.

On their way to Ginger's studio an hour later, Maddie and Sean took a detour to Tombstone for lunch at Nellie Cashman's Café with Ike McWarder. They were already sitting at a table when Ike came shuffling into the cosy, if battered, café, obviously glad to get in out of the wind.

"Rotten day," he muttered as he sat down. "Hi-ya, Sean," he said a little more cheerfully. "You feelin' okay?" he asked Maddie, giving her hand a little squeeze where it rested on the table. Ike was one of three people Maddie had told about being pregnant—and that number did not yet include Sean. Only Jerry, Ike and Ginger had been let in on the secret.

"The wind gets me down is all," Maddie answered.

Sean sat quietly and played with his Game Boy.

Brenda-Nellie suddenly appeared at their table somehow balancing three glasses of water in one hand and grasping three plastic menus in the other. She too was less than her cheery self. Relieved of their burdens, her hands were quickly stuffed into the pockets of her jeans. Even the café reflected the lousy day and was almost entirely empty

"Miserable day," she muttered. Maddie noticed that as Brenda-Nellie's right hand came out of the jeans pocket, her rosary beads came with it. "Just doing a little Holy Saturday meditation as I move about the place." She half-grinned at Ike in a gloomy sort of way. "There's little enough else to do." She stood quietly for a moment, then added, "There's something about this time of year that makes me very sad...you know. And we don't even have our dear little church here any more to comfort us."

Hanna-Nellie waved listlessly through the service window from the kitchen.

"This wind's gonna make for a pretty miserable barbeque tomorrow," Ike grumbled.

"But you're still going aren't you Ike?" Brenda-Nellie asked.

"Guess so," he answered

It was the most tasteless cheeseburger Maddie had ever eaten—especially when she harbored the conviction that she might very well loose it at any moment. No doubt the problem was with her mouth and not Nellie Cashman's kitchen. Regretting the decision to spend time with all those gloomy people, she hustled Sean back into the Audi and headed for Bisbee.

At any other time in her life—any previous time, that is—Maddie's thoughts might not have taken the particular direction they did as she drove that day. A woman does not need to have had a spiritual awakening as Maddie had experienced it, to recognize the miracle of conception and new life. But her new religious awareness led her to see that miracle happening inside of her differently than she might otherwise have done. She knew the biological facts of sperm and egg, joined together by a moment of pleasure and excitement. She had read the books and seen the photographs of the growth of the fetus. She had morning sickness, sensed how uncomfortable she would become and how the birthing process would bring her the greatest pain she had ever felt in her life. But somehow those things mattered little to her. The miracle was so great that it overshadowed every other consideration.

But Maddie anticipated at any moment that she would hear a voice, or see a light—or have some other experience of the sacred coming from…wherever it was such experiences originated. She hoped she would have a sign. Probably she even expected one, something blinding, astonishing, profound. She remembered the day she flew to San Diego.(Can that only have been a month ago?) There was the music that was not there and the insight about God's lack of gender. She thought about her name being called. Or just yesterday she "talked" to Art in the oak grove and knew that communication had somehow happened? What about an acute awareness like Jeremiah's watching the potter and seeing that as a metaphor for the way God would recreate the Chosen People as they came out of exile? Couldn't such a new awareness give her a way to understand her new life?

But nothing happened. There were no voices, no music, no visions, no new awareness, no sense of peace. Had God suddenly abandoned her? Was she being punished for her audacity or error? Was she feeling the power of centuries of human judgment making her question herself and her conception of this child? Trying to turn it into her "sin?" No matter how hard she tried, she had no comforting sign or spiritual experience. No matter how hard she thought or prayed, nothing happened. For a few minutes, she even experienced the deepest loneliness and feelings of abandonment she had ever felt, with the one exception being the day Art died. She even thought belatedly about driving into Tucson to go to Temple. That urge was enormous, but it was Sean's last full day before he had to return to California to get back to school on Monday. She wanted to spend the day with him.

Then, just as she went through the short tunnel and began to negotiate the winding, canyon road on the final leg into Bisbee, suddenly she got it. There was more than the rotten, windy day and the depressing theology of Holy Saturday, Jerry's immature, and—yes, selfish—behavior and the still-open wound of Art's death, the nastiness of the vigilantes and government policy on the border—both racist and exploitative. Transcending it all was the irrepressible joy she felt about the simple, natural process that was happening inside of her body. What other sign did she need? The joy was enough. More than enough.

"It might work," Ginger said after sitting quietly listening to Maddie as she paced around the studio talking. "It just might work and draw them to the Tombstone airport. They've certainly been watching it. Get them to show their hand." The afternoon sun streamed through the huge west windows of Ginger's studio. It was not far enough into the hot season yet that she had to pull the heavy mechanical shutters over the window to keep the sun from turning the studio into a furnace. "What do we have to lose by trying?"

"Exactly. Either they fall for our little drama or they don't. All we lose is a little time," Maddie said. But this conversation with Ginger was not precisely as Maddie had expected it to be. Instead, it was complicated by the presence of potter and shop owner, Harriet Lawson...and Cord. Both of them were at Ginger's place when Maddie got there, and it was without warning that she had been suddenly confronted by the awkward presence of the unsuspecting father of her unborn child. They had, like Maddie, come to Ginger's place seeking justice against Charlie Snow and Alex Cloud. Ginger had already filled them in on what had been learned and suspected.

Cord, who was always quiet in a group, seemed to Maddie to be extra quiet. Not that she blamed him. Besides, his mood matched the day. "There is some risk in this plan of yours," he said at last to Maddie, addressing a point somewhere above her left ear.

"There's always risk," Harriet answered for her. "In everything." She seemed to be less than her usual cheerful self.

"Did Father Jerry agree to go along with it?" Cord asked of anybody.

"I don't know," Maddie answered, looking Cord directly in the eye for the first time. His return gaze was unwavering. She saw sadness and anger there. Despite her joy, she could share the sadness about something that was over, and she understood the anger. "We haven't been able to reach Jerry."

Maddie was relieved when Cord and Harriet left.

Making sure that Sean was out of earshot, Ginger asked, "How bad is the morning sickness?"

"Rotten, but then I don't have anything to compare it with, do I?"

"Still happy about the baby, though?"

"It's one thing I'm really sure about," Maddie answered simply and clearly.

"Cord doesn't know, does he?"

Maddie shook her head.

"Are you going to tell him?"

"I don't know. Probably some day. It would be unfair not to tell him that he has a child. But I don't think I have any obligation to share my pregnancy with him. It's…it's too intimate. I don't want to have that kind of intimacy with him."

"You know, you don't have to feel bad about this, about Cord. It's okay. Enjoy being pregnant," Ginger smiled widely and knowingly, "at least while you can." She reached out and lightly touched Maddie's arm, grinning. "Is that your phone?" Ginger asked suddenly. Maddie also heard the muffled ringing coming from her purse.

"I guess it is." Maddie scrambled to reach the cell phone. "Hello," she said.

"Hi." It was Jerry Hanning. "Sorry I've been so hard to reach. I've been busy." His voice seemed distant, emotionally remote.

"Thanks for calling. I'm at Ginger's place. When are you getting to Bisbee?" Her words felt stilted to her.

"I'm on my way now—with Sadie and with Ginger's girls, too. I've been waiting for the wind to calm down a bit, but it just doesn't seem like it will. We're driving."

"What a come-down for you that is," Maddie tried a small joke. There was no joking response.

"What's your idea?" he asked soberly.

"Tell you when I see you." Maddie felt sick in the pit of her stomach—and it was not a late-day return of the morning sickness. It was Jerry. He seemed so cold, so disengaged. He also sounded depressed. It had probably not been any better day for him than it had been for the other people she had been around. And now he could not even fly Three-Eight Bravo.

Jerry finally arrived with the three girls in tow, thereby transforming Sean's lonely evening into fun. The children and Maddie alone seemed not to share the glum mood that seemed to pervade the day. Jerry was clearly depressed. It could have been Maddie's imagination, but she thought he warmed as the evening passed. But there was no personal conversation between them, and mostly Jerry even avoided eye contact with her. At times she sensed a deep compassion and tenderness in him. At other times he seemed so depressed that nothing appeared to matter to him—not even the kids and their high spirits. She also sensed anger. But her overwhelming experience of him that evening was one of someone who was very depressed.

Maddie tried to put herself in his place, to experience the world as he experienced it and to feel the feelings he must be feeling. But she couldn't do it. The depths of his apparent despair eluded her. She even began to feel a little angry. How dare he treat her in this way? How dare he respond to something so filled with joy and hope—or at least filled with joy and hope for her—by being such a jerk? Was he so full of himself that he couldn't be there for her? The more she thought about it, the less she harbored understanding and concern for Jerry Hanning. Too bad for him, if that's the way he wants to be! It was good that she learn this part of him now. A little anger seemed just the antidote for Maddie. Anger felt better than the despair everyone else seemed to be feeling.

Maddie and Jerry parted without having shared a single touch or private word the entire evening. Jerry went to the Simmons House with Sadie, and Maddie returned to the Twisted K with Sean. That separation seemed so unnatural, so lonely, and so unhappy to her. The tears she shed alone in her room that night were her way of capitulating to the misery of the day. But despite the tears, she felt in no way fundamentally different than she had all day: joyful about the new life growing inside of her.

CHAPTER TWENTY-TWO

Easter

Faith in God means believing that anyone can be transformed, regardless of the past. To write off whole groups of people as intrinsically racist and violent is to use the very same arguments that are employed to support racism.
—Walter Wink

Jerry Hanning stood apart from the gathered clusters of high-spirited people, a cold bottle of Negra Modello in his hand. Other guests, mostly parishioners from St. Peter's, laughed and gabbed with each other sharing the euphoria of Easter Day as they moved in and out of the Tucker's Rocking T Ranch home. Only the nasty wind that had so dominated the last two days, seemed to be missing. The day shone clear, bright and still, the sun gleaming and sparkling over the surface of the swimming pool that, though its water still remained much too cold for swimming, delivered a brilliant alternative to the dry countryside beyond the walled yard's careful grooming. Creosote and mesquite were just coming into bloom with their tiny yellow flowers. Clusters of pansies, geraniums, freesia and alyssum, some in large clay pots, others in hanging baskets and still others in small beds alongside climbing roses, all cheerfully announced Easter Day in differing heights, hues and scents—a continuation of the celebration all had shared in the church that morning. Jerry watched Mrs. Elspeth Findlay fussing over the flowers is if they were the domain of the altar guild. His glance passed to Jim Brown who was holding court from a straight-backed deck chair. The retired lawyer was well along in his recovery from heart surgery and used the moment to bask in both the sun and the good wishes of his church friends. Brenda-Nellie laughed loudly and contagiously. Gathered around the charismatic figure of Ike Clanton McWarder, the parish children sat in a far corner of the yard: Jerry's Sadie, Ginger's two girls, Maddie's step-son, Sean, and the two Curtain boys, who had accompanied their mother, Jillian, to church and now to the Tuckers' barbecue. Curtis Curtain was nowhere to be seen. Jerry wondered what Ike was up to with the kids and what had happened between the Curtains. All he knew for sure was that Jillian and her boys alike seemed high-spirited and full of life.

Jerry felt ashamed of himself for his reaction to Maddie's pregnancy. Excuses about the suddenness and the timing of her revelation just didn't wash; he expected better of himself. That was his first mistake, thinking that somehow he might rise above that kind of knee-jerk reaction just because of his pastoral experience and perspective. Indeed, he had to acknowledge a visceral reaction in himself that made him no different than other men he had known. He hated the thought of Maddie having sex with someone—with Cord. Her pregnancy forced him to acknowledge those mostly-hidden feelings. Of course, he had known that she and Cord were seeing each other, and had made the natural, though unacknowledged, assumption that they were sleeping together. So why did her pregnancy bother him? Was it a moral judgment? Did he somehow think less of her because she now carried a permanent mark of her intimacy like a brand? Finally, he admitted to himself that her news had bothered him because of the deep—and, admittedly, possessive—feelings he had for her. How had he thought that he could simply shut her out of his life, could turn off his feelings for her, just because she carried a child? It had crushed Jerry's ego to know that Maddie was pregnant with another man's child right at what he had expected to be the beginning of their relationship. What lousy timing. Still, the phrase, "get over it!" kept running through his mind. Finally, an important shift in his thinking had begun as he started thinking of this child as *Maddie's* baby rather than as *Cord's*. How patriarchal and sexist it was to identify a pregnancy or child with the father exclusively, as if the baby were a possession of *his* and not a gift of *hers*. He resolved to deal with his possessiveness and ego

That brought him around to his second mistake: the way he had acted toward Maddie for the last two days. He only hoped that it wasn't too late to get started again on a more positive foot than he had been on since Good Friday evening. If only he could finally set aside his initial revulsion. It was Easter now, and he knew that his emotional resurrection was long overdue.

Jerry and Maddie had seen each other for the first time that morning from across the crowded church. There had been no opportunity for them to talk, but their frequent eye contact had said much, especially as Jerry's glances flashed his solitary message, "forgive me for being so stupid." Maddie seemed to understand those pleas as she radiated joy throughout her being, showering her excitement and happiness in all directions, though still understandably cautious where Jerry was concerned.

After church and before they went to the barbecue, Jerry had finally caught a moment alone with her and, as he bent over to whisper in her ear, he felt her breath on his freshly shaved cheek—Lent was over!—and the tickle of her hair on his nose; both sensations sent little thrills of excitement through him. "Can we talk?" he asked.

Maddie looked up at him as he stood straight again, almost a full head taller than she, and smiled with the hope and expectation that this special morning generated. "Of course. I'm taking Sean to catch the plane in Tucson after the barbecue. I'll be back home later this afternoon. Oh, and happy Easter, Jerry," she said as she reached out and hugged him lightly.

"Happy Easter, Maddie," he said as he hugged her back.

Holy Saturday had been terrible for Jerry. Beginning with his confused feelings about Maddie, everything in his life had seemed to be in question. But one threat loomed menacingly: what—and when—would he hear from the bishop about his ill-fated and inappropriate relationship with Kate Becker? Would he be summarily fired from the Bisbee congregation? That would be the simplest and cleanest action for the bishop to take. Or perhaps he would be suspended for a disciplinary period—or brought up before an ecclesiastical court. That seemed pretty unlikely. He hoped for a reprimand and told to get on with the work in Bisbee, where he could point to some early success. Holy Week and Easter attendance figures had soared above those of recent years. Clearly some good things were happening. But no amount of success excused his crossing the line with Kate, and he knew that.

Jerry wrenched his thoughts back to the barbecue and watched as Maddie and Ginger, each with glass in hand, moved together around the patio. They were quite an eye full—Ginger in yellow and Maddie in white—as they greeted people they knew, but otherwise stayed deeply in conversation with each other. If Jerry still wondered about his feelings for Maddie, the small flutter he felt in his chest as he watched her relieved him of that doubt.

Glancing around the crowd, Jerry spotted Alex Cloud, Hank's foreman and the primary target of the little drama about to be staged, as he stood with a small cluster of Sulphur Springs Valley ranchers. Jerry wondered about Alex's influence and leadership in such a group of ranchers, while he was, himself, only an employee of one of them. Undeniably, Alex had a certain charisma, a magnetism used more for evil than good just now, it seemed. At first Jerry could not see Charlie Snow, the other target, but as he followed Maddie and Ginger with his eyes, he spotted Charlie deep in conversation with another rancher Jerry did not know. He could not help but admire the way the two women slowly but—at least to him—relentlessly worked their way toward Charlie. He decided to drift that way, positioning himself beside Jim Brown but no more than five yards from where Ginger and Maddie stood with their backs to Charlie Snow. Jerry watched and listened as Maddie's and Ginger's voices rose in what appeared to be an intense conversation between them. He could not make out all the words, but he had no doubt that Charlie Snow could—as they intended him to do. He imagined them saying what they had agreed they would say: that two male UDAs waited desperately for a way to get to Phoenix; that they should take that risk themselves at least one last time; and that the next morning should be perfect for a flight from the lonely Tombstone airport.

Jerry watched Charlie's attention become visibly riveted on Maddie and Ginger as they talked animatedly with each other. His eyes followed them after they drifted off in Jerry's direction. Then the tiniest of smiles appeared on Charlie's face as the two women reached Jerry. Charlie abruptly disengaged from his interrupted conversation and made a beeline to Alex Cloud.

"We got 'im," Ginger whispered to Jerry as she and Maddie passed by where he stood.

Jerry just nodded, but he could see from Charlie's agitated behavior that Ginger was right. Charlie certainly seemed to have taken the bait they had dangled in front of him. Now it all depended on Alex Cloud also biting. Jerry watched as Charlie drew Alex aside and began having an animated and whispered conversation with him, at one point making a gesture toward Maddie and Ginger. Judging from the angry and resolute expression on Alex's face as Charlie talked, he had also swallowed the hook. Jerry watched as the two men looked intently at the backs of Ginger and Maddie as they walked through the patio door into the house. Jerry glanced over at their consummate host, Hank Tucker, also a part of this small conspiracy, and gave him a thumbs up gesture. Hank understood and smiled back rather soberly and unhappily. Nothing would have pleased Hank more than to find out that Alex Cloud— and, yes, even Charlie Snow—were in no way implicated in events at the Tombstone airport and in the death of Bisbee artist, Harold Jenkins.

Not long after the little drama that she and Ginger had performed for Charlie Snow, Maddie left to get Sean to Tucson in time for his flight back to California. "You know," she said to Jerry as she was leaving, "Sean has asked if he can come back and stay with me this summer."

"What did you say?"

"Of course, I said 'yes.'" She smiled at him. "Though I will have a few things to explain to him by then—for instance, why I'm putting on weight."

Jerry tried to appear unaffected by Maddie's little joke.

"Seriously, I don't quite know what to say to him about...well, you know. I don't want to hurt him."

Jerry maintained a judicious silence, but showed her that he understood her dilemma by reaching out and touching her arm. Then she had had to go.

"I'll call you when I get home," she said as she left.

When they spoke later on the phone, Maddie assured Jerry that Cord had no idea that he was going to be a father."What about you, Jerry? Do you think you can accept my child?" she asked.

"I'm not sure, but I think so," he answered her honestly, hoping that he could. "Let's deal with that when the time comes. We still have a lot of getting acquainted to do."

"I know."

"You'll be in Tucson tomorrow, then?"

"Yes. My mother is expecting me. Once we've finished with...with those creeps tomorrow morning at the Tombstone airport. I'm going to her place. I've already told her my big news. Once she got over the shock of having an unwed pregnant daughter, she became very excited."

"Uh-huh," Jerry responded, remaining noncommital about his feelings.

"You know, Jerry, this child really is very important to me. I'm sorry that it happened this way, but I'm not sorry it has happened."

"I know that."

The Monday morning sun peeked with seeming reluctance over the hills that ringed the eastern approach to the Tombstone airport. Jerry's Skyhawk arched lazily at ten thousand feet on reduced power. Cord sat beside him with a pair of binoculars, ready to call the alert should anything happen. At any moment Maddie would appear from the west as usual and make a careful landing that would bring her beside the windsock as before. Hank should soon appear in his Bonanza from an easterly direction. Now if only the bad guys would show up.

"Somebody's down there," Cord said suddenly. He looked intently in the binoculars. "It's a white, large-body pickup, parked down the road a ways with its hood up—as if it's stalled."

"Charlie Snow," Jerry said simply. He felt uncomfortable having Cord in the airplane with him and could not honestly say that he had ever liked the young sculptor, mostly jealousy over Maddie, he realized. Now the resentment was acute as he thought about Cord's child—Maddie's child!—growing inside of her. It was all he could do to be civil to Cord.

"Three-Eight Bravo? Are you there Jerry? Four-Five Lima," Maddie asked on the same open frequency they had used before.

"Roger," he answered. "We're circling at ten thousand feet," Jerry answered. "No sign yet of Hank. Three-Eight Bravo."

"Seen anyone below? Four-Five Lima."

"Affirmative, Four-Five Lima. There's a white pickup parked down the road. I'm sure it's Charlie. I imagine the other one...ah...Alex is with him. It was damned clever of Hank to keep the keys to the SUV. Alex would never use his own antique car for something like this. Puts both of them together where we can keep an eye on them. Three-Eight Bravo."

"Antique? I don't understand. Four-Five Lima."

"Alex's only car is a forty-nine Studebaker in mint condition. A real collector's item. He'd never use that for anything...risky." Jerry paused. "Are Refugio and his nephew on the ground? Three-Eight Bravo."

"Far as I know. He should be lighting his bonfire any minute now. That will force Alex and Charlie's hand and leave them no doubts about what's happening—or at least what we want them to think's happening." Maddie paused. "Should we go ahead without Hank? Four-Five Lima."

"We can't," Jerry answered. "He's the one who knows the Border Patrol people and will be calling them when we have something to say. I don't even know their frequency—unless you know it. Three-Eight Bravo."

"Sorry. No such luck. Four-Five Lima."

"No? Then let's wait as long as we can for Hank. Three-Eight Bravo."

"I see another plane's lights," said Cord into his microphone on the intercom. "Over there." He pointed toward the northwest.

At first Jerry only saw the blinking navigation lights, then a flash as the sun's rays momentarily gleamed off the cowling of the other plane. Jerry estimated that the other craft was flying at about eight thousand feet as it came directly toward their position above the Tombstone airport from the direction of the town. "He must have flown over the Border Patrol check point to make sure the guards are there...or something," Jerry muttered. As he watched, the other plane banked gently to the left and then to the right, skirting around the empty landing strip below. "He's staying well clear,"

Jerry added, and then he pushed the call button. "Bonanza Three-Four-Four Uniform. Are you there Hank?" There was no answer. "Hank? Are you there Three-Four-Four Uniform?" Still no answer.

"Now I see Maddie," Cord said. "She just came around those hills." Cord pointed toward the southwest.

The plane's lights seemed to hug the ground. Jerry guessed she held at close to pattern altitude, a thousand feet above the surface at about fifty-five hundred feet. That gave her very little clearance over the hills that ringed the area to the southwest. "Everything's looking good," he muttered, mostly to himself.

Hank Tucker had awakened very excited that Monday morning. He liked mornings and always felt especially energized on the ones when, waking up, he knew that he would soon be out flying in his Bonanza. How he loved that airplane! He lay still in the bed listening to the soft, deep breathing sounds of his wife sleeping beside him. Hank felt very good about yesterday's barbecue. It always pleased him to have people at the Rocking T, and yesterday was no exception. Besides, Alex and Charlie Snow seemed to have fallen for the little drama that had been staged for their benefit, thus setting themselves up for the reckoning that they certainly had coming. His anticipation of their comeuppance provided some of his excitement.

Hank quietly slipped out of bed and went into the bathroom where he already had clothes laid out so he could dress without waking Teresa. The wall clock read 5:20. Still time to have coffee and maybe a donut. Sure why not? This was a special day. In the kitchen, Hank busied himself making a pot of coffee, warming up a small thermos to carry an extra cup with him in the Bonanza and put one of the homemade donuts on a napkin in front of him. He sat down at the round kitchen table and stirred cream and sugar into the cup of coffee. He broke the donut in half and began to raise it to his mouth.

"What the hell's that?" Hank asked himself aloud, the donut piece suspended in mid-air on its way to his mouth. He listened. No doubt about it, he had heard the unmistakable sound of his Bonanza as its engine caught and then settled into a low rumble. "Alex! Shit!"

Hank dropped the uneaten donut on the table in front of him and bolted for the door. He was in time to feel the backwash from the Bonanza's propellor sending a shower of dust and dirt behind it as it taxied to the far end of the runway. Hank stood there helpless as the plane began its takeoff run back toward the house. He continued to watch the plane bank sharply away from the house and climb westward toward Tombstone. Rummaging in his pocket for the keys for the old Dodge Ram, Hank sprinted for the house as he punched the numbers for the Border Patrol into his cell phone.

Hank shared the road that morning with only two other vehicles: a slow-moving spreader load of manure pulled behind a John Deere tractor and one lone car. He completed that headlong run all the way from the Sulphur Springs Valley to the Tombstone airport in record time. It had only taken him a minute to pick up his old Colt .45 revolver in the house before he drove off. Hank doubted that he would actually shoot anybody with it, but it made him feel better knowing it was beside him. The Colt gave him a kind of artificial courage that came from carrying a firearm. Hank knew the statistics that more danger came from having a weapon in one's possession than from being unarmed—but he still felt a kind of reassurance from the Colt's ready presence. It meant that *he* meant business. Sometimes a man had to put himself at risk. When he finally did pull into the airport—would he ever get there?—he knew he would feel better knowing the Colt rested there beside him. The Dodge Ram's speed topped ninety as Hank hurtled down the road toward the dirt cut-off for the eastern end of the Tombstone airport.

Maddie reached up and opened the Skyhawk's overhead air vent. The nausea seemed to abate somewhat because of the cold freshness of the outside air.

"You okay?" Ginger asked from the right-hand seat.

"Just a little nausea, that's all."

"Oh God, it's the worst. I remember." Ginger changed the subject abruptly. "There's the pickup truck. There. Beside the road."

"Can you see anything of Refugio?"

"I...yes, there's his fire now." A tiny spark showed on the ground right beside where the windsock stood in the shadowed early morning dark. The fire was meant to be very clear and visible from the ground, leaving no doubt about there being someone waiting there for an airplane. Though Charlie Snow and Alex Cloud would not know it, the men standing there lighting the fire were perfectly legal citizens and carried full IDs to prove it.

"Jerry, everything seems ready on the ground. Shall we go ahead? Four-Five Lima."

"I still can't imagine what's going on with Hank. Do you copy, Three-Four-Four Uniform?" There was still no response from the Bonanza. "Maybe

305

he's talking with the Border Patrol. Let's give him a minute. Surely we'll hear from him any second now. Why don't you turn off, Maddie—at least for now. Just to be safe. Three-Eight Bravo."

"Roger." Maddie began a slow, sweeping turn as she also quickly gained an extra three hundred feet of altitude as a margin of safety over the rough terrain. Another wave of nausea almost gagged her.

"Three-Four-Four Uniform. Are you there Hank?" Jerry called. There was still no answer.

The three airplanes continued their widely separated circling patterns, dancing a slowly rounded minuet at arm's length.

"Do you think Hank could have forgotten what frequency we're using?" Maddie asked after what seemed like a long time. "Four-Five Lima." The only intervening sounds besides the separate roars of the individual aircraft engines had been Jerry's repeated attempts to raise Hank Tucker.

"I suppose it's possible he's forgotten it. But that doesn't seem like Hank. Three-Eight Bravo."

"That pickup truck down there," Ginger said suddenly over the radio. "It's beginning to move."

"Yes. She's right," Cord affirmed. "It's…it's going into the airport."

"Oh, damn. I'm supposed to be on the ground by now. We'd…I can't leave Refugio and his nephew down there alone and so vulnerable. Jerry, I'm going to change frequency just for a couple of minutes. To call Libby ATC for a relay to the Border Patrol. Four-Five Lima."

"Roger, Four-Five Lima. I'm going to be right behind you, Three-Eight Bravo." Jerry cut the power and began a rapid loss of altitude as he also began to position the Skyhawk for landing on the Tombstone runway. At that moment the Bonanza's light was only just visible as the much faster airplane's elliptical pattern carried it well beyond the immediate airspace over the airport. The wind on the ground appeared to be as nearly calm as it ever gets, making landing perfectly possible in either direction. Westward would keep the sun out of their eyes, and the hills ringing the airport in the east were a bit farther from the end of the runway than on the west end—some added margin in case of error.

Maddie also cut back her power and made a tight bank to the left bringing her almost immediately into position to set Four-Five Lima down on the eastern end of the runway. The altimeter showed fifty-three hundred feet— just eight hundred feet above the landing strip—and a rate of descent of over five-hundred feet per minute. She and Ginger would be on the ground in two minutes. Her call to Libby Air Traffic Control was quick and to the point. "Libby, there's some strange activity at the Tombstone airport. I think some friends of mine are in trouble. Will you please call the Patrol in Tombstone and the Sheriff?" she asked. "Eight-Six-Four-Five Lima."

"Roger, Four-Five Lima. Will you be landing?"

"Affirmative, Libby Control. Four-Five Lima." Maddie saw that the pickup truck, clearly visible with its white paint and headlights on bright, had entered the runway from the west end as she spoke to Libby AFB. But the pickup truck was behaving very oddly. For some reason it drove politely well off the center of the strip, moving very slowly, seeming to stop for a time and then start up again, not rushing to make the expected capture of illegal aliens and people who helped them. She and Ginger had set up that expectation so carefully for Charlie Snow's benefit the day before that she couldn't imagine the source of his apparent reluctance.

"See how slowly he's moving?" Maddie asked Ginger over the intercom, fighting back yet another wave of nausea. "What do you suppose Charlie's up to?" Maddie reset the radio from having called on the Libby Air Force Base frequency, returning it to the one where she would find Jerry—and presumably Hank.

"I can't imagine," Ginger answered. "Or…maybe I can." She pushed her call button to include Jerry Hanning and Cord in the conversation. "What if Charlie Snow is alone in the pickup truck down there? And what if it's…*him*…Alex…up there in the other plane, not Hank? Being alone in the truck would make Charlie cautious and insecure, wouldn't it? And that's what it looks like to me. That would also explain why we haven't heard from Hank. If it's *him* after all, he would have no way of knowing the frequency. Even if he did, would he communicate with us? "

"Jerry, I'm going to land. I don't feel good about Refugio and his nephew being down there alone. Four-Five Lima," Maddie said suddenly and emphatically.

Charlie Snow watched from his slowly-moving pickup truck as Maddie's Skyhawk touched down at the eastern edge of the runway and made its rollout toward the windsock at mid-field. Charlie's truck was still moving slowly down the side of the runway from the opposite end, and he was at a loss as to what he should do. "Where the hell is Alex?" he kept asking himself as he looked around for any sign of the Dodge Ram. He had a sense that he needed to make a move toward the fire that he saw burning brightly from beside the windsock, but he had no idea what he would do about the people who lighted it when he got there. That gave Charlie reason enough to drive slowly. He stuck his cigarette between his lips, and, the smoke curling up into his eyes, he reached around and with one hand released the clamp that held his old 30.06 rifle in the rack behind his head. He had already loaded its magazine full. He took a full drag on the cigarette and then removed it from between his lips, thinking about how Alex had been the senior partner in this operation. Up to now, Charlie's participation had been pretty small. This morning he had his chance to be included in something more direct—like the time Alex had run the car off the road in the Santa Ritas. This morning would be different than the last time he had confronted these bleeding hearts at this airport. He didn't see how he could have missed when he shot at that airplane a couple of weeks before, but maybe he made his mark on it with a bullet hole anyhow. Charlie smiled. He levered a cartridge into the magazine of the rifle.

Charlie wondered which plane had just landed, the priest's or the other one. The two Cessnas looked so much alike. Then he saw that a second plane was also making a landing—another Cessna. Double teaming them again, he thought. But they had their own two-pronged approach this time—if, that is, Alex would ever get here. He wished he hadn't forgotten his cell phone so he could call Alex and find out what was happening. Despite the sun in his eyes, Charlie could see the other Cessna clearly as it began its touchdown and rollout. The first one to land had only just reached the windsock, which still hung limp in the calm air of early morning. Charlie stopped his truck there on the side of the runway to see what would happen next. Then he spotted something else. At the far end of the landing stip a dust cloud rose up behind a speeding car that had left the tarmac and raced along the dirt road toward that same end of the runway where the two airplanes had just touched down. Charlie lifted up his binoculars and, shading the end against the brightness of the morning sun, looked at the fast-moving vehicle. No doubt about it, the Dodge Ram. Alex finally, he concluded, relieved. Charlie wondered what had delayed him. He rolled down the window to throw out the cigarette he had been smoking and heard the throb of yet another airplane engine. Now what? Charlie craned his head to look out the window. Hank Tucker now, too? So he *had* changed sides. This time the aircraft engine's sound was coming from the opposite direction, from behind Charlie Snow. A broad smile broke out on Charlie's face.

Jerry Hanning had finished his rollout behind Maddie's Four-Five Lima and leaned his engine until it stopped. Maddie and Ginger were standing beside the fire with Refugio and his nephew, Bobby. Bobby looked every bit the part of an illegal immigrant. Both he and Refugio wore jeans, rough work shirts and felt hats. But Bobby was even less what he seemed than Refugio. His Spanish was little better than Jerry's own. A University of Arizona engineering graduate student and third generation citizen of the United States, Bobby had only been to Mexico a couple of times as a tourist, and his father had denied him the opportunity to speak Spanish in the home when he was growing up. Jerry and Cord got out of the Skyhawk and joined the others around the fire.

Looking in the direction of Charlie's Snow's pickup, Jerry saw that Hank's Bonanza was making its final approach for landing—only from the west end of the runway. Jerry did not envy his landing, whoever the pilot might be, with the sun in his eyes.

"Look," Cord said suddenly, pointing back toward the east end of the runway. The dust cloud was unmistakable. "What now?" he asked.

"Yes. What now, indeed," Jerry replied, watching first the speeding SUV then shifting back to the approaching airplane.

The pilot of the Bonanza throttled back for his landing, and from the distance the wailing sound of a siren broke through the softened sound of the Bonanza's idling engine

"What's that idiot doing?" Maddie asked suddenly, pointing toward the Bonanza as Jerry and Cord stepped up beside her.

Jerry's eyes followed her pointed finger toward the landing aircraft, and he saw immediately what had alarmed her. Charlie Snow's truck had started up again, moving more quickly this time. Suddenly it veered into the center of the runway—right where the Bonanza would have to make its landing rollout. By this time the truck was little more than fifty yards from where they stood beside the windsock.

Perhaps because Alex Cloud had the sun in his eyes or became distracted with everything else that was going on—nobody would ever know exactly what happened—but the landing Bonanza did not immediately respond to the white pickup truck's incursion into the middle of the runway. Finally, and agonizingly to the observers on the ground, a roar of the Bonanza's engine came as the plane belatedly attempted to resume flight. At first it seemed to jump over the pickup truck, which turned and, tires spinning, hurtled furiously back toward the side of the landing strip. But the Bonanza's airspeed must have been too low and the nose-up attitude of the plane too severe. Instead of rising smoothly, effortlessly and elegantly into the air as only a Bonanza can do, it seemed to pause slightly in midair and then slowly begin to fade toward its left wing which stabbed through the air like a knife making a vertical cut. Down it sliced toward the creosote and ironwood bushes covering the caliche-hard desert soil.

"Nose down, you idiot. Level it out," Jerry shouted helplessly. He heard a door slam and glanced at Hank Tucker standing beside the Dodge Ram, a look of horror on his face. Jerry looked back at the Bonanza just as its stall drove the airplane into the ground on the other side of the runway directly opposite from where they stood. There was a slight cartwheeling motion as first the left wing, then the nose and finally the right wing sliced into the creosote and ironwood landscape. Then came the explosion and the fire.

"Oh, my God," Ginger said, horrified at what she was witnessing, not even thinking that the pilot of that plane was the one who had hurt her so brutally.

"That dumb shit!" Hank whistled through his teeth.

"Which one? Alex or Charlie?" Jerry asked.

"Both of them," Hank answered.

The crackling of the fire of the burning airplane in the still morning air greeted the simultaneous arrival of two Border Patrol Blazers and a Cochise County Sheriff's cruiser—just in time to head off the fleeing Charlie Snow, who had turned his truck back toward the main entrance to the airport.

Hank Tucker had a stricken look on his face. It was an expression that mixed horror over the certain death of someone he had known for many years and sadness over the total loss of his airplane.

Maddie instinctively went to Jerry, who put his arm around her. Almost without thinking about it, he began reciting from the Prayer Book, "Depart, O Christian soul, out of this world; in the name of God the Father Almighty who created you...May your rest be this day in peace."

The Border Patrol left Charlie Snow to the deputy and pulled up beside the two airplanes and the SUV.

"What's going on here?" one of the guards asked.

Jerry paused before answering. "We have a story to tell you," he said at last. "A long and not very happy story."

Another siren broke the early morning quiet.

"Fire Department," said one of the guards.

"Gonna need it," said Hank Tucker quietly looking at the burning wreckage. "Really gonna need it, all right."

Ginger sobbed quietly beside the bonfire. Jerry pulled Maddie closer as they stood wondering what to do next.

The feeling of shock continued on to Nellie Cashman's Café where they sat later nursing cups of coffee and each other. A plate of Hanna-Nellie's fresh sweet rolls on their table went largely untouched. The horror of the fiery crash that had killed Alex Cloud followed by hours of questioning by the police and Border Patrol had left them all exhausted, so they had piled into Hank's SUV, and had gone into Tombstone. The breakfast crowd at Nellie Cashman's had nearly all finished and gone by the time they got there just after ten o'clock, leaving the place mostly to them and the two Nellies who hovered lovingly while pretending to go about the business of running the restaurant.

Jerry broke a long period of silence by saying, "I don't know what else you could have done, Hank."

Hank shook his head. "I should have known that keeping the keys to the SUV would be an invitation to Alex to take the Bonanza this morning." He cleared his throat. "Every time I think of him burning alive in that plane I want to puke."

"You aren't responsible for any of Alex's bad judgment," Jerry said, "or his bigotry—which are what got him into trouble in the first place. And you certainly can't chastize yourself for his poor pilotage," Jerry responded.

"That's the odd part of it," Hank said. "Alex was a fine pilot. I can't imagine him making such a stupid mistake, not even with the sun in his eyes and Charlie Snow on that runway in his pickup." He sat thoughtfully for a moment and then shook his head. "No, he would never have made as fundamental an error as that."

Ginger looked up and stared intently at Hank. "Are you suggesting that he deliberately crashed that airplane?" she asked.

"I don't know what to think," Hank answered. He hung his head and shook it slowly from side to side, peering over the top of his eyeglasses at the others around the table.

"Well, I don't believe it was deliberate," Maddie inserted emphatically.

"Not even with him realizing that we were all there waiting for him?" Cord asked with a sarcastic edge in his voice. "Seems just like the kind of thing that someone like him might do."

"He didn't know we had set a trap for him, and he didn't have time to make that kind of decision in any case," Maddie snapped back at him. The tension between them awkwardly filled the room. "I say he acted instinctively…and panicked. Kind of froze, forgetting everything he had ever known about flying. I know that feeling." She brushed an errant tear from the corner of her eye.

"I think Maddie's right," Jerry inserted. "We all saw what happened. It looked like pilot error to me, a classic case of man-handling the controls and failure to avoid a takeoff stall."

"My instructor speaks," Maddie said with a shallow little smile as she reached for one of the sweet rolls, breaking it into two uneven pieces and taking a bite from the smaller portion.

"Do you think there'll be a service for Alex at the church?" Jerry asked Hank, shifting subject.

"I imagine so. He *was* a member. Will that be hard for you—conducting it, I mean…after all of this?" Hank answered with his own question.

"Yes, I guess it will be," Jerry replied. "But, still, it's what needs to happen. What about his family?"

"They're all gone now," said Hank. "All except for a sister he hasn't spoken to in years. Still, she's the next of kin. I know Alice slightly. I'll call her," he added.

Jerry looked down at his hands as a heavy quiet rose up between them. He could hear Hanna-Nellie banging pots in the kitchen. Brenda-Nellie busied herself making a fresh pot of coffee. Hank shifted his position and leaned back in his chair. Ginger played absently with her spoon, trying to sort her complicated feelings about Alex Cloud, his effect on her life and the way he had died; it would take her a long time finally to settle all of it, if she ever did.

Finally, Cord broke the silence. "I really do need to be getting back to Bisbee for an appointment. If I can have a ride? That okay, Hank?" He stood up.

"No problem." Hank, too, rose to his feet

"Actually, I haven't said anything yet." Cord stared pointedly into Maddie's eyes, glaring at her with the intensity of a former lover with still-unresolved issues. Both looked away suddenly and Cord continued, "But my father has had a mild stroke…and…and my mother really needs me to come home. I've decided to go. Permanently."

Maddie and Jerry shared a quick glance. He could see in her eyes a combination of pain and relief, guilt and sadness. He knew this would ease her immediate decision-making, would put off her decision of whether or not to share her child with its father. Neither of them said anything.

Ginger said simply, "I'm sorry. That makes me very sad."

"You're leaving...for good? " Brenda-Nellie asked from across the small dining room. "I'm so sorry."

"Yeah. The movers are coming at noon to give me an estimate," Cord continued, ignoring the expressions of dismay and surprise around him as well as the non-reactions from Maddie and Jerry Hanning. "I'll turn my house over to the realtor I bought it from. Anyhow, I really do need to get back to Bisbee—one way or another."

"I'm ready to go," Jerry said.

"Me too," Ginger injected quietly, still very much within herself. "Mind if I ride all the way back home with you?" she asked Hank. "No offense, Maddie, but I don't think I can get back in that airplane right now."

"Yes, I know what you mean," Jerry said thoughtfully to her. "I was just imagining how it's going to feel taking off from that airport again...especially this morning with that still-warm wreckage sitting beside the runway." They paused for a moment, sharing vivid memories of the firemen putting out the blaze, removing Alex's charred body, burned beyond recognition, and, finally, in the saddest moment of that terrible morning, the paramedics unit driving slowly and deliberately away from the Tombstone airport with what remained of Alex Cloud.

"Flying from there *is* going to be really weird, Jerry," Maddie said. "Still," she added abruptly, "we all have our own lives to get back to, don't we?" She stood up and looked down into Jerry's eyes with an expression at once resolute and hopeful. "I'm ready to go."

"Yes," he answered simply, getting up. "Our own lives."

Hank pulled out his wallet. Brenda-Nellie waved him off with a dismissive gesture. "It's on the house," she said. "See ya in church."

"Right." Jerry grinned back at her, knowing that the quiet interior of St. Peter's would feel like a welcome sanctuary, a place of sanity in a world that seemed to have gone mad. "See you in church."